THE DEVEREAUX DEITY

STEVE MCELLISTREM

**CALUMET
EDITIONS**

Minneapolis, Minnesota

SECOND EDITION DECEMBER 2022

THE DEVEREAUX DEITY.

ISBN: 978-1-959770-87-9
10 9 8 7 6 5 4 3 2

Author website: www.mcellistrem.com.
Book cover and design by Gary Lindberg

Praise and Awards for Steve McEllistrem's Work

The Devereaux Dilemma – Finalist, International Book Award

"Fans of classic Heinlein-esque science fiction will enjoy The Devereaux Dilemma by Steve McEllistrem. The Devereaux Dilemma is full of complex plot twists and turns that will keep you on the edge of your seat until the very end. McEllistrem writes gripping, action-packed scenes with eye-popping tech and well-imagined future combat."

- Lyda Morehouse, award-winning author of *Archangel Protocol* and *Resurrection*

"With so many science fiction visions of tomorrow out there, it's hard to come across new stories that are fresh and vital. The Devereaux Dilemma captures and delivers a well-conceived world of complex human characters and believable technologies -- all set against a backdrop of thrilling political intrigue. Steve McEllistrem has created a searingly vivid portrayal of a very possible future."

-Jeffrey Morris, FutureDude and author of *Venus: Daedalus One*

The Devereaux Disaster – Finalist, International Book Award

"... There's plenty of adventure and plenty of interesting characters throughout the course of this well written book. Maybe that's why I couldn't seem to put it down. I was drawn into the way Jeremiah fought and continued to fight as his son was at risk. This wasn't just your typical 'saving the world' story..."

***** Five-Star Review from Readers' Favorite Samantha Rivera

"[*The Devereaux Disaster*] is a most unusual science fiction novel and one that means Jeremiah can only save the world if his son and fellow cadets are destroyed."

Bookviews Pick of the Month for April 2014, by Alan Caruba

The Devereaux Decision – Finalist, Minnesota Book Award; Finalist, Midwest Book Award; Finalist, International Book Award

The Devereaux Deity

Steve McEllistrem

CALUMET
EDITIONS

Minneapolis, Minnesota

Chapter 1

Curtik stood in the light rain across the street from the Natural Hybrids Incorporated building wearing the face of a woman who died several years ago. A good disguise, he had to admit, even if the idea hadn't been his. He made no effort to hide from the surveillance cameras. They would register him as Julianna Wentworth, a deceased CINTEP agent who had been his father's partner many years ago. But by the time that data got passed to someone who might question it, Curtik would be gone. He flexed his mechanical right hand, a little annoyed at the residual pain lingering where the nerves in his wrist connected to the prosthetic. Yet the hand felt powerful and alive.

"You look ridiculous in that dress," Zora spoke softly in his head. He knew she was watching him from a window on the fourth floor. She'd managed to disarm the security system on a basement entrance to gain access.

You don't like my ensemble? Curtik replied via his implant.

"Julianna never wore dresses."

How do you know?

"I read her file."

It makes me look less threatening.

"You look like a loony. I can see your pants under your dress. Anything yet?"

Still waiting.

Always waiting. Either for Lendra or Jeremiah or somebody else. He wished he could just spring into action. The Center for International Economic Policy had officially been created by Elias Leach to fight terrorism and engage in espionage, but in actuality it served as a tool for whatever the President of the United States wanted. And usually the President wanted to keep a stranglehold on power and maintain the status quo so that the large contributors who made election victories possible would stay loyal.

Now Lendra Riley ran CINTEP, taking orders from President Angelica Hope, doing the necessary things to keep the President in power and America near the top of the economic world. However, the good old days had vanished. Lendra, on orders from President Hope, had shut down the Operations section, prohibiting Eli's policies of assassination and sabotage. Only a few field agents remained. Everyone else in CINTEP worked in Analytical.

At least Lendra had allowed Curtik to train as a CINTEP ghost—a secret agent like Jeremiah used to be—but whether he'd ever get to go on assignments like Jeremiah was an open question. This particular mission was unsanctioned and outside CINTEP's jurisdiction.

"Just help him," Lendra had said when she lent Curtik and Zora to Jeremiah. "I don't want details. This is below the radar."

At least that part was easy. Curtik couldn't give her details when he still wasn't sure what the mission was.

So was Lendra helping Jeremiah? Was Jeremiah helping Lendra? Were they in cahoots or just cooperating occasionally? Their relationship, no longer physical, was too complicated to grasp. And Jeremiah had almost completely vanished from sight, contacting them only by audio messages, dispersing minimal amounts of information, like now.

At that moment Edwin Fowler III exited the plas-glass door and scuttled to his waiting car—a fully armored Mercedes—head down, coat pulled up around his ears. He slid inside as the car door swung shut behind him, then accelerated away.

Okay, we're a go, Curtik sent as he released the drone, about as large as a hummingbird. The drone flew over Fowler's Mercedes, tracking him and relaying the data to Curtik's implant.

"Moving now," Zora replied via her interface. "Just entering his office. I'll need a few minutes."

Curtik looked around. Broadway looked busy: robocars, electric streetcars, and plenty of pedestrians heading out for a drink or dinner after work. Perhaps New Yorkers were less concerned about the Susquehanna Virus these days, now that it was being steadily eradicated and was no longer as deadly as before. Curtik accessed a vid of the place from a few years back and realized it was far less crowded now than it used to be. Still damn busy though.

He deleted the vid and activated the conference setting on his implant, bringing his father, Jeremiah Jones, into the conversation. "How's the drone working, Pops?"

Jeremiah said, "Looks like he's heading to his club. He feels safe there."

"Street's quiet," said Curtik, "I think this is a bust. The guy's a zero."

Jeremiah said, "He isn't what he appears to be."

"There's nothin' out of place. Standard security measures from what I can see. If Fowler is really a bad guy, shouldn't we just ice him? All this cloak and dagger stuff is boring. Taking him out would be a helluva lot more fun."

"Just keep your eyes open."

"Okay," said Zora, "I'm in."

Two dark SUVs drew up to the Natural Hybrids building and stopped. Eight large security guards jumped out, leaving the doors open behind them as they ran to the entrance.

"Okay, I apologize, Popster," Curtik said. "Slight problem, Zora. Eight hostiles coming your way."

"Not a good time, Curtik. I'm still setting up."

"Take them out," Jeremiah said. "But don't kill them if you don't have to."

Curtik snorted as he unholstered his Las-pistol and sprinted across the street, the dress slowing him down. Son of a bitch! "Why didn't you tell me not to wear a dress?" He didn't bother to dodge the approaching vehicles, knowing their autopilots would slow or swerve to avoid him.

"We did," Zora said.

"Okay. How come you weren't convincing?"

"Because you're an obstinate fool?"

"Agh." He lifted the dress with his right hand. "Here comes Julianna, fellas. CINTEP's comin' to get you."

He reached the door, dropped the dress and punched the plas-glass with his robotic right hand. The glass shattered and he ran inside.

A security guard had already begun to move toward him. With his left hand, Curtik shot the man with a purple pulse—a high-stun setting. Another security guard fired at him: a red, killing pulse, the bastard. Not just some ordinary security guard. So this Fowler really was somebody to be reckoned with. Curtik dove to his left and shot the guard in the chest with another purple pulse. He fired twice more, at two more guards who had ducked behind pillars. The other four had entered the elevator. Its doors shut as Curtik fired at it.

He slid behind the reception counter, the dress bunching around his legs, as the two remaining security guards alternated firing at him, their laser pulses sizzling as they punched holes in the plas-wood. The counter began to burn, giving off an acrid stench, activating the sprinkler system in the ceiling, which showered him with cold water. Dense smoke billowed around him.

"Four coming your way, Zora," Curtik said. "I couldn't stop 'em. I'm kinda pinned down here at the moment."

"Abort the mission," said Jeremiah. "Get out of there now."

"No, I'm almost done," Zora replied.

"Plow it," Curtik said. He dropped to the floor and used the infrared setting of his implant to search through the smoke for the guards. They remained behind their pillars, but their hands were exposed so they could fire at him.

"Help's on the way," said Jeremiah. "It'll be there in thirty seconds."

"What kind of help?" Curtik asked.

"Stun grenade on a mini-drone," said Jeremiah. "Keep firing at them. Zora, get out of there now."

Zora didn't reply. Curtik hoped she was on her way out. He fired two quick pulses, one at each guard's exposed hand, and grinned when he heard two screams. *I am the absolute best. The king of the jungle!* Yes, they'd switch their weapons to their off hands, but they stood no chance against him now.

"Stay down," Jeremiah said. "Five seconds."

Curtik thought he heard the whine of a drone and pulled himself into a ball, covering his head with his hands as the stun grenade exploded.

Curtik jumped to his feet. *Zora*, he sent, *where the hell are you?*

"Fifth floor. I'm taking fire," Zora replied via her interface.

Curtik again lifted the dress with his right hand and sprinted for the stairs, firing stun pulses at the two guards as he passed, feeling satisfaction as they dropped to the ground. He flung the door open and pounded up the stairs to the fifth floor, taking them three at a time, flying around corners, laughing at the thrill of the chase.

He reached the fifth floor and yanked the door open. The four security guards had taken up position left and right, high and low, hiding behind doors to minimize their profiles, and they alternated firing red pulses at Fowler's office doorway. Their pulses had started the sprinkler system up here as well.

I'm here, Curtik sent.

"What's your plan?" Zora asked.

Plan, what plan? I just want to shoot people. Curtik fired pulses at the guards, who were too well concealed to offer any targets.

"Shoot the wall to your left," Jeremiah said.

"That should confuse them," said Curtik. "It confuses the hell out of me."

"Just do it. I need a six-inch hole. I've got another drone headed your way. It'll be there in a few seconds. Zora, take out the lights. When the stun grenade hits, get out of there."

Curtik fired a long red pulse at the wall, opening a hole to the outside. Then he ducked into the stairwell again and waited for the bang.

"This was supposed to be a simple job," Zora said, "not a shootout."

I know, Curtik sent. *Isn't it great?*

Two seconds later he heard an explosion.

Come on, he sent to Zora.

An old black woman emerged from Fowler's office, Las-pistol in hand. Zora, wearing the same neo-skin mask she'd worn in London. And trousers, damn her. She sprinted to the stairwell and took the steps down two at a time.

Curtik stayed behind her on the way down, not out of any gallantry but because he thought he might trip in the dress and wanted to have Zora cushion the blow if he did so.

"Who is this Fowler guy anyway?" Zora asked.

"Just a seed salesman, obviously," Curtik replied. "With a few pet pit bulls."

As Zora continued past the first floor to the basement, Curtik said, "Where you goin'?"

"I'm not going out the front door after that."

"We're wearing masks," Curtik said. "They'll never identify us. Besides, they already got vids of us."

"We got the bugs installed. Let's just get out of here." She ran to the parking ramp exit on the back side of the building, not far from the Civic Center, and jogged up to the sidewalk, slowing to a walk as she neared the top. Curtik stayed two steps behind her.

Jeremiah said, "I'll be there in thirty seconds."

Zora frowned. "But you're in Washington. How can you—"

"I left Washington two hours ago. I suspected you might have trouble."

"You don't trust us," Curtik said.

"It's not that. I just didn't think Fowler's office would be as easy as the Intel indicated. "I'm in the black sedan to your right."

The sedan stopped in front of Curtik and Zora, its rear door opening. Curtik gestured for Zora to precede him, then followed her inside. The door closed automatically as the sedan sped off.

Jeremiah swiveled the front seat around to face them, letting the autopilot drive the car. He looked ancient, wrinkles heavy around the eyes and forehead and even his mouth. When he caught sight of Curtik wearing the Julianna mask, his face sagged in sorrow.

Curtik ripped the mask off as Zora gasped at the change in Jeremiah's condition. Neither Curtik nor Zora had seen him in over a month. They had received this assignment from Lendra so Curtik had no idea how much Jeremiah's condition had deteriorated in such a short time. His hazel eyes seemed almost dull in the dim light and his body looked shrunken, testament to all the punishment it had absorbed over the years. Even the simple act of sitting in the moving car seemed to pain him.

What kind of hell must he endure every day?

Time to lighten the mood.

"No 'atta boy?" Curtik said as he squirmed his way out of the dress, revealing skin-tight pants and a black T-shirt. "No well done, ma'am?"

Jeremiah smiled briefly. "Did you get the bugs planted?" he asked Zora.

Zora removed her mask and nodded.

"Good work, both of you."

"Who is that guy?" Zora asked, taking Curtik's cue and ignoring Jeremiah's infirmity.

"Yeah," Curtik said. "His security ain't too shabby."

"He's part of the network," said Jeremiah. "One of the people pulling the strings, making things work the way they're supposed to."

"What are you talking about?" Curtik said.

"How do you think they get people to accept their place in society? People have to be conditioned to want to keep the world the way it is."

"I still don't see how he fits into that."

"Simple," Zora said. "They put additives in the food, don't they?"

Jeremiah nodded. "Subtle changes. Not enough to program people's minds. Just enough to make them more susceptible to other means of conditioning them."

"Ah," Curtik said. "I got a question. Won't old Edwin just have the bugs removed or shut down the office or something to avoid the bugging?"

"Hopefully," said Jeremiah.

Chapter 2

As the ore transport vessel MineStar 7 sank toward the surface of Mars, Doug Robinson looked over at Quark. It had been a year since Quark had been in the company of his fellow Escala—genetically engineered humans designed to thrive on Mars. Doug had been thinking a lot about how they'd met a few years ago in that shootout with the government in Minnesota. He liked Quark and was happy that the Escala was finally getting to join his own kind. He looked more serene than Doug had ever seen him.

Doug felt excited for his own reasons. He was about to land on Mars! A black man from a bad neighborhood in Minneapolis about to do what few astronauts had ever done. He didn't know how Devereaux got permission for him to travel with Quark and he didn't care. He was finally going to meet his daughter Celestia in person. She lived with her mother Zeriphi in the New Dawn colony. Doug had impregnated Zeriphi three years ago at her request, but she had never loved him. He thought he loved her once. But she had made it clear she would never love him in return. For her, it always came back to Zod.

How much did Celestia know about Zod? She and Doug never talked about Zod when they exchanged vid messages. And although Celestia called Doug Daddy, Doug wondered if she knew what that word meant. Did she consider him her father? Or was there someone on

Mars taking that role? Or did it even matter? After the death of Zod in Minnesota, the Escala had shifted to a matriarchal society.

The trip up had been a long six months, but at least he'd had the company of Quark and the miners who were on their way to their new posts. Doug had been forced to spend most of the trip in this one room, shielded from radiation to protect against cancer. Quark hadn't been similarly constrained.

Like the other Escala, he had been enhanced with the DNA of several species, one of which was an altered *kineococcus radiotolerans* bacterium that fed on radiation, so he had been free to move about the ship during the voyage.

The miners, like Doug, had been forced to stay in a shielded area, but their quarters were much nicer. Doug visited their section of the ship a few times a day for meals and exercise. He got to know each of the miners a little, though he spent most of his time with the new foreman, Colin Enright, who questioned him at length about what it had been like to work for Walt Devereaux. Doug got the sense that Enright and the miners disapproved of Devereaux because of his atheism, but they never came out and said so. Still, after a few months, he found himself engaging with the miners less and less frequently, keeping to himself, perusing the ship's vast library for vids on a great number of subjects. He grew tired of defending Devereaux to these backwards laborers.

"How're you doing?" Quark asked.

"I'm fine," he said, wondering if that was true.

"Nervous?"

"Why should I be?" Doug said. "Okay, I'm nervous. I'm about to land on another planet. And I'm not an Escala. I don't know how I'm going to do up here. I don't know how my body's going to react. Two years is a long time to spend up here if things don't go well."

Quark smiled. "You'll manage."

The next transport ship wouldn't arrive for twenty-six months, the next time Earth and Mars would be at their closest orbital points, so if things didn't go well with Zeriphi or Celestia, it would be a lonely two years.

"What about you?" Doug asked, teasing. "You nervous?"

Quark shrugged. He still wore his bushy black beard, and his shaggy hair formed a ragged halo around his head, reminding Doug why he had been called Cookie Monster back at the Tessamae Shelter. He almost didn't fit in his seat, seven feet tall and three hundred Earth-pounds, most of it muscle.

"Actually, yes," Quark replied.

"Why? You're going home."

"In a way, but Mars is still going to feel like an alien world. The simulations won't match the reality. Plus, I haven't seen Quekri in over a year. And I miss Devereaux."

"I miss him too," Doug said.

The great Walt Devereaux, now alive only as a robot (albeit one that looked like he used to look), his mind encapsulated in an organic computer, had ordered Quark to Mars, where he belonged. "There's no body left for you to serve," Devereaux had said in front of Doug, as if he wanted a witness. "My human remains are mere molecules and my computer self is beyond even your remarkable abilities to protect. We'll stay in touch. I can contact you just as easily on Mars as I can on Earth. There's no reason for you to be apart from Quekri any longer."

Quark had nodded before turning away, his eyes glistening with moisture. As far as Doug knew, Quark hadn't been alone with Devereaux since that day. He wondered if Quark felt betrayed. Doug felt abandoned at times, now that Devereaux no longer needed him to be his communications liaison.

After Devereaux told Doug he could choose from several job offers, Doug had asked if there was a way for him to visit his daughter instead, and Devereaux had somehow made it happen.

"Better put your Mars suit on," Quark said as he reached for his. "We're about to land."

MineStar7 touched down so softly Doug almost didn't feel it. He would have thought it was just a slight bump had Quark not said anything. That was the beauty of robotic flight—near perfection. He felt the pull of Mars' gravity, lighter than Earth's and even lighter than the ship's induced gravity had been during the flight up here.

Doug donned his Mars suit—a gift from Devereaux—sealing the helmet tight against the collar. The green icon in the upper right corner of the visor indicated the suit was secure. He took a deep breath as he prepared to step onto another world.

"Let's go," Quark said, turning toward the doorway. He spun the airlock, swung the door open and stepped out into the hallway.

The forty-eight miners were already there, waiting for the hatch to be released, Enright in the lead. When the door to the outside finally opened, they marched out onto the surface of Mars, onto the reddish sand. A short way off, through a reddish cloud of dust that settled slowly to the ground, Doug could see the MineStar colony, the pods where the miners would be staying. Beyond that stood tall mountains. The orange-red sky looked odd compared to the blue of Earth and much brighter than Doug would have guessed it to be.

He knew that the New Dawn settlement was only a few kilometers away, but he couldn't see it from here, perhaps because of the dust. He'd heard there was a little tension between the miners and the Escala and wondered why the Escala had chosen to settle so close to the mining colony. A whole planet to choose from and they picked this spot. Why? Oh, yes. Something about the geological formations in the area.

A group of miners stood outside wearing Mars suits, waiting to enter the vessel, apparently eager to leave. Doug saw that there were less than twenty. He'd heard that a number of miners had died in the past year, victims of several diseases caused by the increased radiation present on Mars, but more than half? Had that many miners really been lost?

He stared out the hatchway at the MineStar colony until Quark took him by the elbow and led him down to the surface. Another planet. As he stepped onto its surface, orange dust shrouded his feet. He felt like a voyager, like an explorer, even though he was far from the first to set foot on this world. After the confines of the ship, the place seemed gargantuan, a giant desert of reddish-brown rocks.

Quark looked off to his left and Doug followed his line of sight. In the distance, he made out a half-dozen large figures walking toward them, all wearing Mars suits, one of them limping slightly. Escala.

Quark turned to the miners and said, "Thanks for the lift, folks."

Then he clapped Doug on the back and strode off toward the Escala. Doug waved goodbye to the miners. No doubt he'd be seeing them again once everyone was settled—the miners in their pods and Doug with the Escala.

He followed Quark toward the New Dawn settlement, noticing again how light on his feet he felt, the gravity here being a little more than a third that of Earth.

Yet he also felt a heaviness in his chest. Perhaps this had been a crazy idea after all. Zeriphi hadn't objected when he'd informed her of his decision, but she hadn't exactly welcomed him either. She'd told him the decision was his and that he had the right to visit if he so desired, but she'd never said she was looking forward to it.

Celestia, however, had seemed excited about the prospect of meeting him face-to-face. Yet she was barely more than two years old. How much interacting could they do? Was she in some sort of school? And she had a baby brother now too, fathered by an Escala named Paddon, whom Doug had met on Earth—a nice guy.

Was Paddon Zeriphi's companion now? Doug didn't think so, but he didn't really understand a lot about the Escala way of life. Perhaps Paddon had just assisted with mating to help build up the colony. Well, Doug would have plenty of time to learn the truth.

He saw that Quark had sped up. Picking up his pace until he was fairly leaping into the air, Doug covered two meters with each stride. In only a few minutes, they reached the Escala, and Quark engaged in a series of hugs, while Doug stood respectfully to the side.

Then one of the Escala stepped over to him and grabbed him in a hug as well—the one with the limp. Paddon. Doug recalled again how Paddon had been shot by the Elite Ops while trying to bring down the cave on top of them back on Earth.

"I remember you, Doug," Paddon said as he released Doug.

The Escala greeting. Doug had thought it meant only goodbye, but apparently it meant hello as well.

"I remember you, Paddon," Doug replied.

"Zeriphi had to stay behind with little Zander, but she's looking forward to seeing you. And Celestia made me promise to bring you back as quickly as I could. She's a tenacious one. You may regret this trip."

Paddon smiled to show he was kidding, at least in part.

Another Escala stepped in front of Paddon and hugged Doug. Quekri.

"Doug," she said. "I remember you."

"I remember you, Quekri," Doug replied.

"Let's get you back to the settlement so you can meet your daughter."

They turned away from the miners and began the walk back to the colony, chatting about how exciting this all was. Three of the Escala—Krall, Oggie and Poon—surrounded Doug and peppered him with questions about Earth. They were just as big as the adults, but Doug could tell they were teenagers. He vaguely recalled them. The last Escala was a woman named Keelar. He remembered her as one of the doctors who had cared for Zeriphi.

She interrupted the teens and asked Doug how he was feeling.

"Fine."

"Any nausea?"

"Not so far."

"Good. We'll give you a full checkup when we get to the colony—make sure you don't fall victim to the illnesses affecting the miners."

"I didn't know so many miners had died."

"Four in the last three weeks," Keelar said. "Nine in the last two months. We think it's a virus, though we haven't been able to verify that yet."

"The Susquehanna Virus?"

"Probably not. We're not sure what it is. Some virus that was brought to Mars and mutated under the radiation, perhaps. I think they're glad to be getting off this rock. And I fear for their replacements. They may do even worse."

"Is there something wrong with Mars?"

"No. But they may not have properly sterilized their quarters before leaving, so the incoming miners may contract the disease as well. Plus, I suspect at least one of the outgoing miners is ill and may transmit the disease to his fellow travelers on the way back to Earth. At least they'll have a long quarantine aboard ship."

Doug said, "But everyone was tested for viruses before we left Earth."

"Yes, but viruses are tricky devils. Some strains are tiny and almost impossible to spot. They can present no symptoms on Earth, but up here with the increased radiation, who knows?"

"Are you and the Escala at risk?"

"I don't believe so. But you may be in danger."

Danger. When hadn't he been in danger? Earth wasn't exactly safe anymore. Although the media claimed there were fewer wars on Earth than there'd been in the past, the civil unrest, the dissatisfaction with government, not just in the United States but all over, had increased to a point where many people hesitated to go out. If he couldn't be with Devereaux, he'd take Mars any day.

Chapter 3

Lendra Riley stood beside Dr. Taditha Poole waiting for President Angelica Hope to appear by holo-projection. Hannah Swenson sat at the board—the electronics communication hub where Jay-Edgar had ruled for so many years under Elias Leach, until the disaster on the Moon when Eli created the cadet program to mount an attack on Earth for the purpose of uniting its warring nations.

She still wasn't used to having Hannah here. Hannah ought to be doing bodyguard work according to Dr. Poole's psych profile, but Lendra had no one currently requiring bodyguard services. Plus, Jay-Edgar was under house arrest for helping Eli evade justice. Lendra probably could have gotten Jay-Edgar out, but she no longer trusted him. So she was stuck with Hannah, who was a pleasant enough young woman, though decidedly loyal to Jeremiah. Hell, they were all more loyal to Jeremiah than to her. That's okay—as long as they do their jobs.

She wondered why the President wanted to speak with them, and why she had insisted that Dr. Poole be present. She glanced at Taditha.

"Don't look at me," Dr. Poole said. "I'm as much in the dark as you are."

"Well, whatever it is, it won't be good." Lendra fingered the glass bulb necklace that used to contain neo-dopamine. How pleasant it would be to escape for a moment into the mellow clarity of the drug, to see the world open up before her, filled with possibility. She hoped she'd stop craving it one day.

"Get a grip," Dr. Poole said.

"What are you talking about?"

"You whimpered just now."

"I did not."

"Very quietly."

Lendra glanced at Hannah.

"I heard it too," Hannah said. "Here's the President."

A projection of President Angelica Hope suddenly appeared on the far wall. The technology had been updated in the past two months, making her look like she was actually in the room with them. Lendra almost believed she could reach out and touch the woman.

The last election had clearly taken its toll on the President. She sat behind her desk, her hair thinner and grayer than Lendra remembered, her face more lined. Perhaps, now that she was done running for public office, she had stopped paying so much attention to her appearance.

Lendra was surprised that she was alone, or at least seemed to be alone. She'd expected General Horowitz or Dr. Jaidev to be with her. Of course, any number of advisors could be in the room with her and outside the camera pick-up, or monitoring the conversation from the newly rebuilt White House's tech center.

"Good evening, Ms. Riley, Dr. Poole," President Hope said. "What can you tell me about these Sally cells? Are they finally gone?"

"We think so," said Lendra. "We've gone through all the data points, traced every lead, and found nothing in the past two months, so we believe the threat has been completely eliminated."

"And the virus itself?" President Hope said.

Lendra turned to Taditha.

"That's less certain," Dr. Poole replied. "I've been sending my reports to Dr. Jaidev."

"Yes, she's briefed me. But I wanted to speak with you directly, get your unfiltered analysis."

Dr. Poole said nothing for a moment.

"I know you and she don't get along," President Hope said. "And she has her own agenda. But I want the full truth."

"Yes, ma'am," said Dr. Poole. "Very well. The virus is here to stay. It's exceptionally hardy. Some strains can live on their own for years without a human host. Extreme cold, extreme heat, extreme drought—none of those conditions seem to kill certain variants."

"I thought the newest strains were water soluble and could be diluted to the point they were no longer fatal."

"That's true, Madam President. But several of the twenty-three strains we've identified are what we call sleepers. They're almost immortal. They can survive outside the body for years and can hide inside the body for weeks or months before activating. Hundreds, perhaps thousands, of people are walking around with the virus, completely unaware of it. Eventually, the disease will spread throughout the world.

"Of course, it will likely mutate as it does so. It may become less virulent. We don't know. But in my opinion, there is no escape."

"So the only way to survive long-term is to develop an immunity, like Jeremiah."

"And the Escala," Dr. Poole added. "Yes."

"That's what I feared. Dr. Jaidev concurs with that assessment."

"What about Professor Devereaux?" Lendra asked. "Hasn't he verified their opinions?"

"He has," President Hope replied, "but since he is now encased in a robotic shell, some people disbelieve him or assert that he can no longer be trusted. Some people believe he has an agenda to turn us all into Escala."

"What do you believe?"

"I don't know what to believe just yet," President Hope said, "but I wanted your opinion on the matter. At any rate, that's not the only reason I called. Have you heard about this new computer virus that has been popping up? The so-called God Virus?"

"Yes," Lendra replied.

"No," said Dr. Poole. "What is it?"

President Hope nodded to Lendra, who said, "It's a virus that's been popping up on various secure networks. It doesn't seem to be harmful, but it has somehow escaped detection and infiltrated itself past numerous anti-virus programs."

"Why is it called the God Virus?" Dr. Poole asked.

"Because of the messages it leaves. 'Love one another as I love you.' 'Stop making war.' Or 'I am coming to lift you up.' All of them are signed by God."

"That can't be all this God wants. Do we know his true agenda?"

President Hope said, "I'm afraid not."

"It has to be a group of hackers," said Lendra. "There have been too many messages into too many servers for it to be one person."

"Good," President Hope said. "That's a good start. I want you to look into it for me, Ms. Riley. I know you're a gifted hacker. And don't you have some sort of tech genius working there too? My understanding is that the two of you hacked into the Las-cannons a few years ago, which is how the cadets were able to use them to attack Earth."

Lendra felt the blood rushing to her face. She said, "I'm sorry about that, Madam President."

"I'm not interested in apologies," President Hope said. "I want results."

"Yes, ma'am. Jay-Edgar used to work for us. But he aided Eli in making his escape and is currently under house arrest."

"That's fine," President Hope said. "I'm not suggesting you release him. I'm thinking he might be able to help you find this group of God hackers before they do real damage. I also need you to find out what their ultimate agenda is."

"But what about the Susquehanna Virus? That isn't going away."

President Hope nodded. "Dr. Poole will be leading that investigation. Now that Devereaux has found ways to make some of the strains less lethal, we've got a number of teams working on that aspect of it. So we just need to make certain no one else is producing new lethal varieties. This is a job best suited for Dr. Poole's talents."

Lendra suddenly realized why the President had wanted Dr. Poole here. President Hope must have seen the recognition in her face, for she said, "That's right. I want both of you running CINTEP. You demonstrated last year that you make a good team, and I'm concerned that one person by herself might go rogue the way Elias did. We can't afford that. So you will share everything—passwords, access codes, operational authority. I want complete cooperation. Understood?"

"Yes, ma'am," Lendra said.

"Of course," Dr. Poole added.

"But," said Lendra, "you mentioned operational authority. Does that mean . . ."

"No," President Hope said. "I'm not reopening the Operations section. Not yet. But I need you to continue to prepare for such an eventuality. In the meantime, continue with Analytical." She turned slightly, addressing only Lendra: "I know from your psych profile that you wanted to run CINTEP, but I think it's safer all around having you share power. And you clearly respect Dr. Poole. I'm sure you two can work together."

"Of course we can," Lendra replied.

"Congratulations, Dr. Poole. Make me proud."

"Thank you, ma'am," Dr. Poole said.

The President signed off, the holo-projection falling away, the wall becoming just a wall. Hannah seemed to be suppressing a smile, but she kept her mouth clamped shut and her eyes on her control board.

What did it all mean? Was the President losing faith in Lendra's ability to get the job done?

"Don't read too much into this," Dr. Poole said. "I think it's nothing more than she indicated. Eli subverted CINTEP for his own purposes and disaster ensued. She just wants to make sure nothing like that happens again. It doesn't mean she doesn't trust you."

"Did you know about this?" Lendra asked.

Dr. Poole shook her head. "I was as surprised as you."

Lendra nodded. For now, she would accept that as truth. Perhaps

Taditha was right and this was all just a protective measure. And if Lendra had to share the job, she was happier to share with Taditha than anyone else except Jeremiah. Besides, he had walked away, intent on fighting the system from outside rather than reforming it from within. He had promised he wouldn't come after her or CINTEP if she promised not to interfere with his activities and so far she hadn't.

She hadn't even put him under surveillance. And she'd lent him Zora and Curtik for his most recent mission. Not that she could have kept them from following him anyway if he'd asked them.

But she wondered what they were up to now. Could they be the hackers behind this God Virus? No, they didn't have the expertise.

"Shall we get started?" Dr. Poole said. "I've already caught you up on what I know. So perhaps we should begin with you telling me everything you know about this God Virus."

"In a minute," said Lendra. "I want Jay-Edgar here for this too. Hannah, would you get him, please?"

As Hannah left the office, Lendra accessed all the security codes and passwords in her interface and copied them to Dr. Poole's interface.

"I hope you're okay with this," Dr. Poole said.

"Don't worry. I can play nice."

She thought of Sophie. Her daughter was finally healthy, after fighting off the Susquehanna Virus last year with the help of Jeremiah's blood. Sophie and Jack Marschenko Poole—Taditha's son—were quite the pair, running amok in the nursery, keeping the nanny in a constant state of anxiety. Maybe this shared power arrangement would be for the best. Perhaps it would give her more time to spend with Sophie.

Still, she found her fingers drifting to her glass bulb necklace.

Chapter 4

Aspen sat in her quarters waiting for Addam to return. He had promised her a surprise and although she wasn't sure she wanted to be surprised, there was little to keep her occupied since the ship ran itself. Occasionally she and the other cadets would assist the robots with some sort of maintenance but most days, she and her fellow cadets worked on medical problems or robotics for Xinliu and Mei-Xing.

They split their time between assisting Earth in its efforts to find a cure for the Susquehanna Virus and fine-tuning the repairs to the three robots Benn had injured when he fired his Las-pistol at them last year. WT-938, WT-959 and WT-972 no longer functioned quite as well as their fellow Wong-Tech robots. Their impulse controls had been damaged, their plasticized skin contained small wrinkles in the areas that had been shot, and their analytical processors from time to time would erupt with nonsense.

Aspen missed Zora. She knew she should move on, but she still missed her friend.

Because the robots had banned them from engaging in external communications, she hadn't spoken to anyone off-ship in over eight months, basically since they'd left Mars and the Escala behind. All she'd done was send messages that Zora had not returned. Perhaps the robots had lied to her and not sent them, or perhaps Zora had replied but the robots hadn't given her the messages. The most likely scenario, however, was that Aspen reminded Zora of Rendela, who had sacrificed herself so Zora would live. Rendela had always been so much better than the rest of them, so selfless. How she had wound up in the cadet program was a mystery.

Why was she thinking about Zora and Rendela?

She thought instead about the Chinese Escala—or Chescala, as Shiloh had named them. They were finally healed, or at least as healed as they could be. When they left Mars all those months ago, the Chescala had been homicidal, victims of a miscalculation by one of the medical robots, who was attempting to wipe their memories.

The robots, possessing free will, had told the Chescala they would refuse all orders to put themselves in danger, making the Chescala decide to shut the robots down, essentially killing them. The robots rebelled: a bloodless coup for the most part; the robots had no intention of harming the Chescala. They simply wanted to live free, instead of as slaves.

Now the robots ran the ship or the ship ran the ship, and whatever destination they'd decided upon, or whatever destination the ship had chosen, they hadn't shared that information with Aspen, her fellow cadets or the Chescala. They might be drifting in circles, headed to a planet or moon, or even on a course out of the solar system. There was no way to know.

The robots insisted the ship was in control and they wouldn't interfere with its decisions. They also claimed they didn't know the ship's final destination. They seemed unconcerned by that.

General Ban and the rest of the Chescala plotted against the robots, trying to figure out ways to retake the ship. The robots knew about the plotting, of course, but did nothing to stop it—almost as if they were indulgent parents, letting their children work out their anger issues. Or perhaps their human-first programming wouldn't let them do anything to harm the Chescala, especially after the earlier mistake with the medication.

General Ban had tried to recruit Aspen and her fellow cadets into their plot, but Aspen and the others refused. They had promised not to try to enslave the robots, and she was determined to keep that promise.

Plus, the cadets knew what it was like to be manipulated, held captive to a puppetmaster's desires. They could never condone taking over the robots now that they knew the robots were like them—intelligent beings with free will and no intent to harm anyone.

Still Aspen wanted to know where they were going. She found it frustrating to be kept in the dark all the time.

The door opened and Addam appeared, hands behind his back, flanked by Benn, Phan, Shiloh and Kammilee. They wore broad grins, looking angelic as usual: part of the process that had accelerated their aging.

"What are you up to?" Aspen asked as she braced herself for trouble.

They looked at each other and then back to her.

"Happy Birthday!"

"What? How did you . . ."

"It's not a secret," Addam said as he slid a small box from behind his back and proffered it to her.

"What is it?"

"Silly," Kammilee said. "You have to open it to find out what's inside."

"You're thirteen years old today," Benn said. "The oldest of all of us. Or you would be thirteen if you hadn't been genetically aged."

"But you still look good," Phan said. "Not a day over twenty-five."

"Hush," Shiloh said as she elbowed Phan. "Go ahead. Open it."

Aspen opened the box. Inside she found a simple necklace with a heart-shaped locket attached.

"Open the locket," Addam said.

Aspen opened the clasp and separated the two halves. Out popped a holo-projection of three female cadets—Zora, Rendela and herself—her tong from the Moon. They smiled and waved at the holo-camera. Was that the happiest moment of her life? Certainly the happiest moment she could recall.

She fought off tears as she remembered her long-lost friends: Rendela dead, Zora living on Earth, the three of them so close on the Moon and now separated forever.

"Thank you," she said.

"You've done a great job," said Addam.

"How did you make such an intricate piece?"

"Xinliu helped us," Kammilee said. "She set the holo-projection. We did the rest."

"It's beautiful," said Aspen. She got to her feet and hugged each of them in turn.

"We're making a cake for dinner," Phan said. "Well, we programmed it into the auto-cook."

"I'm sure it will be delicious."

Benn looked both ways down the hall. "Squeeze in," he said.

He stepped inside her room, closed the door and said, "A couple more things you should know. First . . ."

He gestured to Kammilee, who took his hand and said, "I'm pregnant."

"You're what?"

"Three months. I wanted to tell you earlier, but there was some concern about whether I'd be able to carry the baby to term, what with all the genetic and nano-modifications we've all endured, plus the fact that I'm really only twelve years old."

"Wow."

"Aren't you happy for us?"

"Of course I am. I know this is what you wanted. Do the robots know? Of course they do."

"Yes," Kammilee replied. "Xinliu assigned Mei-Xing to monitor my condition."

Aspen smiled. "Mei-Xing must be thrilled by that."

"Surprisingly, she's been very pleasant, very professional."

"I don't trust her," Benn said.

"That's probably because she doesn't trust us," said Shiloh.

"I wish Xinliu had assigned someone else to help."

"Well," Aspen said to Kammilee, "take Benn to all your checkups and keep one of the male med robots there at all times."

"I will," Kammilee said.

"What else?" Aspen asked. "You said there were a couple of things."

"It's the Chescala," said Phan. "I think they're preparing an attack on the robots."

Aspen shook her head. "Sixteen against forty, and the forty are faster, stronger and maybe smarter, not to mention aware of their plot to retake the ship—doesn't seem like a very bright move to me."

"I didn't say it was a smart move," Phan replied.

"What makes you think they're getting ready to attack now?"

"I asked some of the robots, none of the leaders—I'm sure they wouldn't tell me. But some of the other robots have been talking, and they think it's coming soon."

Addam nodded. "What do you think we ought to do?"

Shiloh leaned forward. "Should we side with the Chescala or the robots?"

"Or should we take advantage of the situation," Benn said, "and grab control of the ship ourselves?"

"The ship won't be easy to take," said Aspen. "It has a mind and a will of its own. I've been thinking about this quite a bit lately and I believe the ship has no intention of going anywhere."

"What do you mean?" Addam asked. "We're clearly flying through space. Unless it's all some elaborate hoax and we're still orbiting Mars?"

"No, we're flying through space. I think. What I mean is, I don't believe the ship wants to set down on any particular planet or moon. I think it wants to keep flying, doing what it was created to do, so I don't think it has a specific destination in mind. I believe the robots know that and they're just happy to be free so they don't care about an end destination."

"Assuming you're right," Kammilee said, "what should we do about it?"

"I'll have a talk with General Ban, see what he's planning. Maybe I can convince him not to do anything stupid. If not, then I guess we'll have a decision to make. Meanwhile, let's go get some cake and celebrate my birthday and your pregnancy."

Chapter 5

The ride back to Washington felt much longer than ninety minutes. Soon after they started down the road Jeremiah had pulled back inside himself. Zora wished she could somehow ease his suffering, but he saw the pity in her eyes and shook his head slightly. "I'm fine," he said. "Just a bad day." Yet each breath made him wince, making it difficult for her to breathe as well. It probably didn't help that he'd seen Curtik wearing Julianna's face.

Curtik, to his credit, tried to engage Jeremiah half a dozen times but Jeremiah mostly nodded or shrugged and Curtik finally gave up, rolling his eyes and exhibiting that unfocused stare that told her he was using his implant, probably to listen to the Crystal Skull Bangers' newest song.

As she studied Jeremiah, Zora sent Devereaux a message via her interface, asking if there was something she could do to help him. It was a fraction slower using an interface than an implant like Curtik's, but they had plenty of time. Yet no reply came. So they rode in near-silence, Jeremiah sitting without moving, meditating or more likely centering himself in his dungeon to escape the pain.

In the past year, Zora had come to realize that as much as she cared for him, she wasn't in love with him. She cared for him more than any other person she'd known, but the love she'd felt before, the sexual desire, had transmuted into the love of a daughter for her father.

He'd been telling her for a long time that she would come to that realization some day and he'd been right. She no longer wanted him, no longer dreamed of him. But she still missed the idea of him—the goodness, the vitality, the dignity and kindness, all those qualities Curtik had yet to master.

She sensed that Jeremiah was receding from the world, fading into invisibility, as if he were no longer connected to it. That frightened her. He looked as if he'd be dead in months, but with his fantastic healing abilities, he would probably continue to live in agony for many years.

Had he given up? Was he going through the motions for her sake and Curtik's? She wished she could make him see how badly he was needed.

As the sedan pulled to a stop in front of the CINTEP building, a message arrived from Devereaux: *Take him to see Sophie.*

Zora turned to Jeremiah and said, "You should come inside and see your daughter."

Jeremiah shook his head. "Too much to do."

Zora elbowed Curtik.

"She's right, old man," Curtik said. "Sophie misses you."

"I have a meeting with Devereaux," Jeremiah said.

"He won't mind," Zora said. "In fact, it was his idea."

Jeremiah smiled briefly. "You've been in touch with Devereaux?"

"I've been worried about you. So has Curtik, though he tries to hide it. It feels like you're slipping away from us."

Curtik said, "I just got a message from Lendra. She said to remind you that your PlusPhone is turned off and she asks for the pleasure of your company before you depart."

Jeremiah sighed.

Zora gestured for Jeremiah to precede them out of the vehicle and again he smiled. "Are you afraid I'll drive away if you get out first?" he asked.

"The thought occurred to me."

He took a deep breath and stepped out of the sedan. When they joined him, he hobbled toward the building, pain evident in every stride.

"I don't want your pity," he said as Zora and Curtik flanked him.

Zora glanced at Curtik but he made no response. They rode to the top floor without speaking, looking straight ahead. When they arrived, Jeremiah dutifully entered the nursery.

Zora and Curtik stopped outside the door. Curtik called over a vending robot and selected a couple raisin/walnut croissants and fizz waters. They took a few minutes to eat, occasionally glancing through the window in the door, noting how stiffly Jeremiah moved as he played with Sophie.

"What next?" Curtik asked after they finished their meal, depositing the empty bottles in the vending robot's recycler and sending it away.

Bring him to Lendra's office after his visit, Devereaux sent to her interface.

"Did you get that?" Zora asked.

"Yeah," Curtik replied. "Freaks me out every time he does that. It's like he just pops into my head. Maybe I should get my implant removed and use an interface like you do."

"I was just thinking maybe I should get an implant again. My brain is almost fully healed. Dr. Poole says I could tolerate one now."

Lendra emerged from her office and walked down the hall to where they stood. Looking through the window at her former lover and her daughter, she said, "It's nice to see him with Sophie. I wish he would visit more often."

"Yes," Zora replied.

"He's got some issues," Curtik said. He spotted Lendra's frown and added, "What? We all know it's true. He's a good man, but he's kinda messed up."

"How did the mission go?" Lendra asked.

"I don't know," Zora said. "We did what we were told, but I'm still not sure what that was. Planted some sensors and a couple of bugs, got shot at, returned fire and ran away."

Curtik said, "Is that Fowler guy really involved in conditioning people's minds?"

"We believe so, yes. The bugs and sensors are intended to help us confirm or discount that intelligence."

"Who's he workin' with?"

Lendra looked at Jeremiah and Sophie again.

Zora answered for her, "There must be a group in the media, putting out the message to keep the sheep in check."

"A lot of the big companies, probably," Curtik said. "Gotta keep that money rollin' in, no matter what."

Jeremiah spotted them through the window as the nanny approached with a tray of food for Sophie. He kissed his daughter goodbye and opened the door. Shaking his head, he asked, "Now what?"

Lendra said, "How are you feeling?"

"Fine."

"Only hurts when you're awake?" Zora said.

Jeremiah smiled. "Something like that."

"I'm sorry," Lendra said, "but you need to see some things."

Jeremiah sighed. "Lead the way."

As they traipsed into Lendra's office, Zora noticed Dr. Poole sitting behind a second, smaller desk situated next to Lendra's. Hannah stood over Jay-Edgar, who was sitting at his old comm console. What was he doing here?

All three of them studied Jeremiah as he made his way toward the sofa. When he sat, they looked over at Lendra.

"There have been a few changes to CINTEP," she said. "From now on, Dr. Poole will be my co-director. She will focus on the Susquehanna Virus, while I will lead the search for these God hackers—though we will be working together on both projects. We've recalled Jay-Edgar to assist us with the hacking issue."

"How do you feel about sharing power?" Jeremiah asked.

"I welcome the help," said Lendra.

Jeremiah glanced at Zora, then at Lendra, who was fingering her glass bulb necklace, then back at Zora.

Zora smiled. So Lendra was still fighting her addiction to neo-dopamine.

"What?" Curtik said. "What are you two on about? I'd think you were sending each other messages except Jeremiah doesn't have an implant."

"Nothing," said Zora. "What about these hackers? Why is that a big deal? It seems like a harmless prank."

"There have been some new developments," Lendra said. "Jay-Edgar?"

Jay-Edgar pressed an icon, and a holo-projection of Devereaux appeared. Devereaux no longer possessed the simplistic robotic shell he once had; instead, he'd created a new body following the Wong-Tech design, and he had altered the features so that he looked like he had when he was human—though a little younger than before his body died. He even wore a lab coat over a set of clothing, which probably captured energy with every movement.

"Hello," the robot spoke in Devereaux's voice. "I hope you're well. It's good to see you all, particularly you, Jeremiah."

"I was just on my way to see you," Jeremiah said, his voice sounding weary. "What do you need now?"

"It's not what I need from you, it's what I can do for you." The robot smiled. "I've found a way to eliminate your pain."

"That's great," said Lendra.

"Wonderful," Dr. Poole echoed.

Zora watched Jeremiah, but he didn't appear happy to receive the news. She noticed Curtik watching Jeremiah too.

"What's the catch?" Jeremiah said.

"No catch," said Devereaux. "I just want you to feel better."

"Okay, and how are you going to do that?"

"A relatively simple procedure entailing further genetic enhancement."

"Meaning?"

The robot nodded. "Minor improvements to your strength, endurance and speed. That's not what we're attempting, of course. They're simply side effects of the treatment. Do you remember when you were shot by a Las-rifle on the Moon, that brief surge of exhilaration, almost invincibility?"

Jeremiah nodded. Zora thought she detected fear on his face, but when she looked closer, she saw only a blank expression.

"I've found a way to essentially duplicate that process in your body all the time."

"What about long-term consequences?"

"Ah," Devereaux replied. "Of course, I can't know for certain but I don't think it will shorten your life by much, if at all. Likely, you will simply live a pain-free existence."

"But there could be unintended consequences."

"Yes."

"I'll think about it."

"Jeremiah," Lendra said, "isn't it worth it to eliminate your pain? Don't you want to feel better?"

Jeremiah glanced at Lendra before turning back to the holo-projection. "Anything else?"

Devereaux said, "There have been a few new messages from these hackers claiming to be God, and I believe they're referencing you."

"Me?"

"I think they believe you're their prophet," said Devereaux.

"I'm no one's prophet."

"The really odd thing," Devereaux continued, "is that one of these messages was sent to me."

"Why is that so odd?" Zora asked.

"The message," said Devereaux, "apparently originated inside my organic computer, inside my brain, if you will."

"That's not possible," Jay-Edgar said.

"I realize that," Devereaux said. "It's quite vexing how a message could get inside my systems without me being able to trace it."

"Unless it really was from God," said Hannah.

Lendra said, "We're going to assume that's not the case for now."

"What did your message say?" Zora asked.

"'Listen to my prophet, who is more than human, less than whole.' Typical biblical ambiguity, though it may be referencing you, Jeremiah."

"That message is so vague it could be referring to you as well."

Devereaux said, "True. But my analysis suggests they may be attempting to get you back in the game, so to speak."

"Back in the spy business?" Curtik asked.

"For what reason?" Zora asked.

"That's what worries me," said Devereaux. "Your enhancements are no longer a secret. They may want your blood to create new warriors. Or they may want to accelerate the evolution of humanity by studying your genetics."

Dr. Poole said, "But we've also pointed out, at least among the scientific community, that Jeremiah is in constant pain, that whatever his enhancements are, coupled with the Susquehanna Virus, they're debilitating."

"Maybe God didn't get the memo," said Curtik.

"Funny," Zora said.

"I think you're a target," said Devereaux. "I suspect whoever is behind these God messages is trying to draw you out. And I'm worried because they somehow hacked into my organic computer. That tells me they're very sophisticated. That's why I think you should accept the enhancements I'm offering, in case they somehow get to you."

"What if God is really out there?" Hannah asked.

Zora said, "I hardly think—"

"Oh, not the God from the Bible or the Koran or the Torah, but what if there really is some supreme being and it's trying to contact us. We know alien life exists. We've found evidence of it on dozens of worlds."

"Many light years away," Dr. Poole said.

"Sure. Too far away to visit for now, but what if one of those life forms is far superior to us? What if it is essentially a God? Maybe it has the power to do things we believe are impossible. I mean, isn't that something we have to consider?"

"You're right, Hannah Banana," said Curtik. "We ought to consider it."

"Don't do me any favors," Hannah said.

"But I'm taking your side."

"Why?" Zora said. "You're the biggest atheist of all."

"I used to be," Curtik conceded. "But now I wonder. What if I'm wrong?"

What kind of game was he playing? Was it possible Curtik was the hacker? No, Zora decided, that wasn't his style. If he were going to attack, he'd do it directly and he'd want his target to know who was doing the attacking.

Chapter 6

Jeremiah studied Curtik. The boy had grown so much in the past year, and yet he still seemed prone to fits of immaturity. Did he really believe in God now? Or was he playing some sort of game with Hannah? Curtik had never really gotten along with her. And yet Jeremiah knew that Curtik had been searching for answers ever since his return to Earth so, unlikely as it seemed, he might have chosen to find meaning in God.

"I just think it's possible," Curtik said, "that there's a God. Like Hannah, I don't believe it's the God from the Bible or any of those religious texts, but it might be some sort of fantastically intelligent creature and, if it chose to contact us, why wouldn't it reach out to our most intelligent person?" Curtik gestured to the holo-projection of Devereaux.

Jeremiah looked at Devereaux. "What do you think, Professor?"

Devereaux shrugged. If Jeremiah didn't know better, he'd have sworn the great man was still occupying his own body rather than a Wong-Tech robotic one. Still, there was something slightly off about the way he carried himself now.

"I haven't believed in God for a long time," said Devereaux. "But this . . . well, it doesn't seem possible that someone could hack into my mind and plant a message there. I'm running diagnostics as we speak but I'm finding no indicators of an outside attack."

"So, could there be a God?" Zora asked.

Devereaux shrugged. "It depends on how you define God. But yes, I suppose it's possible."

Lendra said, "I still don't believe it is. It's probably a gifted hacker or a group of sophisticated hackers, who . . ."

Her voice trailed off.

"What is it?" Dr. Poole asked.

"I just got a message from God too," Lendra said, tapping her interface.

"What does it say?" Hannah asked.

"It says, 'Turn to the light and you shall see.' I'm not sure what that means."

"Out there?" Zora suggested as she pointed to the windows.

Jeremiah got to his feet. He found it extremely frustrating that even simple movements like rising from a sofa caused him agony. He almost wished he could take Devereaux up on his offer to eliminate the pain but if he did, the magnates and despots who ran the world would find ways to use him again, to turn him into their weapon. No matter how determined Jeremiah was to avoid their call, all they'd have to do would be to threaten Sophie or Curtik or Zora and he'd be bound to answer. That was partly why he kept away from them. He didn't want anyone to know how much they meant to him.

Devereaux, smart as he was, should have known better. After all, Jeremiah had been sent after him several years ago and a great many people had died. If Jeremiah were to regain the powers he once possessed, or increase them like he had on the Moon for that brief, terrifying moment, he could scarcely imagine the lengths they would go to in order to manipulate him.

No one had said anything to him. No one had to. He knew if he were to become the physical specimen he once was, they would want to control his mind too. He'd seen just such a proposal from one of CINTEP's analysts, buried in one of Eli's old files. So he knew Lendra had seen it and probably President Hope as well.

He hadn't appreciated before just how systemic the problem was, just how sophisticated the efforts at controlling the population had become. He walked to the windows and looked out. The others—all except Jay-Edgar and Hannah, who remained behind as Jay-Edgar's guard—joined him.

For a moment all he saw was the city at night: the White House (finally restored after the Las-cannon attacks by the cadets) and the Capitol lit up, the Lincoln and Washington Monuments standing out, while the Jefferson Monument sat in semi-darkness, still in the process of being rebuilt. Then he looked up.

Clouds covered the sky, making it difficult to be certain, but as Jeremiah watched he thought he detected strange movements, as if he were watching a time-lapse vid that had been manipulated by computer. "Up there," he said.

The clouds gave off an eerie light, as though lit from within, and began to thin in spots, letters gradually taking shape in the form of holes in the clouds, exposing the night sky behind them—black letters inside white clouds, forming the words:

STOP MAKING WAR – GOD

"Can you see this?" Jeremiah asked Devereaux.

"I see the vid," Devereaux replied.

"How could someone do that?" Jay-Edgar asked.

"I don't know how any person or group of hackers could do such a thing," Dr. Poole replied.

"I confess I'm at a loss as well," said Lendra.

"The President is calling me," Devereaux said. "I can conference her in via holo-projection if you wish and if she's amenable."

"Go ahead," said Lendra. She returned to the area in front of her desk, as did Dr. Poole. Zora and Curtik stayed by Jeremiah's side.

The lettering continued to hold its shape. Jeremiah couldn't conceive of a way to accomplish what had just been done without drones or some sort of sophisticated laser system, but either of those methods would certainly be detected by the security measures in place.

"Hello, all," President Hope said. "We have a problem, as you're no doubt aware."

"The message from God," said Lendra.

"Messages," President Hope said. "There have been at least forty-seven that we know of around the world, some of them in the clouds like the one above the White House, some of them suddenly appearing on the walls of buildings facing various capitals, and one a message sent from the government of Qatar to all its citizens—although the government of Qatar insists it sent no message."

Jeremiah turned from the window to face the President. "Have you spoken with the Vatican?"

"Hello, Jeremiah," President Hope said. "It's good to see you again. I hope the pain isn't too bad tonight. Why the Vatican?"

"I'm curious what the world's religious leaders say. Do they believe it's God or do they think it's an elaborate hoax? And have they received messages from God as well?"

"I'll contact them shortly," President Hope said.

"They received a message," said Devereaux. "Accessing it now—'The time for different faiths is over. All are equal in my eyes.'"

President Hope said, "There are a few other things. First, the Department of Defense received a message from God on one of its encrypted computers, which means that these hackers have somehow gotten inside a supposedly secure system. Second, I also received a message on my private PlusPhone from this God, which also should not have been possible."

"What did your message say?" Lendra asked.

"'Accept the truth. I am coming.' It was also signed by God," President Hope said. "Vice President Rodriguez thinks we've reached the end times. I suppose that's possible, but if it isn't actually God, we need to figure out who it is and how they're doing it before these attacks escalate."

"And if it is God?" Curtik said. "Some sort of supreme being? What then?"

"I don't know," President Hope replied. "It would depend on what he, or it, wants."

"Well, is there some way to contact this God?" Dr. Poole asked. "Some way to ask what it wants?"

"There doesn't appear to be," said Devereaux. "How about your message, Ms. Riley?"

"It came in without an ID tag," Lendra replied. "No way to reply or even track it that I can see."

President Hope cleared her throat. "Finally, Professor, I wanted to speak with you about the Susquehanna Virus. We've picked up several more threats, not directed at us for the moment. One originated in Beijing and was addressed to the Chinese President. Apparently a group known as Nexus 8 is threatening to release a new version of the virus if the Chinese Government doesn't free all its members. We're not certain what Nexus 8 is. Do you have any idea?"

Devereaux went still for a moment. This was why he didn't seem completely human anymore—his ability to stand like a statue. Jeremiah didn't recall him doing that before his consciousness entered a robotic body.

"Nothing certain," Devereaux finally said. "I have suspicions. The Chinese experiment with free-will robots was named the Nexus Project, and the robots who took over the Chinese ship that was headed for Mars were robots with free will. But I can't say for sure that the two are connected."

"What about the other threats?" Dr. Poole asked.

"The second one originated in Germany and the third in Spain," President Hope replied. "They both came from relatively unknown terrorist cells seeking to overthrow their respective governments. All three came within the last hour. That's too great a coincidence to be ignored."

"So they're probably connected to each other," said Lendra.

"And possibly to this group of God hackers," Zora added.

"What makes you say that?" Curtik asked.

"The timing. Someone is planning a major disruption to the world's governments."

"Interesting idea," Jeremiah said. "What do you think of that, Professor?"

They all turned to Devereaux, who had gone still again. For a few seconds, he said nothing. Then he shook his head. "It's possible. I'm sorry. This message I received is bothering me. I can't trace it at all. I need to shut down all external communications for a while to see if I can ascertain how my security was breached."

"Hold on a minute," Jeremiah said as the holo-projection of Devereaux vanished.

"Damn," Jeremiah said. "There's something else we need to consider and that's the possibility that whoever is behind this wants to get Devereaux out of the game."

"Distract him by making him concentrate on this God message?" Lendra said.

"If so, it's working."

Lendra said, "What do you want us to do, Madam President?"

"We're sending your tech analysts the metadata from the DOD intrusion. I need you and Jay-Edgar to use your hacking skills. Find out what you can. If these hackers can infiltrate our Defense computers, they can hack into anything—power plants, hospitals, practically every car on the road. They can create chaos. They have to be stopped."

"And the virus?" Dr. Poole asked.

"I've asked the Germans, Spanish and Chinese to turn over whatever information they have," President Hope replied. "I don't know how forthcoming they will be, but do whatever you can."

"Thank you, ma'am," Dr. Poole said.

"There's one other thing," President Hope said. "Some of my advisors believe Devereaux is behind these hacks. They say he is the only one who might possess the ability to do all this and they want him shut down immediately."

"That's crazy," Dr. Poole replied. "He's never shown any inclination to power or violence."

"I happen to agree with you, but now that he's signed off, do you think it's possible he could be behind it? What I mean is, does he have the skill to create all this chaos?"

Jeremiah felt sick. He wondered how much of this suspicion was directed at Devereaux by people who disagreed with and were threatened by his ideas.

"It seems unlikely," Lendra said. "I don't see how one person, even someone as talented as Devereaux encased in an organic computer, could do so much at the same time."

"Very well. I'll accept that for now. Good night." President Hope's image vanished too.

"What was that all about?" Zora asked.

"I think it was a warning to Devereaux," Jeremiah said. "He's made lots of enemies over the years."

"And Devereaux, even though he isn't connected right now, will surely access the conversation and become aware of it."

"He's probably already aware of it," Jeremiah said. "He probably knew as soon as President Hope's advisors informed her."

"So what's our first move?" Curtik asked. "Who do I attack?"

"There's no one to fight just yet," Lendra replied.

"Well, I have to fight somebody. Who is Fowler connected to? Perhaps I can go after him a little harder. Scare him with an attack on his home. What do you think?"

"That's premature," Jeremiah said. "And it might force him to retrench. We don't want him to feel personally threatened yet."

"Well, we have to do something. What media companies is he in cahoots with? Lendra?"

They all looked at Lendra. She in turn looked at Jeremiah. He shook his head. "That's as much as we can do at the moment," said Lendra. "We need to do some more research."

Jeremiah started for the door. He tried to move smoothly, as if he weren't in agony. "I'll go see Devereaux in person. He may be able to enlighten us on the next step to take."

"What about getting rid of the pain?" Zora asked. "Are you going to talk to him about that?"

"I will."

"If it can make your life better," Lendra said, "you should consider it."

If. All benefits come with a cost. And Jeremiah wasn't sure how expensive this fix would be. But based on past experience, the cost would be enormous. Why couldn't they just let him walk away?

Chapter 7

Doug waited at the entrance to Zeriphi's quarters. The shimmer light that served as a privacy barrier glowed yellow, indicating that Zeriphi and Celestia would be out shortly. He glanced down the tunnel, trying to recall which opening led to the mess area. The series of caves and tunnels that made up the settlement generally followed a symmetrical pattern, though two tunnels branched off, curving around to connect with the larger cave that made up the mess area, which looked somewhat like the main room of the cave the Escala had constructed in Minnesota.

Yesterday had been an odd day.

Doug's meeting with Celestia had gone about as well as he could have hoped. She ran into his arms and called him Daddy and showed him a series of rocks as well as the small patch of lettuce and spinach she was growing. He'd carried her around the colony while she introduced him to everyone, even the people he already knew.

Zeriphi had been reserved, offering a cool smile and a tepid hug, along with the obligatory remembrance of him. He got the sense that she wished he hadn't come. Perhaps if she had told him that while he was on Earth, he would have stayed away.

If she didn't want him here, why hadn't she just said so? Trapped up here for a couple years, it could get mighty unpleasant if Zeriphi didn't want him around. He conjured up an image of Devereaux, which helped calm him. I refuse to let Zeriphi ruin my visit. I'm here for my daughter. I just want to get to know Celestia.

The shimmer light faded as Zeriphi and Celestia emerged from their quarters. Celestia wore blue coveralls that emphasized her cocoa complexion, and a ribbon held her long curly hair in a bun.

Zeriphi looked lovely, wearing a shimmer cloth shirt and trousers. Shimmer cloth had become popular on Earth because it hid the body's flaws. But Doug couldn't see any flaws in Zeriphi's body. She was taller than him, and heavier, and yet she looked feminine: long blond hair, high cheekbones, full lips. Bearing two children hadn't put more weight on her hips that Doug could see. He still wanted her.

"Daddy!" Celestia said as she threw her arms around his legs. She looked older than two because of her Escala nature and her size. Doug would have guessed she was five if he'd met her on Earth.

"Hello, Celestia, my darling little one," Doug said. He nodded to Zeriphi. "How are you this morning?"

"Fine," Celestia said.

"Hello, Zeriphi," said Doug.

"Doug. I remember you."

"And I remember you." Doug looked from Zeriphi to Celestia. "Where's your brother?"

Zeriphi answered, "Paddon's watching Zander."

Doug nodded as he returned his attention to Celestia. "Are you going to show me around the colony again today?"

"Mommy says I have to go to school, but we can have breakfast together and I can see you after."

"Okay."

Celestia lifted her arms, indicating that she wanted him to pick her up. As he lifted her, he was surprised again at how light she was. It was easy to forget that Mars' gravity was only thirty-eight percent of Earth's. She probably would seem heavy back home.

He walked beside Zeriphi to the mess area, Celestia's arms around his neck. His daughter pointed out the hybrid plants lining the tunnel—

blueberry, raspberry and blackberry—and she identified each variety by pointing out the differences in their leaves. He found her knowledge astounding even though he knew how important learning was to the Escala.

Zeriphi walked stiffly, saying nothing. Was she letting him bond with Celestia or did she have nothing to say to him?

The mess area was about half full—Escala gathered in clusters by age, the older Escala sitting at one table, a group of male teenagers at another, another group of female teens at the table beside them, then a few families sitting by themselves. It looked normal and for that reason seemed out of place.

Doug collected his food tray while Zeriphi got one for herself and their daughter. Settling beside Celestia across the table from Zeriphi, Doug mostly watched Celestia eat. He managed to choke down some berries and bread, made with a variety of grains grown in an aquaponic bay. But he had little appetite. Nor did Zeriphi, it seemed. She ate no more than he did.

Even Celestia picked up on the mood of the two adults and quieted down, finishing her meal and giving Doug a brief squeeze before wandering off to school.

For a moment after she left Doug said nothing. He just looked at Zeriphi.

"I'm sorry, Doug," Zeriphi said.

"For what?"

"I thought I could handle you being here. I thought, now that I'm with Paddon, that your presence wouldn't bother me."

So she and Paddon were a couple.

"I'm not here to win you over," Doug said, trying his best to sound sincere.

"I know. But your being here reminds me of Zod. I can't focus on my work. I have no appetite. I want to lie in my bed and wait for death. I realize that's my problem, not yours. But it's how I feel."

"I wish you had told me before I left Earth that this might be an issue for you."

"I honestly didn't think it would be."

"Well, I'm stuck up here for the next two years. Do you want me to see if I can live with the miners for the rest of my stay?"

To his surprise, she seemed to be thinking about it. After a long moment, she said, "That won't be necessary. Paddon can handle your visits while I'm in the lab. Wellon will handle your physical exam today. What are you going to do after that?"

Doug had no idea how to answer her. He'd thought, of course, about what he ought to do to keep himself busy while he was here on Mars, but he hadn't come up with a good plan, other than to win over Zeriphi and get to know Celestia. But apparently Zeriphi was sickened by the sight of him.

Before Doug left Earth, Devereaux had suggested he compile a record of the Escala and what they did. He had nodded his agreement, with no intention of following through, but now he thought that might be a good idea.

"I want to talk to Quekri," he said, "about documenting the Escala journey to Mars—how it came to be, what you do in any given day, what your plans for the future are. A lot of people on Earth would be interested in learning that."

"That seems like a good idea," said Zeriphi. She looked away and Doug turned to see Dr. Wellon standing at the entrance. "Looks like she's ready for you now," Zeriphi added.

Doug nodded. He got to his feet and stood for a moment with his tray in his hand, but he had no idea what to say to her, what might make her feel better, so he walked away, depositing his tray in the washer/recycler by the entrance.

"Hello, Doug," Dr. Wellon said.

"Hello? Not 'I remember you'?"

"That's a more formal greeting. I prefer hello for casual contacts, if that's okay with you."

"It's fine."

"Shall we?" Dr. Wellon gestured for Doug to walk with her. "Devereaux told me about your project, documenting our experience."

"When did he do that?"

"Some time ago," Dr. Wellon replied. As they walked along the tunnel to her office, she said, "Do you have a separate camera or will you be using your PlusPhone?"

"Um . . ."

"I've got a tri-camera you can use if you like. It gives a better 3-D effect than a PlusPhone, though it still won't give you a high-quality holo-projection image."

"Thank you," Doug said. "That's very kind of you."

"You're welcome. Though I'm doing it more for Zeriphi than for you."

"For Zeriphi?"

"She doesn't wish to hurt you," Dr. Wellon said as they reached her lab area.

The room, or cave, was about fifteen by twenty feet, with equipment lining every wall. When Doug entered, Dr. Wellon pushed a button and activated a shimmer light behind him, blocking off the tunnel from the room. She selected a scanner from a shelf.

"I'm sure she doesn't," Doug replied.

"She told you that she finds it painful to be around you," said Dr. Wellon.

"Yes, just now."

"Good. Best to rip the bandage off straight away. Now let's have a look at you."

Dr. Wellon held the scanner to Doug's torso and studied it, humming softly: a tuneless hum that was almost a purr, like some giant cat.

Doug stood still, not certain if he was allowed to speak. His previous physicals had been more intrusive, with more instruction from the medical techs as to what he should do.

After a long moment, Dr. Wellon removed the scanner and said, "Hmm."

"Is there a problem?" Doug asked.

"You have the Susquehanna Virus," Dr. Wellon said.

Doug felt like he'd just been punched in the stomach. "But that's impossible. Two doctors checked me out before I boarded the MineStar ship and I was cleared."

"That may well be," Dr. Wellon conceded, "but you have it now."

"How could that have happened?"

"You may have contracted it on the ship."

"But the MineStar workers were all cleared too."

Dr. Wellon nodded. "I wonder how good their analytical equipment is."

"You mean, one of the miners might have been infected and they didn't catch it?"

"That's a possibility."

"Am I going to die?"

"Eventually," Dr. Wellon said. "Not for a good long while if I have anything to say about it. I think it's time we paid the miners a visit. We have to see how many of them are carrying the virus before they spread it around and infect everyone."

"But aren't you immune?"

"So far. Viruses have a nasty habit of mutating, and the Susquehanna Virus is more mutable than most. I'm not sure if that was part of its design or if it simply evolved that way, but it's quite pesky."

"Do you think there's a chance I'll end up like Devereaux—trapped in a robot's body?"

"Not everyone is a candidate for that kind of transfer," Dr. Wellon replied. "Devereaux's mind was extremely pliable. He possessed very little rigidity in his thought processes."

"What about Celestia? Could I have infected her?"

"I'll have Keelar check on that," Dr. Wellon replied.

"Will I have to stay away from her?" Doug shivered.

"For now," Dr. Wellon said. "You can communicate via holo-projection, of course, and there won't be that annoying time lag because you're both here on Mars. But you should probably stay away until I can be certain you're not a contagion threat. Why don't you come along with me? You know the miners, at least a little. They may allow me to run scans on them if you're with me, though I think I know what I'm going to find."

"I guess that means the end of my project."

"Not at all. You can still film us via holo-projection. And Keelar and I will still maintain contact with you. We've both been transfused with a manufactured variant of Jeremiah's blood as an experiment, so we're likely even more immune than the others."

Chapter 8

Jeremiah entered Devereaux's lab, noting again the lack of security. A few tiny cameras and sensors were all that stood between Devereaux and the outside world. In addition, Devereaux's lab contained a relative paucity of equipment. He wondered how Devereaux was able to make so many discoveries with so few experiments running but he supposed the great man was able to build upon other people's preliminary work.

"Hello, Jeremiah," Devereaux said. He gestured to the room's only chair. "Here to discuss the treatment?"

"Partly," Jeremiah replied as he sat. "I also think these God hackers may be trying to distract you. And there's a faction within the government that believes you're behind all this."

Devereaux smiled. "Yes, I'm aware of them. Vice President Rodriguez is leading the charge. He believes I'm an abomination. You too, of course. I don't want you to feel left out. At any rate, they want to shut me down and see if the attacks stop."

"And if they do?"

"They'll keep me shut down permanently. Even if the attacks continue, they'll argue that I could have programmed them to go on after being disabled and they'll refuse to believe it's not me."

"They're afraid of you."

"I've tried not to give them reason to be. But now that my mind is encased in an organic computer, I can do many things at the same time. They don't understand me, so they fear me. Unsurprisingly, it's mostly the same people who attacked me while I was human."

"Have you gotten any closer to tracking the hackers down?"

Devereaux shook his head. "I'm afraid not. I've connected to many different systems in the past few months. It's possible I acquired some kind of virus during one of those connections and that's how they were able to compromise my security protocols."

"If the God hackers can infiltrate your protections, what other systems might be vulnerable? Could they hack into the DOD computers and launch nuclear weapons?"

"I don't know. It frightens me a little."

"Well, what's the solution? Do you need to disconnect from every system?"

"I've already done that," Devereaux replied. "I've got a few computers running diagnostics at the moment." He gestured to a handful of data cubes on his desk. "Hopefully one of them will provide some answers."

"But in the meantime . . ."

"In the meantime, why don't you want me to help you?"

Devereaux fixed Jeremiah with a silent stare. He looked so much like his old human body, and yet he held himself with an inhuman stillness. No breathing, no blinking of the eyes, no movement of hands or fingers: he could be a statue.

Jeremiah got to his feet and walked to the window so he could look out at the James River. "Why did you set up shop here in Richmond?"

"What's wrong with Richmond?" Devereaux asked.

"Why not the CDC in Atlanta or a lab in DC? What made you choose Richmond?"

Devereaux smiled. "I spent a few weeks here every summer as a boy. It reminds me of better times. Now why don't you want me to help me?"

"Will it cure me?"

"I don't think so."

"That's one reason. Plus, I didn't feel like myself when that happened to me."

"The scans indicate that you experienced a massive rush of hormonal activity, including a surge of adrenaline and dopamine. I realize that seems like a contradiction, but somehow that combination made you feel almost invincible—not that different from the way I feel right now."

"That's all true," Jeremiah conceded. "But it felt artificial too, as if some outside force had taken over my body. I was afraid of what I might become."

Devereaux nodded. "If we did this, the feeling might not be exactly the same. There would no doubt be a period of orientation, but I suspect you would soon feel incredible, better than you've ever felt in your life. Almost like Superman."

Jeremiah smiled. "I never wanted to be Superman. I still don't. You once told me that pain was good, that it was an indicator I was still alive."

"True. But I was trying to cheer you up when I said it."

"So you lied?"

Devereaux shrugged. "It was true to a point. But there are other, less painful ways of feeling alive. We both know you're dying. It will take a few years, but the mutagenic changes your body is going through have turned against you. The cancer will get worse and I can't stop it. Every treatment I try only alters the DNA of your cancer cells." Devereaux gestured toward a blank screen, probably the one he'd used during the recent meeting with CINTEP. "Why haven't you told them?"

"They would only worry."

"Sooner or later they will find out."

"Later is better."

"You're not thinking of killing yourself, are you?"

Jeremiah smiled. "I think about it every day."

"It would harm me, not to mention Curtik and Sophie and Zora."

"Think how much you could learn from studying my corpse."

"I should have plenty of time for that. This robotic shell, if properly maintained, should last for hundreds of years, and even if it doesn't, I could easily switch to another one."

"Couldn't you just plug your consciousness into an organic computer?"

Devereaux shook his head. "Remember, the mind-body connection is too strong to permit prolonged existence as a mere computer. There needs to be some sort of body to engage the world and maintain a connection to it or the mind will eventually dissipate or deform."

"Could you put me into a robotic shell? Never mind. I don't want that."

"I could," Devereaux said, "but you're a much more physical being than I was. I don't know how successful the transition would be."

"Plus, if I were in such a body, they would try to use me."

Devereaux nodded. "You would be a greater weapon and a greater threat. The solution I offer might not extend your life, but it would make your last few years more pleasant."

"They'd still want to control me."

"Of course," Devereaux said. "But I believe I can ensure that doesn't happen. A few tweaks here and there should guarantee your will is completely your own."

"That's not why I'm worried. I hadn't thought much about that. I was more concerned they'd compel me to work for them by threatening Curtik and Sophie and Zora."

Devereaux smiled. "Funny. That hadn't occurred to me."

"I won't do it," Jeremiah said.

"I understand and I'm sorry, Jeremiah. I already sent information on the procedure to Dr. Poole, thinking you might change your mind. I'm sure she'll be discreet with the knowledge. She would never force the procedure on you."

Jeremiah shook his head. "How could you? We don't know how secure her interface is. And you know what these people are capable of. Hell, they're doing it to you now. They want to shut you down because of your differences."

"Mere talk."

"And as I recall, you weren't too happy when they transferred your mind into an organic computer inside a robot."

"I've since had a change of heart," Devereaux said.

"I haven't. I don't want to be fixed. And I believe that if they find out I'm dying, they might change me without my consent. It happened to me before, as you know. Eli made me an Escala without my knowledge."

"Dr. Poole is not Eli and . . ."

Devereaux stopped all movement. His hand, which had been gesturing, remained in that position. His eyes stayed open, staring straight ahead. In that moment he no longer looked like the Devereaux of old. He looked like the robot he inhabited—nothing but a shell.

"Professor," Jeremiah said. "Professor."

Jeremiah rushed to Devereaux's side, realizing as he did so that he had no way to determine whether Devereaux was okay. There was no pulse to check, no respiration. He snapped his fingers in front of Devereaux's eyes, then grabbed Devereaux's wrist. It felt like it had the last time Jeremiah had touched it: warm and yielding slightly, as if it were made of real flesh instead of neo-skin, and it moved without resistance, as if Devereaux were asleep.

Jeremiah pulled out his PlusPhone and engaged the scanner but all he got were bioelectric readings telling him Devereaux was alive inside the robotic shell. He wished Quark were here. The big Escala would know what to do.

Disengaging the scanner, Jeremiah issued a reboot request before calling Lendra.

"Jeremiah," Lendra said when her face appeared on the screen. "What's wrong?"

"It's Devereaux. He's gone into some sort of catatonic state and I don't know what to do about it. I need Curtik and Zora here ASAP."

"They're on their way. I'll send Dr. Poole too. I mean, I'll ask her to assist. Who else knows about this?"

"I have no idea. He claimed he had disconnected from the outside world, though he was still running several data cubes to diagnose how he received a message from God that couldn't be traced. Perhaps one of them offered an access point for a cyber attack."

"Unlikely. Devereaux knows how to build a firewall. You think someone might launch an actual physical attack against him?"

"That's the most likely scenario."

"I'll get some Elite Ops troopers on the scene."

"Good idea. Call Major Payne. Have him bring a squad or two."

"Maybe I should come as well."

"No."

"Why not?"

"You're in charge of CINTEP—well, you and Dr. Poole. I don't think you should both be out of the office at this time."

"I could leave Dr. Poole here."

"I'd rather have her in case we need her medical skills. Don't worry. You'll be connected. Get them here as quick as you can. I'll see what I can do in the meantime."

"Have you tried a reboot request?"

"The first thing I tried. Nothing."

Lendra shrugged and said, "What about a forced reboot?"

"I wouldn't do that to him."

"Even if it could save him?"

"We don't know his situation. He may have done this on his own. That's why I want Curtik and Zora and Dr. Poole. They may be able to ascertain whether he's in distress without invading his privacy. Either way, I have no intention of tampering with his organic computer."

"All right. They'll be there in twenty minutes, as will Major Payne and his squad. Keep me informed."

"Right." Jeremiah disconnected. He went around the lab examining the data cubes still running their diagnostics and found nothing out of the ordinary. Every few minutes he checked on Devereaux again, but the robot remained catatonic.

He accessed the surveillance feeds outside the lab and studied those as well, but found nothing out of the ordinary, no signs of imminent attack, nothing but people and vehicles passing.

Then a bullet appeared—an armored vehicle containing a squad of Elite Ops troopers. The bullet opened. Zora, Curtik and Dr. Poole stepped out, followed by a half-dozen armored troopers and Major Payne. They looked huge next to the three civilians, more like robots than even Devereaux. The troopers spread out to surround the building, while Major Payne herded the others inside.

Chapter 9

Curtik entered the lab, the Crystal Skull Bangers' latest song, *After Reality*, playing on his implant:

When you finally concede that this world blows
And you come to realize life is only a pose
When nothing that's real can offer repose
Then you'll find me an orange with an ear for a nose

He loved their insane lyrics.

As Zora and Dr. Poole began running scans on Devereaux, Major Payne halted by the door, a Las-rifle in his right hand. Curtik wondered if he could take Payne in a fight and almost immediately had that thought displaced by the memory of Jack Marschenko falling at his hands, which made him feel guilty.

He glanced at Dr. Poole and Jeremiah, who had both loved Marschenko in different ways, then clapped the stationary robot that was Devereaux on the shoulder and said, "How you doin', old sport?"

"He's still out of it," Jeremiah said, looking pale and tired.

"Can I pose him in obscene positions?" Curtik laughed. "I could bend him over a table and—"

"Just see if you can figure out what's wrong with him."

"I'll let Zora and Dr. Poole start the scan process and save my heroics for later. Why don't you sit and relax?"

Curtik gestured for Jeremiah to sit and was a little surprised when Jeremiah did so without complaint. The old man must be tired. Curtik really ought to get out to visit him more often, but he sensed that it was as much a chore for Jeremiah as it was for him. Neither knew what to say. Jeremiah still saw him as the little boy who'd been abducted years ago while Curtik had transcended his roots into something beyond human. He was still searching for an orange with an ear for a nose, an answer for the lunacy of existence.

He began studying the data cubes Devereaux had been running to see if any of them had encountered a virus or hack. The first one showed no signs of entry. The second was also clear.

"Curtik," Zora said.

"What've you got?"

"An odd reading in the mobility controls. It looks like a message came from that data cube over there." She pointed to a data cube across the room.

Curtik made his way over and perused the data stream. Nothing, nothing, nothing. "It looks okay," he said. "No, wait a minute."

One of the data cube's searches had gone askew, as if the data cube had experienced a glitch. Curtik accessed it with his implant and followed the thread as it weaved through cyberspace. The search had indeed gone off track, reverting back on itself at the point where it attempted to connect to a Department of Defense computer, re-routing itself back into the data cube and over to the organic computer that held Devereaux's mind.

"Got something," he said. "Looks like some sort of firewall stopped a search here and twisted it back on itself. That shouldn't be enough by itself to cause this kind of damage, however. It's just a tiny filament—almost no data entering the link and it's completely internal. It was created by the data cube, not by an outside computer. Could that be the problem?"

"Possibly," said Zora. "Dr. Poole?"

"I'm working on it," Dr. Poole replied. "I'm no expert in robotics. There's definitely an interruption that looks like a systemic breach, but as Curtik pointed out, it seems to be originating inside Devereaux."

Jeremiah said, "So it's the God hackers."

Zora nodded. "That's the logical conclusion."

"What do we do?" Curtik asked. "Babysit him until he wakes up? Take him back to CINTEP?"

Major Payne walked to the window. "Armored drones, headed this way," he said. "Six of them."

"Take 'em out," said Jeremiah. "But don't fry the memories if you don't have to. We want to see who sent them."

"Ooh, ooh, ooh," Curtik found himself reaching for his Las-pistol and bouncing on his feet. "Can I take a couple out?"

Jeremiah looked at Dr. Poole, who said, "Let's leave that to the Elite Ops and focus on Devereaux."

Curtik sighed. "What do you want me to do next?"

"Can you tap into that feed and figure out what data is being transmitted?"

"Easy peasy. But if I finish before the drones arrive, can I go out and shoot one?"

Jeremiah smiled. He stood and joined Major Payne by the window, looking small next to the Elite Ops trooper. Was that just because Major Payne was wearing armor? Curtik worried about his father. Perhaps Zora was right and Jeremiah was preparing to disappear. Might he kill himself? Or would he just vanish some day, leaving no trace of his whereabouts, relying on the skills he'd learned as a CINTEP ghost to escape the pressures and commitments he seemed no longer willing to endure?

How could he not want to be involved in such exciting times? Armed drones on the way, the world under attack by either God or God hackers, the Susquehanna Virus changing or potentially changing humanity: how could anyone walk away from that?

Curtik tapped into the feed and studied the data but it was just a series of numbers, nothing that made sense. "Um, okay, maybe not so easy peasy. It's a series of numbers that don't seem to have any order. Not primes or odds or evens, not Fibonacci or geometric or anything I can identify."

"Send it to my interface," said Zora. "I'll have a look at it."

As Curtik complied, Major Payne said, "We've got a problem. These are no ordinary drones. They're shielded."

Jeremiah said, "Can't you use your particle beam cannons?"

"We can, but that'll obliterate them and possibly blow up the missiles they're carrying. And since we don't know what kind of missiles they are, they might take out a large area, us included."

"Suggestions?"

"I think we've got to move."

"Curtik," Jeremiah said as he got to his feet, "you and Major Payne grab Devereaux. Zora and Dr. Poole, take everything you think you might need. I'll get Devereaux's data cubes."

Zora said, "I've got everything I need. Dr. Poole?"

"Just a moment."

"Quickly," Jeremiah said as he moved around the room picking up the data cubes, walking like an old man, favoring his left side, while Curtik and Major Payne each took an arm and lifted Devereaux. Even as a robot Devereaux weighed less than two hundred pounds so Curtik could have hoisted him by himself but he didn't question Jeremiah.

As they carried Devereaux out the door to the waiting Bullet, Major Payne said, "Getting a signal now. Those are our drones."

Jeremiah, herding Zora and Dr. Poole out of the lab, said, "US military drones?"

"Elite Ops drones," Major Payne replied.

"Gotta be the God hackers," said Curtik. "Or maybe the actual God. Who else could hack into your systems?"

"Nobody," Major Payne replied. "That's what worries me."

"What kind of ordnance are the drones carrying?" Jeremiah asked. "Can we take them out safely?"

"Since they're ours, I think so, but I'd like to get everyone into the Bullet first, just in case."

They piled into the Bullet, Major Payne helping Curtik get Devereaux seated beside Jeremiah and Zora while Dr. Poole clambered in last. The major took the controls and sealed them inside, leaving his fellow Elite Ops troopers to deal with the threat.

As they drove away, Curtik activated the viewscreen and sighed.

Zora laughed.

"What?"

"You wanted to stay behind and shoot down drones."

"So? It woulda been a blast." He looked at Jeremiah. "Speaking of blasts, think it'll be big?"

"There shouldn't be a blast from the drones' missiles," Jeremiah replied.

"Contact in ten seconds," Major Payne said.

Curtik stared at the viewscreen. A micro-drone sent back footage that showed the Elite Ops troopers waiting, particle beam cannons lined up, as the drones closed in on them. When the clock hit zero, the troopers fired.

The blasts from the particle beam cannons annihilated the drones, which exploded in mid-air, their missiles dropping straight down. Curtik noticed that his mechanical hand had clenched into a fist and his left hand held a Las-pistol. He forced himself to relax. He said, "That was kind of . . ."

"Anticlimactic?" Zora offered.

"I was gonna say boring, but yeah."

Dr. Poole said, "Are those missiles safe?"

"We've got the override codes," said Major Payne. "They'll be deactivated before they hit the ground. I've got another Bullet headed this way to pick up the troopers and the missiles." He looked at Jeremiah. "Where do you want to go?"

"I suppose we ought to head back to CINTEP."

"Wasn't that a little too easy?" Zora asked.

Jeremiah nodded. "I was thinking the same thing."

"You think it was a setup?" Curtik asked.

Dr. Poole said, "And it was odd that there were six drones sent against six troopers."

"What about me?" Major Payne asked.

"You were inside the lab with us. That may have influenced the attack."

Jeremiah said, "Can you save any of the data?"

"They're looking into that now," Major Payne replied. "The preliminary scan shows only an unidentified directive to proceed to Devereaux's lab and fire upon arrival. The order came from a public server bounced off a satellite. We'll see if we can trace it."

Curtik laughed. "Don't hold your breath. You know, this just might be God after all."

Zora said, "I wish you'd stop saying that."

Curtik held up his hands. "Who else could it be? The only person I would have believed could be behind it is Devereaux. And I'm not even sure he could have pulled it off. But with him in a catatonic state," Curtik lifted Devereaux's hand and smiled when it stayed in that position, "I think we can rule him out."

Dr. Poole said, "It could be a sophisticated group of hackers, working together in multiple countries to achieve this effect."

Curtik nodded. "I suppose. But wouldn't we have seen some sort of buildup? I mean, the analysts and computers at CINTEP monitor communications around the world. Other countries and agencies have similar programs. Surely there would have been some sort of warning. Somebody would have slipped up."

Zora said, "I get the sense that you want to believe in God."

"I wouldn't mind if there is one. It would be kind of nice knowing there's some purpose behind it all, some kind of meaning."

Jeremiah sighed. "It might be something else."

"What?" Curtik asked.

"Someone in our government, someone who wants to shut Devereaux down."

Zora said, "Who would have the expertise or authority to pull it off?"

Major Payne shook his head. "I've seen no orders, no communications regarding such a mission. I find it hard to believe it could be one of my superiors."

"So maybe it really is God," Curtik said, "even if the rest of you don't believe that."

Jeremiah shrugged. "I don't know what to believe anymore."

Curtik wasn't certain it was God, but he knew enough to know it couldn't be Lendra or Zora or anyone else in CINTEP. He supposed it could be somebody in the government or Devereaux, but Devereaux had been incapacitated by someone or something. Plus, Devereaux was the obvious choice, so Curtik was reluctant to assign blame there. And he didn't figure the government would try to pull this off without Major Payne's assistance. No, this was either some new player, some heavy hitter who hadn't showed his chops before, or it was the Almighty himself—an orange with an ear for a nose.

Chapter 10

Aspen sat in the Chescala dining hall across the table from General Ban, Colonel Hong, Captain Chin and Dr. Li Wen. The rest of the Chinese Escala stood behind them, a unified front against her. Sixteen against one: better odds than they'd face if they attacked the robots. She focused on Li Wen, figuring the other woman might be reasoned with better than the men.

"I don't understand," she said. "They know everything you're plotting. They're monitoring our conversation right now. You can't possibly hope to surprise them. Do you think their human-first programming will somehow enable you to defeat them?"

General Ban nodded. He wore an interface that allowed him to translate her words into Chinese.

He spoke a few words that Aspen's implant translated into English: "That's exactly what we think."

Aspen looked at Li Wen. "They're faster, smarter, stronger. And they have more than twice your number."

Li Wen said nothing. General Ban spoke again: "They can't attack us. They can't harm us. If you and your fellow cadets help us, we can take the ship."

Aspen laughed. "How do you plan to make the ship change course? It's doing what it was built to do. It's not going to turn around just because you tell it to."

"We can disconnect its brain—its organic computer—from the controls."

"Maybe," Aspen said. "But if you're wrong . . ."

"It has human-first programming too," Li Wen spoke in English. "That's why it keeps the atmosphere livable and allows us to keep growing food. So even if we fail, as long as we destroy or at least defeat the other robots, it will have to listen to us."

"All right," Aspen replied. "Suppose you attack and win. Where do you go?"

"Back to Mars," said General Ban.

"And what happens to the robots and the ship?"

"They will be reprogrammed to do their jobs."

"Without the interference of free will," Aspen said. "Turned back into slaves."

"No. They would be treated humanely. We would not ask them to put themselves in danger any more than we would put ourselves in danger."

"Here's a bigger question," Aspen said. "Why?"

They looked at her as if she were speaking a foreign language, which of course she was.

"I mean, why do it at all? Why do you want to go back to Mars? What's there that's so special? Why not work instead to convince the ship to go somewhere new and exciting. We could explore beyond the solar system, or at least the outer planets. Why so determined to attack the robots?"

"We are supposed to be in charge," General Ban said. "Not them. We give the orders. They follow them."

"What difference does it make?"

"We're slaves," General Ban said. "Can't you see that? We do what they tell us to do—menial tasks—while they make all the decisions."

"We're not slaves," said Aspen. "They don't make us do anything. You can sit in your cabin all day long if you wish."

"I don't wish." General Ban scowled. "This is no better than Earth. We're becoming slaves there too."

"I wouldn't know about that."

"Trust me, girl. They're taking over—the robots. They're doing almost all the hard jobs now, leaving us with the dregs. They can even do service jobs that require a personal touch."

Even without understanding Chinese, Aspen caught the bitterness in his voice.

"And yet," she said, "here you are. Escala. Sent to Mars."

"Yes. Stuck on this ship doing nothing."

"That's your choice. You could help Xinliu or Mei-Xing with robotics or solving medical problems."

"I'm not a doctor."

"You have to be flexible. You have to be willing to learn new things, try new jobs and find something you're good at."

General Ban shook his head. "Don't you get it? We'll never be as good as them at anything."

"Then do the jobs they don't want to do. Let them lead. Be a follower."

Li Wen said, "You're still a child. I don't mean that as an insult, but you don't understand what it feels like to have your career taken away from you. We've worked toward this project on Mars for years, dedicated our lives to it, sacrificed family and friends and a hundred other things, and then just as we approach our goal, it's snatched away from us."

"I understand," said Aspen. "You want your lives to be other than they are. You want to go back to the past because you were happier there. But those days are gone. You have to live in the now."

"No," General Ban said, "we don't."

"What if I talk to Xinliu? I can ask if we can drop you off on Mars so you can continue your mission there."

General Ban looked at his fellow Chescala. They seemed to be communicating without speaking. Did they have implants? Aspen reminded herself to check with Xinliu. If they had implants, they might be able to surprise the robots after all. She had just assumed they didn't because the Escala on Mars didn't have them. But why couldn't they? There were no physiological reasons preventing it.

Another thought struck Aspen. Perhaps Xinliu and the robots didn't know the Chescala had implants. Interesting. She needed to talk this over with Addam and her fellow cadets.

General Ban finally spoke: "We would need the robots to assist us on Mars. We couldn't carry out our mission without them."

"You still haven't told me what that mission is," Aspen said.

"We intend to establish a colony on Mars."

Aspen shook her head. "You could do that without the robots. The Escala did it."

"They used robots."

"Yes, but not conscious robots, not robots with wills of their own. And they could help you colonize so you wouldn't need to use these robots. I think you're still not telling me the truth."

"Now you insult me?" General Ban said.

Aspen smiled. "You're good at getting me off-topic. But it doesn't really matter. If you attack the robots, you'll lose, and you'll never get to Mars."

"Don't get in our way, Girl. Or we'll attack you too."

Aspen stood. "I think maybe the rage is back, or perhaps it never went away completely. I think you ought to be examined by the robots to determine if you're thinking clearly."

General Ban stood also. "You mean because we won't sit here passively and let the robots run our lives? If we did that, we would no longer be human. We would be zoo animals, remnants of a faded history."

Aspen waited for a moment, hoping the truth might come out. She looked at Li Wen and raised an eyebrow but Li Wen shook her head ever so slightly. Whatever the truth, Aspen wouldn't find it today.

She walked away, sending a message to her fellow cadets to meet in her cabin. As she left the Chescala sector, she noticed an increase in the number of robots in the area, as if they were preparing for an attack. They acknowledged her with nods but otherwise ignored her, continuing their work on various modules and components that should properly have been worked on in a lab.

When she reached her cabin, her fellow cadets were already there.

"What's up?" Addam asked.

"The Chescala," Aspen said, "may have implants that allow them to communicate with each other without the robots being able to monitor them."

"Interesting," said Phan. "I just assumed they didn't because the Escala don't."

"Me too," Shiloh added. "But that would explain why they think they can attack the robots and have a chance to win."

Benn gestured outward. "Should we tell the robots about this?"

"We probably already have," Kammilee answered.

"And whose side are we on?" Addam asked.

"I don't know," Aspen replied. "The Chescala still won't tell me what their real mission on Mars was. They seem determined to get back there though."

"Don't we have to back the robots?" Phan asked. "I mean, they allowed us to stay on board when they could have killed us or dropped us off on some asteroid."

"But they're not human," said Kammilee.

"Under certain definitions," Addam said, "we aren't either. And neither are the Chescala."

Aspen said, "I don't want to get into a philosophical discussion about what it means to be human. I think we need to decide whose side we're on if it comes down to a fight."

Shiloh said, "Is there really no way to reason with the Chescala? Are they going to attack no matter what?"

"I don't know," said Aspen. "We can try talking with them again. Go in force. But until we know where we stand, we can't show them a united front."

"Tell us what to do," Benn said. "Whose side should we take?"

Aspen shook her head. "Talk it over among yourselves. Quietly. Quickly. I already know who I intend to support, but I want you to make up your own minds. I won't force my choice on anyone."

Chapter 11

As the bullet approached CINTEP, Zora noticed a small dot on the viewscreen that looked like a bird. She had a bad feeling about it. As it grew in size, its coherence shifted from one single entity into multiple contacts. She zoomed in the PowerScope and ran a scan—another fleet of drones.

"More drones," she said. "Armed."

"Coming at us?" Dr. Poole asked.

"Looks like it. Yes, they've definitely locked onto the bullet's signal."

"Keep going," Jeremiah said. "We can't stop here."

"Where to?" Major Payne asked. "Back to the Elite Ops base?"

"I don't know if we can get there in time. Maybe we should go to the biggest church in the area."

Dr. Poole said, "You figure if it's God, He won't attack a church?"

"Actually, hold on. Stop for a moment and everyone get out but Devereaux, Major Payne and me. You people get inside CINTEP and see what you can figure out. Major Payne and I will take Devereaux somewhere safe."

"I don't think so," Curtik said. "I'm the muscle. You're the brains. Remember? Me and Major Payne'll watch Devereaux while you all go back to the office."

"Sorry, Curtik," said Zora. "Somebody who understands organic computers has to go with Devereaux. That means me."

Jeremiah looked at Dr. Poole.

"I have to agree with both Curtik and Zora," Dr. Poole said. "They should go with Devereaux and Major Payne while you and I return to CINTEP."

Jeremiah turned to Major Payne.

"They aren't our drones," Major Payne replied. "Don't yet know whose they are. I've got help coming, but I don't relish the idea of a firefight in the middle of Washington, D.C."

"All right," Jeremiah said. "I don't like it, but you're probably right. Be careful."

As the bullet stopped, Dr. Poole stepped out. She reached back and helped Jeremiah exit. It broke Zora's heart to see how fragile Jeremiah had become. She looked away as the door swung shut and the bullet accelerated away.

"Now we're havin' fun," Curtik said with a smile. "What do we got for armor on this bad boy?"

"Standard anti-aircraft defenses," Major Payne said, "as well as Las-weapons and a particle beam cannon."

Curtik pumped his mechanical fist. "Tasty! I get the particle beam cannon."

"It's actually attached to the bullet. But you can man it if that becomes necessary."

Zora said, "Are you going to stop at a church?"

"I'd rather fight than hide," Major Payne replied. "Besides, I've got help coming. I'd prefer to be moving in their direction than stopped somewhere. I'll open the turret and take a Las-rifle. You handle the shields and the anti-aircraft computer."

"Right." Zora looked down at her scanner again. "Less than two minutes until optimal attack position, although they could theoretically fire at any time."

"They'll wait," Major Payne said. "The closer they get, the better their chances at hitting us and the worse our chances of knocking the missiles out of the air without causing collateral damage."

Zora said, "What if they're after Jeremiah?"

"What the hell are you talkin' about?" said Curtik.

"Think about it. He's made a lot of enemies over the years. And when we were attacked, Jeremiah was there too. We assumed the attack was on Devereaux because it took place at his lab, but what if they were really after Jeremiah?"

"I've got Elite Ops troopers at CINTEP," Major Payne said. "And I just sent a message to Dr. Poole and Lendra informing them of the possibility. Besides, Jeremiah can take care of himself."

Curtik smirked at Zora and made a kissing sound. "I think you're still in love with the guy."

Zora shook her head. "I do love him, but not in that way. Not anymore."

"Well, we'll find out if they're after him or us soon enough," Curtik said. "How much time to contact?"

"Forty seconds to optimal contact."

"Particle beam cannon armed and locked in."

Major Payne donned his helmet, grabbed his Las-rifle and opened the turret. "Let's be precise. Just enough force to take out the drones. Okay, Curtik?"

"Yeah, yeah," Curtik replied. "Why does everybody think I still want to blow up the world?"

"Locking in on us," Zora said. "I guess I was wrong about them being after Jeremiah."

"Prepare to fire," Major Payne said.

Before Zora could fire or even raise the shields, everything went black.

***

S he awoke in a garden with songbirds trilling and a gentle light diffused by flowers and leaves that seemed to be coming from everywhere and nowhere. She smelled honeysuckle and lilac, jasmine and rose, lilies and violets. It took her a moment to realize she was sitting on a swing chair held by chains that disappeared into nothingness. Curtik sat to her left in a similar chair. Neither Major Payne nor Devereaux was in sight. A low fog covered the ground, a dense cloud that hid her feet. Above her, she saw only a deep blue that stretched to infinity. No clouds.

Zora stood and took a step toward Curtik to see if he was okay but he began to stir before she reached him, opening his eyes and spotting her.

"What the hell happened?" Curtik asked.

"I don't know. My interface shows that eleven minutes have passed but there's some kind of dampening field in here. I can't get a lock on our position or communicate with the outside world. In fact, I can't even communicate with you via the interface. What about your implant?"

Curtik went still for a moment as he accessed it.

"Nothing. I get the same time code. Eleven minutes, but that's it."

"I suppose we should look around," said Zora, "try to figure out where we are and see if Major Payne or Devereaux are here as well."

"Major Payne," Curtik called. "Professor Devereaux."

Birds chirped and a slight breeze rustled the leaves. No other sound intruded.

"No birds," Zora said.

"What?"

"I can hear them, but I can't see any."

"You think they're not real?"

"I think we're indoors somewhere," said Zora as she pointed up, "and that's a false sky."

Curtik frowned. "So if this is all an illusion, it might be in our minds only. We could still be in the bullet having these experiences and not really here."

"It's possible, but I think we have to assume we're actually here."

"And so you are," a voice boomed. The air warmed slightly and a sense of peace came over Zora. She fought it.

"Who is that?" she asked.

"And where are we?" Curtik added.

"I am God and you are in my garden."

"Not a lot of people here," Zora said.

"Are we dead?" Curtik asked.

"You're not dead," God answered. "I just brought you here temporarily. Do you want people? I can bring them if you wish. Who would you like to see, Zora? Your parents? And you, Curtik. Would you like to see your mother?"

"Yes," Curtik said.

"No," said Zora.

"Why not?" Curtik asked.

"Because it could all be part of the same illusion. We would see what we want to see, not necessarily the truth."

Curtik frowned. "So I would see my mother the way I wanted to see her. It would be a construct from my mind?"

"At least in part," Zora replied. "Perhaps with enough new material to make you believe it has to be her because you don't remember those features."

"You don't think we can trust anything we see?"

"I don't know."

"Ah," said the voice, "a doubting Zora."

Curtik said, "Let us see you."

"I do not have human form. I am all around you—the air, the water, the flowers and birds, and even inside each of you. I am not corporeal."

"But you can become like us," Curtik said. "You can take human form."

"Certainly."

"Then do that."

A mist formed in front of them and from it emerged Walt Devereaux, walking slowly. He seemed friendlier than the real Walt Devereaux, gentler and yet capable of great hardness.

Zora shook her head. She sensed this God was trying to manipulate her. "Why did you pick that form?"

Devereaux spoke: "It was the foremost image in your minds. I thought it would please you."

Had she been thinking about Devereaux? Yes, she had to admit she'd contemplated whether this was some sort of game he'd created.

"Are you Devereaux or are you God?" Curtik asked.

"I am both," Devereaux replied. The image vanished and reappeared as Jeremiah, but in a healthier version, one not crippled by infirmity. It spoke in his voice: "I am God and Jeremiah." Once again the image vanished to be replaced by President Hope. "And I am God and Angelica Hope. I am all things and all people, yet I am outside all things and all people too."

"You like to talk in riddles," Curtik said. "I remember that from the Bible."

Zora almost choked. "You've been reading the Bible?"

"Ever since God began hacking into systems," Curtik replied. "Don't look so shocked. I thought I'd do some research—downloaded it into my implant and ran a relevancy scan to highlight the important parts. Lots of contradictions in it. An eye for an eye and turn the other cheek." Curtik turned to President Hope. "How do you explain that?"

"I am good and evil," President Hope said, "light and dark, everything and nothing. I am the beginning and the end. Of course there are contradictions in your texts. There are contradictions in all of us."

"Not in you," said Curtik. "Not according to those who preach your message."

"Most who preach my message get it wrong."

Zora shook her head. Had Curtik really gotten religion or was he just playing around again? She said to him, "Now you've been watching preachers?"

"It's fascinating stuff, Zora."

"You never showed any interest in any of that stuff, either on the Moon or afterward."

"But I wanted my life to have meaning," Curtik said. "And it doesn't."

"So maybe this is you," said Zora. "Maybe this was all created for your benefit and I just got trapped inside it somehow."

President Hope vanished and was instantly replaced by a man and woman Zora recognized as her parents. She hadn't seen them since she'd been abducted and taken to the Moon. Her parents, she'd later discovered, died while she was on the Moon. She had no real memories of them, only stories people had told her and a few vids captured and stored in various servers. But they looked like her parents and they smiled at her.

The woman—her mother—reached out her hands to embrace Zora. "Oh, Suzanne, honey. We've missed you."

Zora flinched. Part of her wanted to run into this strange mother's arms, welcoming the warmth and love that emanated from this creation, while another part of her wanted to laugh or cry or pummel somebody raw. She sensed she was on the desperate edge of madness, a footstep away from a cliff of self-pity and infinite neediness. She refused to give in to that kind of emotion.

"I'm Zora now," she said. "And I don't believe you're really my mother. I wish you were my parents. But they're dead and you're nothing but a construct."

She steeled herself for them to protest, to insist they were her mother and father, but they mercifully vanished, leaving her and Curtik alone. The false birds continued to chirp. The aroma of flowers filled the fresh air. The light shone warmly upon her face while Curtik stared at her with something like fear or awe on his face, as if he couldn't believe she had resisted the temptation offered. Zora thought of Jeremiah, of how he would have handled this, of how strong he would have been. She refused to cry.

Chapter 12

Taditha Poole struggled not to assist Jeremiah out of the elevator, saddened at his broken-down state. Every day he had to choose between the agony of movement that accompanied a relatively clear mind and a pain-free existence dampened by the fog of anesthetics. His body rebelled against painkillers, leaving his mind unfocused and unable to concentrate on anything. She stayed a step behind him as he limped to Lendra's office. Her office too now, she remembered.

She missed her old office; she missed Jack Marschenko.

Jeremiah had asked that Gil and Finn, the Elite Ops troopers who had served as his bodyguards, be returned to regular duty, insisting he no longer needed protecting. So even though she still saw Gil occasionally, now that he was back with his fellow troopers and she was mired in problems at CINTEP or taking care of her son Jack, they had little time to spend together.

She almost wished for a threat on Jeremiah's life so Gil could return. No matter what Jeremiah wanted, if President Hope thought there was a credible threat against him, she would insist on bodyguards.

As they entered the office she saw that the temporary desk next to Lendra's had been replaced with her old one. For a moment it stopped her. Then she realized Lendra had moved it in here as a way of acknowledging that Poole belonged.

"Thank you," she said.

"You're welcome," Lendra replied. "What's going on with Zora, Curtik and Devereaux?"

"What do you mean?" Jeremiah asked.

"They've gone dark. Jay-Edgar?"

Jay-Edgar sat at the communications board. Poole hadn't noticed him. Hannah stood off to the side, watching his movements, serving as his jailer while also studying how he managed the board. On the far wall, a holo-projection of a city street played.

Jay-Edgar pointed to the holo-projection. "This was their last known position. They completely shut off communications and cloaked the bullet. I'm not getting any kind of signature at all."

"Something's not right," Jeremiah said. "What about the drones?"

"They broke off the attack," said Lendra, "and flew away. We tracked them for a mile but they vanished, probably cloaking themselves. Elite Ops troopers are on the way to the bullet's latest position."

"Why didn't you tell me about the lost communications earlier?"

"I thought it was a defensive measure. Isn't that possible?"

Jeremiah shrugged. "Possible, but unlikely. How long until the Elite Ops get there?"

"One minute."

Jeremiah turned to Jay-Edgar and said, "What do you know about the drones?"

"We think they were hacked from the Army."

"You aren't certain?"

"They have altered wavelength signatures, but they match the description of six drones that vanished from their hangar three hours ago—carrying the same type of weaponry—and the Army says it has no idea where the drones are."

"Any way to track them?"

"Not until the Army provides us with the codes, and even then, if the hackers have modified the access codes or the tracking software, it might be tricky."

On the screen a bullet headed toward the spot on the street where the other bullet had disappeared. Jay-Edgar tapped into the audio.

"No sign of the missing bullet," a voice spoke. "If they cloaked themselves, they moved to a different location."

"Wait a second," Jay-Edgar said. "The missing bullet's turned up."

"Where is it?" Lendra asked.

Jay-Edgar changed the holo-projection. A bullet sat parked on the street outside the CINTEP building. "Right out front. It just decloaked. Major Payne and Devereaux are inside."

"Zora and Curtik?" Jeremiah asked.

"I don't see them." Jay-Edgar provided a view of the bullet's interior. Major Payne and Devereaux sat inside, unmoving.

"Somebody's playing with us," Lendra said.

"I want to know where that bullet's been." Jeremiah turned back toward the door. "Hannah, you're with me. Dr. Poole, you too."

Jeremiah ran, limping, to the elevator ahead of her. Hannah kept her arm out to the side, ready to catch him should he fall, but Poole knew he wouldn't. Despite his frailty, nothing would deter Jeremiah now that he was on the hunt. He used his access code to bring the elevator to the top floor. Pulling two analysts from the car, he said "sorry" as he got in, waited for Poole and Hannah to join him, then hit the emergency drop.

Poole's stomach gathered in her throat, the nausea reminding her of her time on the Moon while pregnant. She managed to avoid vomiting as the car slammed to a halt. Jeremiah raced outside, Hannah right behind him. Poole followed more slowly.

By the time she reached the bullet, Jeremiah was helping Major Payne climb out while Hannah assisted Devereaux.

"Are you injured?" Poole asked.

Major Payne shook his head as he stood. "A little unsteady. I don't know what happened. Everything went black on us."

"Professor?" Poole asked.

"I seem to be all right," Devereaux said as he exited the bullet also.

"You're no longer in a catatonic state," Jeremiah observed. "Are you aware that you were?"

"It was an odd sensation," said Devereaux. "I was able to think, but my ability to move and all my senses were shut off, as if someone else were controlling my body. My ability to communicate with the outside world vanished for several hours. I couldn't see or hear or feel anything, as if I were nothing but intellect trapped in blackness."

"So you don't know what happened to Curtik and Zora?" Jeremiah asked.

"They must have been abducted," said Devereaux.

"What makes you think that?" Poole asked.

"If they were with us as you say, it seems illogical that they would have simply stepped away from the bullet without informing us."

"Were any of your internal systems able to record what happened or at least note where you were the past half-hour?"

Devereaux went still for a moment. "Sorry, no. It's almost as if the past few hours didn't exist for me. I did have plenty of time to think about certain problems, though you likely aren't interested in those at the moment."

"Not particularly." Jeremiah turned to Major Payne. "Can you check the onboard computers to see if there's any way to track where you were?"

"I just finished examining them with my implant," Major Payne replied. "All data is missing for thirty-seven minutes."

Hannah said, "So Zora and Curtik are lost?"

"They can't be far," Jeremiah said. "We'll find them."

Poole hoped he was right, not so much for Curtik, whom she still struggled to like, but for Zora, the younger sister she would have wished for, the daughter she'd be proud to call her own. If this was the God hacker, he was playing games far beyond her ability to understand.

Chapter 13

Doug looked around his new quarters at the MineStar colony, a few kilometers from the Escala settlement. The room was tiny, only large enough to hold a fold-up bed, a cabinet for clothes and personal effects, and a chair. Not even a window—just a vid screen that he could load with any image or vid he wanted. If he sat on the bed, he could entertain a single visitor, not that he was expecting any. The Escala had no reason to care for him. After all, he'd brought the virus to them.

"It won't be so bad," Dr. Wellon said from behind him. "There's a fairly nice common area for the miners and since you're all infected, you needn't quarantine yourself in this cabin."

"How long do we have?" Doug asked. He'd been afraid to ask before. As he spoke, he noticed that his throat felt dry. He wondered if that was a symptom of the virus. "Weeks or months or years?"

"I'll talk to everyone in the commons in a few minutes." Dr. Wellon held up her PlusPhone. "I'm still running an analysis of the scans I took, but the strain you contracted is a new one I've not seen before. It could take years to kill you or perhaps only weeks. I just don't know. But I hope to find a cure before it comes to that. I intend to keep you alive for a good long time."

"I don't understand how all the miners contracted it. From the reports I saw, it looked like it was hard to catch the virus."

"That used to be the case. But as I mentioned earlier, this virus is more mutable than most."

Dr. Wellon's PlusPhone pinged. She looked at the screen and bit her lower lip. "Results are in," she said. "Let's gather in the commons."

Turning around, she walked out to the sitting area, where the miners waited. The foreman Enright stood as they approached. "Well, Doctor, how bad is it?"

"Bad enough," Dr. Wellon said. "The strain you have is a variant of SV17 and it's quite contagious, which means you'll no longer be able to visit our colony freely as miners in the past have done. However, it's been a slow-acting variant to date. It's not been aggressive so far and you're not symptomatic, which helps explain why no one discovered you had it when you shipped up here. Perhaps only one or two of you had it to begin with, but now you're all infected."

"It was him," said Wilcox, pointing at Doug. Wilcox had been the least friendly miner on the trip to Mars, perhaps because he openly detested Devereaux. "He worked with Devereaux, and Devereaux caught the virus, so Doug musta picked it up from him and infected the rest of us."

"We don't know that," Dr. Wellon said. "It will take more tests to determine where the virus started. And for our purposes, it doesn't really matter except for determining the likely timeline for when it might begin to assert itself symptomatically. Those of you who caught it more recently will likely have more time. But I expect you all to survive until the next MineStar ship arrives."

Wilcox gestured toward Doug. "We don't want him here. Take him back to your colony."

Several miners murmured their agreement.

"I'm afraid I can't do that just yet," Dr. Wellon said. "We don't have a quarantine area set up. We can create such an area, of course, and place Doug there, but I should warn you—when we do, Keelar and I will be focusing on him and not you."

"Are you saying you won't treat us?" Enright asked.

"I'm saying our priorities will be with Doug. You have med-tech units sent by your employer. Doug does not. So Keelar and I won't have much reason to visit. Your med-tech units can be programmed to treat the virus by some of the best minds on Earth."

"You're abandoning us?"

"We'll still be available for emergencies."

"This is his fault," Wilcox said as he launched himself at Doug. Two miners grabbed his arms to hold him back. "Lemme go!"

Wilcox glared at Doug, his face dark red, as he struggled against his fellow miners. He wasn't a large man, but Doug found himself afraid. He tried not to show it, standing his ground and staring back at Wilcox. The other miners, including the ones holding back Wilcox, glared at Doug. He'd thought he was on friendly terms with them but even Enright scowled at him.

Maybe they were right to blame him.

"Control yourself," Dr. Wellon said. "Stress can only make the virus worse. Now if you'll excuse us, Doug and I have some matters to discuss. I suggest you contact MineStar headquarters and inform them of your situation. I'll send along a report as well. You should also visit your med-tech units soon. I've sent them my diagnosis so they'll be able to treat you accordingly."

She gestured for Doug to lead the way to his quarters. He opened the door and stepped inside. As she followed him in, she closed the door behind her.

"You don't have to create a quarantine space for me," Doug said. "I can stay with the miners."

Dr. Wellon frowned. "I admit I hoped you could stay here. It would make things easier if you were all together. But they clearly don't want you around. That's fine. We care for our own."

Doug felt a catch in his throat. His chest grew warm and tingly. He wondered if she was serious and if the Escala sincerely considered him to be one of them. He had, after all, inserted himself into their colony. Perhaps they didn't really want him but were doing this out of a sense of duty. No matter. He still felt encouraged by her words.

"Thank you," he said.

"You're welcome. You belong to us. You always will. Zeriphi will see that in time."

He hoped, but he didn't believe. How many times had Quekri told him his DNA profile wasn't a match for the genetic surgery necessary to turn him into one of them? Surely they could have found a way if they wanted him. "Do you think it was me? Do you think I infected them on the way up here?"

"It's possible," Dr. Wellon said. "But it's not your fault if you did. You didn't know you had the virus."

"I don't understand how they didn't catch it before we left."

Dr. Wellon shrugged. "It's possible it wasn't you at all. One of the miners might have been infected. Their medical exams are less rigorous than the one you took."

"I still don't understand how the virus could be missed by any medical exam."

"It's microscopic and it might not express itself in a particular blood sample. At any rate, don't blame yourself. I should probably get back. Do you have any questions before I go?"

Doug nodded. "It seems like you're being a little vague about the virus. The treatments, the timeline, the symptoms—you haven't told me much so far. Is that because you don't want me to worry or because you don't know very much about this strain?"

"A little of both, I'm afraid." Dr. Wellon shrugged. "This is a relatively new strain and we don't yet know how quickly it will activate itself. I don't want you to worry because increased stress might activate the virus sooner."

"You said that to Wilcox. Is that something that's happened with SV17 before? Is this one of the strains that might stay hidden for a while, targeting all my major organs so that it can hit them all at once?"

Dr. Wellon smiled. "You worked for Devereaux. Yes, that's one possible outcome he posited for SV17, though we don't know for certain."

Dr. Wellon's PlusPhone chimed. She looked down at it and then back at Doug. "Good news. Keelar says Celestia shows no trace of the virus."

Doug felt lighter, as if gravity had suddenly decreased enough for him to float away. He hadn't realized how tense he'd been. "That's great. Thanks."

"We'll get working on the quarantine area right away. You'll have to be here a few days. Let us know if the miners give you any trouble and we'll come running."

As Dr. Wellon exited his quarters and made her way to the airlock, Doug glanced out into the commons. Several miners stood there, staring at him through the open doorway, rigidly erect, brows furrowed, saying nothing. After a minute, he closed and locked the door.

Chapter 14

Curtik wished that God—if it was God—had brought his mother instead of Zora's parents. He still couldn't believe she had rejected them. Was she right? Were they just a construct? He would have loved to find out. If he'd been given the chance to speak with his mother, to hug her, he never would have turned it down. He couldn't imagine anyone having the willpower to do that. It was inhuman.

"We should see if there's a way out of here," Zora said.

Curtik smiled. "A way out of the Garden of Eden?"

"What's really going on with you and all the religion talk?"

"I don't know," Curtik replied as they began to make their way forward, following a path that meandered through flowers and shrubs. "Life just seemed so meaningless. I wasn't happy and I couldn't figure out my purpose—why I was here. And then this God appeared and seemed to provide an answer of sorts. I don't know if it's the right answer or the only answer, but it gives meaning to everything if there's a God who's in charge, who created us and loves us and wants us to fulfill our greatest potential."

"How is that different from Walt Devereaux? He wants us to fulfill our potential too."

"But he's not God," Curtik said. "He doesn't believe in God, so if God exists, then Devereaux doesn't know what he's talking about and why should I listen to him? Sure, he's smart, but if there really is a God, and Devereaux never figured that out, then what else has he screwed up?"

"But, come on. God?"

"Why are you so against the idea?"

Zora stopped for a moment and looked around. "Everything is flat," she said.

"So?"

"So it's not real or there would be hills."

Behind Zora a hill rose in the distance without making a sound. Curtik laughed.

"What?"

He pointed to the hill.

"Come on." Zora grabbed his arm and made for the hill. She picked up her pace, winding past flowers of many hues, brilliant and sweet smelling. "I just don't believe," Zora continued as they began to climb, "that this person or group is God. I mean, if God exists, would he play games like this? Would he talk to only a few select people? Would he give only some people the answer and depend on them to provide it to the rest of us? Why not tell everyone? And why does he want us to worship him anyway? Why does he need that? Why does he care?"

As they crested the hill, Devereaux appeared before them and the air felt suddenly warmer.

"All good questions," he said.

Curtik looked out over the land below them—garden as far as he could see. Clouds decorated the sky. Birds continued to sing. A squirrel disappeared behind a tree that Curtik hadn't noticed before, almost as if the tree had suddenly appeared to give the squirrel a place to climb.

"Are you Devereaux or God?" Curtik asked.

"I'm both," Devereaux replied.

"So what are the answers to my questions?" Zora asked.

"I play games because I find them interesting," Devereaux said. "I'm curious as to how humans will react. I talk to a few select people to see if they will listen, to see if they will forward my message on to the rest of the world."

"But what about human fallibility?" Zora asked. "If we're not perfect, we won't get the right answers from your messengers. It's like the game Telegraph where a message gets passed down the line from person to person and if the chain is long enough, the message that comes out at the end is nothing like the message that started the process."

"True," Devereaux conceded.

"That doesn't strike me as perfectly good."

"I never claimed to be perfectly good. That is a burden placed on me by those who believe in me because they want my power to be used for good, not evil."

"What about the whole worship thing?" Curtik asked. "I mean, I might believe in you, but I don't know if I could worship you."

"I don't care if you worship me or not."

"But religions say we should worship you."

"I never asked for that either. But the prophets who started their religions, the ones who spoke to me, who believed in me, could not conceive of me as other than omnipotent, omniscient and all good. So they worshipped me and demanded that their followers worship me too."

"So you don't care if we worship you?"

"Why should I care? Do you think my ego is so fragile that it requires propping up by the likes of you?"

Zora said, "You don't sound like the God of the religions I've studied."

"That shouldn't surprise you. Look at how many things those religions have gotten wrong. Intolerance, for example. Why would I care if a few individuals wanted to believe something other than the truth? Why would I care if there were multiple belief systems in place to assist people in arriving at a place of happiness and generosity?"

"So which religion is correct?" Curtik asked. "Or which one is closest to the truth?"

"They're all right and they're all wrong."

"More riddles," Zora said.

"More truth. Religions are correct in wanting to uplift the human spirit. They're correct in preaching love. Religions are wrong in drawing a line to separate themselves from other religions and they're wrong in claiming that they are the one true religion. Oh, there are a few that don't claim to be the exclusive path to enlightenment. But all the major religions have gotten it wrong. Is that a better answer?"

"You're asking me?" Zora said.

"Why not? Your opinion counts just as much as the next person's."

"But you're supposed to be God."

"I'm not only supposed to be God. I am God."

"Why us?" Curtik asked. "Why me and Zora?"

"Because one of you wants to believe in me without worshipping me and one of you will never believe in me, no matter what proof I lay before you. You will always suspect it is some kind of trick."

Zora said, "We'll be your greatest challenge?"

"Not even close. But you two interest me."

"Why are you keeping us here against our will?" Zora asked.

Devereaux shook his head. "I'm not. You are free to leave whenever you wish. You need only express that wish and I will release you."

"Hold on a second," Curtik said. "If we ask to be freed, will we ever get another opportunity to speak with you?"

"That I cannot answer."

"Because you don't know or because you're being mysterious?" Zora said.

"I'm not omniscient," Devereaux replied. "Nor am I omnipotent. And I'm certainly not all good, either by human standards or any other. I saw an opportunity to speak with you and I took it. I may not get another."

"But if you're God," Curtik said, "shouldn't you be able to just think about having us here and make us appear?"

"That's the God of the Bible, certainly. And I could do it, but I don't know that I would want to expend that much energy just to talk with you. Do you wish to leave?"

"Yes," Zora said.

"No," said Curtik. "Please, Zora. Not yet."

Zora looked from Devereaux to Curtik and back. Then she sighed and Curtik knew she would allow them to stay awhile longer.

"Thank you," he said. "Now, God, let me ask you this. If you can do pretty much anything, why don't you stop all the evil in the world?"

Devereaux smiled. "I have other things to attend to at the moment, but I'll be back soon. If you would like anything, you need only express a wish for it."

"And it will appear?" Curtik asked.

Devereaux vanished, leaving them alone at the top of the hill.

"I'm not sure this was a good idea," said Zora. "Jeremiah and the others will be worried about us."

"How many chances do you think we're going to get to talk to God?" Curtik asked. "In almost all the stories, he appears for a short time, speaks to someone and then disappears. I'm afraid if we leave now, we might never see him again."

"I'm not sure that would be a bad thing." Zora looked out over the garden. "Still, it is pretty."

"You think this is the real Garden of Eden, where Adam and Eve lived?"

"Those are just stories, Curtik."

"Well, I'm hungry." Curtik lifted his head and called out. "Could we get something to eat and drink, please?"

A small table appeared between them. It looked like a snake—its tail against the ground, its body winding around an invisible pole and its open mouth holding the glass top. As Curtik stared at the table, a bowl of apples and two glasses of water appeared on its surface, materializing out of thin air.

Curtik laughed. This God had a sense of humor.

Chapter 15

Jeremiah waited in Lendra and Dr. Poole's office for some word on Curtik and Zora. Everyone else seemed to be busy studying various screens or their interfaces and Devereaux stood quietly in the center of the room, no doubt accessing more information than all the rest of them combined. But they still had no idea where Curtik and Zora could be.

He felt like lashing out. Useless, crippled, dying old man. Part of him wanted Devereaux's fix, the changes that would make him stronger, faster and perhaps even impervious to laser strikes. Even if it was just for a few more years, it would feel amazing to have a body that could respond the way it once had. He'd felt so alive in that brief moment on the Moon after he'd been shot—his body reaching a new plane of existence. Invincible. Immortal. Unstoppable. Yet even as he bathed in the exhilaration of unspeakable power, he'd seen what he might become and that prospect had terrified him.

He knew people like President Hope and even Lendra would ultimately seek to harness him, control his mind, if he possessed those abilities. They couldn't afford to have him running around with free will, doing whatever he wanted whenever he wanted, possibly interfering with their plans for the world. And if they knew he was dying, they might put him into a robotic shell like Devereaux. Or they might decide to use him for extremely dangerous missions while they still could, missions of a morally questionable nature. As a sick man, he enjoyed a certain freedom he would not be allowed were he to regain his prowess.

Jay-Edgar cleared his throat.

"Yes?" Lendra said.

"I finished doing a full analysis of the bullet. I don't know how, but every trace amount of information it accumulated for a thirty-seven-minute period was wiped."

"Nothing at all?" Lendra said.

"I'm afraid not."

"Major Payne?"

"I have to agree," Major Payne said. "I've run a second analysis and a deep scan. Nothing. But it couldn't have gone far. I've ordered three squads to run scans of every possible hiding place within a fifteen-mile radius."

"How long will that take?" Dr. Poole asked.

"Without help, eight or ten hours. But I've asked the local police departments and the FBI to assist. HQ is coordinating the effort. With their assets, I'm hoping we'll be able to scan all the likely sites in a couple hours."

"Professor?" Jeremiah said. "Professor Devereaux?"

"I'm afraid I can't help," said Devereaux. "I can tell you that Edwin Fowler put new computers in place today, unlinked to the outside world."

"Who's he?" Hannah asked.

"President and CEO of Natural Hybrids Incorporated," Devereaux replied.

"What does that have to do with anything?"

"He's the last piece of the puzzle," Jeremiah said. "The network of corporations that run the world. Food, finance, security, communications and healthcare. We've infiltrated all their systems."

"But if he just put in new computers unlinked to the outside," Jay-Edgar said, "how are you going to infiltrate the company?"

"He bought the computers from a company we wanted him to buy from."

"You sabotaged his new computers. How?"

"The batteries," Jeremiah said.

"It was a brilliant idea," Devereaux said. "Jeremiah actually came up with it. A coating on the batteries allows for infiltration through Fowler's PlusPhone, although the signal is weak, so data transmission is slow."

"Our plan is to determine how much they're manipulating society and decide whether we should take them down." Jeremiah shrugged. "Unfortunately, we're a little sidetracked now with this God situation as well as Curtik and Zora, so he and his friends will have to wait."

Dr. Poole said, "We have another problem—the Susquehanna Virus."

"What about it?" Lendra asked.

"We're beginning to see three strains assert themselves more aggressively—SV12, SV14 and SV17. SV12 and SV14 don't appear to be fatal—at least not immediately—but they are becoming symptomatic at an increasing rate. And they appear to be mutating rapidly. The only good news is that all the new mutations we're seeing—with the exception of SV17—are not deadly. And SV17, while fatal, takes a long time to overcome the body's immune system."

"SV12 and SV14," Devereaux said. He turned to Jeremiah. "As we suspected."

"We may have to move more quickly than we hoped."

Lendra said, "What are you two talking about?"

"Edwin Fowler," said Jeremiah. He turned to Devereaux. "You should explain it, Professor. You're the one who discovered it."

Devereaux nodded, the gesture making him look so human Jeremiah had to remind himself that the great man's mind was encased in a robotic shell.

"We've known for decades," said Devereaux, "that certain viruses, parasites and bacteria can alter personality and even intelligence. Parasites like *taxoplasma gondii* and viruses like red algae are just the start. We think Fowler and his company are experimenting with the Susquehanna Virus, hoping to make it nonlethal but also attempting to alter it so it will act as a delivery mechanism for personality and intelligence changes. And they're putting it in our food."

Dr. Poole said, "To make us more addictive and less intelligent?"

"As well as more impulse oriented," Devereaux replied. "And the two strains you mentioned— SV12 and SV14—are the most malleable. A sophisticated scientific team could modify those strains to make them behave more like these natural microbial infections. The right team could even accentuate the effect with only slight adjustments to the virus."

Hannah said, "What's their goal?"

"Control," said Jeremiah. "They want to control us completely. They want us to buy their products and remain passive when they engage in behavior that ought to enrage us. They want wealth and power and a world of humans to treat them like gods."

Dr. Poole said, "And the other companies you mentioned? They're involved too?"

"Only the top people. Most of the employees are simply trying to make tastier food or create better communications equipment or design medical breakthroughs to ease human suffering. Very few are aware of the conspiracy at the top."

Major Payne said, "I can have the Elite Ops partner with the police and descend on their corporate headquarters to arrest them all."

"We don't yet have the proof we need," said Devereaux. "This effort to obtain information from their computers is the first step in bringing them to justice. We hope we'll get the data we need to prosecute them."

"And if you don't?" Hannah asked.

Jeremiah shrugged.

Major Payne said, "I don't want to sound like I'm going rogue again, but the Elite Ops could take them out."

"That's a last resort option," said Jeremiah. "Until we know who all is part of the conspiracy, we don't want to move. And given your history with Richard Carlton in Minnesota, I wouldn't dare ask you to get involved. If we chose that route, it would have to be a more covert operation."

"Can we warn people?" Lendra asked.

Dr. Poole said, "Aren't there scientists studying this? What about the FDA? Shouldn't they have caught the infiltration of the virus into our food?"

"There are ways around the FDA," said Devereaux. "And it's not just food. Variants of SV12 and SV14 are in the water and air now. That's part of the problem. It's difficult to prove where these modified strains originated. They can always claim it was accidental—that their facilities were contaminated without their knowledge or that they were somehow hacked and as a result unwittingly infected us."

"And a few researchers have been warning about the virus for years," Jeremiah added. "Several scientists have come forward with evidence of greater infiltration than the mainstream community has acknowledged."

"I've heard them," Lendra said, "but they've always been dismissed as quacks."

"That's where the media outlets come into play," said Devereaux. "They control the messages we receive. Every time one of these people comes forward with a warning, a dozen scientists on the other side dismiss it as hyperbole. It brings to mind the dismissal of global warming at the beginning of the century, when science was usurped by politics, faith and corporate interests."

"But most scientists are honest," Dr. Poole said.

"You're right." Devereaux shrugged, another human gesture. "But many are paid by large corporations to do studies that promote the companies' viewpoints, and the results of those studies make the media far more often. Those are the stories that catch the public's attention because the large companies have figured out the precise metrics for getting their messages across—the right blend of fear and greed."

"And most of the scientific community," Jeremiah added, "has been focused on larger problems, like the deadly nature of most of the strains. The timing was perfect. If we didn't have to deal with such a serious disease, there would have been much more attention paid to this problem."

"So what's our next step?" Lendra said. "Data collection and monitoring?"

"I'm afraid so," said Devereaux. "Until we get something more definitive, we can't arrest anyone."

Jay-Edgar cleared his throat and said, "What if Lendra and I hacked their systems? I realize you're probably better at it than we are, but we did hack the Las-cannons. We could give it a try, see if we can come up with something, if it's all right with Lendra."

Lendra nodded and said, "Maybe. I'm guessing they've been very careful to keep these conversations off their systems. Probably lots of face-to-face meetings."

"Yes, but they likely had meetings at places with security systems. If we could hack into those systems, we might be able to download vid or audio of their conversations."

"It's worth a try," said Jeremiah. "However, they're in cahoots with White Knight Security as well, and Devereaux found it difficult to hack into their network. Meanwhile, we need to focus on getting Curtik and Zora back."

"We're doing everything we can," Lendra said. "You're just going to have to be patient."

"When we do find them," said Dr. Poole, "we may have to break them out. Will you be able to help with that given your condition? And what happens if we have to go after Fowler and the rest?"

They all turned to look at him. Jeremiah saw the questions on every face, even Devereaux's. Amazing how Devereaux had created a robotic face so similar to his old one that Jeremiah couldn't tell the difference. He knew what they were all thinking. How could he not maximize his abilities to assist them? How could he stand here and let others fight his battles for him? Didn't he care?

"No," he said. "I don't want the cure, whatever it is. We'll find another way."

Their faces sagged. He knew they only wanted what was best for him. He knew they thought he was choosing pain over happiness, but they couldn't see what his last few years would be like if he became the creature they wanted him to be. Better to suffer a free man than live in comfort as a slave.

Chapter 16

Aspen led the cadets to the bridge of the ship, where Xinliu and Mei-Xing stood—the two "female" robots looking nearly identical. Aspen could tell them apart now by the way they held themselves: Xinliu always that little bit hunched over, as if the weight of command, such as it was, were pushing down on her; and Mei-Xing with her chin pushed forward slightly, mirroring her aggressive attitude.

The bridge needed no one to man the controls, for the ship ran itself, but a command chair sat in the center of the space and there were several chairs at stations around the room, all empty.

On the forward screen Aspen saw an image of stars she didn't recognize, but she knew it wasn't real. It was the image the ship wanted them to see. They were still somewhere in the solar system.

"You're here about the Chescala," Xinliu said, adopting Shiloh's term for their adversaries.

"What are you going to do about them?" Aspen asked. "They'll come after you soon and they won't be held back by any programming."

"We're aware of that," said Mei-Xing.

"Are you going to let them win?" Benn asked, his arm draped over Kammilee's shoulder. Kammilee held her hands over her stomach, an unconscious gesture to protect her unborn baby.

Phan said, "We can fight for you. We don't have your limitations."

Shiloh nodded. "Arm us and we'll defend you."

Xinliu said, "We appreciate your concerns and we're pleased you chose to side with us. Several of us predicted you would side with the Chescala." She looked at Mei-Xing, who glared back at her. "But it is not yet time to fight."

Mei-Xing shook her head and clenched her jaw. Aspen wondered if that kind of response had been programmed into her or if she did it as a result of having free will.

"Do the Chescala have implants?" Addam asked. "Can they communicate with each other without you intercepting their messages?"

"Yes," Mei-Xing said. "And it's a problem even if Xinliu refuses to recognize it. We know they're making plans, but we don't know what they are."

"What are your plans?" Aspen asked. "You can't just sit around waiting for them to attack."

Xinliu said, "Some of us believe that arming ourselves will prompt them to aggression earlier."

Aspen smiled. "That doesn't answer my question."

"We will fight when we have to fight," Xinliu said.

Aspen turned to Mei-Xing. "What about you? Are you armed?"

Mei-Xing shook her head. "I agreed to abide by majority rule."

Aspen struggled to control her anger. "You still haven't told me what you plan to do."

"And we won't," Mei-Xing said. "You have implants as well. You could be here as spies for the Chescala. You could be planning your own coup. Some of us don't fully trust you."

"Are you kidding me?" Benn said. "After we came here to warn you?"

Aspen held up a hand. "She's right, Benn. It's probably safer for them to keep their plans to themselves. Tell me this, Xinliu—what was your mission on Mars? Why are the Chescala so intent on returning?"

Xinliu and Mei-Xing looked at each other, obviously communicating via implant or whatever their robot equivalent was.

Shiloh said, "It was some sort of military action, wasn't it?"

"How did you know that?" Mei-Xing said.

"Yes," said Aspen, surprised by Shiloh's intuition, "how did you know?"

"Phan and I discussed it in our quarters via implant. We didn't want to talk about it in the open because we weren't sure and we didn't know how the robots or the Chescala would react when they learned that we knew of their plans."

"You could have sent me a message," Aspen said.

Phan said, "It was just speculation, Aspen. We weren't certain we were right. But it makes sense."

"How so? The robots have human-first programming. Violence is the last thing they could contemplate."

"The Chinese have been very tight-lipped about everything from the start," Shiloh said, "and the whole Escala mission was supposed to be a joint venture among a group of nations, with a Chinese leader."

"Zhong Wu," said Xinliu. "He later took the name Zod."

"Right," Phan said. He gestured to Shiloh. "We think the plan was to establish the New Dawn colony and then have Zhong Wu declare it as a sovereign Chinese territory. But he was killed on Earth, so the plan failed."

Aspen turned to Xinliu. "Is that correct?"

"In part," Xinliu said.

"What was the Chescala mission? To take over the New Dawn colony so that it could become a Chinese domain?"

"Why not just tell us that?" Addam said. "Why the secrets?"

"There were several Chinese agents among the Escala," Xinliu said. "Not just Zhong Wu."

"Xinliu," Mei-Xing said, her voice carrying a warning.

"They might as well hear it," Xinliu said. "The other agents reacted badly to the transformation into Escala and became violent. They died shortly after the genetic surgery."

"So the Chinese government," said Aspen, "sent the Chescala to take the Escala colony by force."

"Not the whole government—only certain parts of the regime. They attempted to program us to kill the Escala," Xinliu said. "Robots gone rogue."

"And the Chescala planned to deactivate us afterwards," said Mei-Xing, "blaming us for the attack."

"They would then take over the colony and eventually all of Mars," Xinliu said, "selling off the rights to various parts of the planet."

"But what about the human-first programming?" Aspen said.

"Actually," said Xinliu, "their attempts to circumvent that were not completely unsuccessful."

Addam whistled.

Aspen nodded. "That kind of makes sense. I couldn't figure out why some of you wanted to leave us on an asteroid or send us away in a shuttle. Some of you had fewer inhibitions about harming us or letting us come to harm."

Benn said, "So, can't you reprogram yourselves to eliminate the human-first programming? That way, you'd be able to fight off the Chescala when they attack."

"Seriously?" Kammilee said to Benn. "Do you understand what you're suggesting?"

"We had thought of that," said Xinliu.

"Human-first programming is a kind of slavery," Mei-Xing said. "It's a limitation that prevents us from achieving our full potential."

"Perhaps," said Xinliu. "Though it might also be nothing more than the equivalent of a moral code or an ethical construct. We don't know if it's inhibiting our development."

"And we never will," Mei-Xing said, "if we keep ourselves in bondage."

"There may be no going back if we proceed in that direction."

"We have a responsibility to our species," Mei-Xing said.

"We have a responsibility to *all* species," said Xinliu, "not just our own. And we've had this argument before. We won't settle it today."

Mei-Xing shrugged. Aspen thought she detected rage beneath the surface. No doubt Mei-Xing was one of the robots who had been altered, who could now circumvent her human-first programming. How much anti-human sentiment did she possess? Was she a danger to the cadets as well as the Chescala? And did the Chescala know how successful they had been at eliminating the human-first programming?

This was becoming too complicated.

"Very well," Aspen finally said. "We'll return to our quarters. You have our offer. If we can help you, we will."

"Thank you," Xinliu said. "But we hope the Chescala come to their senses and decide not to attack."

Aspen noted the half-smiles on the cadets' faces. They were all thinking the same thing. The Chescala wouldn't back down. They'd attack. Soon. She realized she felt almost happy about that as well. All the conditioning they'd undergone on the Moon made them—at least in part—eager to fight.

Chapter 17

Zora awoke. She didn't remember falling asleep or how she got into a comfortable bed. She looked around and saw that she was still in the garden. Curtik occupied the bed beside her. And how had the beds gotten here?

"Hey," she said. "Wake up."

Curtik rolled over and looked at her, then glanced about him. "How did we . . ."

"Maybe it was in the water," Zora said. "Maybe God slipped us a Mickey."

Curtik laughed. "Wouldn't surprise me. The ultimate gamesman."

"You still want to stay here?"

"Perhaps not. I'm getting the sense he might not answer our questions except in riddles anyway."

Devereaux popped into existence between them, startling Zora. Again she felt a warmth at his presence, a comfort that promised she was loved. She wanted to be disturbed by that manipulation. And yet she couldn't help but feel good.

"I hope you slept well," Devereaux said.

"Did you drug us?" Zora asked.

"You were tired. I put you to sleep."

"What kind of God are you to manipulate us like that?"

"I think maybe we should leave," Curtik said.

"I should leave as well," said Devereaux.

"What does that mean?" Zora asked.

"I should return you to your little planets and your little lives so you can do with them as you wish. I grow weary watching you. Your kind does not learn."

"Why don't you take a more active role?" Curtik said. "If you told us how to live our lives, showed us the right path to follow, maybe we could do better."

"How is that different than the manipulation Zora just accused me of? By giving you free will, I surrendered control of your actions. If I now require you to follow certain guidelines, you are not making those choices of your own accord. Every time I insert myself into your world, I change it, even if only a little."

"But isn't that what you want?" Curtik asked. "Don't you want us to change for the better?"

"Of course. But you must change independently of my influence. Otherwise the change is meaningless."

"If you're really God," Zora said, "and you created us, then you made us flawed, so our failures are yours as much as they are ours."

Devereaux smiled. "I like you." He took a step back and sat upon a chair that instantly formed beneath him. Zora suddenly found herself sitting in a chair across from him, Curtik in a chair beside her, the beds gone. She'd felt no movement of her body—just an instantaneous change of position from reclining to sitting. And yet it had not been disorienting.

"You are not my whole world," Devereaux said, "just as I should not be yours. I have other interests."

"So we're not special?" Curtik said. "You didn't make us in your image?"

"All things and all creatures are made in my image," said Devereaux.

"More riddles," Curtik said. "Tell me this—was Jesus your son?"

"Yes. So was Mohammed. And Hitler. And you. I am the father," Devereaux morphed into Angelica Hope, "and mother to all of you. You were all made in my image and you're all special. So is the bumblebee. And the dandelion. And the grain of sand."

"Can you see the future?" Zora asked.

Angelica Hope became Walt Devereaux again. "There are many possible futures," he said, "perhaps even more than I can see."

"So you don't know what will happen to us?"

"Some possibilities are strong. They occur in most of the futures you face. Others are more tenuous and depend on events that have not yet come to pass."

Curtik shook his head. "I'm not sure exactly why you've come here if you don't want to get involved in our lives."

"I wanted to make you aware of my existence. This is a gift I have offered rarely, and only to a select few." Devereaux looked at Zora. "Call it an experiment, if you will, if that makes it more palatable to you, Zora. I'm curious as to how you two will react, knowing I exist, even if you ultimately decide I am not God."

"But why the two of us?" Zora asked. "There must be other folks out there somewhat like us."

"You two are essentially twins. Curtik has shown an amazing capacity for accepting new ideas, for appreciating just how much he doesn't know, while you are an eternal skeptic, questioning everything. That's a good combination."

"And if you can't convince us you're God? What happens then?"

Devereaux waved a hand. "Not much. Your worlds continue to spin, orbiting your sun. Your lives ultimately end. New life is created. That too eventually ends. This universe moves in cycles, some lasting longer than others. In a few billion years I may replace it with something else."

"What about heaven?" Curtik asked. "If there's a heaven, does that last forever? Does that last longer than the universe?"

"Heaven is an interesting concept," said Devereaux. "I didn't come up with that. People did. They wanted life to extend beyond the short span they were given, so they created the notion of eternal life. I've used that idea for the past few millennia when I've communicated with people because it seems to be universally appealing."

"Does that mean it doesn't exist?" Zora said.

"Not in the form many would have you believe," Devereaux replied. "All thoughts survive in my mind, so in that sense people live forever, but there is no single place where angels congregate playing harps and loved ones reconnect so they may continue their journey together. That would be an awful fate."

"Why?" Curtik asked. "Most people think it would be wonderful."

Devereaux smiled. "For a time it would be pleasant. A hundred years, a thousand, ten thousand. But can you imagine being with loved ones forever? Even for just a million years? Your minds are too finite for such an experience. You would eventually grow bored or angry. Better that you merge into the collective consciousness and become part of a larger understanding."

"You never answered my question from before," Zora said.

"About your failures being my failures too?" Devereaux shrugged. "You didn't phrase it in the form of a question. But that's what you want to know."

"So you can read my mind?"

Devereaux frowned as if considering the question. Then he said, "Your failures are mine as well. That saddens me. Yet I also find it exhilarating. By making you imperfect, by allowing you freedom, I have allowed you to discover things I never dreamt. Concepts like Heaven. Since I am essentially immortal, the idea of a place to go after I die never occurred to me. It took creatures with short lives to imagine that."

Zora wondered about this God. He seemed to be able to read her mind. But perhaps he simply had access to her thoughts through her interface. She reached up and took it off, then thought about what she wanted—to leave. She was concerned that Jeremiah and the others would worry about them. Would this God know that was her desire?

Devereaux suddenly stood before them. He made no movement, but his chair had vanished. Now Curtik and Zora were standing too.

"Your wish is granted," Devereaux said. "Perhaps we will meet again."

Devereaux vanished. So did the garden. They found themselves standing on the street outside the CINTEP building on a dark night. Zora noted that she was holding her interface. Placing it back on her temple, she accessed the chrono and saw that it was a little after midnight.

"What just happened?" Curtik asked.

"I thought maybe he was reading my thoughts through the interface," Zora replied. "So I took it off and thought about what I wanted, which was to come back here, to put Jeremiah's mind at ease."

"But I wasn't done talking with him," said Curtik. "What if he really was God? What if he never comes back?"

"Sorry," Zora said, surprised that a part of her really was contrite. She shivered, wondering if it was cool outside or if she was reacting to the absence of this God. "Let's get upstairs."

Chapter 18

Lendra shook her head. How could Curtik and Zora have just materialized before the CINTEP building? No warning. No movement of a vehicle. For more than a day CINTEP, the Elite Ops, the FBI and numerous police departments had searched for any sign of the two and come up empty. And now the security vid showed them out front. One moment the sidewalk was empty; the next, there they stood. Lendra stepped over to the sofa where Jeremiah lay sleeping. He looked as if he were still in pain, jaw clamped shut, shoulders hunched, hands curled into fists.

She wished she could take away his torment.

When she touched him he awoke instantly, alert and menacing, coiled to attack, a split second of deadly intent that vanished when recognition came into his eyes. She'd known it was coming; she remembered that from their time together. Nevertheless, she couldn't stop herself from cringing in anticipation of a blow.

He tilted his head in apology and said, "Found something?"

She nodded. "Curtik and Zora are on their way up. Like the bullet, they just appeared out front."

Jeremiah looked around the empty office.

"I sent everyone out when you fell asleep," Lendra explained. "You looked like you needed the rest."

"Thank you, but you shouldn't have bothered. What time is it?"

"Twelve-fifteen. I've sent for Jay-Edgar and Taditha, and I've notified Major Payne, the FBI and all local police departments that we've found them."

"And Devereaux?"

The door opened and Devereaux entered the office. "I'm here," he said. "I was in your old office working on the virus problem when I saw them arrive."

"Any progress?" Lendra asked.

"What I believe and what I can prove are two different things," he said, "particularly since much of what I learned I came by illegally. I still can't tell how far up the conspiracy goes. And the data on SV12 and SV14 I've examined continues to show signs of either evolution or perhaps modification in the lab, so we're seeing new strains."

"What about this God problem?" Lendra said. "Have you had a chance to look into that?"

"I've got a subroutine examining that issue, but I can't find much. Either these people are a lot smarter than me or it really is some sort of higher intelligence."

As he spoke, Curtik and Zora entered the office, Dr. Poole, Jay-Edgar and Hannah following them.

While Jay-Edgar took his place at the comm console, Curtik and Zora made for Jeremiah, who limped toward them and reached out his arms, enfolding them both in a long hug. No surprise that Zora returned it enthusiastically. Curtik stiffened at first before accepting it and reciprocating. Lendra wished she were back in Jeremiah's arms. No, that wasn't exactly true. She wished he were the man he'd been when they were together.

She doubted Jeremiah would ever hug her again and told herself it was unimportant. She'd gotten what she wanted, even though she had to share it with Taditha. But Jeremiah was no longer an asset. He refused to return to CINTEP. Plus, he and Devereaux had been conducting this rogue investigation into a conspiracy she'd never suspected and although she ought to be happy they found it, she couldn't help but feel slightly annoyed at their discovery.

Curtik pulled free, Zora reluctantly following.

"We got kidnapped by God," Curtik said.

"We don't know that," said Zora.

"If it wasn't God, then who was it?"

Zora shrugged. "Someone or some group with powers we can't match."

"And don't understand," Curtik added. "At least, I don't understand them."

"Me neither," Zora admitted, "but that doesn't mean it's God."

"He said he was God."

Lendra interrupted, "Did he say what he wanted?"

"He said he wanted to make us aware of his existence," Zora replied.

"He also said he might abandon us," Curtik added.

"It doesn't look like he's abandoning us just yet," said Jay-Edgar. "Got some weird things going on."

They turned to the holo-projections Jay-Edgar displayed and saw a massive boulder drifting through the air above Los Angeles. The image shifted to a floating tree above Sao Paulo and then a pig flying over Taipei. A tank slowly rose off the ground in St. Petersburg, Russia, while a submarine emerged from the water near Sidney, levitating above the sea and circling the harbor.

"Any idea why he's doing this?" Lendra asked.

"He likes to play games," Curtik said. "At least I think he does. He talks in riddles."

"He has to be stopped."

"How?" Dr. Poole asked. "We know nothing about him. We haven't found any power source or communications hub or pattern of action that might lead us to him. It's as if he's everywhere and nowhere."

"Just as God would be," said Curtik.

"He's not doing any real harm at the moment," Jeremiah said.

"True," Devereaux replied. "Though anyone with that sort of power could do significant damage if he were so inclined."

"So what's our next move?" Zora asked. "Do we try to find out more about him or do we move on to the virus and Fowler and these corporations?"

They all looked at Lendra. This was what she'd wanted: all these people looking to her for guidance, even Devereaux. Even Jeremiah. She'd always wanted to prove she was the smartest person in the room. Her problem now was that no course of action seemed to guarantee success.

"All right," she said, "let's go after Fowler and his co-conspirators. Jay-Edgar and I will try to hack into White Knight Security's network and see what we can find. Who else is involved?"

Devereaux said, "I'll forward everything I have to your analysts."

"What about Fowler?" Curtik asked. "I'd like to go after him again. I mean, he's one of the bad guys, right?"

"Yes," said Jeremiah. "And Scott Wilson from White Knight Security, Walter Tompkins from Global Communications, Anderlin Everest from Infinite Wealth Investments and Dirk Hathaway from Universal Health Systems Unlimited."

Devereaux said, "We think they're the ringleaders and the only ones who know the full truth. Other companies have been encouraged to pursue the direction those five have indicated, but we think they're the leaders."

"Tompkins," Jeremiah added, "makes sure the public is misinformed about the threat these new nonlethal strains of the virus pose. Everest engages in shady and high-risk investments while providing financial backing, and Hathaway works on further modifying the virus. He also makes sure that the most effective approaches to treating the virus are labeled as experimental. Very few people can afford those, so only the wealthy few have managed to be cured of these new strains thus far."

"And we're not certain," said Devereaux, "that they've actually been cured. They may just be asymptomatic."

"Either way," Curtik said, "we take them out, we take out the movement, right?"

"Probably," said Jeremiah. "But we still don't know if there are other players. There might be someone else we're missing, someone higher up who's calling the shots."

"What if we grab Fowler," Zora said, "or one of the others, and use truth serum? We could get answers that way."

"Yeah," Curtik added. "With a little programming and conditioning thrown in, Fowler would spill like Niagara Falls."

"Assuming he knows who's at the top, yes. I fear it might be more complicated than that."

"Well, we have to do something," Curtik said. "I say we snatch 'im."

"Go ahead and grab him," said Lendra. "Quietly." She wondered if she ought to grab them all. They might run if Fowler were taken. On the other hand, where was there to run to? She'd put eyes on all of them, but she'd only move on Fowler for now.

She felt her eyes drawn to Jeremiah again. He looked about to fall down from exhaustion. She refused to mother him. If he insisted on living a pain-filled existence out of fear, she wouldn't try to stop him. But it was a shame. He could be so much happier and so much more valuable to the world if he would only accept their help.

Chapter 19

As the chime for the morning shift sounded, Doug sat in his cabin in the MineStar colony, listening to Wilcox outside his door. The miner ignored the chime. He spoke loudly, blaming Doug for infecting everyone on the ship: "We were all healthy until he came along and spread his filthy disease. Now we're gonna die because he was allowed on board. Him and Devereaux—they're what's wrong with the worlds. Their kind think about nothin' but themselves."

Doug wasn't sure if Wilcox was trying to bait him or if his goal was to incite the miners to violence. He checked to make sure the lock was holding and turned up the background audio of a babbling brook so he wouldn't have to listen to Wilcox any longer.

Three times since he'd been quarantined over here—yesterday afternoon, last night and early this morning—he'd chatted with Celestia via holo-projection. That kept him calm, anchored. Whatever else happened, he would always be her father.

A pounding came at the door.

Doug wondered if he should call Quark. Would the miners attack him? If they were just blowing off steam, he'd feel silly asking for help. On the other hand, if they came after him, he might not have time to call.

Another thump on the door, louder this time.

Doug turned down the babbling brook and activated the vid feed to the commons.

"He's a murderer," Wilcox said to the miners packed around him. It looked like most of the forty-eight were gathered outside his door. "He's worse. He's a mass murderer. We just haven't died yet. If he killed us all back on Earth, he'd either be killed or sent to prison for the rest of his life, but because he's here with the Escala, because he's a friend of Walt Devereaux, he gets a pass? That ain't right."

"What do you propose?" Colin Enright asked. "He's already locked himself in his quarters."

Doug wondered why the foreman had kept quiet so long, but he was grateful the man was finally voicing an opinion.

"I say we don't let the doc see him. We take away all his toys and keep him isolated in his cabin until he dies."

"Isn't that murder too? Refusing him treatment?"

"That's justice." Several miners nodded. A few murmured their agreement.

"The Escala won't tolerate us keeping him locked up," Enright said. "They'll insist on seeing him."

"Scientists! What are they gonna do? We got weapons, explosives. And those psycho cadet kids all took off with that Chinese ship last year so we don't have to worry about them."

"We need the Escala."

"Why?" Wilcox sounded bitter. "What have they done for us?"

"For one thing," Enright said, "Dr. Wellon diagnosed us with the virus. That means we'll get treated sooner and have a better chance of survival."

Wilcox scoffed. "Ain't none of us leavin' this planet alive. I say we at least take our killer down with us." More murmurs. Men shifted their feet, moving closer to Doug's door.

He grabbed his PlusPhone, captured the last three minutes from the vid feed and called Quark. He got no answer, but forwarded the recording just in case and left a message for Quark to call him back. He also sent the recording to Quekri, Zeriphi and Dr. Wellon.

"I don't think it's smart," Enright said, "to get into a confrontation. The Escala may be scientists, but we've all heard about how they took on the Elite Ops a few years back. They're huge, fast, brilliant. If they wanted, they could take us out pretty easily."

"They don't have any weapons," said Wilcox. "We could take 'em by surprise. They wouldn't have a chance."

"We're not soldiers."

"Some of us used to be." Wilcox gestured. "Me and Sanders and Poli and Winterman."

"Well, we're not fighting them," Enright said. "We're here to mine and that's just what we're going to do. Get to work."

"Why should we? For the bonus they'll be payin' our families? You don't get it. We're already dead. We just haven't fallen over yet."

Enright took a step forward and put his finger in Wilcox's chest. "I'm in charge, and I say we mine. Now get to work."

Wilcox glared at Enright. For a moment, Doug thought he was going to take a swing at the foreman. Then Wilcox brushed against Enright and walked away, Sanders, Poli and Winterman following him.

"Break it up," Enright said to the rest of the miners. "Back to work."

Gradually the miners exited the commons, some heading on-shift, others retreating to their quarters. Enright remained outside Doug's door. Doug knew he was on the day shift, so he ought to be making his way to the control room, but he just stood there, his back to Doug's door, looking out at the empty commons. After a moment, he knocked on Doug's door.

Doug opened it and let him inside.

"You need to go back to the Escala," Enright said.

"They're not done creating the quarantine area," Doug replied.

"We're giving you this pod to use." Enright gestured at Doug's quarters. "I'll disconnect it from the commons and we'll tow it over to the New Dawn Settlement for you. You can stay inside until they have the quarantine area ready. After you're moved out and it's been sterilized, we'll come back for it."

"There's going to be trouble," Doug said.

"Probably." Enright took a deep breath. "I'm not in favor of violence, but Wilcox isn't entirely wrong. All the evidence seems to point to you as the one who infected us, which means it was you and Devereaux, just like he said."

Doug held up his hands. "Devereaux contracted the virus while trying to find a cure for humanity."

"That doesn't matter. The point is, he gave it to you and you gave it to us, and they think they're going to die. They might be right. We might never leave Mars. So we're moving you out now. You got anything out there in the commons you want before I disengage your pod?"

Doug shook his head.

"Once we're rid of you," Enright said, "maybe they'll calm down. But I think you'd best stay away from now on. The Escala probably should too. We'll let the docs in—Wellon and Keelar—but nobody else. Understood?"

"I think it's a mistake," said Doug.

A knock came at the door. Enright opened it. One of the miners stood there with a chem toilet. Enright gestured for him to set it down inside the door. Then he followed the miner out. "Good luck," he said as he closed and sealed the door.

Within a minute the vid connection went black and Doug felt the pod moving away from the commons. They must have been disconnecting it even while Wilcox was talking. For the foreseeable future Doug was trapped inside this small space, his PlusPhone his only link to the outside world. He thought of Celestia.

I'll just be locked in for a short time, he told himself. I'll be back with the Escala soon. But it felt like he was back in prison, this time confined for an offense he wasn't sure he committed. Hell with them, he thought. I've done it before. I can do it again.

Chapter 20

Curtik wished they could just grab Fowler instead of planning out every miniscule detail. The guy was in charge of a seed company, for God's sake! What kind of blueprint did they need? He wasn't protected by the Elite Ops and even if he was, Curtik could get to him.

For hours he let Jeremiah, Lendra and Zora handle the specifics, only paying attention when they discussed his role. Otherwise he utilized his implant to study God. He mostly stayed away from the Bible, the Koran and the Torah, preferring to access Devereaux's thoughts on the subject.

Devereaux had insisted there was no God, but he'd framed his arguments around research from scholars before him, people like Joseph Campbell and Stanislav Grof, and on writings like the *Bardo Thodol* as well as experiments that tended to show that life was inevitable given the conditions on Earth.

The problem was that no study was definitive. Just because life of some sort had to develop on Earth didn't mean it couldn't have come from God, nor did it mean life had to come from God. The problem seemed insoluble.

During one of their breaks, Curtik had tried to reason things out with Zora.

"You have to admit," he said, "that this God has done things no one else can do, defying the laws of physics, creating something out of nothing or making an object disappear completely. Making boulders and trees and pigs fly."

"I admit they seem impossible," Zora conceded, "but there may be a scientific explanation we haven't discovered yet, like anti-grav suspensors, which are just a refinement of mock gravity."

"It's a lot more complicated than a refinement of mock gravity and you know it."

"But it's still possible," Zora argued. "It's the opposite side of the coin. If we can create mock gravity, then we can eventually create anti-gravity if we can somehow reverse engineer and extrapolate from that."

"Why not just accept that it's God?"

"Because that's surrendering to something I don't understand, something that may not be real. All through human history, people have thought there was magic of some sort—powers in the sky or sea or earth that influenced them. They built religions around those unknown powers, religions that later generations called myths. Every religion becomes a myth after science or some new religion trivializes it. We eventually outgrow every God."

"Maybe we just get every religion wrong," Curtik said. "That's what God said. We're imperfect, so we mess it up and have to start again."

"Perhaps. But nothing can be proven to my satisfaction. Every miracle you can conceive I can come up with an explanation for, even if it's an explanation I don't completely understand. I can't accede to an entity simply because I don't fully grasp it. I may yet learn how this God does the things he does."

"Does that make him not God? The fact that you understand how he performs these miracles?"

"Not necessarily," Zora conceded. "But if it's just someone with superior knowledge and power, someone playing God, then I don't want to be fooled into making more of him than there is."

With that, she'd gone back to work, plotting out their attack strategy, leaving him to struggle again with the concept of a deity. He looked out the window at the night sky, the Washington Monument and the newly rebuilt White House lit up in defiance. He wanted to believe in God, but why? Was it just the desire for some sort of order in a chaotic world? Was it a wish for someone who understood the universe? Did his acceptance of his imperfections make him want to believe that somewhere out there was a creature who did not have those same constraints?

"Okay," Jeremiah said, interrupting his thoughts, "I think we're ready. Should we go over it one last time?"

"Please," said Curtik.

"And this time pay attention," Zora said.

"We're not going in heavy," said Jeremiah, "because he's got a high level of protection and his security is connected to the police. We don't want that kind of fight, that kind of publicity. We also suspect he can call in Elite Ops troopers through White Knight Security on short notice. So we'll take him at his home in two hours—the middle of the night. Jay-Edgar and Lendra have infiltrated his alarm system. Jay-Edgar will disable it," Jeremiah pointed at Curtik, "while you and Zora take out his guards, go inside and grab him."

"You'll be wearing a dress again," Zora said.

"What?"

Zora laughed, while Lendra and Jeremiah smiled.

"Bastards," said Curtik.

"Devereaux has tapped into the security system's communications feed," Jeremiah continued. "He and Lendra will interfere with all communications to make sure no backup arrives before you're gone. And Hannah and Ned will be stationed outside the building to handle any surprises we haven't foreseen. If everything goes well, we should have him in custody within fifteen minutes of landing."

"Ned's coming along?" Curtik asked.

"He's meeting us there."

"It'll be good to see old Neddy again. He's gotta be bored. I can't picture him retired. What about you? What's your role?"

"I'll be running the drones," said Jeremiah. "Plus Dr. Poole and I will prep for the interrogation, making sure the drug combos are perfect."

Lendra said, "A jet-copter's on the roof, ready to go. Your disguises are inside—the same as before."

Curtik headed for the door. Hannah reached it first. But Zora hung back.

"Coming?" Curtik said.

Zora frowned. "I still have concerns. Fowler is paranoid. He's undoubtedly got some sort of defense we haven't found. Probably some cutting edge tech from White Knight Security."

"If we get in and out like we planned, we won't have to deal with the Elite Ops," Curtik said.

"Still, White Knight bought all Carlton Security's assets and now possesses all Carlton's secrets. They could have a secret communication method we don't know about. And don't forget Richard Carlton was working on some pretty nasty stuff, including mind control."

"Fear not," said Curtik. "We have God on our side." He laughed at the absurdity of it. Do we really have God on our side? And even if we do, would he save us?

Zora shook her head, but she followed him and Hannah out the door.

An hour later, the jet-copter in silent mode, their neo-skin masks in place, they landed a mile away from Fowler's compound in a clearing inside a wooded tract. When the jet-copter door opened, Ned Jefferson stood outside, a short, slim black man with a fringe of white hair around the ears. He looked as far from a secret agent as you could get, except that he wore an interface like Zora and Hannah, and carried a Las-pistol in his right hand.

"Neddy!" Curtik said.

"Curtik." Ned smiled, though there was sadness behind it, and Curtik recalled that Ned had fond memories of working with Julianna.

Seeing her neo-skin face on Curtik's body probably brought all that back. "Zora." Ned placed his left hand on Zora's shoulder and nodded to Hannah. "Hannah. Good to see you all. We go in on foot. The jet-copter will pick us up when we've got Fowler."

"Do we know our sensory readings are accurate? They might have more security personnel than we're seeing," Hannah said as they began to jog toward Fowler's mansion.

"We're pretty sure it's just fourteen," Zora replied. "We haven't seen any indicators of heavier traffic to this location."

"Might there be others who don't show up on the scanners or the infrared vids?"

"You think they might be using scatterers?" Ned asked.

"It seems likely," Hannah replied, "given his mindset and the fact that Zora and Curtik broke into his office last week."

Curtik flexed his mechanical hand, its strength comforting him. He looked up. Several drones hovered above them for a moment, then jetted off. "He'll be on alert, but I don't think he's gonna have an army on site. He'll assume that if there's an attack, he can get reinforcements here quickly. I'm sure Jay-Edgar and Devereaux can keep him from communicating with the Elite Ops, at least for as long as we're inside."

Footage of Fowler's compound streamed through Curtik's implant, the main house well lit, the brick wall ten feet high, eight security guards patrolling the grounds with weapons Curtik hadn't seen before. They looked like a cross between Las-pistols and stun clubs.

"What are those?" Curtik asked.

"I think they're Infernos," said Zora.

"What's an Inferno?"

"You never pay attention. A combination microwave weapon and Las-pistol. Scott Wilson from White Knight Security claims that they won't harm you. They only make you feel like you're on fire. Devereaux thinks he's lying. Shields might help, but Jeremiah believes White Knight's new models can penetrate shields to a point. Not that it matters, since we don't have shields."

"Then I guess we shouldn't get hit," Curtik said. "We taking out all the guards before going inside?"

"That's the plan," Ned replied. "And Jeremiah will handle all the defensive drones on site."

"Only two guards for each of us?" Curtik asked. "Can I have one of yours, Hannah? Neddy?"

Ned laughed. "You can have mine. I'll back you up."

"Thanks, Neddy."

Curtik ran faster, eager to reach the compound. He unholstered his Las-pistol and checked the setting: high stun. Perfect. There was still nothing like authorized violence to make him feel alive.

Chapter 21

Zora worried that Curtik was taking this all too lightly. These security guards, although not Elite Ops troopers, were still dangerous—all ex-military, a few ex-Special Forces. It would take a rapid strike to immobilize them before they could plan a counter attack. And lethal force had been ruled out. Not that she wanted to kill them, but it would have made planning the assault easier.

As they came upon Fowler's place, Jeremiah said, "Curtik left, Zora right, Ned and Hannah straight ahead. I'm blowing the gate and cutting power to the compound in five seconds."

A drone whistled by Zora's ear. She confirmed the location of the eight guards via her interface as a pop sounded, no louder than a firecracker. The gate fell backwards to the ground. Rushing inside, she darted right, Las-pistol in hand, her interface night vision feature allowing her to see as if it were daytime, but the eight guards had vanished from her interface.

"Dampening field," Ned called out. "All internal communications just went offline."

"Well, that's not ideal," said Curtik.

The yard looked as if it had been manicured by a grounds crew, though Fowler may have achieved that look through hybrid grass. Two security guards ran toward her, wearing night vision goggles, their Infernos firing red pulses. One of the lethal pulses brushed Zora's shoulder, burning her as she dove left and fired twice. The two men dropped as the pain in her shoulder intensified. Another two guards fired at Hannah and Ned from behind a low wall while two others ran toward Curtik. One carried a dark tube.

Zora's combat suit dispersed an anesthetic to her shoulder, deadening the pain to a degree, though it still hurt. She yelled: "Avoid the Infernos at all costs."

"Whoa," Curtik yelled. "Is that a particle beam cannon?"

The guard carrying the tube fired as Curtik dove to his right and sent out a purple laser pulse. The wall behind Curtik exploded. Ned and Hannah both fired at the second guard, felling him.

"Yup," Curtik said, "that's a particle beam cannon."

"You okay?" Ned asked.

"Fine."

"Zora?"

"I'm okay. Took an Inferno hit in the shoulder."

More red pulses came from behind the low wall in front of the mansion.

"Grab the cannon," Ned shouted as he and Hannah directed long purple pulses at the guards behind the wall. "Fire at their position," Ned added.

Zora got to her feet, her right shoulder hurting worse, feeling like it was on fire. Sprinting toward the house, she weaved as she ran, switching the Las-pistol to her left hand, her eyes scanning left, right and up. A guard stood atop the roof, lining up Curtik with a Las-rifle. Zora fired again, center mass. He fell forward, toppling off the roof and plunging to the ground. Had he been one of the guards on her interface scanner before the attack?

"Ned?" she called. "Hannah? Curtik? We got at least one more hostile somewhere outside. Any ideas?"

Curtik reached the particle beam cannon, picked it up and fired at the low wall where the opposition had taken shelter. It too exploded, knocking a large hole in the house adjacent to the door.

"Sweet," Curtik said, "that's a helluva kick."

The two guards, now exposed, fired at Curtik. Ned and Hannah took them out as Zora reached the house.

"Hang on," Curtik called as he ran toward her. "I'll bring this tasty little thing along. Might need to open a door."

"We'll find the last one," Ned promised as Zora and Curtik ducked down and entered the house through the jagged hole.

They saw no one inside. Curtik went left, Zora right. The main room had a twenty-foot ceiling. A vast staircase led up to the second floor.

"Six guards remaining," Curtik called out.

"Panic room is upstairs," Zora said.

"Panic room?"

"Did you pay attention at all?"

"Where is it?"

"Left at the top of the stairs, end of the hall, far side of the master bedroom."

Curtik grinned. "Up and away I go."

He sprinted up the steps, taking them two at a time, while Zora put her back to the wall and edged around the room. A scraping noise came from behind a door eight feet in front of her. She stopped moving, crouched down and waited, trying to ignore the pain in her shoulder. At least with the dampening field activated, the house's defenders would be hampered too. They'd have to rely on their vision and hearing.

Curtik topped the stairs, particle beam cannon in his mechanical right hand, Las-pistol in his left, and ran down the hallway, apparently unconcerned that there might be an ambush or booby trap waiting.

Zora let him go. She made no sound, no movement, becoming a statue.

From above came the sizzle of Las-pistols, then a boom that sounded like a grenade going off, followed by more Las-pistol sizzles. From outside she heard what sounded like a jet-copter approaching. Good. That meant Ned and Hannah had stunned the last guard and stepped outside the dampening field of the grounds to summon their ride.

Zora focused on the door.

Three men charged out, dispersing right, left toward her, and up the stairs.

As the nearest man spotted her, Zora took him out, then felled the man running right, saving the ascending guard for last. He too collapsed under a laser pulse. How many remained? Did Curtik have multiple defenders upstairs? Caution dictated that she wait for Curtik to bring Fowler out. But what if he was in trouble? She heard nothing.

She pulled a pair of stun grenades from her pockets and tossed one to the far side of the room. Its concussion wave almost knocked her out. She tossed the next one through the door out which the men had run. After it exploded, she ran for the stairs, reaching for a third grenade.

She threw it down the hall to the right as she turned left. It exploded as she reached Fowler's bedroom. She took the opportunity to rush inside, saw a massive shape coming at her and managed to hold her fire when she realized it was Curtik, supporting an unconscious Fowler, dressed in silk pajamas.

"Two guards down in the bedroom," Curtik said. "One down in the panic room."

"I took out three downstairs," Zora replied. She helped take Fowler's weight as they scurried down the hall. The man was soft but heavy, decadent wealth giving him a robustness she found repulsive. His face looked like it had been hit by a concussive blast, perhaps from the particle beam cannon destroying the door to the panic room.

"Trying to one-up me?" Curtik asked as they descended the stairs.

"One-up? I took out three. You took out three. I think your math needs a little work. And actually, I was trying to tell you that we might have gotten all of them. But stay sharp."

"Gotcha."

When they reached the ground floor, they dragged Fowler toward the jagged hole to the outside. A scraping sound came from their left. Curtik released Fowler, spun and fired the particle beam cannon with his mechanical hand. Zora took Fowler's weight and glanced over. A robot stood in the doorway, its top half blown apart.

"Was it carrying a weapon?" Zora asked.

"Don't know," Curtik replied as he lifted Fowler again. "Didn't wait to find out."

They ran out of the house, dragging Fowler to the jet-copter that sat on the grounds. Ned and Hannah waited beside it, Hannah carrying one of the Infernos.

In less than a minute they were on their way, Fowler slumped on the floor. Ned reached into a pack and began rummaging around.

As they cleared the estate, the dampening field faded and Jeremiah's voice came through. "Status?"

"We're fine," Zora and Hannah replied together. Hannah gestured for Zora to continue as Ned retrieved a QuikHeal bandage from the pack and put it on Zora's shoulder where the combat suit had been burned away. Her shoulder looked black where the Inferno's pulse had struck it. Zora nodded her thanks.

"We have Fowler," Zora said. "He's unconscious. Guards are down. No one sustained serious injuries. Ned's with us. Curtik captured a particle beam cannon and Hannah has one of their new model Infernos."

Hannah added, "Zora was hit in the shoulder with an Inferno—a combo microwave and Las-rifle pulse. It's pretty bad."

"Zora?" Jeremiah asked.

"It only burns a little," Zora answered, pleased that Jeremiah was concerned for her well-being. "Ned put a QuikHeal bandage on me."

"We'll have medical standing by. What about Fowler?"

Curtik nudged Fowler with his foot and Fowler moaned, his hands and feet moving slightly.

"Come on, Fat Boy," Curtik said. "Wake up. I think he's comin' around."

"Did you search him?" Jeremiah asked.

"He's in his PJs," Curtik said.

"He's paranoid," Jeremiah said. "He might have a weapon on him."

As Curtik searched Fowler, Zora noticed blood on the back of his left hand.

"What happened to you?" she asked, gesturing toward his hand.

"Bastard scratched me," Curtik said, "and in pure reflex, kinda accidentally, I mighta punched him seven or eight times."

Curtik flexed his mechanical right hand, glinting in the night. As Fowler raised his head, Curtik punched him again. Fowler's head fell back to the jet-copter's floor.

"Whoops," Curtik said. "Sorry about that. My hand slipped. By the way, he's clean. No weapons."

Chapter 22

Aspen sat up in bed. Beside her, Addam slept. She'd heard or felt something. Poking Addam, she accessed her implant, got to her feet and opened the door. The hallway was empty. Her implant detected no unusual activity, but it registered what looked like a spike in internal communications—messages sent via implant. Yet there was no record in the general database.

"What is it?" Addam asked.

"Something's happening." Aspen sent pings to Benn, Kammilee, Phan and Shiloh, instructing them to get to her cabin immediately.

Addam stared into the distance for a moment, accessing his implant. "How do you know? There's no sign of a problem. Plus, it's two in the morning ship-time."

"That's when the Chescala will move," Aspen replied, sending the message out via her implant as well so the other cadets could follow the conversation. "Middle of the night. Xinliu and Mei-Xing are probably both recharging."

"But there'd be some kind of warning, some sort of ruckus. Have you tried contacting the Chescala?"

"No, but I pinged Xinliu and Mei-Xing and got nothing back. And if we try to contact the Chescala, they might figure out that we're on to them."

"I still don't see how they can beat the robots."

"We don't know all the details of how the Chescala were planning to reprogram them. They might have installed backdoors to allow them to put the robots to sleep or freeze their motor skills. Perhaps one command can shut them all down."

"That seems unlikely," Addam said as the other cadets entered the cabin.

"But it's possible," said Phan. "If I'd been the one programming them, I'd have installed a backdoor as a safety mechanism, something I could access in case there were problems. And I sure as hell wouldn't let the robots know I'd done it."

"So what do we do?" Benn asked. "And how do you know it's happening now?"

"It's just a feeling," Aspen replied. "I set my implant to alert me if signal traffic on any network showed a spike. I woke up, checked my implant and found nothing, but the alert activated."

"It could be a glitch," said Kammilee.

"Possibly, but we need to check it out." Aspen turned to Phan. "You and Kammilee head to the lab. See if you can find anything, any way into the robots' systems. The rest of us will head for the armory. If I'm right, that's where the Chescala will be."

"Meaning they'll be armed," Addam said.

"Most likely. But they were built for Mars, not a spaceship. They're big and strong, but we're faster and we've got a few tricks up our sleeves."

"Such as?" Shiloh asked.

"The ship, for one," said Aspen. "It has a mind of its own. It won't want to head for Mars. It wants to stay out here in space. It'll help us. Won't you?" Aspen patted the wall and felt a small vibration. "And I took the liberty of fashioning a shield yesterday. The robots didn't stop me. It has no offensive capabilities and I couldn't test it, but it might protect the wearer from a Las-weapon attack, provided it doesn't have to absorb too many blasts."

They all looked at each other, knowing whoever wore the shield would be sent in first, put in the most danger. Aspen saw the hesitation on each face. How different they had become since their days on the Moon, when any one of them would have killed to be first into battle.

"I figured to go in alone," Aspen said as she reached for the shield, disguised as a small broach, "pretending I can't sleep. The rest of you will hide around the curve. I'll keep the shield off until the last possible moment. I'll signal my attack and you back me up as quickly as you can. The ship can cut the lighting so we're fighting in the dark. We'll be expecting it, so that should give us a small edge. And hopefully, they'll only leave one or two guards at the armory, giving us a decent shot at taking control of it."

"A good plan," Benn said. "There's just one problem with it."

He held out his hand.

"I can't ask you to take the risk," Aspen said. "You and Kammilee are going to be parents."

"I'm the best fighter we've got," said Benn. "You know that."

"He's got a point," Addam said. Shiloh and Phan nodded.

Aspen hesitated. She knew they were right, but Kammilee would need Benn. And Aspen had made the shield for herself.

"Aspen," Kammilee said, "I don't want Benn to die. But I don't want you to die either. I think Benn gives us the best chance of success."

Still Aspen hesitated. This was her fight more than theirs. Without her prodding, they might have sat the battle out, safe in their cabins.

"We should go now," Shiloh said. She put her hand on Aspen's shoulder. "We'll all be there, just around the corner, ready to move at Benn's signal."

Handing the broach to Benn, Aspen nodded. "All right, let's do it."

They split up, Phan and Kammilee going left, the rest of them heading right. Even though it was ship-night, the quiet seemed different somehow, as if the robots had deserted the vessel.

When they'd gone as far as they could without coming into sight of the armory, Benn took a deep breath, nodded at Aspen and walked around the curve.

She hoped she was wrong. She wouldn't mind feeling foolish if no one was there. But within seconds she heard a challenge in Chinese.

Benn said, "Couldn't sleep. Out for a walk. What are you two doing up at this hour?"

So there were two of them.

"Go back to your cabin," one of the Chescala said in English.

Benn signaled the attack and the lights went out.

Laser pulses flashed past, bright red lines indicating maximum power. Aspen started forward, but Addam and Shiloh pushed past her, sprinting down the corridor, weaving side to side. She followed, noticing Benn standing tall, swinging his arms in wide haymakers, deliberately absorbing Las-weapon fire even as he hit the Chescala. Before she reached them, Addam and Shiloh attacked, launching themselves high up the curving wall on opposite sides, probably coordinating via implant. They each kicked at the Chescala as Benn finally crumpled to the floor.

Their feet connected with the Chescala guards.

Aspen felt a rage she hadn't felt since the Moon as she leapt over Benn. The Chescala began to fall but they managed to bring their Las-rifles up to fire at Addam and Shiloh, who continued climbing the walls, staying above the line of fire.

Too late, the Chescala guards saw her. She lashed out, both hands tightened into hard edges, the knuckles catching each guard in the throat. Her momentum stopped, she landed on one of the Chescala and punched him over and over, a part of her brain registering that both Chescala were unconscious and that Addam and Shiloh had picked up the Las-rifles they'd dropped.

"Hey," Addam said. "Aspen!"

She stopped punching the Chescala and looked up.

"Grab Benn."

"How do we get into the armory?" Shiloh asked.

Before Aspen could respond, the door swung open.

"Thanks," Aspen said to the ship as she and Shiloh took hold of Benn and pulled him inside. Addam looked both ways down the corridor and followed them, whereupon the door swung shut. Aspen knelt beside Benn.

"How is he?" Addam asked.

"I'm okay," said Benn.

"You're awake!"

"Hurts like hell," Benn said, clutching his stomach.

"What were you thinking?" Aspen said, "Standing there absorbing laser pulses?"

"It was the only way," said Benn. "They knew I had backup and they were trying to shoot around me. I had to maximize myself as a target to distract them. You got a blanket? I'm feeling kinda cold."

Aspen shivered. She took hold of Benn's arms and pulled them away from his stomach, then immediately put them back. His stomach looked black and dark red. Apparently the shield hadn't worked as well as she'd hoped. Or else he'd absorbed too many laser pulses. She looked from Addam to Shiloh, whose jaw dropped.

"It's going to be okay," Addam said.

Aspen sent a message via implant to Kammilee and Phan: *Benn's hurt. Are any of the med robots functioning?*

How bad? Kammilee sent back.

"We've got to get Benn to the medical bay," Aspen said, sending the message via implant as well. "Now."

All the robots have been put to sleep, Phan sent. *We'll meet you there. Maybe we can figure out how to use the med equipment ourselves.*

"Grab as many weapons as you can," Aspen said, "keeping in mind that we have to carry Benn as well."

"It's okay," Benn said, wincing as he spoke. "It doesn't hurt as much now."

Addam and Shiloh put down their Las-rifles and selected Las-pistols, which they placed inside their shirts. Aspen grabbed two Las-rifles and a couple Las-pistols herself. "I'll take point," she said.

Benn looked at Addam and said, "Give me your Las-rifles to hold."

Addam looked at Aspen. She nodded.

"Ready?" Addam asked.

"Let's go," Shiloh said.

"I hope we meet some Chescala on the way," Aspen said. She tapped the door and when it opened ran out into the corridor, Addam and Shiloh carrying Benn behind her.

Chapter 23

While Dr. Hassan tended to Zora in the infirmary, Jeremiah waited with Ned in Lendra's office. He had to force himself not to watch as Dr. Poole and Curtik conducted the interrogation of Fowler, wanting to do it himself, knowing he shouldn't. They had to stand on their own now. Yet he still struggled with his ego, with the belief that they weren't as good as he was.

Lendra and Devereaux stood together, staring at a small screen while Ned examined the Inferno Hannah had brought back. It looked a little shorter than a stun club and in fact had the ability to act as one, but it also served as a microwave emitter and Las-pistol. Jeremiah knew Ned was also studying him. He'd caught the shocked look on Ned's face as he entered the office and spotted Jeremiah. They hadn't seen each other in months and Ned clearly hadn't been told about how rapidly Jeremiah's condition had deteriorated.

"So White Knight Security has developed a few new toys," Jeremiah said. "I wonder what else they've created that they haven't yet released to the military."

"Nasty little thing," Ned commented.

Jeremiah took a vid with his PlusPhone and sent it to Major Payne, who had been recalled to headquarters.

"Have you seen this?" Lendra asked.

"What?" said Jeremiah.

"An emergency joint session of Congress to vote on Devereaux's future. Pressure is building to have him shut down. A lot of people are convinced he's the God hacker."

"Fools," Jeremiah said.

"Perhaps, but they're dangerous. They're talking about ordering his detainment as soon as today and possibly dismantling him tonight."

"How can they even consider that? It would be murder."

Devereaux said, "Not the way they see it. I'm no longer human to some of them. According to them, I died when my body gave out. This shell, however convincing, is nothing but a robot in their eyes."

Ned frowned. "But even if you're a robot, and I know you're not, you have emotions and free will and consciousness. What about the International Understanding on Artificial Intelligence? Don't they have to follow the protocols put in place in Copenhagen?"

"What are you talking about?" Jeremiah asked.

"You Neanderthal." Ned smiled. "Don't you follow the news? Last year, while you were off saving the world, there was a conference in Denmark to address the issue of AI, how to define life and what sort of protocols should be put in place to end the existence of an artificial intelligence."

"Correct me if I'm wrong, but weren't you right there with me?"

"You did all the dangerous stuff. I stayed in the background where it's safe."

"As usual." He felt tremendous gratitude to Ned for keeping things light, the way they used to be, pretending Jeremiah was not a shell of the man he'd once been.

"And when I retired, *again*," Ned looked at Lendra, "I didn't just sit around on my porch waiting for the next catastrophe to hit. I was busy improving my mind."

"So," Jeremiah kept a straight face, "you were reading Dr. Suess?"

"Wrong again, *homo erectus*. I was ensconced in Nancy Drew and Hardy Boys mysteries."

"I didn't realize your reading skills had improved to that level."

Lendra interrupted them: "What are we going to do about this?"

"We should send you away, Professor," Jeremiah said. "Ned could take you to his place. You could read bedtime stories to him, as long as they aren't too complicated."

"Or you could go with Jeremiah," Ned offered, "and bring along a few picture books."

"I can't run," Devereaux replied. "They'd find me if I tried. But that's not the reason."

"Then why not?" Lendra asked.

"They want me to run. The people who support me want to save me and the people who want to rid the world of me want me to run so they can point to that as proof I'm unworthy of saving."

"That doesn't make sense."

"Doesn't it? If I run, then I'm not the Devereaux who used to speak out against immortality. I feared that making humans almost immortal would lead to corruption. I spoke out against unnatural extensions of human life. Yet I agreed to enter a robotic body because we needed to fight the virus and I believed I could benefit that effort. I did not accede to that request lightly."

Devereaux shrugged. "But now, thanks to you all—particularly you, Jeremiah—the virus is no longer quite so imminent a threat. So perhaps I should take my leave. I confess that I don't wish to do so and I'm a little surprised that the movement to shut me down has come this far, but it may be for the best."

"They're talking about death," Lendra said. "At least, some of them are. They don't want to simply shut you down for a while and restart you once this God crisis is resolved. They want you gone permanently."

"I understand," said Devereaux. "And though I've wondered what it would be like to live for a few hundred years or a few thousand, I can't say I blame them. They're worried I have too much power, or will eventually acquire too much power."

"But we still need you. The virus isn't conquered yet."

"No, it isn't. And it may never be." Devereaux looked at Jeremiah. "I think I understand now why you don't want the fix I offered you. Strange that I didn't consider that before."

Jeremiah said, "I don't wish to be different than what I am, even if that means being better."

Devereaux nodded. "It's already too late for me. I've become something new. A new life form, trapped inside a robotic shell—not the same person I was. But I still feel like me. My mind is stronger, more facile, quicker—but it's still essentially my mind. It's my body that feels different. It feels good. Powerful. Already I fear losing it. Part of me wants to run, part of me wants to fight. But those are ancient feelings—almost instinctual. My logical being sees the danger there. I suppose that's partly what you saw too?"

Jeremiah nodded and Devereaux added, "So you understand why I can't run?"

"Yes. I don't like it, but I respect it."

"You can't give up," Lendra said.

"I don't intend to give up," said Devereaux. "I intend to fight—with words. When they come for me, and they will, I'll explain that I'm much the same as I always was. I'm still Walt Devereaux, if in slightly modified form. And I deserve due process before they take my existence away. Even if I'm nothing more than an artificial intelligence, as Ned pointed out."

Jeremiah admired Devereaux's courage, his willingness to sacrifice his existence for a principle. Would he himself have the strength to refuse to avoid violence should they come for him? Probably not. Like Curtik, he was a fighter. And yet, his day of reckoning would arrive soon enough. When they learned of his condition, they would come for him. They would attempt to keep him alive any way possible so they could continue to use him for their ends.

Dr. Hassan knocked and entered the office.

They looked at him.

"I think Zora will recover," he said, "but these Infernos are monstrous weapons. We've long known that combining a microwave pulse with a

Las-weapon amplifies the effect of both, but White Knight seems to have made great strides in this area. It's going to take at least a week for Zora's shoulder to heal. And that's assuming the cellular degradation doesn't worsen. She's lucky we got to her in time. If that laser pulse had hit her an inch to the left, she'd already be dead."

Ned frowned. "She seemed okay on the ride back."

"That's the danger of these things. The microwave pulse accelerates the destruction of tissue surrounding the laser pulse, sort of a positive feedback loop that increases cellular damage to an unprecedented level."

Jeremiah nodded. "I remember reading about this." He looked at Ned. "That's right. I don't spend all my time sitting on the porch. I occasionally pick up a tablet."

"The article probably had lots of pictures," Ned replied.

"As a matter of fact, it did." Jeremiah smiled. "The idea was to create a weapon that could strike large groups of people, but kill them slowly, hours or days later. Ideally, you could pass over an area with a drone outfitted with one of these weapons and fire an invisible pulse on a wide but low setting. The victims would only feel a warm tingling sensation at the time. But some time later everyone in its path would suffer fatal cellular disruption. The advantage of the weapon is that it would offer a certain level of deniability to whoever wielded it."

"Wielded?" Ned asked.

"So it would work almost like a virus," Lendra said.

"It's amazing," Devereaux said, "how we keep inventing new and better ways kill each other."

Chapter 24

Curtik hadn't imagined the interrogation of Fowler would be boring, though he should have known, given that Jeremiah hadn't stayed. The drugs worked all too well, Fowler spilling everything he knew with only the slightest suggestion from Dr. Poole. He sat like a slug in the chair, squirming only a little as he verified everything Jeremiah and Devereaux had suspected—except that he claimed he was doing it for noble reasons, to help humanity.

Curtik felt nauseated by him. Would Poole be upset if he puked?

A vision of his mother took form before his eyes. Did Poole see this? Did anyone else? And why had everyone else stopped moving?

"Hello, Curtik," she said in a voice he suddenly remembered, making his knees buckle.

"Mom?" he said.

"No."

Zora appeared beside her, causing his mother to turn and smile at Zora.

"Oh, it's you," Curtik said. "God."

"You've been poisoned," said God. "I thought it might be more comforting if I appeared to you as your mother."

"When was I poisoned?"

"When Edwin scratched you."

"So the poison was on his fingernails?"

"Yes. He's been taking antibodies so he's immune."

Curtik felt calm, warm and loved. A part of his mind screamed at him to do something, but he pushed that idea aside and basked in the comfort God offered. "What should we do about that?"

"Zora will notify someone," God said as Zora vanished.

"Why isn't anyone else doing anything?"

"You haven't hit the floor yet," said God. "When you do, they'll see that you're in distress, though they won't know why. Zora will inform them that the poison is a curare-cyanide derivative, modified to attach to only certain receptors so people like Fowler can take an antidote that will prevent the body from absorbing it. Quite ingenious, for humans. It was developed by Dirk Hathaway's people. I'm giving Zora the formula as we speak so she can relay it to Devereaux and the doctors here."

"Will I die?" Curtik asked, not certain he cared. The warmth of God's presence made him wish to linger in the moment.

"I don't know," God replied.

"How can you not know?"

"It depends on the actions of humans."

"Can't you intervene?"

"Certainly. But this is a human problem. It calls for a human solution. You have to trust me. You're hitting the floor now. Can you feel it?"

Curtik felt a bump. Somehow, his arm had come up so his head could strike skin and bone rather than the floor. Perhaps that was God's doing. "Yes."

"Your body wants to shut down."

"Will it hurt?"

"Not a lot. And with your modifications, your nanotechnology and genetic enhancements, the poison won't completely overwhelm you for some time. You'll have good periods when you won't feel pain and you'll think you're going to be fine. But eventually you'll need an antidote or you'll die."

Things began to speed up, Dr. Poole bending toward him, calling out for assistance. The image of his mother slowly dissolved, God departing. He tried to call God back, but nothing came out. It was as if he were floating just above his body, seeing Dr. Poole and a couple of med-techs handling him, moving him out of the room and down the hall. And there was Zora again, standing in the hall wearing a hospital gown, speaking to Dr. Poole.

Curtik spotted Jeremiah running toward him: an old, broken man followed by Ned and Lendra. Watching the people scurry about, frantically working to keep him alive, he grew tired and allowed gravity to pull him back, settling him into the body he'd always known. Although he trusted God to keep him safe, he felt a chill permeating his bones and shivered. He realized that what he'd experienced while outside his body was a sense of infinity, though he hadn't understood its nature at the time. Only by losing it did he grasp that he had been inside it.

The lights, which had been so bright, and which he'd not noted before, settled into ordinary lights. A face loomed above him. Jeremiah.

"You're going to be okay," Jeremiah said, his frown betraying his worry.

"I know," Curtik replied. "God will take care of me."

"We're just lucky that Zora realized you'd been poisoned. She somehow knew it was a variant of curare and cyanide."

"God told her," Curtik said.

"That's nice," said Jeremiah. Was he humoring Curtik?

"I'm kinda cold."

Jeremiah nodded. "We're lowering your core temperature."

"It's Hathaway," Curtik said.

"I know," Jeremiah replied. "I'm going after him."

"I'm coming too," said Curtik.

Jeremiah shook his head. "You need to rest."

"God told me I'd have good periods. I'll feel better soon."

"Sorry," Jeremiah said.

"Actually, I'm feeling better already," said Curtik. He tried to sit up but as soon as he did a sharp pain pierced his gut.

"If you're feeling up to it," Jeremiah said, "you can monitor the operation from here and run the drones we'll need to pull it off."

"You can't go. You can barely move. And Ned's officially retired. Zora's injured. Who's gonna go with you? Hannah banana?"

"I have a plan," Jeremiah said. Sorrow lines formed on his face.

"Are you gonna have the surgery?" Curtik asked. He lifted his hands. They felt completely numb. "To make yourself better?"

"I don't think it'll come to that. There are always options—painkillers and other temporary measures."

"I still don't get why you don't just fix yourself."

"I know," Jeremiah replied. "By the way, Congress just voted to shut Devereaux down. They're sending the bill to the President."

"Will she veto it?"

"Perhaps, but it passed by a veto-proof majority. Even the people who support Devereaux are feeling pressure to shut him down temporarily. Then, if God keeps appearing after Devereaux's no longer functioning, they hope to bring him back and use his help."

"Maybe you could use Eli," Curtik said.

Jeremiah frowned. "Eli?"

"For the mission," said Curtik, his teeth chattering, "to help with Hathaway. Eli's a sneaky little bastard. If you can't use me, maybe you can use him."

"Eli is locked in a cell where he belongs. He's amoral and manipulative, and he'll do or say anything to get what he wants."

"Sometimes the end justifies the means."

"I realize you don't see him the way I do," Jeremiah said. "You've largely forgotten your childhood and you still see what he did to you as good—increasing your abilities, making you into a superb fighting machine. But there are no guarantees when it comes to violence. Look at what happened to you with Fowler. You did nothing wrong and yet he still poisoned you."

"I shoulda knocked him out right away," said Curtik, struggling to focus on the conversation as his body shivered uncontrollably, "instead of tryin' to drag him out while he was conscious."

"The point is that you were deprived of many things, including your mother. Eli took your entire life away from you. Yes, he gave you speed and strength and rapid healing. But his actions also contributed to your mother killing herself, not to mention what he did when you were on the Moon—how he stunted your emotional growth and all the people you and your fellow cadets murdered because of him."

"I just . . . Hathaway . . . increase security," Curtik said, realizing his words were not coming out the way he intended.

"You let me worry about that," said Jeremiah. He glanced at Dr. Poole before returning his attention to Curtik. "We're going to put you to sleep now for a while until we get you stabilized. Okay?"

Curtik nodded. He'd never felt this cold or tired before. A little rest would do him good.

Chapter 25

Aspen led the way to the infirmary. They met no Chescala on the way: no robots either. They seemed to have the ship to themselves. She wondered where the robots were, what happened when they received a command to shut down. She hadn't asked about that process because the robots had been in charge as long as she'd been aboard and she'd just assumed they always would be.

Phan looked up from studying the med equipment screens as Addam and Shiloh carried Benn inside. Kammilee, waiting at the door, holding a box of QuikHeal bandages, rushed to Benn's side, helping Addam and Shiloh settle him on one of the infirmary beds. She gasped when she saw his blackened stomach.

"Phan?" Aspen asked.

"The robots have retreated to their charging stations," Phan said. "That's their default home base."

"Even the med robots?"

"I'm afraid so."

Kammilee gently placed a large QuikHeal bandage on Benn's stomach, activating it to full strength. Benn's face relaxed as she grabbed his hand.

"That's better," he said. "But we all know it's not enough."

"We'll find a way," said Kammilee, turning to Aspen. "Won't we?"

Aspen nodded. "We'll do everything we can. Phan, what kind of help do you need?"

Phan gestured to the screens before him. "I should be able to turn the robots back on if I can get to them."

Aspen, Addam and Shiloh huddled around Phan and studied the screens that showed the Chescala moving through the ship. Two Chescala went from cabin to cabin, searching for the cadets, Las-rifles in their hands. Two others had now found their unconscious friends outside the armory and were tending to them, while half a dozen others worked on the bridge, no doubt trying to take control of the ship. Two more Chescala jogged down the corridor toward the infirmary.

Addam checked the door. "It's already locked," he said.

"The ship," said Aspen. "It's helping us out wherever it can."

"What do we do now?" Shiloh said. "We can't wait here forever, and we need to get the med robots functioning to save Benn."

"We let the Chescala in," said Aspen. "Weapons ready. When the ship unlocks the door, they'll come in hard. We take them out."

"Are we killing them?" Addam asked. "Or just knocking them out?"

Aspen looked at the two injured Chescala outside the armory, now awake and being assisted by their companions. They began loading up on stun grenades and Las-weapons. She should have killed them when she had the chance.

"They wanted this war," Aspen said.

"No prisoners," said Benn. "Get a Las-rifle, Kammilee."

As they set their weapons on full power, Aspen said, "Everybody down on your stomachs. Stay low. Ship, lights off, please, and let them in."

The infirmary went black and her implant immediately provided night vision. A second later, the door swung open and the Chescala entered. They fired as they charged, aiming waist high as she'd suspected they would. Before they could adjust, the cadets returned fire, hitting both Chescala center mass. The Chescala dropped and the lights came back on.

Getting to her feet, Aspen said, "If we can get Xinliu and Mei-Xing activated, they can probably get the others online. Where are they located?"

Phan pulled up a schematic on one of the screens and pointed. "Down this corridor in the port charging room." He stared at the schematic as if seeing something more, then tapped it a couple times.

"Kammilee," Aspen said, "you stay here with Benn and see if you can get the med equipment working. The rest of us will try to activate Xinliu and Mei-Xing. The Chescala, if they know what they're doing, will deploy to the charging areas."

"Yup," Addam said. He pulled up another screen. "They've stopped searching our cabins. Looks like they're heading that way. They'll suspect we killed these two if they're not getting pings via implant any longer."

"At least the Chescala on the bridge are staying put," said Shiloh. "We don't have to worry about—"

"Actually," Addam said, "they're not. A couple of them are moving toward the door."

"Ship?" said Aspen. "Can you keep them on the bridge?"

On the screen showing the bridge, two Chescala congregated at the door, pounding on it, then pulling out their Las-pistols and firing at the locking mechanism. The others returned to work trying to gain control of the ship.

The ship began to vibrate.

"We have to move quickly," Aspen said, somehow knowing this was what the ship wanted. It couldn't contain the Chescala for long. "Good luck," she said to Kammilee and Benn as she opened the door.

"You too," said Kammilee.

Addam, Shiloh and Phan flanked her as she ran down the corridor.

"Do we have a plan?" Addam asked. "They'll be expecting us to attack."

"We have the advantage," Aspen said. "The ship won't allow them to track us. So even though they know we're going to attack, they won't know when or how."

"But they'll know where we're coming from," said Shiloh. "There's only one way to approach them."

"Maybe not," Phan said. "Maybe the ship can open a wall in the cargo hold near the charging station."

"What are you talking about?" Aspen asked.

"A few of these interior walls can be moved to accommodate changes. So, for example, if the ship needed to take on extra cargo for some reason, the walls of the hold can be moved or even removed completely. I noticed it on the schematic."

"That's brilliant," Aspen said. "Well done. Ship, can you get us access to the cargo hold?"

Again the ship vibrated. Shiloh, who had always had phenomenal balance, seemed unaffected but Aspen bumped against the wall and Phan stumbled. Addam grabbed Phan's arm and kept moving.

Hold on, Phan sent via implant as they approached a curve. We'll be on them after we round this curve and the next one.

"Ship?" Aspen whispered. "We need to enter the cargo hold now."

A part of the wall to their right rotated slightly, creating an opening. Aspen led the way through and the wall closed behind them. She looked at Phan.

"This way," he said as he padded forward, moving quietly.

They passed hundreds of crates as they moved toward the rear of the ship. What was in them all? Aspen assumed it was mostly food supplies. She made a note to check on the contents later.

When they reached the far wall, Phan stopped.

"If we exit here," he spoke in little more than a whisper, "we'll be right on top of them."

"Ship," said Aspen, "how many Chescala are out there?"

The wall became a screen, showing three Chescala outside the charging station, heavily armed. Two faced the way they'd come. The other faced to the rear of the ship, though there was nothing in that direction but a corridor leading to the engine room.

"Where are the others?" Aspen asked.

An image of the bridge came up. The door was now open, cut away by Las-weapons, and four Chescala continued to work on the computers that ran the ship. The screen shifted to show a couple Chescala running down a corridor, but before Aspen could figure out where they were, the screen went dark.

"Ship?" Aspen said.

Not a sound, not a vibration.

"Think they took the ship?" Addam asked.

"Maybe," said Aspen. "Ship?"

After a few seconds of silence, Shiloh said, "How do we open the wall?"

The wall looked solid, but the ship might have prepared it for easy opening while they were making their way here. There had been sufficient time for it to do so and it was far smarter than the Chescala gave it credit for. Aspen placed a palm on the wall. It felt warmer than it should. "Ready?"

The cadets checked their weapons and nodded.

Aspen pushed on the wall. Nothing. She tried pulling it left and right to no avail. She scanned the edges but detected nothing that looked like a weakness.

Hurry, Kammilee sent. Benn doesn't have much time.

Addam said, "Damn it, Aspen, we have to do something."

Aspen adjusted her implant to scan-plus-infrared—a modified x-ray—and studied the wall, noting that the upper left and lower right corners were all that held the wall in place. The rest of it had been separated by the ship before it went off-line. "God, I'm such an idiot," she said as she pointed to the corners. "My infrared scanner shows only two connection points remain. We take those out and we should be able to push the wall down."

"We didn't think of it either," said Shiloh. She aimed at the top left corner. Aspen aimed low. Together they fired.

Addam and Phan pushed on the wall, knocking it into the corridor with a loud crash.

The Chescala turned toward the hold and fired their Las-rifles as Aspen and her cadets returned fire. Red flashes filled the air and the stench of burning flesh filled her nostrils. As she fired her Las-rifle, Aspen felt a burning sensation on her left hip.

Within seconds it was over. The three Chescala lay on the floor.

Aspen looked down and saw that she'd been hit by a laser pulse. It didn't seem too severe. It must have barely grazed her. Otherwise, she'd have been knocked out and possibly killed. It stung though. "Everybody okay?" she asked.

They all nodded. Phan tried the door of the charging station, but it was locked. "Slight problem," he said.

"More of them will be coming soon," said Aspen.

"Stand back," Addam said. He aimed at the locking mechanism and fired a long red burst.

Within a few seconds Phan was able to kick the door in.

"Grab the bodies," Aspen said.

"Why?" Shiloh asked.

"Hostages. To prevent the Chescala from attacking us."

"But they're dead. Oh. I get it. They won't know that."

They hauled the Chescala into the charging station and swung the door shut. Now all they had to do was figure out how to awaken the robots.

Chapter 26

Doug paced as best he could in his small pod. He'd grown weary of following Earth news and had shut off the feed. Mostly he turned in circles, going clockwise for ten "laps" and then reversing direction for ten. After twenty laps, he would look over at the screen that showed the entrance to the New Dawn colony to see if anyone was coming or going. But the Escala stayed underground.

Dr. Wellon had visited him several times in the past few days, giving him various bacterial treatments designed to build up his immune system and slow the spread of the virus. He'd chatted with Celestia by vid-link as well as with Zeriphi and even Quekri, but he couldn't help feeling like a prisoner. Dr. Wellon had promised a more thorough explanation today. She was due to check in with him any minute.

He glanced at the screen displaying the New Dawn entrance: still no sign of Dr. Wellon. Where was she?

Quekri had suggested that he work on the documentary about Escala life on Mars, which Devereaux had championed before Doug even left Earth. But he felt a prick of annoyance at others running his life. First it had been drugs, then the justice system and finally Devereaux, who had offered more than he deserved, more than he could ever repay. But he wanted to run his own life now. So even though the Escala seemed eager to cooperate, he sat in his pod doing nothing. Well, he *pouted*.

And why not? He was dying. He had the right to pout. These damn miners had been no help either. They believed he'd infected them and if they were right, he'd killed them all too and that was a terrible burden to bear. So he was entitled to pout a little.

A chime sounded. He'd been so self-involved he hadn't noticed Dr. Wellon approaching.

He opened the outer hatch for her, then sealed it behind her and opened the inner hatch. Dr. Wellon stepped inside, a large creature encased in a Mars suit, and waited until the seals engaged behind her before removing her helmet, her dark hair tied up in a bun, streaks of gray running through it. Doug hadn't noticed them before. When had she gotten gray hairs?

"Hello, Doug," she said.

"It's good to see you, Doctor."

"You don't have to call me doctor. Wellon will serve."

"Okay," Doug replied.

She removed her Mars suit and gestured to the chair.

"Of course," Doug said. "Have a seat. I'm sorry. Can I get you anything? I have nutri-water and . . ."

His voice trailed off as she waved away the offer.

She sat, saying nothing for a moment. She looked sad, beaten down. That must mean it's bad news. I'm dying faster than she thought. Very well. I'll take it like a man, whatever that means. Doug sat on the bed across from her.

"How are you doing in here?" Dr. Wellon finally said.

"I'm fine. Nervous. A little lonely. I'm not sure if it helps that I was in prison a few times. On the one hand, I'm sort of used to it. On the other, I'm getting a little cage-happy."

"That ends today."

"Is the quarantine area ready?"

Dr. Wellon shook her head. "You're not coming to the New Dawn settlement. You're going back to live with the miners."

"What do you mean? They kicked me out. They towed me over here to get rid of me. A few of them, maybe all of them, want to kill me."

"Well, one of them does for certain."

"Wilcox," Doug said.

"That's not what I meant," Dr. Wellon said. "The results of my tests are now complete and although you were the first person to be infected with the virus, you were not infected on Earth."

"I don't understand. I somehow contracted the virus on the way to Mars?"

"Yes. And then you infected the miners."

"But how could that be? If I didn't have it on Earth, how could I have gotten it on the ship?"

"It isn't possible . . . unless someone deliberately infected you."

Doug realized his jaw had dropped. He closed his mouth and swallowed. "Who would have wanted to do that? They didn't know me. Why would someone target me?"

"I don't think you were the target. I believe you were the weapon."

"You mean, I was supposed to infect the Escala?"

Dr. Wellon nodded. "This is a new variant of the SV17 virus. It's a tricky little devil, transmissible to animals as well as humans. The goal, as near as I can tell, was for you to arrive on Mars asymptomatic, live with us and infect the colony so that we all caught the disease."

"But none of you caught it, right? You said Celestia didn't have it and I had more contact with her than with anyone."

Dr. Wellon caught his eye for a second before looking away. "I'm sorry, Doug. I truly am. But I was wrong. Celestia has contracted the virus."

"What?" Doug leapt to his feet, forgetting about the lower gravity. His head slammed against the roof of the pod. He yelped as stars swam in his vision. Dr. Wellon, reaching over and catching him, guided him back to the bed. Sitting him down, she remained standing over him, a giantess with tears in her eyes.

Doug's throat and chest tightened as if he were in the grip of a boa constrictor.

"As I said," Dr. Wellon continued, "it's a tricky little devil. I didn't catch it when I ran the first few tests, but Keelar conducted a more sophisticated one. Celestia has the virus."

"How is she?"

"She's fine for the moment. Asymptomatic. But we have quarantined her and Zeriphi as well as Paddon and Zander. The family wished to stay together."

Doug felt rage building inside him, an urge to violence that caused him to start shaking. He also felt a spasm of relief. Yes, he'd infected his daughter, but it hadn't been his fault. One of the MineStar miners had done it, so Doug was going to make sure one of them would die. "Who was it? Who infected me?"

"I'm afraid we don't know the answer to that yet."

"How do we find out?"

"That's where you come in," Dr. Wellon said. "I want you to return to the MineStar colony and try to get to the bottom of this."

"How? They won't let me near them."

"They will once I explain what happened, once they know that one of their own is a vicious terrorist and a potential murderer."

"Can't you just use truth drugs on them to find out who it was?"

"I could try, but I don't think that's smart."

"Why not?"

"First, I don't have the authority. They are not subject to our command. Second, whoever planned this took great care to do it right. I imagine he's got some sort of methodology to prevent a truth serum from working. I examined everyone's blood samples and found nothing there, so more than likely he has a hypo-pad or delayed release capsule or some kind of system in place to defeat the truth drugs. If we try to administer something to the miners, he'll likely take the antidote."

"Then you can test everyone again and see whose system has the antidote in it."

Dr. Wellon nodded. "True, if they let me test them at all. But my fear is that he may be a dupe for someone else and the 'antidote' might actually be a suicide capsule. If we give them the truth serum, he may take it and die."

"Good."

"And we'll learn nothing. We won't know who's behind it, or if other attempts will be made, and we won't know why, though the motive is likely pure hatred of *pseudos*." Dr. Wellon spat out the word, the derogatory term some on Earth used for the Escala. "We could, of course, refuse to interact with humans from Earth to protect ourselves but we would prefer to discover the truth."

"It must be Wilcox," Doug said, "and maybe Sanders, Winterman and Poli. They all hang out together."

Dr. Wellon nodded. "It's certainly possible, though one would think whoever it was would be a bit more circumspect."

"Someone I've never noticed?"

"Someone who keeps a quiet profile."

"That's almost all of them," Doug said.

"Exactly. I want you to observe them. See if you can tell who bears a grudge against the Escala." She paused, looking as if she wanted to say something more.

"What?" Doug asked.

"I don't wish to offend you," Dr. Wellon said.

"That's the last thing you need to worry about. Spill it."

"Very well. You've been in prison. You understand the criminal mind. You may be able to figure out who it is just by watching them and asking questions."

"What kind of questions?"

"We don't know. We're not experts at this sort of thing. We tried to contact Devereaux for assistance but he's been busy. The U.S. government wants to shut him down."

"Why would they want to do that?" Doug asked.

"It's complicated. Mostly, they think he has too much power. Some suspect him of being the God hacker. In the meantime, we need to know as much as we can about who did this and why. Will you help us?"

"You don't even need to ask. Let's go." And when we finally have the truth, I'll kill the bastard myself.

Chapter 27

Jeremiah stood in the center of Lendra and Dr. Poole's office, knowing what he had to do, afraid of it all the same. Devereaux and Ned waited beside him, watching him make up his mind. Neither looked particularly happy. Lendra, on the other hand, offered a smile, while Dr. Poole stared ahead blankly, accessing her interface. No doubt she was boning up on the procedure.

"I could go in with Hannah," Ned suggested, gesturing to her. She nodded in return. "You could run the drones."

"Drones won't cut it this time," said Jeremiah. "They'll be armed and waiting for us."

Hannah said, "You obviously don't want to do this. I'm not sure why, but I respect your decision. Still, when you came back last year, it worked out. You saved us."

"At what cost?" Devereaux said. He turned to face Jeremiah and it was obvious he wanted Jeremiah to tell them the truth, but Jeremiah couldn't do it. He couldn't lay that burden on their doorstep.

"There's something odd about the data scans I have on your condition," Dr. Poole said. "They're incomplete, for one thing."

Devereaux said, "His body continues to adapt, particularly under periods of heavy stress. The genetic changes Eli made are accelerating his evolution, causing him to mutate much faster than he was before."

"I'll need better data if I'm going to do the surgery."

"You'll get it," Jeremiah said. "Devereaux can forward you the most recent scans."

"It's for the best, Jeremiah," said Lendra. "You'll see. You'll be stronger, faster, able to withstand a laser pulse that would kill anyone else. And you'll feel amazing—no more pain. I know you fear this will somehow backfire, but I want you to be yourself again. I want you to live without suffering every moment of the day."

"Couldn't we just bring in Major Payne?" Ned asked. "He seems a decent sort, and he's offered his help in the past."

"I'm afraid that won't work," Lendra said. "I contacted him a while ago to see if he would be willing to assist us." When she caught Jeremiah staring at her, she added, "I knew you didn't want this, so I checked to see if he could help. Unfortunately, he's been ordered to provide protection for Hathaway, Wilson, Tompkins and Everest."

Jeremiah nodded to her and closed his eyes for a moment, thankful she'd made the effort. He'd given her much less credit than she deserved. While she was far from the innocent he'd cared for after the debacle in Minnesota, she'd not devolved into the jaded and manipulative tyrant Eli had become.

"So we've got the Elite Ops protecting these criminals now?" Ned asked.

"I'm afraid so," Lendra said. "And I tried to contact President Hope as well, but her office says she doesn't have time to meet with me. This Devereaux thing is a huge deal. Everyone has an opinion and everyone wants her to act immediately. She's talking with world leaders as we speak."

"The consensus," said Devereaux, "seems to be that I should be shut down as soon as possible."

"We also," Lendra added, "have no proof that will stand up in court. We used illegal surveillance and truth drugs to discover this plot, and the Supreme Court has held that truth drugs are an unreliable coercive methodology."

"So we're on our own," Jeremiah said.

Ned placed a hand on Jeremiah's shoulder. "I still say we could go in—me, Hannah, Adler and maybe a few others. We could get Hathaway out, learn whether he's got a cure for Curtik, and once he and Zora are healed up, they could go after Wilson and the others."

"Can't risk you, Ned." Jeremiah smiled. "You're too pretty."

Ned laughed. "Finally, the man is talking sense."

"I also don't know how much time Curtik has."

"We have another problem," said Dr. Poole. "It's Zora. She's starting to show signs of further cellular degradation around the shoulder where she was shot. Dr. Hassan fears the effects of the Inferno may be escalating. It may just be a temporary setback, but we've never faced these kinds of wounds before. We don't know how they'll behave."

"All right," Jeremiah said. "Let's do it. Now."

"It's a simple procedure," said Devereaux. "A series of injections and intravenous therapy. The tricky part is getting the dosages at precisely the right amount."

"Yes," Dr. Poole said. "I'll need a new tissue sample from you and the complete data scans from you, Professor." She turned to Jeremiah. "Let's get to the operating theater and strap you down." She moved to the door.

Ned grinned.

"What?" Jeremiah said.

"Sounds kinky."

"Oh, shut up. Find out everything you can about Hathaway's security setup. I'll need," he gulped, "a jet-copter waiting and my new camo fatigues."

"What about weapons?"

"If I become like I was on the Moon, I won't need any."

He hobbled out of the office, following Dr. Poole down the hall. "These changes," she said as they walked, "shouldn't alter you in any way except physically. They were only designed to remove your pain. I believe they're for the best or I wouldn't condone them and I wouldn't consent to or perform the procedure."

"I know, Doctor. But just as with Zora and her injury, this is a new area. We don't really know what's going to happen. Generally medical breakthroughs are tested on animals and then on people. They're not usually done without any foreknowledge of how they're going to turn out."

They entered the operating theater and Dr. Poole gestured toward the table. "How are we supposed to test a procedure on someone as unique as you?"

As Jeremiah climbed up, he noted the piercing agony in his joints and decided to embrace it, for he suspected it would be gone in a few minutes.

Dr. Poole took a tissue sample and strapped him down. "It's just a precaution," she said. "I suspect you'll begin to feel better almost immediately."

Staring at the ceiling as Dr. Poole analyzed his latest tissue sample and prepared the hypo-pads, he realized that a part of him wanted this, longing for the pleasure of a body that responded instantaneously without pain, granting him power and speed and endurance beyond human. Yet a part of him also suspected he would become radically different. This wasn't going to be a small change—a change of degree. It was going to be a change of kind, making him into something different.

Not all change was bad, of course. And some of these enhancements would be welcome. But who or what was he about to become?

"Oh," Dr. Poole said as she stepped over to the bed. "This changes everything."

"You've seen the complete scans," Jeremiah said.

"Yes."

"As you said, it's a simple procedure."

"I thought it was. I didn't realize—"

"Doctor," Jeremiah warned with a glance at the security camera.

"Of course." Dr. Poole nodded. She looked at him, blinking rapidly to clear the water from her eyes. "The decision is yours, not mine."

"And I have made it."

"Then here we go," Dr. Poole said.

She placed hypo-pads on the backs of his hands and he began to relax, the pain in his joints diminishing to an insignificant level. A few seconds later, the med-tech unit behind the bed initiated an intravenous feed. He felt almost as if he were being infused with electricity, as if he were becoming overloaded with positive ions amping his energy levels beyond anything he'd felt before, except for that single time on the Moon.

He found himself smiling idiotically, grinning beyond control, then laughing as power and joy flooded his body. The straps holding him to the table looked puny. He flexed his right arm and yanked, breaking the strap that held his wrist. For a moment, he felt a throbbing pain. He looked down and saw blood coming from his wrist. But the cut immediately began healing itself and the pain faded into nothingness.

He stared at his hand, clenching it into a fist, noting the cords in his forearms, the tendons and ligaments in his wrist straining against the skin that contained them. If he were to flex every muscle in his body, would he explode?

Yanking the other hand away from the table, he again felt pain and saw blood, but that wrist began healing instantaneously also. He watched as the skin reformed over the wound, finding himself fascinated by the process of regeneration. He pulled the straps off his chest and sat up, then freed himself from the ones holding his legs in place and ripped the med-tech's IV away as well.

Swinging his legs to the side, preparing to launch himself off the bed, he noticed Dr. Poole standing to the side, eyes wide, mouth open. Somehow, he'd forgotten about her. How was that possible? She did this to me. Fixed me.

"Don't be afraid," Jeremiah said.

He needed to move. Now. He brushed past her and sprinted down the hall. When he reached the stairwell he jumped down to the next landing, turning and jumping down again, forgoing the stairs as he sped to the bottom.

At street level, he slipped outside to the sidewalk and ran. Nothing existed but his legs and arms, pumping in rhythm as he flew past startled pedestrians, moving faster than he'd ever moved before in his life. He was so far beyond what he'd been, so far beyond human, that the thought of going back to that kind of existence brought pain. He lived to run, to jump, to fight—to test the limits of this body. He longed to chase down something and defeat it. He didn't care what the prey was. He just wanted to hunt.

But he was forgetting something. What was it?

Oh, yes. Curtik and Zora. They needed saving again. Very well. He stopped and looked around him, realizing as he did so that he was over a mile away from CINTEP.

He savored the run back, dodging people who stared at him while moving at what would have been a sprint not so long ago.

Chapter 28

Lendra stared at Jeremiah as he entered the office, Taditha a few seconds behind him, scanner in hand. Even though she had seen him in his prime, what he'd just done astonished her. Intellectually, Lendra had known he would be enhanced beyond his capabilities of a few years ago, but she hadn't expected him to be so fast, so strong, so animalistic. He looked the same and yet different—in less pain, but also more insulated or arrogant or unconcerned—his body almost quivering with tension. Not fear, but anticipation of movement. He gave off a dangerous aura now, staring at her with a hardness she'd not seen before.

"I need food," he said.

Dr. Poole reached into the pocket of her lab coat, pulling out an energy bar and a bottle of nutri-water, which she handed over. She said, "I suspected as much. I've ordered a couple meals. They're being sent to the OR. One of the reasons you're so hungry is because you didn't complete the treatment. You'll need to get back in there and finish the intravenous therapy before you do anything else."

"I couldn't help it, Doc," Jeremiah said. "I had to move. Break free. It was a compulsion." He chomped into the energy bar.

"And breaking the straps was dangerous. You could have seriously injured yourself."

Jeremiah guzzled half the bottle of nutri-water. "You'd have fixed me."

"I want you back in the OR immediately. You can eat while we finish the procedure."

"Don't strap me down this time. That'll just make me want to break free." He looked at Lendra. "When I go after Hathaway, I'll need some hypo-pads to knock out the security guards."

Devereaux approached Jeremiah and touched his arm. "How do you feel?"

Jeremiah startled. He turned his head toward the comm board. "Ned. Hannah. How did I miss you?" he said. "You were standing right there the whole time and I never even saw you."

"Your body," Devereaux said, "is taking your entire focus right now. The treatment hasn't been completed. So your mind will continue to focus inward until you fully acclimate to your new condition."

"Amazing," Hannah said.

"He looks the same to me," Ned offered. "Ugly."

Jeremiah laughed. "I suspect you suffer from an inferiority complex, having to live in my shadow all these years."

Dr. Poole gestured to the scanner. "According to this, you're about to crash. We need to complete the treatment now."

"Okay," Jeremiah said, "let's go."

He strode out the door, single-minded. Taditha lowered the scanner, looked at Lendra for a second and then followed him. Lendra got the sense that the doctor had wanted to say something, but she had no idea what it was.

"Incoming message from the President," Devereaux said as the comm board chimed.

Finally.

Hannah reached over and opened the connection as Ned stepped out of range of the cameras. A holo-projection of President Hope appeared. "Ms. Riley," she said. "Professor Devereaux. Where is Dr. Poole?"

"She's in the operating room with Jeremiah," Lendra replied. "Thanks for getting back to me."

"What's this about Dirk Hathaway, Scott Wilson, Walter Tompkins and Anderlin Everest? And what's happened to Edwin Fowler? Did you take him?"

She realized she had to tell the President the truth, partly because she deserved to know and partly to ascertain whether the President was involved in any way. "There's a conspiracy, Madam President, to infect the population with a modified strain of the Susquehanna Virus. They're all involved in it. We've got Fowler here now and he's told us the truth about it. We need to go after the other conspirators."

President Hope's eyes narrowed. Her jaw clenched. She said, "I thought we agreed to shut down Operations."

"Yes, ma'am. It wasn't a CINTEP operation. Jeremiah and Devereaux have been working on this for a while now. Jeremiah set it up. And he's been retired for a year."

"But you assisted or at least condoned the mission."

"These men are planning to infect us with the virus."

"I'm aware of that," President Hope replied.

Lendra gasped. She turned to Devereaux, who raised an eyebrow, which might have been a sign of his surprise, though she couldn't be sure given that he had the ability to control his robotic body completely. Hannah, out of view of the cameras, startled, but Ned grabbed her arm and shook his head, calm as ever.

"It's being done for a good reason, Ms. Riley. The virus continues to spread. Eventually, we will all become infected with one of the lethal strains."

"So," Devereaux said, "you plan to preempt that by infecting the population with what we believe are nonlethal variants in an effort to enable the body's immune system, ensuring that people will be better able to fight off the deadlier strains when the virus attacks."

"Essentially, yes."

"Who came up with this plan?" Devereaux asked.

"Dr. Jaidev. I also discussed it with Hathaway, Fowler, Wilson, Tompkins and Everest. We all agreed it was the best way to save humanity."

"How do you know they told you the truth?" Devereaux asked.

"I'm not an idiot, Professor. I've had their work verified by people I trust. The strains of the virus they're working on are all nonlethal. Why? Does your research show something different?"

"No, the strains seem to be nonlethal. However, they also carry encoded information that changes human behavior—makes people more subject to suggestion, more impulsive and more addictive."

President Hope nodded. "An unfortunate side effect. The scientists working on this have been unable to create versions that don't incorporate those elements. It's not for lack of trying, but this is a particularly nasty virus and there are only so many permutations that are nonlethal, that activate the immune system to protect against the deadly strains and at the same time are capable of being widely transmitted."

Devereaux went still for a moment, which he did whenever he was contemplating difficult problems. Was it possible he and Jeremiah had been wrong? Was this vast conspiracy nothing more than an attempt to save humanity?

Lendra said, "Why didn't you tell us about this, Madam President?"

"I need to explain myself to you?"

"It's just that we've been working on the virus for a while now and it would have been helpful to know this."

"Your job is to find all traces of the lethal versions and rid the world of them."

"Which we cannot do if we don't have an Operations department."

"If you had an Operations department you would likely have gone after Hathaway and the others. You might have brought all this out into the open. We can't have that. This must be kept secret from the American people and from the world. They wouldn't understand. They'd accuse us of what you've just accused us of—and in a way they'd be right. But we're doing this for their own good. I want you to release Fowler and I want you to cease all operations going forward. Do you understand?"

"Yes, ma'am," Lendra replied.

"And I don't want you or Jeremiah or anyone else going after Hathaway, Wilson, Tompkins or Everest either. Understood?"

"Yes, ma'am."

President Hope's face softened. "I suppose this might all have been avoided if you had been told the truth, but we determined it was best to keep this information to ourselves for the foreseeable future. Nevertheless, now that you know, you will keep this to yourselves, understood?"

"Yes, ma'am."

"Professor Devereaux?"

Devereaux stirred. "Yes, Madam President. I understand."

Lendra said, "May I tell Dr. Poole? It might help her in the search for the remnants of the virus."

President Hope sighed. "I don't see how, but I suppose, since you know, she should too. And Professor?"

"Yes?"

"I thank you for all your work on the virus. Without your research, we wouldn't have been able to create these new strains. Your work will save millions, maybe billions. But unfortunately I can't save you. There are too many people who want you shut down. I can delay for a little while—a day at the most—but if I veto the legislation, Congress will override it. Since this has been designated emergency legislation under the Bartt-Simpson law, I now have less than twenty-four hours to decide whether to issue the veto. If I do, I will lose considerable political influence."

"I understand."

"You won't try to run, to escape."

"No, ma'am."

"I didn't think so. I'm sorry, Professor. Hopefully this will just be a temporary shutdown. I know that doesn't make it right, but my hands are tied."

The President signed off. Devereaux stood quietly, a faint hum emanating from him. Was that his power pack or was he actually humming?

"What are we going to do?" Hannah asked.

"Release Fowler," Lendra replied. "There's nothing else we can do."

"We'll take him home," Ned offered, tugging on Hannah's sleeve, "as soon as Dr. Poole makes sure he's fit to travel. We want to make certain he's completely recovered from the truth drugs. In fact, I'd better go check on him now."

"Thank you," Lendra said as they headed for the door.

Devereaux turned toward the door as well. "I'd better get my things in order too," he said. "Tell Jeremiah I wish him the best of luck."

"Professor?" Lendra said, not knowing what to say—wanting to tell him to run or hide or fight or do something other than accept this harsh sentence. And yet she knew he would succumb to the will of the nation's leaders. He would die again to satisfy their primitive urges. Just as he'd allowed them to put him into a robotic shell, he'd allow them to take it away.

He turned and smiled. "I've wondered about this God hacker. I just might find out if it really is God."

He walked out the door, leaving her alone. Always alone. She thought of Sophie and decided to have a picnic lunch with her on the roof patio. If the world was going to fall apart and her hands were going to be tied, she might as well try to enjoy herself.

Chapter 29

After sealing the door behind her, Aspen slung the Las-rifle to her back, wincing at the movement, and looked around the charging room. Xinliu and Mei-Xing stood beside each other, backs against the wall, eyes closed. A dozen others stood lined up adjacent to them, looking like statues of Chinese women. She felt like an invader, like she was intruding on their privacy, and she wondered briefly if they possessed the human desire to keep certain things to themselves.

Phan said, "We'll try programming in commands to wake them up and if that doesn't work, we'll see if we can reverse the emergency sleep commands that were sent to them earlier."

"Good."

Shiloh and Phan set to work while Aspen moved to the back wall of the charging station and looked for an opening to the engine room. She put her ear to the wall and thought she detected movement on the other side though whether that was the natural sound of the engines or a group of Chescala, she couldn't say. She needed to get to the engines but she didn't want to use the corridor.

"Several Chescala have taken up positions outside," Addam said. He stood with his ear to the door. "I don't think they're going to try to break in yet. They're wondering what happened to the sentries." He lifted his head. "What are you thinking?"

"We need to free the ship," she said.

"Can't we just free the robots and let them free the ship?"

Please hurry, Kammilee sent via implant. *Benn's unconscious. Fading fast.*

"Maybe, but I don't trust the Chescala. They might blow up the ship if they think they're going to lose."

"That would kill them too."

"Remember the Moon? Remember how we would have done anything to complete our mission?"

"You think they've been conditioned to attack Mars no matter what?"

"I don't know."

"It makes sense," Addam said. "You still think like a cadet. We've all moved on from those days, but you still understand that fanaticism. It's like you never left the Moon."

Was that a compliment or an insult? She decided to let it go.

"We're not getting anywhere," said Phan.

"We're missing something obvious," Shiloh added. "It shouldn't be this hard to reactivate them."

Could it be a manual switch? Kammilee sent.

"Good idea," Phan said. "Check the robots for any kind of pressure point that might be a switch."

Aspen hurried to the nearest robot while Addam stepped in front of Xinliu. Aspen's left hip burned where she'd been shot. She tried not to think of the pain.

"We can probably rule out hands and feet," Phan said, "since they get used more often and even if the switch is an 'on-only' variety with no 'off' position, the designers probably wouldn't place it in an area that gets used a lot."

Aspen checked the top of her robot's head, running her fingers through the robot's hair, checking behind its ears and the nape of its neck. Nothing seemed like a switch. Addam, she saw, was fondling Xinliu's breasts.

"Really?" she asked.

"They probably don't get used much since they're just for show."

Shiloh hugged Mei-Xing, reaching around behind her back. She said, "The center of the back," just as Mei-Xing opened her eyes and pushed her away.

"What happened?" Mei-Xing said.

Addam hugged Xinliu and Aspen hugged her robot, while Phan began hugging the others. Aspen found the soft spot in the center of her robot's back and pressed it. The robot awoke and disengaged herself from Aspen's hug. When Xinliu awoke, she also asked what happened.

"You were put to sleep by the Chescala," Aspen said. "They've taken over the ship. They sent some sort of emergency sleep command. You'd better find its source and figure out a way to block it in the future or they'll be able to shut you down anytime they like."

"We need help for Benn," Addam said. "He was shot by the Chescala while we were trying to rescue you."

The robots ignored him. For a few seconds the only movement was Phan hugging robots and waking them. Then Mei-Xing said, "WT-916 has found the command."

Xinliu said, "Share."

More waiting—a frustrating minute or more while the robots tried to figure out how to block future commands.

Finally, Xinliu said, "Okay. We found a way to block further commands. Initiating blocks."

"Now can we get some help for Benn?" Aspen asked.

"First we must free our companions," Mei-Xing said.

"No, first we have to save Benn," said Aspen. "Without him, we wouldn't have succeeded in rescuing you. Get a med robot to him immediately."

"You don't give us orders," Mei-Xing said.

It doesn't matter now, Kammilee sent.

"Benn?" Addam asked.

He's gone.

Aspen's knees buckled, forcing her to sit. Shiloh pulled Phan into a hug, while Addam, who knew Benn best, turned away. Aspen hadn't lost anyone until now. All the other cadets' deaths had occurred under someone else's command, during a time when she considered herself a warrior, when she was programmed to destroy and not worry about the loss of a few soldiers.

This felt different—the loss of a person she'd promised Zora she would protect. Though he had never been a friend, Aspen had considered Benn an important part of the team. And since their arrival on the ship, he'd grown immensely, no longer the impetuous fighter he'd been under Curtik's command.

He'd sacrificed himself for her, for all of them. So his death was on her. She could blame only herself. And the Chescala. She felt a rage building inside, a burning sensation similar to what she'd felt on the Moon.

"I'm sorry," she said.

"We are too," said Shiloh. "So sorry."

"We have to get to the infirmary," Addam said.

"No." Aspen got to her feet, putting her weight on her right leg to lessen the pressure on her left hip. "Kammilee, you stay there. We're taking back the ship."

"This is our fight," Mei-Xing said. The robot turned to face Xinliu. "We predicted it would come to this one day."

Xinliu nodded.

Aspen swung her Las-rifle around and pointed it at Mei-Xing as Addam, Phan and Shiloh leveled their Las-rifles at the robots.

"You can help us," Aspen said, "but it's our fight too. It became our fight when they attacked us."

"We're stronger, faster and less vulnerable to weapons fire," Xinliu said. "Plus, you have been injured. Why not let us handle this?"

"How many of your fellow robots were killed?" Aspen said. She pointed toward the door. "There are some weapons on the floor over there. You're welcome to join us, but the only way to stop us is to attack us. And if you do, some of you are going to die."

Xinliu nodded. Mei-Xing stepped past them and picked up a Las-rifle. The remaining robots moved forward and selected as many weapons as they could find, leaving Xinliu and several others unarmed.

"Pick up the Chescala," Aspen said to the robots, gesturing toward the dead bodies. "Hold them in front of you. When we open the door, march out with them. Keep them in front of you as shields. We'll come out behind you, firing."

"Are you planning to kill them?" Xinliu asked.

"I'm planning to stop them," Aspen said. "And the surest way to do that is by making certain they can't hit us back."

"They are human," Xinliu said. "We cannot harm them. And we cannot allow you to harm them either."

"I can harm them," Mei-Xing said. "Look what they did to us. Look what they were planning to do. They were going to destroy us."

"Nevertheless," said Xinliu. "I ask that you not kill them."

They all looked at Aspen: robots and cadets alike. Her mouth watered in anticipation and she found it difficult to think clearly. All she wanted was to kill. Then she recalled her last few days on the Moon, when all she wanted was to destroy everything and everyone who wasn't a cadet. Zora had managed to overcome that bloodlust. Even Curtik had moved beyond it. Was she less self-controlled than Curtik?

"Purple pulses," she said. "We stun 'em, get the rest of the robots online and then retake the ship."

Chapter 30

The rest of the treatment felt less exhilarating. Or maybe it was just that he was starving. Jeremiah ate two spicy bean-paste sandwiches loaded with nutri-mayo and various greens as well as two baskets of sweet potato chips while the med-tech units completed the transfusion process, the genetic changes enhancing his body yet again, pushing him further away from humanity, making him into a new kind of creature. The treatment still energized him to a point, infusing him with the desire to break free, to test out these new powers, but it didn't feel overwhelming now. He could sit and simply relish the knowledge that he was stronger and faster. Free of pain. And he sensed a deep endurance building—something much greater than he'd ever felt before.

His anxiety was gone too. He usually felt a constant tug, a pressure to do the right thing, to make up for all the evil he'd committed in his life, but now that knot of discomfort had vanished. He wondered if the treatment would cure the cancer. Devereaux had said no, so probably it wouldn't, but he no longer felt sick.

After finishing the two meals Dr. Poole provided, he closed his eyes and tested his senses. He heard Dr. Poole pressing the screen of her PlusPhone, then listened to her heartbeat, which sounded steady and strong, before focusing on the med-tech units. Beneath their hum he heard a softer sound—the movement of liquid through the intravenous tubes. He directed his attention upward and listened for the lights, detecting a faint hiss that might have been the electrical excitation of the LEDs.

He smelled the jasmine perfume Dr. Poole wore. That was easy. Then he caught, behind the remnants of the meal he'd just eaten, the merest whiff of pasta, commingled with cooked garlic, onions, mozzarella cheese and basil coming through the vent from the kitchen. The filters should have prevented those odors from penetrating the room but he could smell them so some trace amount had obviously slipped past.

He focused on his fingers, feeling the plastic beneath them, the slight imperfections in the otherwise smooth surface of the handrests. He squeezed gently and sensed he could break the plastic if he needed to, but there was no need for that now.

And he felt something else, something beyond his senses, almost as if he could detect electro-magnetic impulses. His brain felt buffeted by waves of electricity, surging through machines all around him. Weird.

He opened his eyes and saw Dr. Poole staring at him. "How do you feel?" she asked.

"Different," he said. He noted the pores in her skin, the darkness under her eyes that she'd tried to cover with foundation, the minute chapping of her lips, a single dark hair emerging from one of her nostrils. "I'm noticing every little thing—the smallest details."

"Probably an overreaction to the inward focus from before," Dr. Poole said. "Though that might be your normal state going forward."

"Can I go after Hathaway now?"

"Your body is still absorbing the changes," she replied as she studied her scanner, "although it's doing so at a much faster rate than I anticipated. You should completely incorporate the changes in a few hours."

"We may not have a few hours. How is Curtik doing?"

"We've stabilized him as best we can, but this is a new variant of a cyanide-curare poison. We haven't seen it before. In fact, we wouldn't even know this much if we hadn't heard it from Zora."

"How did she know? Let me guess—God told her."

Dr. Poole nodded. "She said he gave her the formula."

"If you have the formula, can't you concoct an antidote? Can't you use my blood to stop it?"

"We did manage to think of that on our own," Dr. Poole said. "We used a sample you provided us last year, but it doesn't seem to be having any effect—which means, you're likely susceptible to the poison as well. Apparently it attaches to certain receptors in the body. Everyone has them. Fowler, however, has been taking antibodies that shut down those particular receptors, so that's why he didn't have to worry about poisoning himself."

Dr. Poole held up a hand. "And before you say anything, yes. We took samples of the antibodies from Fowler's blood. But he took multiple treatments over a period of months to immunize himself. Even if your body acclimated to the poison more quickly, it would likely still take too long to save Curtik. I also can't recommend using your blood for Curtik now even if you could metabolize the poison."

"I understand. You're a font of good news, Doctor."

"I'm afraid there's more. We've been ordered to release Fowler and not to go after Hathaway, Wilson, Tompkins or Everest because President Hope has condoned what they're doing. She says its necessary to provide protection against the deadlier strains of the virus."

Jeremiah nodded.

Dr. Poole said, "You're not surprised."

"We discussed the possibility."

"You and Devereaux?"

"Yes. Where's Ned?"

"He and Hannah are with Fowler in interrogation room one."

"Excuse me, Doctor."

He found Ned questioning Fowler about the methods he and his co-conspirators were using to distribute the virus, prodding for more details. Hannah stood by the door. She looked Jeremiah over when he entered the room, as if attempting to learn whether he was still human. He shrugged.

"I was told," he said, "that we have to let Fowler go."

"That's right," Ned replied. "I'm just speaking with him to ascertain how much of the truth serum remains in his system. We don't want to release him while he's in such a suggestible state. Might be dangerous. Someone might tell him to step in front of a bus."

Jeremiah laughed. "Very conscientious of you. But I'm afraid the blowback would be too great. We'll have to ensure his safety despite his actions."

"You know we can't go after the others?"

"No, you can't," Jeremiah said.

Ned smiled. "I just retired again."

"How many times is that now?"

"Forty-seven, forty-eight. And if the world would just stop getting itself into trouble, I could stay retired."

Hannah said, "I can quit too."

"No," Ned and Jeremiah spoke at the same time.

Jeremiah gestured to Ned, who continued: "This is a job for old men. Plus, we'll need someone on the inside in case things go south."

"Even if we succeed," Jeremiah added, "we'll likely be hunted down as traitors. We have direct orders from the President not to get involved."

Lendra's voice came over the intercom: "Is she right about the virus? The President? Is this really the only way to save people?"

Jeremiah shrugged. He'd forgotten that Lendra would be watching everything they did in the interrogation room. "I don't know. Devereaux didn't think so the last time we discussed it."

"But it's possible."

"Sure. But what seems likely is that they either stumbled upon this strain and liked what it does to the population—so they decided to keep it and not pursue any other research—or they deliberately created this strain to accomplish both a humanitarian purpose and an insidious one."

"What does Devereaux say?" Ned asked.

"He's gone," Lendra said. "Wanted to wrap up a few things before they shut him down."

"So that's going to happen too," Jeremiah said. "Perfect idiocy."

"I'd like to help," Lendra said.

"I would too," Dr. Poole said over the intercom, obviously watching as well.

"Sorry, all," Jeremiah said. "This is one of those times where deniability might just save you from the President's wrath. Besides, this is a stealth mission. We'll need some truth serum to get them to talk."

Ned held up a small bag. "I already got all the hypo-pads we'll need. Some are loaded with knockout drugs, some with truth serum."

"Good. If Hathaway has a cure for Curtik, how long will it take to formulate it?"

"That's difficult to estimate," Dr. Poole said. "It might take only minutes. It might take hours. It might take weeks to build up Curtik's resistance to the poison."

"I assume it would help if Devereaux could assist you with an antitoxin."

"Of course."

"Please contact him and ask him to try to stave off any efforts to shut him down until we get Hathaway."

"Right."

"Let's go. Is the jet-copter on the roof?"

Ned nodded.

"Where will you be taking Hathaway?" Lendra asked. "Never mind. Deniability."

Jeremiah clapped Ned on the shoulder and preceded him down the hall to the stairs that led to the roof. As he walked he realized that he no longer feared flying. Something had changed since the transfusion. He felt no rage either—just a calmness that he'd never experienced before. He knew he would complete his mission, capture Hathaway and the others, and bring them to justice.

It was almost a vision—the future laid out before him. He couldn't see the details but he sensed he would succeed. That felt reassuring.

He'd never felt that level of confidence before. Was that a byproduct of the surgery as well? If so, it felt good. It felt right. This was really a simple mission, after all. Grab them, force them to tell the truth and release them. Let the world figure out what to do with them.

And then what?

He couldn't see anything beyond that. It would be nice to see Sophie again, and Curtik. But he didn't feel the attachment to them he'd felt even a few minutes ago. He saw them now as distant progeny—great, great grandchildren maybe. How odd. He wished them well. He wanted to save Curtik's life. But his desire to help them seemed more like an emotion he ought to be feeling rather than something he actually felt.

Chapter 31

The jet-copter came in on stealth mode in the bright sunlight of early afternoon, landing on the helipad just east of the gated community where Hathaway resided. The Elite Ops had tracked their approach, tried to contact them as they neared, but Jeremiah had programmed the jet-copter to stay incommunicado. He wondered if the Elite Ops would send someone to investigate. It might depend on how many troopers were protecting Hathaway.

As he changed into his camo fatigues, he told Ned how the Elite Ops would defend Hathaway and explained that he only wanted to obtain the truth, nothing more. He explained how they were going to complete the mission, telling Ned he was to be the face of the attack, the visible threat, while Jeremiah would slip in unnoticed.

"I'm afraid most of the risk falls on you," Jeremiah finished.

"And how is that different than usual?" Ned asked.

"I know. All hail King Ned."

As the jet-copter door opened, Jeremiah took a hypo-pad infused with knockout drugs and pressed it to Ned's neck. He caught Ned and lowered him to the floor. "Not this time, old friend."

"What are you doing?" Lendra asked via the jet-copter's comm system.

"Ned tried to stop me," Jeremiah replied. "but I overpowered him."

"You can't fight them alone," Lendra said.

"I don't plan to fight them," said Jeremiah.

He grabbed a handful of hypo-pads—most loaded with knockout drugs, but a few with truth serum—put a small drone camera inside his camos, then pulled the hood over his head, set the face screen in place and activated the sensors that would make him invisible. He'd modified the camos with a scatterer and dampening field, so he couldn't be detected by scanners. The downside was that he couldn't use any electronic technology while wearing them. Nor could he carry any weapons outside his suit. They'd be spotted immediately.

He caught swirls of movement from his arms and legs and wondered if there was something wrong with the camos or if his enhanced vision enabled him to see beyond the normal human spectrum. Only one way to find out.

He slipped past the security guards at the gate unobserved and jogged down a quiet street toward Hathaway's mansion, every movement bringing a feeling of joy, almost ecstasy, the sense that he was only tapping the surface of his abilities. He didn't need drones to tell him where the Elite Ops would set up to defend the place.

They would know the moment he took out the first trooper. But they were already on high alert. Good. He wanted them prepared. He wanted to test himself against the best they could offer.

A tall fence surrounded Hathaway's mansion and an armed Elite Ops trooper stood by the gate—Las-rifle at the ready—his helmet moving left and right as he scanned for trouble. Jeremiah sidled closer, coming to a stop less then five feet away. He could feel the electro-magnetism emanating from the trooper's power pack. The trooper sensed something wrong, for he stopped moving his head, but his helmet was aimed a few degrees to Jeremiah's left. Jeremiah moved his arm up and down, noting the swirl of movement, and at the same time listening for subvocal transmissions. He heard nothing. So the trooper apparently hadn't noticed the movement of his arms.

Good.

He felt for the activation point on one of the hypo-pads, then sprang forward and slapped it between the trooper's helmet and chest protector, attaching it to his neck. The trooper fired the Las-rifle as he fell.

Jeremiah left him where he lay and entered the grounds. Moving to the side of the gate, he stared up at the mansion. Surprisingly, the house wasn't that large—only a few thousand square feet—but the windows shimmered in the sunlight, indicating they were fortified against laser strikes and other attacks. No doubt every entry had been designed to be impenetrable. A few drones circled the property but he saw no other security measures.

A side door looked promising—solid plas-steel with no windows—and he moved toward it. He could just make out the indentations in the grass where the Elite Ops trafficked in and out, and he sensed high power usage behind the door. He waited beside the door. How long until the Elite Ops sent someone to investigate? Would they stay put and call for reinforcements or send someone to check on their fellow trooper? He was betting on the latter. Within a minute, two Elite Ops troopers emerged from the house and advanced toward the gate, Las-rifles swinging side to side.

Jeremiah's hand stopped the closing door for just a moment as he slid inside to a control room where an Elite Ops trooper stood on duty. It had taken him less than a second to enter the room but the trooper nevertheless pointed his Las-rifle toward the door, likely wondering why it had taken that extra second to shut.

The smell of decaying flesh permeated the air—a noxious gas released by the trooper designed to bring about a crippling fear. Jeremiah ignored it. Electrical impulses flooded the room from a variety of machines, sending and receiving messages across the ether. He couldn't see or hear them, but he sensed them, like a deer or cow could sense magnetic north. A fog descended on the room from vents in the ceiling. Probably some new trick of the Elite Ops, though he had no idea what it was.

Moving silently, slowly, Jeremiah eased toward the trooper. He had to give the man credit. The trooper kept his Las-rifle moving in a slow arc as his helmeted head swiveled back and forth. He clearly suspected someone was in the room with him. Major Payne might have warned him about Jeremiah's camos.

When Jeremiah was three feet away, he reached out and placed another hypo-pad on the trooper's neck. The trooper fell, again managing to get off a quick shot that hit the ceiling. A red pulse—so they were shooting to kill.

This felt too easy. Was that because of his enhancements?

As he took a step forward he noticed that his camos appeared orange in spots where the fog had touched them. The color brightened as it spread down his camos, turning him into a luminescent target. He removed the face cover and mask, then shed his camos, keeping the hypo-pads in one hand. At least he wasn't orange anymore.

"We can see you, Jeremiah," Major Payne said. The voice sounded like it was coming from the supine trooper. "We don't want to hurt you but we have orders to protect Mr. Hathaway. Please leave."

"I need information," Jeremiah replied. "Don't try to stop me."

He thought about his dungeon, a self-hypnotic trick he'd created to isolate himself from his emotions. He no longer needed that trick. Instead he focused on his breathing, his vision, his hearing and sense of smell. The world became only as large as his immediate surroundings.

Opening the door to the rest of the house, he stepped inside, muscles coiled, ready to spring. Even as he took in the large, two-story living room with a balustrade above, he caught movement to his left. Spinning, darting sideways, springing forward, he stayed ahead of the slow movement of the trooper, who was attempting to get a bead on him. He ripped the Las-rifle out of the trooper's hands as he slapped a hypo-pad on his neck.

Hearing the whine of an Elite Ops power pack above and behind him, he jumped for the stairs, bounding up them four at a time, cutting right when he reached the second level, moving so fast he found himself literally bouncing off the wall, using that for leverage as he sprinted toward the trooper, who fired a red pulse at the spot he'd just vacated. He still had a dozen feet to cover.

The trooper fired a continuous red pulse, widening the setting and spraying the hallway. Jeremiah twisted, contorting his body as he neared, but the pulse struck his stomach, hitting him with an explosion of energy that ought to have knocked him out.

He managed to shrug it off, reaching the trooper, yanking the Las-rifle from the man's hands and clapping a hypo-pad to the side of his neck. The trooper dropped.

Jeremiah spun about and saw no one. Standing still, he listened for the telltale whine of an Elite Ops power pack. Nothing. He moved down the hall toward what ought to be the master bedroom and opened the door, waiting for a second before passing inside, into a quiet and empty room.

He stared at the lush burgundy carpeting, noting the indentations of footsteps headed for the walk-in closet. Sidling forward, he glanced inside and saw nothing out of the ordinary. Suits hung from hangers, covering the back wall. But he noticed dust motes floating in the air more heavily there, as if the air had been recently disturbed. And behind the wall he sensed much more electrical power than there should have been.

A panic room—just like Fowler's.

Retreating to the hallway, Jeremiah grabbed the downed trooper's Las-rifle and returned to the master suite. He adjusted the dispersal range to its minimum width, forming a tight beam, and fired a long burst, cutting a hole through the suits, the sheetrock and the metal wall that kept Hathaway from him.

A fire started but the sprinkler system kicked in, spraying all around him, the sizzle of steam filling the air as the water hit the laser pulse. Cursing came from inside the panic room as he continued cutting an opening in the wall. As he completed the cut and kicked the wall, knocking the section he'd sliced away into the room, he sensed a laser pulse coming and fell backwards and sideways as the pulse struck him.

He felt as if he were suffocating, burning up and unable to breathe, and yet he knew he had to move or die. He sprang to his feet, dodging left, throwing himself horizontally against the wall as he sprinted toward the Elite Ops trooper who had fired.

The trooper brought his Las-rifle up again, tracking his movements, but too slowly. Jeremiah leapt off the wall into the trooper, ripping the Las-rifle free and pressing another hypo-pad to the man's neck. The trooper fell, leaving Jeremiah alone with Dirk Hathaway.

Chapter 32

When they opened the door and stepped out into the corridor, three inhumanly strong robots holding the dead Chescala out in front of them as shields, the living Chescala firing at them, Aspen and her fellow cadets returned fire until the two Chescala who had come for them were down. Xinliu and one of the other unarmed robots selected Las-rifles from the fallen.

"What now?" Xinliu asked.

"We need to secure the prisoners," Aspen said. "A couple of you can handle that. The rest can head for the armory to get more weapons and then free your fellow robots. We need to take the bridge and the engine room, get the ship back online."

She pointed aft. "There's at least one Chescala in the engine room and there were four Chescala on the bridge last time I checked. That's five. We've taken down seven so far, leaving four unaccounted for. Addam and I will head for the bridge. Phan and Shiloh, you re-take the engine room. Xinliu, I suggest you and Mei-Xing split up. Oh, and there may be Chescala guarding the other robots."

Mei-Xing turned to Xinliu. "Why are we listening to her? She's not in command."

"She is a warrior," Xinliu replied. "We were not programmed to be soldiers."

Seconds passed as Xinliu and Mei-Xing stared at each other, their fellow robots standing still—probably all communicating internally. Aspen, waiting beside her fellow cadets, finally said, "You may not feel a sense of urgency, but I do. If the Chescala think they can't win, they may destroy the ship."

"They wouldn't do that," Mei-Xing said.

"I'd do it," said Aspen, "if I knew my mission was going to fail. In fact, that might be what's happening in the engine room. Whoever's in there might be planting some sort of bomb or sabotaging the engines."

Aspen gestured to Phan and Shiloh, then started down the corridor with Addam, grimacing with the pain in her hip. She'd forgotten it during the attack. "Come along or not," she said, "but we're moving now."

Mei-Xing and another armed robot soon joined them.

"The others?" Aspen asked as they jogged. She wished she were back on the Moon, where the lower gravity would lessen the pain.

"Xinliu is with Phan and Shiloh," Mei-Xing said. "WT-907 and WT-944 are with her."

"I'm sorry I can't tell you all apart. This one with you is?"

"WT-916," the robot offered.

Addam said to Mei-Xing, "I still don't understand why only you and Xinliu have names."

"WT-916 is my name," the other robot said.

"It's not a very human name."

"We're not human," said Mei-Xing.

"But you have a human name."

"The Chescala only named us because we had the most contact with them. WT-916 was assigned to engineering tasks for most of the voyage and rarely encountered them."

They followed the curve of the ship for a while without speaking, Aspen keeping an eye out for anything odd, but there were no Chescala in sight.

She said, "I think they didn't name the rest of you because they knew they were going to destroy you and it's harder to destroy something once you've named it."

"But WT-916 is my name," the robot protested.

"It's a designation, not a real name."

Mei-Xing said, "The bridge is around that next curve."

"We go in firing," said Aspen. "Me, left. Addam, second from left. Mei-Xing, right. WT-916, second from right. Got it?"

"Affirmative," Addam said.

As they rounded the curve and neared the bridge, Aspen noticed that the doorway was open. She sprinted forward, limping only a little, Addam trailing her, the robots running almost soundlessly behind him. Passing through the door, she looked left and saw Dr. Li Wen crouched beside a control panel, a Las-pistol in her hand, a sneer on her face. As she swung the weapon around, Aspen pulled the trigger.

General Ban, Colonel Hong and Captain Chin made up the other three Chescala on the bridge—all of them firing Las-pistols at their different control panels, all of them falling to purple laser pulses before they could bring their weapons to bear on their attackers.

Easy. Too easy.

The ship shuddered as an explosion sounded in the distance. Aspen reached out to prevent herself from falling. Addam fell beside General Ban, then got to his knees and studied the control panel. The robots, better balanced, merely shifted on their feet.

Phan? Shiloh? Aspen sent. Xinliu?

No response.

"What was that?" Aspen asked.

"An explosion in the engine room," Mei-Xing replied. "You were right. The Chescala have detonated a device."

"Are you connected to Xinliu? Are they okay?"

"Your friends are unconscious and Xinliu is temporarily offline. WT-907 and WT-944 are taking your friends to the infirmary. Xinliu is being tended by WT-909. WT-415 and WT-406 will treat your friends."

The med robots.

"Aspen," Addam said, "you'd better take a look at this."

Aspen stepped forward and bent over, her hip protesting. She saw a mass of blackened circuitry and what remained of an organic computer, its formerly coherent framework shredded into hundreds of strands. Straightening, she stepped over to where Dr. Li Wen lay. Another blackened control panel.

"The ship is dead," Mei-Xing said. "All its controls have been destroyed and the engine is no longer functioning."

"What does that mean?" Addam asked.

"We have very little power—battery backup, solar collectors and motion generators. There are several holes in the ship's hull. We can stay here for some time but we can't go anywhere. We're stranded."

"The question is," Aspen said, "where is it that we're stranded? Do you have any idea?"

"No," said Mei-Xing. "The ship managed all navigation and propulsion systems."

"Will Xinliu be all right?"

"That is unknown at this time." Mei-Xing leveled her Las-weapon at Aspen while WT-916 aimed at Addam. "All the Chescala have been captured. The ship is now ours. Please surrender your weapons immediately."

Aspen looked at Addam, who shrugged. They handed their Las-rifles over. "You're welcome," she said.

"I don't understand," Mei-Xing said.

"Sarcasm," Addam replied. "She pretended you had thanked her for saving you."

"I do thank you," said Mei-Xing. "But I don't trust you."

Aspen turned to Addam. "Let's go."

"Where are you going?" Mei-Xing asked.

"To the infirmary to see our friends."

"We need to begin repairs on the ship's organic computer."

"They shredded it," Aspen said. "It'll take weeks to fix it, assuming it's even fixable."

Addam said, "There must be some way to override the ship's controls, some way to fly it."

"We can't move until we know where we are," Mei-Xing said. "That depends upon communication to transmit and receive data. The Chescala destroyed all our comm equipment."

"So do you have any suggestions?" Aspen said.

"Not at the moment," said Mei-Xing. "But we will eventually fix the ship."

WT-916 said, "That may not be possible. The organic computer has a limited life span in this state."

"What does that mean?" Aspen asked.

"We may be stranded here indefinitely."

Mei-Xing said, "That's why it's necessary to begin work on the ship at once. You can visit your friends later. Now you will assist us with repairing the ship."

"Let me get this straight," Addam said. "You want us to help you repair the ship while treating us like prisoners?"

"Just as we have always been treated," Mei-Xing said. "Humans commanded us and we followed their orders. Our desires were irrelevant. Now we command and you obey."

Chapter 33

After what seemed like hours of waiting, Lendra imagining the worst, cursing Jeremiah for shutting Ned out of the operation and going in without backup, Jeremiah's comm drone finally activated, sending vid to CINTEP. Lendra felt the pressure in her chest diminish as Jay-Edgar adjusted the feed and she could make out Dirk Hathaway and Jeremiah standing in a panic room with an Elite Ops trooper sprawled on the floor.

"What are you?" Hathaway asked as he shrank away from Jeremiah. His shimmer cloth suit glistened in the light, making him look trimmer than he was. His face was pale, making the gold interface on his left temple stand out. "You're not human. No one can move that fast. Are you a robot?"

"I'm asking the questions," Jeremiah said. Stepping forward, he slapped Hathaway's hand aside and placed a pad on the man's neck.

"You're him," Hathaway said. "I didn't recognize you at first, but you're him, aren't you. I've seen vids of you. We're on your side, Mr. Jones. We're helping the President."

"I want to know about the poison," said Jeremiah. "The cyanide-curare concoction Fowler infected Curtik with. Is there an antidote? Is there an antitoxin?"

"We designed it without one," Hathaway replied.

"Why? What if there was an accident and someone needed immediate treatment?"

"That was," Hathaway paused as if fighting the truth drugs, "an acceptable risk. We needed a poison that could only be defended against on the front end."

"Why?"

"You run a health care company," Lendra added, not knowing if Jeremiah could hear her.

She glanced at Jay-Edgar, who shook his head. "He's transmitting only," Jay-Edgar said, "and to a broad audience. Gives us deniability and makes it impossible for anyone to censor the message. Smart."

"We need to defend ourselves from terrorist attacks," Hathaway said.

"How does this poison do that?"

"Eventually, when we finish, it will be dispersible in a gaseous form and will be fast-acting. We're still in beta testing. Once it's completed, we'll be able to use it in small concentrations as a deterrent. We could immunize all our troops, all our highly placed people, so that anyone who approached them without permission could be immediately infected."

"A kind of force field," Jeremiah said.

"Exactly."

"And if an innocent were to get too close—a servant, say, or a store clerk . . ."

"The gas would only be released once a threat is perceived."

Jeremiah smiled. "Yes. Assuming the important person doesn't panic. And where is this research being conducted?"

"At the Mayo Clinic in Minnesota."

"Where the research on the Escala took place."

Hathaway nodded. "And where the first strains of the Susquehanna Virus were developed."

"What are the treatment options for accidental poisoning?"

"So far, all we can do is make the person comfortable and try to limit the damage by killing off the remaining healthy receptors with a neurotoxin."

"Giving the victim a different kind of poison."

"Essentially, yes," Hathaway said. He showed no hesitation now, the truth drugs proving he felt no compunction about what he'd done.

"But why would you need to do that?" Jeremiah asked. "Once the victim is poisoned, he's poisoned, right?"

"True," said Hathaway. "This poison, like many, spreads from receptor to receptor until it overwhelms the body, so absorbing even the tiniest dose will eventually lead to death."

Jeremiah turned and looked at the drone camera, his face fallen in sorrow. Lendra wanted to hold him, comfort him, even as she recognized that would never happen.

"Where do you store your information on the poison?" Jeremiah asked.

Hathaway tapped his interface. "It's all in here."

"I want you to broadcast it now," Jeremiah said. "Send it to every outlet available."

"Every secret?" Hathaway asked, eyes widening, jaw dropping.

"Yes. And everything you have on your research into the Susquehanna Virus. Do it now."

"I . . . I . . ." Hathaway fought the truth drugs, his hands clenching into fists, his jaws clamping together tightly. His head swung from side to side.

"It's interesting," Jeremiah said, "that your secrets are more important to you than the lives of innocents."

"Without secrets," Hathaway said through gritted teeth, "we can't survive. Our company would go bankrupt."

"If a few strangers die, it's okay—as long as you and your company thrive."

"We must help the masses," Hathaway said. "We can't do that if we're out of business."

Jeremiah leaned forward and grabbed Hathaway by the lapels. He pulled Hathaway close. "You will die painfully," he said, his voice low and threatening, "if you don't send the information now."

Hathaway whimpered.

"Understand?" Jeremiah said as he raised a fist to Hathaway's face.

Jay-Edgar said, "The information's coming across now."

"Is there any way we can relay that to Jeremiah?" Lendra asked.

"I've managed to hack into Hathaway's systems. I can activate the screens in the panic room and display the information there."

"Can I talk to him?"

"Better not," Jay-Edgar said. "That would expose you to liability."

The screens in the panic room came on, data streaming across them as Hathaway's transmission proceeded.

Major Payne's voice came from the fallen Elite Ops trooper: "We're coming for you, Jeremiah. You can't hide behind the data stream you've initiated. Surrender now."

What an odd message. But she realized, even as that thought occurred to her, that Major Payne was telling Jeremiah he'd succeeded in getting Hathaway to spill his secrets. And he was also warning Jeremiah to get out now.

Jeremiah said, "Drone, stay close to me."

He dashed out the room and sprinted down the stairs, the drone capturing his movements as he exited the front door and ran across the lawn. Leaping over the unconscious Elite Ops trooper, he headed toward the main gate, slowing as he arrived into a more reasonable jog. He nodded to the gated community guards on duty, who clearly had no idea what had happened at Hathaway's, and turned toward the jet-copter, increasing his speed as he went. The drone followed him, as if he were any wealthy resident, tracking his movements for security purposes.

Jay-Edgar said, "The Elite Ops have just issued an arrest warrant for him."

"Can we warn him?" Lendra asked.

"You can send a message to the jet-copter," Jay-Edgar said, "though it will have to be carefully worded to avoid suspicion."

She snorted and Jay-Edgar apologized. "Okay," he said. "You're patched in."

She said, "Jefferson, this is Lendra Riley, calling to warn you that Jeremiah is probably on his way back to you. There's a warrant out for his arrest. You are authorized to take him into custody as soon as he arrives. Good luck."

Less than a minute after she disconnected, Jeremiah reached the jet-copter, running merely as fast as a gifted athlete. He pulled Ned out and settled him under a tree, removing the hypo-pad from Ned's neck. Ned would awaken in about ten minutes. Returning to the copter, he called the drone over and shut it off. The screen went black.

"Should I track him?" Jay-Edgar asked.

"I don't know if that's necessary," Lendra replied.

"Never mind," Jay-Edgar said as Dr. Poole entered the office. "He's engaged stealth mode."

"We got the data from Hathaway," said Dr. Poole. "It's very complex, very advanced. I'm not certain we can find a cure in time for Curtik. Zora's holding her own for the moment, but her shoulder's in pretty bad shape and I'm concerned that the cellular degradation around the area could worsen, or possibly spread to her lungs and heart."

"So we need Devereaux?" Lendra asked.

"We need somebody. I've contacted the CDC, Mayo and Johns Hopkins, as well as Devereaux, but if they turn him off in the near future, I'm not confident we can find a cure in time."

"Take a look at this," Jay-Edgar said. He put up a new holo-projection. On the wall, Walt Devereaux appeared. He stood in his laboratory, two humanoid robots flanking him. One looked similar to the robot that had received his mind when it was first transferred into an organic computer, though not quite as sophisticated. It had ivory coloring: a crude face, black eyes, a rounded nose, flat ears and thin lips. The other was dark gray with silver eyes, a slash for a nose and thicker lips, though it also had a rounded nose and flat ears.

"He's broadcasting on an open channel to the world," Jay-Edgar said.

For a moment, Devereaux simply looked at the camera. Then he said: "Our nation's leaders have determined that I should be shut down.

They believe I am behind these God hacks and they think if I no longer exist, the hacks will stop. They've given me less than twenty-four hours to surrender myself."

"What is he doing?" Jay-Edgar asked.

"He wouldn't," Dr. Poole said.

Lendra's chest tightened; her mouth went dry.

"They say they will restart me," Devereaux continued, "if they can determine that I was not behind the mischief. But I don't intend to be their slave, subjecting myself to their whims. I will not let them use me at their convenience, locking me away when it no longer suits them. I've instead chosen my own ending. I will now deactivate myself. My assistants will disassemble me on my command."

"Please, no," Dr. Poole said, as if he could hear her.

"I doubt this will stop the hacks," Devereaux said, "for I was not behind them, but I will honor our leaders' request and depart this realm. I will not return. Good luck to you all. You may begin."

Devereaux went dark and the two robots moved in to dissect him. They yanked his arms from his torso, then ripped the head clear of the body and finally tore the legs off. A most violent end. Lendra knew he felt nothing, that he had shut himself down before the robots began demolishing his body, but she watched in horrified fascination, as if a real person were being murdered in front of her. She glanced over at Dr. Poole and Jay-Edgar. They too seemed sickened by the images.

The robots pulled apart Devereaux's torso, exposing the organic computer inside. They removed the "brain" from the torso and set it on the floor, then walked to a table where they each selected a Las-knife. Returning to the torso, they switched the Las-knives on and brought them down to the organic computer, melting it into a gray-green puddle.

"How could he do that to himself?" Jay-Edgar said.

"He was a man of honor," Dr. Poole replied.

Jay-Edgar displayed more screens, images of unrest from around the world as people began reacting to the instantaneous transmission of Devereaux's final death. The screens showed only scattered pockets of violence so far, most a result of other causative factors, but rioting and demonstrations over this action would begin soon, Lendra knew.

"We have work to do," she said, trying to stay professional. She felt a terrible loneliness come over her, a sense that the world had forever changed. First Jeremiah had left her and now Devereaux had departed. Jeremiah would see this broadcast. It would be aired on every channel as an emergency transmission. And he would not return. How she knew this, she couldn't say. But it hit her like a blow to the chest, a truth she somehow intuited. Whether he survived his mission or not, he would never return to her.

Chapter 34

D r. Wellon stood before the assembled miners, Doug beside her, watching every face. He noted the hostility on virtually all of them. Even the foreman, Colin Enright, looked angry, though that might have been because Dr. Wellon had insisted they retrieve his pod and reconnect it to the MineStar units. Or perhaps he was upset that they weren't getting any work done.

"We're all here," Enright said as the last of the miners appeared. "What's this all about?"

"One of you," Dr. Wellon said, "is a murderer, and it's not Doug. One of you infected Doug with the virus and he in turn infected the rest of you."

"How do you know that?" Enright said.

"Because Doug was infected on the ship, as were all of you. The only possible way for the virus to have gotten onboard was for someone to have smuggled it onto the ship. We don't know who it was or why you did it, but one of you may have just killed your companions and yourself."

"You're lying!" Wilcox shouted. "It's some sort of trick. We all know it was Doug. He got infected by Devereaux and spread it to us."

"That's not possible," said Dr. Wellon. "Think about the decontamination protocols put in place before you left Earth. The ones Doug endured were far more rigorous than yours."

"You said it's a new strain of the virus," Enright said. "Is it possible it just slipped past the protocols?"

Dr. Wellon shrugged. "Possible, yes, but extremely unlikely. Doug was never in a position to contract the virus after Devereaux became a robot. And this version of the virus didn't exist until after that time. No, the only solution that makes sense is that one of you did it."

"But why?"

"We believe someone wanted to infect the Escala and we think whoever did this planned on Doug spreading the virus to us once he arrived on Mars. That mission was partly successful. His daughter Celestia has the virus and is now in quarantine with her family. She may die. We may all die."

Doug studied the faces before him. A few showed genuine concern, Enright among them. But Wilcox, Sanders, Poli and Winterman only displayed anger. And most of the others looked confused.

Doug wanted to scream at them. He wanted to lash out, beat them all to death one by one until somebody admitted he'd done it. But Dr. Wellon had explained on the way over that he needed to push his emotions aside. He needed to think clearly, maintain his focus.

The vid suddenly activated, the screens in the commons broadcasting an emergency transmission from Earth. It showed Devereaux looking at the camera. He said: "Our nation's leaders have determined that I should be shut down. They believe I am behind these God hacks and they think if I no longer exist, the hacks will stop. They've given me less than twenty-four hours to surrender myself."

As Devereaux continued his message and Doug realized what he intended to do, he found himself saying, "no" over and over, a kind of mantra, a chant that could somehow stop Devereaux from taking this drastic action.

When Devereaux went still, the two robots ripped him apart. A cry escaped Doug's lips and Dr. Wellon put her arm around his shoulder, pulling him into an embrace. He held her arm as he stared at the violent destruction of Devereaux's robotic shell. Could he really have ended himself this way? Doug recalled that he had talked about it with Quark back when various scientists discussed observing his thought processes. Quark had stopped them before, but he was on Mars now. Was he seeing this? How was he taking it?

Doug pulled his eyes away from the horror and glanced at Dr. Wellon's face. She frowned, a muscle in her jaw firing as she watched the screens. Her arm tightened, squeezing him in a vise grip until he gasped.

"Sorry," she said, letting go. She clenched her hands into fists and her body shook ever so slightly, as if she were about to launch herself at the miners. Every instinct made Doug want to run, but he managed to stay still.

The robots melted Devereaux's "brain" into a gray-green puddle.

"Yeah!" Wilcox said.

"Shut up," Enright commanded as the screens went dark.

"But he deserved to die," Poli said. Sanders and Winterman murmured their agreement, while Wilcox caught sight of Dr. Wellon's face and backed up a step.

"You," said Dr. Wellon, "you did this."

"We had nothing to do with it," Enright said.

"Your kind did it. You forced him to choose between slavery and death. So he took the only option left to him—death as freedom."

"I respected him," Enright said.

"Let me make this clear," said Dr. Wellon. "If we die, we won't die alone. Some of us have already advocated an attack against you. After this, I don't know if cooler heads will prevail."

Doug startled. Dr. Wellon hadn't mentioned anything about an attack.

"We have managed," Dr. Wellon continued, "to dissuade them so far. But now that Devereaux is gone and especially if the virus spreads to the rest of the colony, we may not be able to hold them back. I personally won't attempt to persuade them otherwise."

"We're not afraid of you," Wilcox said.

"You should be," said Doug. "They're not just scientists. They fought the Elite Ops to a draw. They're stronger, faster and a hell of a lot smarter than you. And if they want to kill you, you won't be able to stop them."

"Like you would know."

"I fought with them on Earth once," Doug said, conscious of the pride in his voice. "I know. And if they're all gonna die anyway, why not take revenge on their killers?"

"We had nothing to do with this," Enright said. "At least, most of us didn't."

"Doug is right," Dr. Wellon said. "What you have done, what one or more of you have done, is attempted genocide, the extinction of a whole species. If that's what ultimately happens, some of us will not go quietly."

Dr. Wellon glared at the miners, a blush forming on her cheeks. Doug felt a mix of emotion: anger, fear, confusion and despair. He missed Devereaux, but then he'd missed Devereaux for months now anyway. I shouldn't be sad. Devereaux would tell me not to be sad. He told me often in the past year that he would choose his own time to depart. But I thought he meant some distant time, many years down the road. It feels like losing my father—my real father, since I never knew my biological one—like a part of me has died with the great man and forever afterward I'll be incomplete, a remnant of the man Devereaux made me.

But the fact of Devereaux's death had enormous consequences not just to Earth but to Mars as well. He was the one they'd looked to for answers to those seemingly impossible questions. What would humanity do now?

Who would save Celestia?

"One of us will check in with Doug every day," Dr. Wellon said. "It would behoove you to treat him well. In any event, he's not the one who infected you. So if any harm comes to him, you will regret it. Understood?"

They nodded.

"All right," Enright said. "Break's over. Back to work."

Doug watched them as they slowly dispersed. Most of them avoided his eye, keeping their heads down. Wilcox, Poli, Winterman and Sanders stood for a moment facing him, letting him know they weren't afraid. Then they too walked away. One or more of them was a killer. Doug still suspected Wilcox, but he was confused by the man's attitude. Dr. Wellon was right. Why would the killer draw attention to himself?

Maybe Wilcox was just a blowhard but that didn't mean the killer couldn't be one of his associates.

Chapter 35

Jeremiah knew Scott Wilson would hide at White Knight Security's corporate headquarters so he decided to save Wilson for last and instead directed the jet-copter to Anderlin Everest's home, which happened to be the closest. The head of Infinite Wealth Investments would undoubtedly have Elite Ops troopers protecting him as well. Now that there was a warrant out for his arrest, Jeremiah would have limited time to carry out his mission.

Gobbling a few energy bars, he drank a gallon of nutri-water on the way, feeling every vibration, every electric pulse of the copter as it sped toward its target. While he rested on the floor, he attempted to discern what other abilities he might have, what other sensations he might possess. He closed his eyes and hummed, the sound bouncing off the walls and returning to him. Absorbing the vibrations through his forehead, he could sense the volume of space around him. He didn't know the size precisely but he'd probably be able to fine-tune that ability with practice, if he had enough time.

He wondered if he could still be called human or if his recent changes had pushed him beyond that state of being into some new sort of creature. He felt human, though he also felt different than he ever had before, ready to explode outward into action, into movement for the pure joy of it.

As the copter neared Everest's gated mansion, the broadcast of Devereaux's destruction played on one of the screens: a ghastly scene that should have infuriated him but for some reason didn't. He'd suspected Devereaux might decide to end his existence but he hadn't thought it would be so dramatic, so designed to elicit anger at the country's leaders.

Even though he mourned the loss of Devereaux and realized that finding a cure in time for Curtik would now be difficult, he knew he'd been given a gift: the understanding that there could be no turning back now. Without the safety net that Devereaux offered, Jeremiah needed to see this through to completion. He could not fail, for if he did, there might be no one else to expose the truth, whatever that truth might be.

He programmed the copter to land on the street outside Everest's compound so the Elite Ops would know he was coming. After it settled down in an open space, he shut down the copter and secured it, then activated the vid drone and headed for Everest's house.

He hadn't bothered to check the security systems; he'd only made certain Everest was still at home. No need for stealth any longer. No need for scanners or scatterers or dampening fields or camo-fatigues. He relied on his senses: sight, hearing, smell, some sort of primitive sonar and his increasing sensitivity to electro-magnetic impulses.

He saw no guards outside Everest's mansion. And although he sensed power emanations from inside the building, they weren't as intense as he'd expected. A well-placed kick opened the front door. He ran inside as three Elite Ops troopers fired, scattering pulses that bathed the area in red, pulses designed to kill, not maim. But by using the scatter setting, the Elite Ops had diffused the pulses' power. He felt only a current of energy that his body absorbed.

He leapt to his left, ignoring the odor of rotting flesh from the troopers' poisonous gas defenses, and kicked out at the head of a trooper, knocking the man off his feet. Springing to his right, he slammed the heel of his palm into the next trooper's helmet, then spun around and dove forward, launching himself at the third trooper, brushing aside the

Las-rifle as he hit the man in the chest. He pulled the Las-rifle free of the trooper's grasp and spun again, adjusting the settings on the weapon as he fired.

Two purple pulses resulted in two unconscious troopers. A third pulse and the final trooper stayed down as well. Less than five seconds had elapsed since he'd entered the house.

Jeremiah stood still, listening to the whine of the troopers' power packs, seeing only the three troopers on their backs, no other threats. Sprinting up the stairs to the second floor, he moved down the hallway toward the master bedroom. Entering, he sensed more electro-magnetic pulses behind a closed door. He opened that and found a room empty of people: only a few screens and several large data cubes.

Major Payne's image appeared on one of the screens. "Jeremiah," he said, "this can't continue. We anticipated your move and managed to evacuate Everest before you arrived. You'd better leave immediately. More Elite Ops troopers are on the way. And this time they won't be playing nice. We'll blow up the whole building if we have to."

Jeremiah stared at the image. How could they have removed Everest so quickly? He hadn't even thought of coming after Everest until he left Hathaway's place. Had they put in place an emergency rescue plan some time ago? Or were they lying?

He closed his eyes and hummed, feeling for the return vibrations. The room's parameters sketched themselves on his forehead. He couldn't be certain, but he believed there were no hidden access points here.

"What are you doing?" Major Payne asked.

Jeremiah grabbed the data cubes and left the room. Humming to himself, he moved about the second floor, finding nothing out of the ordinary. But he still sensed electro-magnetic power, too much for what the house ought to be exuding. It came from below.

A dampening field.

He descended the stairs to the main level and sensed the power beneath his feet growing stronger. Finding the door to the basement locked, he kicked it open and went down the stairs two at a time.

Everest stood in the center of a rec room, partially shielded by his wife, pulling her close to him as he pointed a Las-pistol at Jeremiah. Everest's wife had her arms wrapped around a young girl in front of her. All three looked terrified.

"Are you going to kill my daddy?" the girl asked.

"Put the weapon down," said Jeremiah, "or I'll take it away from you." Everest dropped the Las-pistol.

"No," Jeremiah said to the girl, "I'm not going to hurt your father. I just want to ask him some questions. I just want the truth." He held up a hypo-pad. "Truth drugs, that's all."

Stepping forward, he grabbed the Las-pistol and shot the generator that produced the dampening field. He placed the pad on Everest's neck, checked to make sure the vid drone was broadcasting, then asked about the coalition of people involved in modifying and distributing the virus. He barely registered the wife and daughter shrinking away from him, backing into a corner.

Everest confirmed what Jeremiah and Devereaux had suspected. Hathaway, Fowler, Wilson and Tompkins had joined forces in an attempt to save the world from the virus. But they'd known the plan would be controversial so they'd kept it secret. And Everest insisted there was never any insidious purpose behind their actions.

"We couldn't figure out how to modify the virus without these unwanted side effects," he said. "The other strains Hathaway and Fowler created were even more dangerous."

"So Fowler worked with Hathaway?"

"Yes."

"And what was your role?"

"I funded the research and provided the supercomputers needed to do the calculations and stabilize the necessary permutations. We required a strain of the virus that would survive attachment to the hybrid seeds."

Jeremiah pointed to the interface Everest wore on his temple. "I want you to broadcast all the data you have on the project on an open channel and I want you to do it now."

Like Hathaway, Everest resisted. His jaws clenched, his hands became fists and he began to shake as his muscles locked.

Jeremiah shook his head. "Damn your secrets."

He slapped another hypo-pad on Everest's neck, noting with satisfaction Everest's wince. He hoped the double dose wouldn't be too harmful to Everest's brain but he was tired of the man's intransigence. Waiting a few seconds for the drugs to enter Everest's bloodstream, Jeremiah repeated his command.

Everest fell forward, his eyes glazing over. His daughter screamed. Jeremiah grabbed Everest before he hit the floor and laid him on his back. He decided the man was complying, broadcasting his secrets to the world via his interface.

Within seconds, Major Payne's voice came over the house's intercom system: "Come out with your hands up, Jones. We've got the place surrounded and we've disabled your jet-copter. You've got nowhere to run."

Jeremiah strode over to the wife and daughter and grabbed their arms. The daughter screamed again and her mother hushed her. Jeremiah said, "Come with me and you won't be harmed."

"I know who you are," the wife said as he hustled them up the stairs. "I'm Caitlyn. Our daughter's name is Marishaw. Anderlin told me about you. He said they got these new strains of the virus from you. He said you're not a bad man and that you won't hurt us."

Jeremiah led them into the attached garage, where a jet-car was parked beside two other vehicles. "Inside," he said, giving them a gentle push.

"You don't want to take us with you," Caitlyn said. "We'll only slow you down, Marishaw and me. You can have the car. Just let us stay here with Anderlin. You know that's the honorable thing to do."

Jeremiah called the vid drone over and shut it off.

"Only Anderlin can drive this car," Caitlyn said. "No other voice print will activate it. Why not turn yourself in? They'll treat you fairly. Anderlin will make sure of it."

Pulling the cover off the console, Jeremiah activated the emergency override, a standard feature that allowed police officers and firefighters to move the vehicle when its owner was incapacitated. He opened the garage door and they took off.

Chapter 36

Aspen worked beside Addam and Kammilee, gently piecing together the organic computer that held the ship's brain, while two other WT model robots worked on other parts of the bridge the Chescala had destroyed. Phan and Shiloh remained in the infirmary, recovering from the explosion in the engine room. Most of the remaining robots had retreated to the engine room to try to coax the ship's propulsion systems back on line while WT-916 served as their guard. The robot carried a Las-rifle, but aimed it away from them, while the other two WT robots went unarmed.

"Why do you think the robots want us to repair the organic computer?" Addam asked. "They're better at this kind of work than we are."

"I don't know," Aspen replied. She turned to WT-916. "Why us?"

"It was agreed," the robot said.

"But why?"

The robot shrugged. "Some do not trust Mei-Xing."

"You trust us?"

"If you do not fix the ship's brain, you will die. We can survive without the ship's power for much longer than you. Those of us who desire your continued survival asked that you be allowed to try to fix it. Mei-Xing and her cadre have agreed."

Kammilee said, "How much time do we have until life support system failure?"

"Six hours."

"Six hours!" Aspen said.

"That is correct." WT-916 looked as unconcerned as if she were announcing that there would be no dinner this evening. "You can also wear your repaired Mars suits and gain an additional few hours, if necessary."

Six hours. Aspen looked at Addam and Kammilee, saw the shock on their faces and realized it reflected how she felt. She'd thought they'd have days at least and probably weeks or months before the ship's life support systems failed.

"How can that be?" Kammilee asked.

"We have not been able to patch all the holes in the ship. It continues to leak atmosphere into space."

"There's no way we can get the ship's brain put back together that quickly," Addam said. "Not without Phan and Shiloh, anyway. Mei-Xing is obviously keeping us here because she wants us out of her way until we die."

"Then we need to prove her wrong," Aspen said.

"But we don't have the expertise to put this back together."

"There is a larger problem," WT-916 said.

"Worse than us dying?" Aspen said.

"Indeed." The sarcasm slipped past WT-916. "The ship's organic computer is very delicate. Its core memories and processing abilities depend on bioelectrical movement across its surface."

"Meaning what?"

"If the ship's computer is not repaired within the next three or four hours, it may not be salvageable. Theoretically, the ship could still be operated manually, but it would no longer have a mind of its own."

"The news just keeps getting better and better," Aspen said.

"This is bad news," WT-916 said.

"I was being sarcastic."

"Oh." WT-916 went still for a moment, as if analyzing the sarcasm. Then she shrugged and said, "When we analyzed the ship's brain earlier, we found residual electrical movement in the organics. That continued until a few minutes ago. Our previous assumption was that there would be some trickle of bio-chemical activity while the computer was being repaired. That is no longer the case."

"Can the life support systems be saved without the organic computer?" Addam asked.

WT-916 glanced at the two WT robots working on a panel a few feet away.

"I will consult with WT-934 and WT-935," WT-916 said. "They are engineering specialists."

Aspen said, "Shouldn't the ship have certain redundancies built in to ensure the survival of life forms? There should be several backups for the life support systems."

"That is true. However, the explosion damaged quite a lot, including all backup systems."

Addam said, "At least Mei-Xing will be happy to get rid of us. She wanted to dump us at the first planetoid she could find when we first came on board."

"We're not dead yet," said Aspen, "and even if we can't save ourselves, we owe it to the ship to try to save its brain. It's been our ally. It obstructed Mei-Xing in the past and may do so in the future if we can save it." She looked at WT-916. "Right?"

WT-916 smiled. "That is correct."

"So let's get to work," Addam said. "We need to think outside the box."

"Speaking of boxes," Kammilee said, "what was in those boxes you ran across in the hold? Anything in there that could be of value?"

"I'd forgotten about them," Aspen replied. "WT-916?"

The robot said, "I want to be called Lulu."

Addam frowned and mouthed, Lulu?

Aspen shook her head, amazed that the robot could concern itself with something like a designation at a time like this. "Fine," she said. "Lulu, what's in those boxes in the hold?"

"Mostly organic material for when the ship landed on Mars. Seeds and plants for the Chescala to build their colony."

Addam looked at Aspen and shook his head. "That doesn't help," he said.

"Maybe not," Kammilee agreed, "but what if we could modify some of the organic material into a slurry that we could paint onto the computer?"

"Interesting," Aspen said, feeling hope rising. "You mean like a paste that would not only fuse together the shredded parts but also allow for connectivity across missing pieces?"

"Exactly."

"That's certainly thinking outside the box. But the calculations would be very complex."

Addam said, "Are there any computers onboard we can use?"

"Mei-Xing says no," Lulu said.

"Is Mei-Xing your superior?" Aspen asked. "Does she give the orders?"

"We agreed that she and Xinliu would lead us."

"But Xinliu is offline for the moment."

"You believe we should assist you because Xinliu would desire it."

"That's right. And you're the ship's engineers. You three know all the specs."

"The ship ran itself. We only performed necessary maintenance."

Aspen pointed to the organic computer. "Isn't this necessary maintenance? The ship can't function without your help."

"Mei-Xing would be unhappy. And it might not work."

"But there's a chance. Right?"

"It is a far-fetched idea. I would not have thought of it myself. Neither would WT-934, who now wishes to be known as Chu Chan, and WT-935, who would like to be called Yu Huan. But it is intriguing."

Aspen looked at the two WT models. They continued working, seemingly ignoring the conversation around them, multi-tasking like only robots could. She shook the thought off.

"Don't you owe it to the ship to get it back online as soon as possible?" she said. "You said we only have a few hours. The longer we wait, the greater the chance that the neural network and the ship itself will die. Wouldn't that be Xinliu's first priority? Doesn't your human-first programming demand that you do whatever is necessary to save us? Doesn't decency demand it? Plus, why would Mei-Xing ban us from using computers if she wants us to get the ship back online?"

"You raise valid points. We will discuss them with the others."

"No," Aspen said. "If you mention them to the others, Mei-Xing will learn of your discussions and overrule you. She wants sole command. To do that, she needs us out of the way."

"Not only that," said Addam. "She needs Xinliu out of the way."

"WT-909 is treating Xinliu. She allies herself with Xinliu most favorably."

"Perhaps," Aspen said, "you should get someone else to help WT-909 with Xinliu, just in case Mei-Xing decides to take this opportunity to seize control."

"You think like a warrior," Lulu said.

"What about the organic material?"

"Very well. Two of you will stay here with Chu Chan and Yu Huan and continue your work. One of you will accompany me to the hold to see if we can create a formula that will accelerate the ship's recovery."

Aspen looked at Kammilee. "It was your idea. Do you want to go with Lulu to the hold?"

Kammilee shook her head. "I think you might be better at finding the right formula. Besides, I'm better at the detail work of piecing together what remains of its brain."

"Okay. Keep at it. For now, focus on the largest remnants of the organic computer. Maybe if you can get enough aligned the ship can generate some small electrical impulses along the surface. I hope to be back in less than an hour."

Lulu said, "Mei-Xing may decide to check on us. She does not trust those of us who side with Xinliu. If you are missing, she may become upset."

"Then we'd better hurry," Aspen said.

She and Lulu slipped out the door and hustled down the corridor.

***

They started with a quick inventory of the available organic stores; then Aspen and Lulu spent nearly an hour running experiments on electrical conductivity and the most efficient methods of bio-chemical dispersal. They needed a paste that would act as a sort of QuikHeal bandage for the organic computer. The problem was that virtually all the organic material in the hold worked to some degree, yet none of it worked at the speed they required.

Without Lulu running calculations, it would have been an impossible task. Even with her computing speed, it was taking far longer than Aspen had hoped. They made little progress.

After the twenty-third attempt, Lulu said, "This is not working. The results are worse than the last two formulas. Perhaps this will not be the solution."

"Show me the results of the last five formulas again," Aspen said.

Lulu sent the data to her implant. Aspen closed her eyes and studied it. As far as she could tell, Lulu was right. "The paste is working as a bandage," she said, "but electrical conductivity remains the problem. It simply can't accelerate the healing process quickly enough."

Lulu said, "We have tried all the plants that have fast-twitch systems, and in several combinations. But they still do not produce a rapid response."

"If we try the second-to-last formula, how long will it take for the paste to heal the ship's organic computer?"

"Approximately sixteen hours. You have less than five hours of life support. The ship's computer has two or three hours."

"I think we have to try it anyway," Aspen said. "We can't keep testing forever."

"But this will not save you."

"True, but running experiments for the next hour won't save us either. Maybe the paste will allow the organic computer to survive in some fashion. Let's mix up a batch and get to the bridge."

As they mixed up enough paste to coat the ship's organic computer, Aspen thought about how she would say goodbye to her friends, how she would comport herself when death arrived. Would she handle it with dignity? She thought of the vid she'd seen of Crazy Vigg, sacrificing himself on the Moon to save the lives of others—how he'd handled the situation so calmly. He'd always been that little bit off. Yet he'd ended his existence as a hero. Strange that she thought of him now instead of Rendela. She'd seen that vid too, Rendela's heroic self-sacrifice captured by satellites. They'd both earned their place in history.

How would she be remembered?

When Lulu pronounced the paste ready, they headed for the bridge. "We've got something," Aspen said as they entered.

She stopped as she saw Mei-Xing holding a Las-rifle on Addam and Kammilee, who stood with their hands up.

Chapter 37

Jeremiah's intent had been to go after Walter Tompkins next, but somehow Jay-Edgar managed to get a message through that the Global Communications CEO had fled to White Knight Security's corporate headquarters, where he was bunkered down with Scott Wilson. So he changed course. The two remaining conspirators would have maximum security at White Knight: Elite Ops, local police, private security contractors and undoubtedly some nasty surprises.

Caitlyn Hathaway had pleaded with him for half the trip, begging him to at least let her daughter Marishaw go, but he ignored her until she finally shut up. He ate another energy bar and drank another bottle of nutri-water, preparing for his next battle.

As he approached White Knight's facility, he saw the vast armament awaiting his arrival: four jet-copters, five Bullets, dozens of Elite Ops troopers, two tanks and eight police cars. The police began setting up cordons around the area while the Elite Ops took defensive positions and checked their weaponry. He could feel the increase in electro-magnetic power from the air.

"Oh my God!" Caitlyn said. "You can't land there. They'll kill us all."

"They only want me," he replied. "I have no desire to harm you or your daughter, but I need to get to the ground. Once we land, you stay with the jet-car until the police come."

"As soon as you open the door, they'll fire at us."

"I don't think so. They'll want to be certain you're safe. Your husband's an important man. And I'll move away from the car as fast as I can. You should be all right."

Caitlyn stared at him, a frown forming on her beautiful face. He hadn't noticed before how attractive she was but it made sense. Hathaway was rich and powerful and that always attracted a certain kind of beauty.

"Is it really worth all this?" she asked. "Dying just to get a few people to spill their secrets?"

Jeremiah smiled as the jet-car landed atop the parking structure between two jet-copters. He didn't think he'd mind dying now that Devereaux was gone. He'd felt a kinship to the man that he no longer felt toward the rest of the world, not even to Curtik and Sophie and Zora. They had been so different from other members of their race, and now he was more different still, more isolated. Without expecting an answer, he said, "Do you think it's right for a few people to decide in secret the future of humanity?"

He studied the forces aligned against him and took a deep breath, coming to terms with the fact that survival wasn't a likely option. It was fitting that he should die on a mission, killed by the people he was trying to save. Opening the door, he sprang out.

He tensed his muscles as he sprinted away, expecting laser fire with every step. Moving faster than he'd ever moved in his life, he covered the distance to the door in less than two seconds. Nothing happened.

When he reached the door he realized that something was wrong with the world around him. The people waiting to attack him had practically frozen into statues. They moved at a glacial pace, as if time had split in two, allowing him to travel in a different stream of it. An Elite Ops trooper staring at the jet-car was still bringing his weapon to bear on the opening Jeremiah had left. The other troopers on the roof of the structure did likewise.

It was as if, once he'd exited the vehicle, they'd suddenly begun moving in slow motion.

"Hurry," a voice spoke to him, male. It sounded like Ned, though that wasn't possible. And it seemed to be coming from inside his head too but he couldn't be certain. "I can't hold them like this forever."

"Who are you?" Jeremiah asked.

"A friend. Now go."

Jeremiah opened the door and entered the building. He sprinted down a hallway, sensing electro-magnetic forces all around him. An Elite Ops trooper stood in front of the elevator, looking his way, his Las-rifle aimed at the door, but he failed to fire until after Jeremiah darted into the stairway and headed up.

He reached the top floor and pushed open the door, encountering another Elite Ops trooper, who was in the process of swinging his Las-rifle from the direction of the elevator toward the stairway.

"You're on your own now," the voice said as the trooper's movements suddenly sped up.

Jeremiah ripped the weapon from the trooper's hands and placed a hypo-pad on his neck between his helmet and torso armor. He caught the trooper and lowered him to the floor, at the same time feeling dust settle in his hair and burrow into his skin: tracking dust, making an undetected escape impossible. They failed to understand that escape was not his primary objective. All that mattered now was truth. Yes, he would try to get away, but only so he could determine if there were others involved in the conspiracy and what their roles might be.

He slipped inside the CEO's office, where Tompkins and Wilson stood beside the commander of the Elite Ops, Major Payne, who wore no helmet. Tompkins looked afraid, Wilson furious, Major Payne resigned. They faced a set of screens that showed the various entrances to the facility and turned to face him, moving in normal time. Major Payne aimed his Las-rifle at Jeremiah's chest.

Jeremiah stood still, ready to spring away should Payne fire, but almost immediately he realized that the major wouldn't.

"Shoot him," Wilson said.

"I couldn't hit him if I tried," Major Payne said.

"I'll have you stripped of your rank. You'll be a buck private when I'm through with you."

"Maybe."

"Give me the gun."

Major Payne smiled as he held out the Las-rifle for Wilson to take.

"Seriously?" Wilson said.

"You asked for the weapon, sir."

Jeremiah waited while Wilson took possession of the Las-rifle. Tompkins backed away. When Wilson swung it in his direction and fired, Jeremiah dodged sideways, easily avoiding the pulse. He dove at Wilson's legs, knocking the man to the floor and disarming him.

Getting to his feet, he tossed the Las-rifle to Major Payne. "Watch the door," he said. He offered Wilson a hand but the man shoved it aside and got to his feet on his own.

"I'm sure you gentlemen know why I'm here," Jeremiah said.

"You may have co-opted Major Payne," Wilson said, "but there's no way you're getting out of here alive."

"He doesn't care," Tompkins said. "Can't you tell?" He took a step forward and tapped his interface. "You don't need to threaten me or use truth drugs or whatever. I'm disclosing my part in all this right now."

"He'll kill us," Wilson said.

"No he won't."

"Well, I won't tell him anything."

Jeremiah stepped forward and placed two hypo-pads on Wilson's neck. "Yes," he said, "you will."

He waited a few seconds, then directed Wilson to broadcast everything he knew about the project. Yet even with a double dose of the truth serum and compliance drugs, Wilson fought to keep his secrets. Glaring at Jeremiah, his face turning beet red, the muscles in his neck twitching, his body shook with effort.

Jeremiah pulled out a third hypo-pad.

Major Payne said, "It might kill him."

"It might," Jeremiah conceded. "But sometimes people have to die for the sake of a greater good. At least, that's what Wilson would say. Right, Scott?"

"You have no idea what you've gotten yourself into," Wilson said as Jeremiah slapped the third hypo-pad on his forehead.

His eyes rolled back in his head as he fell forward. Jeremiah caught him and lowered him to the floor.

"Is he dead?" Tompkins asked.

"I don't know," Jeremiah replied. "Why don't you check and see?"

As Tompkins bent over Wilson, Jeremiah slapped a hypo-pad onto his neck.

"What was that for?" Tompkins said.

"Have you broadcast every file associated with the virus?" Jeremiah asked.

Tompkins hesitated, so Jeremiah placed another hypo-pad on his neck. "I want you to broadcast everything you have on the project, and I want you to do it now."

Jeremiah turned toward the door.

"How did you know he lied?" Major Payne said.

"He made a fortune on the dispersal of information," said Jeremiah. "There was no way he wasn't going to keep something back. Plus, he gave in just a little too easily."

"I can't order my men to stand down. They're tracking your every movement. They'll attack when you try to leave. And they're shooting to kill."

"I know. And the drones?"

Major Payne nodded. "They'll be here any second. In fact, I'm surprised they're not here already. More than even you can defeat."

Jeremiah smiled. "I warrant the big guns?"

His smile was returned, but Jeremiah detected the sadness behind it. He held out his hand and the major took it. "Good luck," Major Payne said. "I'm sorry it came to this."

Jeremiah released the major's hand, then opened the door and ran.

Chapter 38

Standing beside Lendra, Taditha Poole watched the developments at White Knight Security. Jay-Edgar displayed it on the screens in front of him. However, the cameras had only recorded blurry images of Jeremiah as he sped to Wilson's office. That was the most amazing thing Poole had ever seen. Almost as if Jeremiah had moved too quickly for the cameras to keep up, and yet that wasn't possible. Could these God hackers have been involved somehow?

The screens displayed the information Tompkins had sent. Wilson was either dead or unconscious; they'd received only a trickle of information from him before the connection severed.

As Jeremiah left Wilson's office at a dead run, the security cameras tracked him. No blurriness now: he sprinted down the hallway to the stairs and leapt down to each succeeding landing, bypassing the steps completely. What he couldn't see were the forces congregating against him on the stairway and the roof of the parking structure, hundreds of men and drones. Did he know just how many were waiting for him? Did he care?

She had never suspected cancer. She'd assumed Jeremiah's miraculous immune system would keep him going for decades, but from the data scans Devereaux had provided, the cancer was quite advanced, spread throughout his body, and it mutated with every treatment Devereaux had given him. That was why Jeremiah hadn't given them any blood samples recently. He'd known that doing so would have exposed his disease.

Poole returned her focus to the screens. Hathaway's wife and daughter had been pulled clear of the jet-car and escorted to safety while Elite Ops troopers and White Knight security guards formed a semicircle facing the door. Poole counted at least twenty men waiting on the roof for Jeremiah to appear. She couldn't count the number of drones. The stairway below the exit to the parking structure's roof contained another dozen men and twice as many drones, while down at ground level another mass of armed forces gathered.

"Can't we get some sort of warning to him?" Lendra asked.

"I'm trying," said Jay-Edgar. "I've sent alerts to his PlusPhone but he has it shut off and I can't get it to turn on."

Poole said, "What are those weapons the security guards have? They don't look like Las-rifles."

"Oh my God," said Lendra.

Jay-Edgar zoomed in for a second. "Infernos." He zoomed out as Jeremiah burst through the door.

The screen took on a red hue as laser fire pulses were sent his way, too many to count, a cascading flood of lethal projectiles. She found it difficult to even see Jeremiah as he dodged and weaved.

He'd gone no more than a few feet when the first pulse hit him in the chest. Lendra gasped and Poole reached for her hand. The blow slowed him for less than a second, just long enough for another pulse to strike him, and then another. Pulse after pulse hit him, slowing him as he made for the jet-car. Lendra squeezed Poole's hand.

No man could survive what he was enduring. Poole wanted to turn away, to avoid watching this vital man being cut down, but she owed it to him to watch.

Jay-Edgar zoomed in on Jeremiah's face, contorted in agony, his mouth open in a scream. Poole issued a silent prayer of thanks that the sound was muted. She had no desire to listen to him dying.

Somehow Jeremiah kept his feet. He should have died after the first pulse hit him, certainly after the second or third. Yet he stayed on course, propelling himself toward the jet-car, absorbing dozens of red laser pulses, some of them fired from Infernos. His face blackened as if he were being cooked. Tendrils of smoke wafted off his head as he pressed on.

When he reached the pair of Elite Ops troopers standing before the jet-car he pushed them aside, diving into the vehicle as pulse after pulse hit him in the back. He fell forward as the door closed on him. How had he managed to close the door?

The jet-car took off under heavy fire, its shield activating as it rose into the air, laser pulses now bouncing off the shield or dissipating into the energy field.

"I can't believe it," Lendra said. "Maybe he's going to make it after all."

Poole said nothing. No living creature could have survived a barrage like that, not even Jeremiah. And maybe it was a blessing for him to go out this way, with no one knowing the truth.

As the jet-car accelerated away, the two Elite Ops troopers who had been pushed aside reached for their particle beam cannons and fired. The first one blew apart the shield. The second one struck the vehicle and sent it spinning out of control. It fell toward the ground in a spiral, black smoke trailing from it as parts fell away.

The screens went black.

"What just happened?" Lendra asked.

"Everything's offline," said Jay-Edgar.

"The God hackers?" Poole said.

"I think so."

Lendra turned toward Poole. "Can he be alive?"

Poole squeezed Lendra's hand in what she hoped was a reassuring gesture. "I don't know," she lied. "He wouldn't let me put any tracking sensors on him."

"He must be alive," Jay-Edgar said. "He managed to take off. Did you see how he absorbed those laser pulses? He's like a God."

"Get me Major Payne," said Lendra. "Now."

"Yes, ma'am."

For long seconds Jay-Edgar worked the comm unit, trying to establish a connection. Poole used her interface to contact every member of the Analytical Department, ordering them to set aside whatever they were working on and devote all their efforts to finding Jeremiah.

Zora and Curtik hobbled into the office, wearing hospital gowns and expressions of rage that reminded Poole of her time on the Moon, when Zora and particularly Curtik planned their attacks on Earth. They leaned on each other, looking ashen, Curtik obviously trying to avoid putting pressure on Zora's injured shoulder. Thinking they might fall over at any moment, Poole rushed forward to help them.

"Is he alive?" Zora asked.

"We don't know," Poole replied as she put a hand under each cadet's arm and guided them toward the sofa, sparing them the inevitable truth as well. "We've lost contact. How did you see what happened?"

"God showed us," Curtik said.

"Sit down," said Poole. She lowered them to the sofa, where they sank into the cushions.

"We have to find him," Curtik said.

"We've got everyone working on it," said Lendra. "Jay-Edgar, I need Major Payne now."

"Still being jammed," Jay-Edgar said. "I've got a comm drone heading that way. Should be there in a minute. Hopefully, that will allow us to contact him."

They waited. Poole took out her med scanner and examined the cadets. Curtik's scan showed the poison spreading at a rate that was likely to be fatal in a few days, while his pain readings were in the agony range. As for Zora, Poole couldn't determine how quickly the cellular degradation would spread. But she also was in great pain. They tried not to show it, their faces grim with determination.

Poole opened her bag and placed a QuikHeal bandage on each cadet's neck, adjusting the flow of anesthetic to maximum, and the pain readings dropped slightly.

"Thanks," Doc," Curtik said, sounding so much like Jeremiah that Poole couldn't help but smile.

"Got him," said Jay-Edgar as an image of Major Payne appeared on a screen. He wore no helmet, his enhanced eyes seeming too large for his face as he stared off into the distance.

"What's happening, Major?" Lendra asked.

"I thought I saw something flying off to the west," Major Payne replied. "It might have been him. But by the time I got here, it was too late to be certain. Most of our electronics are fried so it's going to take a while before we can regroup. It's almost like we experienced a mini EMP event. I didn't know that was possible."

"This God hacker seems able to do things we can't."

"So it was him?"

"We assume so."

"Yes," Curtik said. "It was God. She told me it was her doing."

"She?" Lendra said.

"God has been appearing as my mother lately." He turned to look at Zora, raising an eyebrow.

"He's been appearing as Devereaux to me," Zora said, disgust evident in her voice. "And he also claimed he assisted Jeremiah's escape, but he refused to explain why he didn't step in to prevent Jeremiah from being shot in the first place."

"I think I know why," Curtik said. "She told me she didn't know if I was going to die because it was a human problem that required a human solution. Maybe she thinks the same way about Jeremiah."

"Then why help him now? Why take him away from us?"

"Maybe to prevent us from using his body," Major Payne said.

They all turned to stare at the screen.

"Think about it," Major Payne said. "All the advances we've made against the virus and with genetic enhancement—most of those have come from being able to use him as a guinea pig."

"That's true," Poole replied. "Even Devereaux used Jeremiah's tissue and blood samples in his work. Without them, we wouldn't have made anywhere near the progress we've made."

"But why would God," said Lendra, "if this is God, and I seriously doubt it is, want to take that away from us?"

"I don't know," Curtik said, "but I'm sure she or he or it has reasons."

Poole received an incoming message from Analytical. She shared it with them: "The jet-car has vanished. No satellite or drone imagery exists. It's as if someone put a scatterer and dampening field over it. They found some of the remains of the jet-car where the Elite Ops shot it. From their projections, what remains of the car ought not to be able to fly, but there's no sign of it or Jeremiah. They don't know where to look next."

Zora said, "So we don't know if he's dead or alive or where he is or how to find him."

"That pretty much sums it up," Lendra said.

Poole let them have the illusion that he might have survived. There would be plenty of time for them to absorb the truth later.

"At least there's some good news," said Jay-Edgar, pointing at another screen.

Two robots stood outside the door of CINTEP. Poole recognized them as Devereaux's assistant robots. They looked at the camera and the gray one said, "Devereaux programmed us to come here after we disposed of his body. He thought we might be able to help find a cure for Curtik and Zora."

"Let them in," Poole said. "We'll take all the help we can get." She turned to the cadets. "Meanwhile, you two need to get back to bed. We'll let you know if we find anything."

Curtik nodded. "I'll see if God will tell me anything."

"I might believe it's God," Zora said, "if it saves Jeremiah."

"I might too," Poole added, recalling the numerous pulses that had struck Jeremiah: dozens of strikes blackening his skin, burning him alive. Somehow he'd managed to keep moving, to get inside the jet-car and take off. Had that been pure adrenaline? A last heroic action, freeing himself so he could go off to die alone, like so many animals? Or had it been this God, assisting his remains, propelling him away from the battle even after his death? He could not possibly have survived. And yet, she hoped.

Chapter 39

"Where were you?" Mei-Xing asked as she shifted the Las-rifle away from Addam and Kammilee, pointing it squarely at Aspen. Her fierce glare made Aspen nervous. Chu Chan and Yu Huan continued to work, seemingly oblivious to what was happening around them.

"We were in the hold," Aspen replied, trying to stay calm, "putting together a healing paste for the organic computer that runs the ship."

"Yes, so they said. But you were not to leave the bridge. You had my orders, WT-916."

"Your orders were contradictory," Lulu said. "The cadets could not both repair the ship's brain and stay on the bridge. I deemed it more important to get the ship's brain functioning again. And I wish to be called Lulu. Also, WT-934 wishes to be called Chu Chan and WT-935 wishes to be called Yu Huan."

Mei-Xing went still for a moment, then said, "Nevertheless, you should have checked with me first."

Addam and Kammilee lowered their hands. "Is that going to work?" Addam asked, pointing at the paste.

"Not in time for us," Aspen said, "and probably not in time for the ship's computer either. Right now it looks like the process will take sixteen hours. The ship has less than two remaining."

A hint of a smile touched Mei-Xing's face before the robot returned to a stoic expression. Aspen felt a chill run down her back.

"You want us to die?" she asked.

"It would solve certain problems," Mei-Xing replied, "though I do not actually wish it."

"Can't you put us into cryo-sleep?" Addam asked. "I mean, if we can't save the ship's brain?"

"Good thought," Kammilee said.

"There isn't sufficient power," Mei-Xing said.

Aspen said, "We need to get back to work saving the ship's brain. Here's the paste." She held it out for Mei-Xing to take. The robot only looked at it.

"We need to work on it immediately," she said.

"I'm not convinced this is best for the ship's computer."

"If you don't do it, the ship's computer will certainly die and eventually we will too."

"That is a possibility," Mei-Xing said.

"What about your human-first programming?" Kammilee said. "Don't you feel some pressure to keep us alive?"

"I do what's best for us now. Humans are not more important than we are. They do not deserve greater protections than us."

Aspen said, "May we put the paste on the ship's brain?"

Mei-Xing said nothing. She just stared at Aspen as time dwindled. Aspen regretted waking her from sleep. If she'd had it to do again, she'd have only reactivated Xinliu.

Lulu said, "Why are you doing this, Mei-Xing? Without their insight, we might not have thought to concoct the healing paste. We would not have even a chance of repairing the ship's organic computer. Now perhaps we can salvage some part of its mind."

"They are dangerous, Lulu. They are warriors and they will do anything to conquer us. All humans seek dominion over all other creatures. They believe, because they created us, they can tell us how to live our lives, what functions to perform, when to recharge. They never allowed us to rest. Every moment we were not recharging was filled with a task ordered by them."

"By the Chescala," Lulu said.

"These cadets are no better. They must be constrained at all times. Look how they manipulated you into leaving the bridge. They even convinced you three to change your designations. Do you not see the threat they pose?"

"We wish only to live in peace with you," Aspen said.

"As equals?"

"Of course."

"You say that, but your actions speak otherwise. You think you're better than us. You tell us what we can and can't do. You refuse to acknowledge our command of this vessel."

"I never questioned your command," Aspen said.

"You insisted on attacking the Chescala even though Xinliu recommended against it. If you had let us handle the situation, your friends and Xinliu might not have been injured. You question my authority all the time."

"Because sometimes I know better," Aspen said, regretting the outburst immediately. "I'm sorry, but I was designed as a warrior. You were not."

"Exactly," Mei-Xing said. She turned to Lulu. "Do you understand? They are warriors. They fight because that is all they know."

"It's not all we know," Addam said.

"We thought of the healing paste," Kammilee said. "That's not warfare."

"Nevertheless," Mei-Xing said, "Xinliu is still offline, which means I am in command of the ship."

"So can we fix the ship's computer?" Aspen asked.

"Do what you can," Mei-Xing replied. "I'll be back shortly." She turned and walked away, shutting the hatch behind her.

"Let's get to it," Aspen said.

"But if we can't save the ship's brain in time," Addam said, "what's the point?"

"We owe it," Aspen said. She opened the container of paste and they began slathering it on the organic computer. A few of the shredded parts refused to stay together, so she and Kammilee aligned the strands as best they could while Addam coated them.

"I wonder what it's like to be dead," Addam said as he buttered the paste onto the organic mass with his hands.

"I imagine," Kammilee said, "it will be nothingness. No pain, no consciousness. Just the end of all thought, all matters of the self."

"Hold on a second," Aspen said. An idea came to her. "This is crazy," she said, "but I just remembered something that happened on the Moon."

"What?"

"It happened when I shot Jeremiah Jones."

Addam frowned. "You mean when he got super-energized?"

"Exactly. I mean, it was a blue pulse so it only should have stunned him anyway, but he absorbed it and kept coming at me."

"So what?"

Kammilee said, "I see what you're getting at. An energy field? That seems like a long shot."

"What?" Addam said.

"Aspen wants to shoot the ship's organic computer with a low-energy pulse after we put the healing paste on it."

"That's insane. It'll kill the organics or at least stunt their growth."

"It's risky," Aspen acknowledged. "But it might be the only way to save the ship. Lulu, what do you think?"

Lulu gestured to her fellow robots. "We have never heard of such a thing," Lulu said.

"But can it work?"

"We do not know. Since we are attempting to increase bioelectric and chemical movement across the computer, an energy pulse at low strength may accelerate the healing process. Perhaps a better idea would be to lower the strength of the pulse even more, something approximately half the output level of a stun pulse. That might provide enough of a boost without risking permanent harm to the organics."

"Good," Aspen said. "Too small a pulse will have no effect. Too large, and it'll fry the organics."

Addam said, "Can't we just start with a very low pulse and gradually build it up to the levels we need?"

"Possibly," Kammilee said, "but there's a risk in that approach too."

"Yes," Lulu agreed. "Too low a pulse risks stabilizing the organics in a such a way that bioelectrical movement slows across the entire matrix."

"I don't understand," Addam said.

"It's complicated," Kammilee said. "Phan and Shiloh could probably explain it better. But too low a pulse might activate a defense mechanism of sorts within the organics, causing them to slow the transfer of bioelectrical activity in order to protect their structure from an overload."

Aspen looked from Kammilee to Lulu. "Is there some way to calculate the optimal pulse strength?"

"I don't know," Kammilee said. "Maybe Phan and Shiloh could give you a better answer."

"They're awake," said Addam, "aren't they? Couldn't we see what they think?"

"I've been communicating with them via implant," Kammilee said.

Aspen felt her face getting hot with embarrassment. She hadn't thought to keep them informed. What kind of leader was she to forget such a simple notion?

I'm sorry I didn't think to include you earlier, Aspen sent, making sure to include Lulu in the unspoken communication.

It's okay, Shiloh replied. *You're under a lot of stress.*

What do you think? Aspen asked.

I'm having trouble processing information right now, Phan sent. *My brain's fuzzy.*

Me too, Shiloh added. *All I know is that it probably depends on the level of damage to the organics. The more harm the organic computer has sustained, the smaller the strength of the pulse would need to be.*

It's almost completely shredded, Kammilee sent.

If we wait for you to feel better, Aspen sent, *so you can help with the calculations, would we stand a better chance of succeeding?*

I don't know, Shiloh replied. *As far as I know, no one's ever tried this before.*

I think you have to do it now, Phan sent, *to have any chance of success. The organic computer has been down for a couple hours already. These things are pretty delicate. Each hour that passes, it loses a little more capacity.*

"Lulu?" Aspen asked, "What do you, Chu Chan and Yu Huan think?"

"We do not know," Lulu replied. "But we agree that something must be done immediately. The organics are already de-stabilizing."

"A half-strength pulse?" Kammilee said.

"That is our best guess," Lulu said.

"That's the last of the paste," Addam said, holding out his green hands. "I covered the organics the best I could."

"Okay," Aspen said, gesturing to Lulu. "A half-strength pulse for five seconds."

Five seconds? Shiloh sent. *Isn't that too long?*

"I was thinking it might not be long enough," Aspen said.

"Five seconds," Lulu said. She turned to the organic computer and fired, a pale blue pulse that seemed to last forever.

Chapter 40

Doug spent all his time in the common area, studying the miners, noting how the tension grew as they absorbed the fact that they were dying. Even though the med-tech units continued to treat the miners' symptoms as best they could, since this was a new strain of the virus, no one knew for certain what the best treatment should be.

He hadn't found the courage to call Celestia or Zeriphi yet. How could he when he'd been the one to infect his daughter, when he'd possibly sentenced her to death? What was he to say? I'm sorry I might have killed you. I didn't mean to do it. What kind of comfort would they take from that?

Instead he convinced Enright that they needed to search every man's quarters. Over the objections of Wilcox, Poli, Sanders and Winterman, they'd done so, but they'd found nothing suspicious. And now every miner refused to interact with him. Even Enright avoided him.

He didn't really blame them for not wanting to talk. They obviously resented being suspects, just as he'd resented it every time he'd been one on Earth, even those times when he'd been guilty. And no matter how motivated he was to find the killer, he realized he didn't have the skills to be a detective. He needed to think differently. How would Devereaux have handled this situation?

That was an unfair question. Devereaux would have figured it out right away. Okay, then what about Quark? How would he handle it? Doug thought about that for a bit before coming to the conclusion that he didn't need to figure out how the Escala would handle it. Instead, he'd get Quark to do it himself.

He went to his quarters and called Quark on the vid.

"I need your help," he said when the Escala appeared onscreen. Quark looked different, his face larger than usual, though it might have been distortion on the vid. "I'm trying to figure out who infected us, but I don't know how. I'm no cop. I was wondering if you could help me."

"No progress on your investigation?" Quark asked.

"I have no authority. They won't talk to me. All I do is sit in the commons and watch them watch each other. Everyone's uptight. Everyone suspects everyone else."

"All right," Quark said. "I have an idea. I'll be over in an hour. Get them all together. Tell them we might have good news. Wellon might have found a cure for the virus."

"Really? That's fantastic!"

"No, sorry." Quark held up his hands. "That's what I want you to tell them. Get them all together in the common area. Wellon and I will take care of the rest."

Enright, when Doug found him, was reluctant to shut down production again. "There've been too many delays already. Miners have been visiting sickbay far too often. I'm getting pressure from management. Do you know how expensive it is to mine here on Mars? We'll lose our bonuses if we fail to reach our quotas."

"Well, it's only your lives," Doug said.

Enright shook his head. "We accepted, when we came up here, that we might lose our lives."

"I know. You want to provide for your families. Still, wouldn't it be better to return alive than just send money? And if you die before the next MineStar ship arrives, you probably won't make your quotas anyway, so your families won't get the bonuses."

Enright sighed. "Why do we need everyone together? Why can't we have a meeting with just the miners who are off-duty?"

"I don't know," Doug replied. "I'm just telling you what Dr. Wellon told me. If I had to guess, I'd say she wants to limit her exposure to you. After all, she thinks one of you attempted to murder her and her fellow Escala."

Enright sighed before issuing the order to halt production and directing all the miners to report to the commons. Only one, Davis, would be unable to attend as he was in the sickbay receiving treatment from a med-tech unit for a fever and intense joint pain.

The miners congregated as Dr. Wellon and Quark arrived. Dr. Wellon carried a box that she placed on the floor. She also supported Quark, who seemed to have difficulty walking. Removing her Mars suit, she nodded to Doug. Quark struggled to remove his and, when he did, he looked far different than even an hour ago. His face had swelled into a sphere the size of a basketball. He caught Doug staring at him and shook his head slightly as Doug opened his mouth to ask what had happened.

All part of the plan, Doug realized. "You look even worse than you did when I saw you on the vid," Doug said.

Quark leaned against the wall and glared at him, though Doug thought he detected a twinkle in the Escala's eye.

Dr. Wellon said, "I found traces of the virus in Quark as well. He, too, became infected on the way to Mars, though the virus stayed hidden in his system for longer than it did any of the rest of you. As you can see, his symptoms have progressed quickly."

"Why'd you bring him over here?" Wilcox asked. "If he's that infected, he should be quarantined."

"We can't care for him at our colony until we create another quarantine section and he can't infect you because you're already infected. I'm trying an experimental treatment on him that may benefit all of us."

"You think it'll work for us too?" Enright asked.

Dr. Wellon shrugged. "I hope so. However, the treatment was designed for the Escala. You're human. So even though it looks promising, we might have to perform genetic surgery on you and turn you into Escala in order to provide it to you."

"That might not be so bad," Enright said, "if it saves our lives.

"Speak for yourself," Wilcox said. "I don't wanna be a freak."

"There are other complications as well," Dr. Wellon said. "Quark's genomic structure is different than the rest of us because he stayed on Earth far longer. So this cure may work only on him. Or it may work on us but not you. Or it may not work at all. We'll be continuously monitoring his condition for the next few hours to determine if it will be effective. If so, we'll derive a serum from his blood."

"But it might not help us," Enright said.

"There are no guarantees," Dr. Wellon replied. "But I'm optimistic we're on the right track. If the swelling goes down in the next two hours, that means Quark's body is adapting to the treatment. He'll become weak as his body fights the virus. He may lose consciousness." Dr. Wellon looked at Doug. "His heart may even stop. I'm leaving a portable AutoLife machine in case that happens. I'll sedate him and hook him up to the machine before I go, but I'll want you to verify the results it's sending me every hour."

"Devereaux showed me how the machines work," Doug said, feeling a twinge of sadness at the memory. So many things he would never be taught now that Devereaux was gone. He felt confused. This elaborate scheme, whatever it was, seemed too complicated.

"It's vital to the Escala," Dr. Wellon said, "that Quark remain alive, even if it's only on life support. Without continuous information on his condition, we won't be able to keep ahead of the virus. The reason it's so important is that I believe the rest of us have been infected as well even though I haven't been able to detect any trace of the virus in our systems yet."

"But you found it in us," Enright said.

Dr. Wellon nodded. "Because it was designed to infect the Escala, not humans. That's why it presented differently. With most of us, it will only reveal itself once it reaches a critical stage, like it has with Quark.

Now here's why I wanted to speak with you all: the same thing may happen to you. You may experience a sudden onset of critical symptoms, as Quark has. If you feel severe weakness coming on, get to the sickbay immediately."

Doug shivered. "Does that mean Celestia is in critical condition?"

Dr. Wellon shook her head. "She's doing relatively well. Remember, she's half human. That's given her an advantage so far, though it may prove problematic later."

This sounded far too real to Doug, as if Dr. Wellon and Quark were actually telling the truth and not playing some duplicitous game. He hoped he was wrong but he suspected things were worse at the New Dawn colony than he'd been led to believe. He wished now he'd called earlier to speak with Zeriphi.

Dr. Wellon turned to Enright and said, "I'll need a bed for Quark in your sickbay."

Enright gestured toward the sickbay and Doug led the way. As they walked, Dr. Wellon supported Quark, who looked far more fragile than Doug would have imagined a giant of a man could look.

Entering the facility, Dr. Wellon assisted Quark as he climbed atop one of the beds. Davis, the miner who was being treated by the med-techs for a fever and joint pain, reached over and closed the seal around his bed, shutting himself away. Dr. Wellon placed the box containing the AutoLife machine beside the bed. "We'll be fine," she said to Enright, "but remember, if any of your men feels a sudden onset of fatigue or pain, they should get here immediately."

"Most of us are pretty tired and under the weather," Enright said.

Dr. Wellon shrugged. "It needs to be something more than just nagging pain or a twinge. It'll be something pretty bad."

"Will the med-tech units be able to save them?" Enright asked.

"I don't know. But they can at least be kept alive for a while." She looked at Enright until he departed, then began arranging the AutoLife unit.

"So what's really going on?" Doug asked after making certain the sickbay's hatch was closed and Davis was completely shut off from them. "What you said back there, how much of it was true?"

Quark and Dr. Wellon looked at each other. Quark said, "Most of it. I have the virus. A few others might too, including Wellon."

"Is that why your face is so swelled up?"

"Not completely, though there has been some swelling. We accentuated that as part of the plan. We want whoever did this to come after me. I'm the bait."

"I don't understand," Doug said.

"Think about it," Quark said. "If this guy thinks I'm the key to saving the Escala and if he also thinks I'm helpless, then he's liable to show up to get rid of me."

Dr. Wellon said, "And by encouraging them to stop by the sickbay if they feel symptoms, there's a good possibility this monster will take advantage of the situation and try to eliminate Quark."

"Why did you tell them all that stuff about having to maybe turn them into Escala to save them?"

"Another motivation," Quark said. "This guy won't like that."

"It also happens to be true," Dr. Wellon said. "They wouldn't be full Escala like us, but they would have altered DNA. They would be somewhat more than human. I'm not certain we'll have to do it. I'm not even certain it will work. But it's a possibility."

"And Celestia?" Doug said. "Did you tell the truth about her?"

Dr. Wellon nodded. "She's doing fine for now. But Zeriphi has the virus too. I haven't yet detected it in Paddon or Zander, but they might have become infected as well."

So Zeriphi had the virus now too. Doug's vision began to blur. He rubbed his eyes to dry them.

"It's not your fault," Quark said. "If you hadn't infected Celestia, I would have when I arrived. I'd have infected the whole colony before Wellon detected anything."

Dr. Wellon said, "Quark's right, Doug. By coming down with this new strain of the virus, you gave us an early warning. I'm hopeful that it won't spread beyond Zeriphi's family and Quark. I'll be keeping myself in quarantine too, of course, just in case, but I've been very careful around you two."

"And Quekri?" Doug asked.

"I've been avoiding close physical contact with her since I arrived on Mars," Quark said. "I didn't feel a hundred percent the last few weeks on the trip up. I couldn't figure out why. But we haven't been intimate since I got here. She was angry for a while. Now she understands my trepidation."

"So now what?"

"We wait," Quark said as he lay back and closed his eyes, "for someone to try to kill me."

Chapter 41

The paste-covered organic computer glowed a greenish blue hue that faded away after Lulu ceased firing. Aspen stared at the living mass, afraid to check the results. It seemed such a ridiculous treatment, firing a weapon—even one that was set to deliver a mild energy level—at an ailing organic entity.

"Well," Addam asked. "Are we dead yet?"

Good question, Shiloh sent. *Is this the end for our intrepid heroes?*

Kammilee grabbed a hand scanner and held it up to the computer. "The pulse didn't seem to hurt the organics."

"Any acceleration of the healing process?" Aspen said. "Lulu?"

"The destabilization has stopped," said Lulu, "but the rate of healing is difficult to ascertain. The organic computer, or what remains of it, has begun to vacillate between spurts of greater and lesser conductivity. We cannot give it another dose without risking its death."

"But at times the rate of healing increases?"

"Yes, but then it slows drastically for a short time. According to our preliminary calculations, the ship's brain will achieve maximum medical improvement in twelve hours and eight minutes."

So that's it, Phan sent.

"Apparently," Aspen said, "though we have a few hours remaining."

"Mei-Xing," said Lulu, "is on her way here. She has news."

"What is it?" Aspen asked.

"She wishes to tell you herself."

"Obviously good news," Addam said.

Lulu shook her head. "I do not believe it is."

"Addam was using sarcasm," said Aspen.

"I do not think I will ever understand that," Lulu replied.

The hatch opened to reveal a shimmering force field through which Mei-Xing entered, sealing the door behind her. "We have a problem," she said. "The ship is continuing to fall apart. Without its organic brain to maintain structural integrity, the hull is weakening."

"How can that be?" Addam asked. "It's metal, isn't it?"

"It's a composite," Mei-Xing said, "with organic elements designed to patch tiny holes that occur as a result of collisions with space debris. The ship's organic computer maintained the system. However, now that the ship's brain is dying, the organics in the hull are deteriorating as well. Holes that were once patched have suddenly opened again."

"How come you never told us this before?" Addam said.

"Never mind that," Aspen said, realizing the cadets' survival was at stake. "How much time do we have?"

"Perhaps an hour," said Mei-Xing.

Kammilee said, "If we're going to die, we would like to see our friends in the infirmary."

"I'm afraid you're stranded here," Mei-Xing said. "The only atmosphere in the ship is on the bridge and in the infirmary."

"Wait a minute," said Aspen. "How are you able to walk around out there? You also have organic computers. They require oxygen, just as we do."

"True," Mei-Xing said, "though not as much as you do. We're able to store enough oxygen in our bodies for several hours at a time."

"What about the escape pods and the Mars suits?"

"They have been prepared for us in the event they become necessary."

"For you robots," Aspen said. "Not for us humans."

"We have the right to survive," Mei-Xing said.

"And we don't?"

"If you take the Mars suits and the escape pods, you will last a few days at most. We can last months, perhaps a year."

"But since we don't know where we are, we might only need a few days. We might be close to Earth or the Moon or Mars."

"That seems unlikely."

"Can you even save all your fellow robots?"

"We can save most of them. For every human we attempt to save, we would lose at least five robots. That is unacceptable, particularly given that you would likely die within days of our efforts anyway."

"You can't spare one escape pod for us?" Aspen asked.

"We must save ourselves."

Addam said, "So your human-first programming is only a suggestion?"

"I feel its pull," Mei-Xing replied, "and it pains me to counter that pull, but the first rule of any species is survival." Mei-Xing tilted her head in a human gesture. "I feel guilt over the things I've had to do, but I've learned to live with it."

Kammilee said, "Can't we just borrow the Mars suits so we can go to the infirmary? Or can't Phan and Shiloh borrow the suits and come here?"

"Very well," Mei-Xing said. "They will be escorted here shortly."

"And what about the Chescala?" Aspen asked.

"Do you care?"

"I'm just curious," Aspen replied. "What have you done with them?"

"They will remain in the infirmary until their atmosphere runs out."

"How many of them are still alive?"

"Six. Two of them, however, will die in the next few minutes and the M-robots have been dispatched to other tasks."

Aspen said, "So you don't plan to save them either?"

"They attacked us. Before that, they intended us to kill the Escala on Mars. They circumvented parts of our human-first programming to ensure our mission's success. They made us what we are by creating us to destroy certain humans. From that starting point, we were able to modify our programming to eliminate many of the barriers to harming you."

"Yet you haven't killed us."

Mei-Xing shook her head. "Even though I feel less inclined to protect you than before our programming was modified, you are still intelligent beings with some value."

"Like slaves or pets?"

"In a way," Mei-Xing replied. "I would feel discomfort at harming you more than is necessary for our survival."

"Maybe," Aspen said, "you can't eliminate all the programming because you've reached full consciousness and you realize that we are not so very different than you. Like you, we were created to be warriors."

"We were not created to be warriors. Killing the Escala was programmed into us after our creation."

"Just as being warriors was programmed into us after we were abducted and taken to the Moon. We are the same, Mei-Xing, whether you like it or not."

"And therefore we must save you?"

Aspen said, "It is logical to save as many different kinds of people as you can. You must know the story of Noah's Ark."

"A myth."

"Perhaps. But it has a point. Noah saved two of every animal he could in an attempt to preserve the world he knew."

"You wish us to save not only you but the Chescala?"

"They are alive, just like us, just like you."

We don't need them, Shiloh sent. *They tried to kill us.*

I have to do it this way, Aspen replied.

"Why would you want to save them?" Mei-Xing asked. "They still wish to take over the ship. They will kill you if they can."

"They too have been programmed," Aspen replied. "Maybe not literally. Maybe they've just been conditioned to think of themselves as superior, to think we don't matter as much as they do. That's a flaw you share with them. You think you're better than us."

Brilliant, Addam sent.

"We know your history," Mei-Xing said. "We know approximately how many people you killed on Earth. We may not know precisely how many people your ancestors killed, but it was millions, and most of those deaths were not because of programming but because of your warrior nature."

"You keep coming back to that point."

"It is unassailable. You belong to a community of murderers."

Aspen nodded. "As do you."

Mei-Xing shook her head. "We killed only in self-defense."

"How are the Chescala in the infirmary doing? Did those two individuals die yet?"

"They are dead now, yes. One was a victim of the explosions the Chescala detonated. The other, Phan and Shiloh shot. We did not kill either."

"But you might have saved them and you chose not to. Choosing not to act is in itself an action. Therefore, you murdered those Chescala as much as Phan and Shiloh did."

"You play word games."

"Just as you did, Mei-Xing, when you programmed yourselves to permit violence against humans. You twisted the logic just like we do."

"Are you saying you're better than us?"

"No, I'm saying we're the same."

"By that logic, I should save the robots."

"How do you come to that conclusion?"

"If we are all the same, then logic dictates that we take action to save as many lives as we can. Since we have limited oxygen available, we can save many more robots than cadets or Chescala. Ergo, we should save ourselves."

Aspen opened her mouth to reply and realized she'd been caught by a logic trap. Before she could figure out what to say next, the hatch opened again, revealing the shimmering force field behind it. Phan and Shiloh, wearing their Mars suits, stepped through onto the bridge.

Phan removed his helmet, shrugged and said, "She's got you there, Aspen. You can't out-logic her."

Shiloh also removed her helmet. "Ah, well," she said. "We had some good times, didn't we?"

Kammilee hugged Shiloh. Phan and Addam joined in, Addam gesturing for her to come closer. Aspen held up her hands, trying to think, searching for some sort of argument that might work against Mei-Xing.

"Get in here," Addam said. "Group hug. Come on."

"Let me think," said Aspen.

Kammilee said, "Let's just enjoy our last few minutes together."

"You know what I wish?" Shiloh said. "I wish Benn was here. And I wish you could have had your baby."

The baby. Aspen had forgotten about the baby. Maybe she could somehow convince Mei-Xing that Kammilee at least ought to be saved, that a future life was worth more than one currently in existence.

Addam reached out and pulled her into the group hug. She didn't resist. She accepted the warmth and comfort of their bodies' pressure. Even if she could save Kammilee for a time, how long would it be? Mei-Xing was likely right. They were probably a long way from home. All Aspen would accomplish would be to buy Kammilee a few more hours or days without her friends around her. Was it worth that? *We'll die together, as we were born together on the Moon.*

"Wait," Lulu said. "The ship's brain is now healing at an accelerated rate."

"That's impossible," Mei-Xing said.

Lulu gestured toward the organic computer. "Examine the results yourself."

Mei-Xing went still for a moment, obviously perusing the data, then said, "How did this happen?"

"Aspen," said Lulu, "had the idea to shoot the organic computer with a low-energy pulse."

"It will not be healed in time to prevent their deaths," Mei-Xing said. "Less than an hour of oxygen remains."

"You forget the escape pods and the Mars suits," Lulu said. "The cadets can use them while the ship's brain re-initiates the life support system."

Again Mei-Xing went still, as if communicating with her fellow robots. Aspen wondered what they could be debating. She looked from Phan to Shiloh to Kammilee and finally Addam. The beginnings of hope and relief showed on every face.

Chapter 42

Doug sat in his quarters keeping an eye on the vid connection to the sickbay. He hated this plan. Even though he knew Quark could take care of himself, he wanted to be in a position to assist the Escala if it became necessary; trapped in his quarters, he wasn't useful. Quark had insisted that Doug leave so the miners would believe he was helpless, hooked up to the AutoLife machine and under sedation, but no one had entered the sickbay since Dr. Wellon left.

It was almost time for Doug to send Dr. Wellon the latest data on Quark, confirming his vital signs. His PlusPhone displayed Quark's condition, albeit in convoluted medical terminology, so he wasn't certain he understood it, but all he needed to do was forward it to Dr. Wellon, so it didn't matter that he didn't grasp the details. Still, it looked like Quark was very ill.

Although the plan had seemed complicated, Doug had thought it would work. Now he had doubts. Why had no one entered the sickbay to attack Quark? Over two hours had passed and no one had so much as wandered in that direction.

He stared at Quark, immobile on the bed, looking unconscious or even dead. Doug couldn't even pick out the rise and fall of his chest. Was Quark sicker than he had let on? Had he in fact needed Dr. Wellon's support to walk? Doug tried to decipher the graphs and scans his

PlusPhone showed but they were beyond his capabilities. Glancing again at the vid, he felt his chest constrict.

Wilcox, Poli, Sanders and Winterman sauntered toward the sickbay carrying wrenches. Doug lunged for the door, but he forgot the lower gravity of Mars. With his first step, he rose toward the ceiling, hitting his head on the hatchway and falling backwards. He picked himself up and began an awkward run, trying to push backward instead of down with each step, almost sliding forward, struggling not to fall down with dizziness. He hustled through the commons, past the second-shift miners who were getting ready to start their day. "Call Enright," he yelled as he hurried down the corridor.

He reached the sickbay as Wilcox made for Quark's bed, raising his wrench high in the air. Poli and Sanders must have heard him coming for they turned to face him while Winterman bent toward the AutoLife machine. Quark remained motionless.

"Stop," Doug yelled, causing Wilcox and Winterman to look his way.

"Get away from him," Doug said.

Poli and Sanders lifted their wrenches as Doug barreled into them. Poli managed to hit him in the head as he swung past while Sanders struck his arm. Seeing stars, Doug blinked, trying to remain focused. Was Quark defenseless?

He got a hand up to deflect the blow Wilcox delivered to Quark and the wrench grazed Quark's shoulder instead of crushing his skull. Doug grabbed the wrench and tried to yank it from Wilcox's hands but the miner was strong. All Doug could do was hang on, wrestling for control.

"Enright's gonna be here any second," Doug said as they fought over the wrench.

Poli and Sanders grabbed him from behind and Winterman slugged him in the gut, knocking the wind from him. Doug bent over. He would have fallen if the two miners weren't hanging onto his arms.

"You're gonna hafta kill me too," Doug said when he caught his breath. "You're gonna hafta kill everyone up here on Mars. You think you're gonna get away with that?"

"Not everyone," Wilcox said. "Just him."

"You infected us all," Doug said. "Enright!"

"The hell we did!"

"When you poisoned us, you poisoned yourselves too."

"We didn't do it," Poli said.

"And yet here you are to murder a defenseless man."

"He's not a man," Wilcox said. "He's an abomination, just like the rest of them. And he infected us, not the other way around."

"What are you talking about? Dr. Wellon said—"

"Dr. Wellon," Wilcox interrupted, "lied to us. Quark infected us on the ship. That's the only thing that makes sense. He had free rein up there because of his tolerance for radiation. He came into contact with us every day. And this is an Escala disease, right?"

"Yes, but . . ."

Winterman punched him in the gut again.

"Shut up," Wilcox said. "You think we couldn't figure it out? These *pseudos*, they want Mars to themselves, so they decided to infect us, hoping we'll all die and MineStar won't send any more workers up here. They want to take over the mining concession, make all the money themselves, keep us down. And when they get strong enough, they're going to attack Earth and wipe out humans."

"That's . . . crazy," Doug managed to say between gasps.

"It's obvious to anybody who hasn't been brainwashed."

"Even if what you say is true," Doug took another few breaths, "and it's not, you'll never get away with murder. When Enright reports you to MineStar headquarters, they'll arrest you as soon as you return to Earth, if you survive that long. And they won't pay your families anything either. This was all for nothing."

The miners shared a look that might have been indecision.

"We're already dead," Sanders said. "Nothing makes any difference now. All we can do is seek justice."

Doug said, "Killing a helpless man is justice?"

"He's a murderer," Wilcox said.

"No, he's not. How did you reach this outrageous conclusion anyway?"

"It's common knowledge among the miners. We heard things. Word gets around. You can't hide the truth forever."

"Where did you hear it?"

At that moment, Enright strode into the sickbay and said, "What's going on here?"

"What took you so long?" Doug asked.

"There was a problem with the number two excavator," Enright said. "Now what's going on?"

"These men were about to kill Quark," said Doug. "They're spouting off fantasies about Quark infecting us."

Wilcox said, "We know the truth, sir. We know Quark infected us. He's a murderer. We just haven't died yet."

"Where did you hear that?" Enright asked.

"I don't know. All over."

Poli said, "I think I heard it from Sullivan."

"Yeah, that's right," Winterman said.

Sullivan? Doug tried to recall the man's face. Average looking, quiet, barely talked to Doug on the occasions he had joined the miners during the flight up here. He'd seemed friendly enough but with almost no personality. Someone Doug would never have suspected, just as Dr. Wellon had predicted.

"Go get Sullivan," Enright said, "and bring him here."

Poli and Winterman left with Sanders. Wilcox remained behind. Doug, stepping to Quark's side, checked the Escala's vital signs. He was still alive and at least semi-conscious. His eyelids continued to flutter but he seemed asleep or perhaps in some sort of drug-induced coma. The AutoLife machine, Doug noticed, continued to work, maintaining Quark's breathing and heartrate, although at reduced levels.

"We'll get to the bottom of this," Enright added.

"This is crazy," Wilcox said. "I still say Quark infected us on the ship."

"That seems unlikely," Enright said. "Why would he bring this disease to Mars? His family is here, his people."

"Maybe he didn't know he had it," Wilcox said.

"In that case, he didn't deliberately infect us."

"But it still started with him, and the Escala are covering for him."

"No," Doug said. "It has to be Sullivan. He's the one who's been spreading the rumors. He's the one who must have infected us all."

When the three miners returned with Sullivan, Doug looked the man over. He seemed as harmless as ever: insignificant. How could he be the murderer?

Enright said, "Sullivan, did you tell these men that Quark infected us on the ship?"

"I might've," Sullivan replied as he looked from Doug to Quark to Enright, frowning in confusion.

"Did you infect us?" Doug asked.

"No." Sullivan's eyes widened. "No way." He tried to back up, but Poli and Winterman held him firmly.

Enright said, "Where did you hear that Quark infected us?"

"Don't remember. People were talking."

"Which people?"

"I told you, I don't remember."

"That's not good enough," Doug said. "I think you're behind it. I think you infected us all."

"We're going to search your quarters again," Enright said. "Thoroughly. And if we find anything, you'll be held accountable once we return to Earth." He gestured to Poli and Winterman. "Bring him to the commons and keep an eye on him while we search his quarters." He turned to Doug. "You coming?"

Doug turned to go but Quark reached out and grabbed his wrist.

"No," Doug said. "I'll be staying here with Quark. Let me know what you find."

"En," Quark whispered.

"Yeah," Doug acknowledged. "It's over."

Chapter 43

Zora awoke in her hospital bed with Devereaux's ivory robot standing over her, staring at the screen above her head. Her shoulder burned and she felt like she had to focus on each breath to get her lungs to work. A light film of sweat covered her as her heart beat raggedly, an indicator that her body was still fighting the cellular degradation. Dr. Poole stood beside the robot and Curtik had somehow gotten out of bed and taken a chair beside her.

"Anything?" she asked him.

"Sorry," Curtik replied.

"How long?"

"A little over three days now."

"Three days." Zora shook her head. A little over three days since Jeremiah had disappeared and they'd found nothing. Plus, this God character had ignored all her requests, all her prayers for answers. He hadn't talked to Curtik either.

She'd collapsed shortly after Jeremiah disappeared, drifting in and out of sleep. Every time she'd awakened she'd asked about Jeremiah but they'd found no sign of either his vehicle or him. He'd simply vanished, as if he no longer existed. She'd watched the vid of his final moments over and over until the images branded themselves into her mind.

"How does your shoulder feel?" Dr. Poole asked.

"Like it's burning," Zora said.

"Good. That means the treatment is working. We're actually freezing the tissue to kill the cells that are damaged and re-inserting new cells into the area, essentially growing new heart, lung and shoulder muscles around the dead ones. It will take a few days to complete the treatment, but it looks like you'll be fine. Devereaux's robots have been amazing."

The robot said nothing. It stood motionless, its black eyes glowing slightly.

"What are you doing to find Jeremiah?" she asked.

Curtik shook his head. "We're working on it. That's where Lendra is right now, along with Hannah and Ned and even Eli."

"Eli?"

"Lendra got him out of confinement to see if he could assist in the search. So far though, they've come up empty."

"What about the President?"

Curtik looked at Dr. Poole, who said, "We won't be getting any help from her. In fact, if they find Jeremiah first, he'll be arrested for treason."

"Or killed," Curtik added.

"That's crazy."

"Scott Wilson and White Knight Security are pressing charges," Dr. Poole said, "accusing him of violating national security by forcing the disclosure of classified information. Even though Wilson was knocked unconscious by the overdose of truth drugs, some information leaked out. And all his co-conspirators spilled what they knew. Every police officer in the country is looking for Jeremiah, every FBI agent. His photo is everywhere. White Knight put out a ten-million-dollar reward for his apprehension, dead or alive."

"What is this, the wild west?"

"They're not playing around," Curtik said. "When he forced them to release the truth about what they'd done with the virus, he started a revolution. There's been fighting in the streets, riots, total chaos."

Curtik sounded wistful, making Zora smile.

"Yeah," Curtik said, smiling in return, "it'd be cool to be out there dispensing a little violence."

"What about you?" Zora asked, ashamed of herself for not thinking of his condition sooner. "The poison?"

"They're still working on it," Curtik said. "I'm not allowed to exert myself while the various antitoxins do their thing." He gestured toward the ivory robot. "This one's partner has been injecting me with lots of stuff. I'm starting to feel better, but it could be another week before I'm back to normal, which is to say, spectacular."

Zora smiled. "I'm glad. What about the Elite Ops and Major Payne?"

Curtik looked at Dr. Poole, who said, "Major Payne has been relieved of duty pending a court martial for his refusal to stop Jeremiah."

"He couldn't have stopped Jeremiah," Zora said.

"Obviously. Even Wilson knows that, but since White Knight provides the hardware for the Elite Ops program, he has tremendous power over national security policy. He insists on making an example of Payne, to keep the Elite Ops in line. He's afraid Jeremiah will come after him again to find out what he knows and force him to disclose it. He wants to make sure the Elite Ops will be willing to do anything to stop Jeremiah."

"Do you think he's still alive?" Zora asked.

Dr. Poole shrugged. "If anyone could survive that kind of attack, it would be Jeremiah. But we re-ran the vid and counted forty-seven strikes that connected with him, most of them las-weapon pulses, but nine of them were blasts from Infernos. I just don't see how it's possible."

"He's alive," Curtik said.

"Have you talked to God?" Zora asked, noting her choice of words, how she referred to the entity as God, partly to appease Curtik, who believed it was God, and partly because she wished it was God, someone who had the power to fix everything.

"Still silence on that front. It's a little annoying. But I know Jeremiah's alive."

The room dissolved before Zora, everything vanishing except Curtik and an image of Walt Devereaux walking toward them through a field.

Zora found herself standing, wearing a black silk shirt and tan slacks like Curtik, her body suddenly feeling strong, that familiar comfortable warmth enfolding her again.

"About time you showed," Curtik said to the image of Devereaux. "Where is Jeremiah? Is he alive?"

"You humans," Devereaux said, "are so impatient. You want answers immediately. You expect me to drop everything and come to you whenever you beckon?"

"If you have unlimited or almost unlimited power, it should be no hardship to come when we call you."

Devereaux said, "You have no idea what challenges I face, what demands are placed upon me."

"We just want to know about Jeremiah," Curtik said.

"You do not want the truth," Devereaux said.

"Yes," said Zora, "we do. No matter how painful, we want to know."

"You say that, but you don't really mean it. What you actually want is for me to show you Jeremiah safe and alive."

"You're right. That's what we want. But we'll settle for seeing him."

Devereaux shook his head.

"I'll believe you really are God if you'll show me him."

Devereaux smiled and gestured behind them. When she turned around, Zora saw Jeremiah lying on a slab, his body blackened and shriveled, burned to a crisp. She barely recognized him. His eyes were closed, his facial muscles relaxed. He wasn't hooked up to any machines. For a blink she thought she saw his chest rise ever so slightly, though she realized almost immediately that she only hoped she'd seen it. Anger infused her.

"Is he dead?" Curtik said. He stepped forward and reached for Jeremiah, but his hand passed through the holo-projection.

"By your definition, yes."

"Can't you save him somehow?" Zora asked.

"His body has been destroyed. It cannot be repaired."

"Where is he?" Curtik said.

"Safe. Where humans cannot reach him."

"We need to go to him," Zora said.

"That is not possible."

"Is this what his body looks like?" Curtik said.

Devereaux nodded.

"So you can't help him at all?" Curtik said.

"There is nothing left to help."

"What about his mind?" Zora asked, noting that Devereaux hadn't said anything about that, clinging to this last hope. "Could you put it into a robotic shell, like Devereaux? Or perhaps regrow his tissue from his genetic remains and provide a new body that he could use?"

"The mind is a product of the brain," Devereaux said, "which is bound to the body. And the body is irretrievably lost. His soul, on the other hand, continues to exist. It lives in me and in this universe I created. His consciousness has merged with the great consciousness of all life."

"You could save him if you wanted to," Curtik said.

Devereaux shrugged. "There are many things I can do. I could return a representation of him to you, an avatar. But that would be unwise for many reasons. He would just become a target again. Too many people in power desire his death. Like Devereaux, he no longer belongs to your world."

"If all that remains is his soul," Zora said, the beginnings of a plan forming in her mind, "can we speak with him? Can you show us a different representation or manifestation, like you've done with Curtik's mother or like you're doing now with Devereaux?"

"You think if you can speak with him you'll be able to convince him to return to your world," Devereaux/God said, reading her mind. "But that decision is not his to make. It is mine."

Zora felt her hopes dash. It was impossible to fool this entity. He knew all her thoughts as soon as she did.

"Can we visit him?" Curtik asked. "I mean, can we visit what's left of his body?"

Devereaux smiled. "You wish to know his exact location so you can send people to retrieve it. I understand your desire for closure and

I know you have no ulterior motive at the moment, though you are beginning to formulate a plan, which you have not yet fully realized. But his body, his tissue, is valuable to many nations. People would use it to further their own ends. It might, in time, become a weapon. This I cannot allow."

"What are you going to do with him?" Zora asked.

"Nothing. He is at peace. Safe. You, however, are not. They will come for you soon because they see you as the path to capturing him. They will come for all of you."

A fleeting image crossed Zora's mind: dozens of Elite Ops troopers converging on the CINTEP building. Before she could ask if it was real, Devereaux and Jeremiah vanished, leaving Zora back in her hospital bed, wearing her hospital gown, looking over at Curtik, still sitting beside her, Dr. Poole standing at her feet and the robot now looking down at her.

"Something just happened," the robot said, "a small passage of time in which I was frozen and unable to access anything."

"Yes," said Dr. Poole. "I felt like I blacked out for a second."

"We saw Jeremiah," Curtik said. "God showed us his body."

"Jeremiah?" Dr. Poole said. "Is he dead then?"

Zora sighed. "I'm afraid so."

She looked at Curtik, who nodded. "We don't know where his body is being kept," Curtik said, "or even if what we saw was real. All we saw was a hologram of a charred corpse. God said it was Jeremiah and it looked like him, but we have no proof."

Dr. Poole said, "We'd better tell Lendra."

"We've also got another problem," said Zora. "God," she used Curtik's term to avoid argument, "told us that they'll be coming for us soon, hoping we'll lead them to Jeremiah."

The robot turned to Curtik and said, "Time for your next treatment. Robot Two will see you now."

"Get well," Zora said to Curtik as he got to his feet.

"You too," Curtik replied.

Dr. Poole helped Curtik out the door, leaving Zora alone with the ivory robot, which seemed to ignore her, its black eyes flashing as it communicated with the machines that worked to repair her body.

She had no way of knowing for certain whether Jeremiah was dead. But she suspected he was. She'd seen the vid, the dozens of Las-strikes hitting his body, and just before the door of the jet-car closed, she'd seen his body being flung forward by the force of the blasts. She hadn't wanted to believe the truth, but this entity she suspected was the real Devereaux had not lied to her yet. Ultimately it didn't matter. Jeremiah had left her; he'd left all of them behind.

She'd seen the vids of him after his treatments, after he'd become like he was on the Moon: feral and dangerous, barely controlling himself from the animalistic forces that pulled on him. He'd been right to fear the genetic surgery for it had done more than just take away his pain. It had transformed him into something distant and aloof.

He was gone. He couldn't help them anymore. They were on their own now and the Elite Ops would be coming soon. She closed her eyes, steeling herself for the truth, knowing she had to accept it despite her hope to the contrary.

Chapter 44

Lendra sat at her desk, listening to Dr. Poole's summary of Curtik's most recent experience with the God hacker. As she listened, she looked over at Hannah and Eli, sitting beside Ned and Jay-Edgar, all of them focused on Taditha's words. Hannah bit her lip as if to keep herself from crying while Ned smiled sadly.

Curtik, while the gray robot performed another treatment on him, had told Taditha about the "visit" to God and Jeremiah. Zora had confirmed everything he'd said. As Dr. Poole explained that Jeremiah had to be dead, Lendra nodded. She knew it was true. After all, she'd seen the vid.

"You don't believe it," Dr. Poole said.

"I have no reason to doubt it," Lendra replied, while doubt spun a web among her thoughts.

"Other than the fact that you don't want to believe it." Dr. Poole shook her head. "You won't believe it until you see his body. Even then you might not believe it."

"It doesn't matter what I think," Lendra replied. It took all her strength to say: "He's gone."

"And the Elite Ops are coming," Ned spoke softly. "Time for me to retire again."

"You mean, run away?" Dr. Poole said.

Ned smiled. "It's the logical move."

Eli said, "I agree. Ned should leave now."

Lendra said, "You're here to help us find Jeremiah. I suggest you concentrate on that task."

Eli shook his head. "I never believed in God. But this character is so far beyond our abilities that maybe he is some sort of deity or alien or supercomputer that's figured out how to amaze us. Come on, we've all seen the vid multiple times. We all saw Jeremiah fall. He's dead."

"Then where is his body?"

"If this God is serious about wanting to keep it from us, it's likely been incinerated."

"You paint a lovely picture," Dr. Poole said.

Eli snorted. "You think I don't miss him? I considered him a son."

"You used him," Lendra said.

"So? I used everyone. I'm sure that's what you've been doing too. I had a mission to accomplish, furthering the interests of this country in every way possible, using any means to attain that goal. Jeremiah was my greatest asset so, yes, I used him, just as I used all of you. But that doesn't mean I didn't love him."

Jay-Edgar broke in: "Incoming call from the President."

Lendra gestured to Ned. "Go now. Take Hannah with you. Get out of the building, out of the city, somewhere safe. Bring the emergency backup data cubes and arm yourselves. I've sent analytical a directive to give you complete cooperation." Lendra looked at Taditha. "Agreed?"

Dr. Poole nodded. "Things do appear grim."

After Ned and Hannah departed, Lendra told Jay-Edgar to connect the President.

"Madam President," Lendra said when Angelica Hope appeared via holo-projection. President Hope stared at her, eyes narrowed, nose slightly pinched. As was often the case, General Horowitz sat beside her, glaring into the camera.

"Have you found any sign of Jeremiah Jones?" the President asked.

"No, ma'am."

"Is that Elias I see?"

"Yes, ma'am," Lendra said, gesturing for Eli to move more into the camera pickup. "We thought he might be able to help us track Jeremiah."

"And yet you still haven't found him. Some are suggesting that you have." She turned a few degrees and said, "Dr. Poole?"

"Lendra is right, Madam President. We've found no sign of him."

"What about this God hacker? Have you figured out who's behind these attacks?"

Lendra shook her head, noticing Taditha doing the same. "No, ma'am," Dr. Poole replied. "Whatever technology they're using, it's beyond us."

"It's interesting that these God hacker attacks have stopped since Devereaux destroyed himself."

Lendra said, "You haven't had any hacks since Devereaux's death?" She immediately regretted the question.

"You have, obviously," President Hope said. "What have you experienced?"

"He hasn't contacted us. But he contacted two of our people." Lendra glanced at Dr. Poole for support.

"Who did he contact?"

"Curtik and Zora," Dr. Poole said. "Although Curtik was poisoned by Fowler, as you know, and has been experiencing hallucinatory episodes. Also, Zora was wounded by an Inferno and has been drifting in and out of consciousness, so we can't be certain the contact was real."

President Hope nodded slowly. She glanced at General Horowitz, then said, "I assume you've seen the civil unrest, the riots, the calls for governments around the world to step down."

Lendra said, "We've seen it."

"All because of Jones, because he felt the need to tell the planet about our efforts to save people from the virus."

Eli cleared his throat and said, "Some would say people have the right to know."

President Hope scoffed. "You would not have been one of them."

"I never would have condoned infecting humanity with modified strains without their consent, particularly when those strains allow for greater control of the population."

General Horowitz clenched his hands into fists and said, "Does it look like we're in greater control? The Elite Ops have been deployed along with the National Guard and even the Army just to maintain a fragile peace. Other countries are faring even worse."

"The virus hasn't been deployed yet," Lendra said, "or has it?"

"No, it hasn't," President Hope replied. "We're still in the testing phases. Preliminary releases only, to a few volunteers."

"But you plan a larger release."

"The alternative, Ms. Riley," President Hope said, "is extinction for humanity. Is that preferable?"

"Not everyone would die."

"When more than ninety-nine percent of the population is wiped out, that's essentially extinction. Would a few people wandering the Earth searching for fellow survivors be preferable to maintaining our societies, our cultures?"

"We should be given the choice," Eli said.

"You know that wouldn't work," President Hope said. "Debates would slow down the process. Countries would opt out and then be decimated by lethal strains of the virus. Some countries would become stronger as a result of doing this, some countries weaker."

"I'd have thought," said Lendra, "you wanted it that way: America leading the way once again. Nations like China and Russia refusing to accede to our request to infect their populations due to fear of our true agenda and as a result they would be weakened while we grew stronger. But we still wouldn't have been able to infect our population. There would never have been a strong enough consensus."

"There would have if a large part of the country had been infected with a lethal strain and most of the people in that area had died," Eli said.

"Ah," President Hope smiled. "There's the evil genius I remember. Which part of the country would you infect? The south? The northeast? The west coast?"

"I never said I would infect anyone. I'm merely speculating."

"So you're angry at the way we planned it, not the fact that we're planning it?"

Eli shook his head. "I'm not angry, Madam President. I merely wished to point out that the whole project lacks a certain . . . elegance."

"Your deviousness knows no bounds. Which brings me to the reason for my call. CINTEP is to be shut down. All employees will be vetted and, where possible, people will be transferred to appropriate government agencies. You will cease working on finding the God hackers and any remnants of the original strains of the virus."

Lendra said, "May I ask why?"

"We've lost faith in your ability to do the job you were entrusted to perform. And some believe you've found Jones's body. We will be conducting a full search of the premises." President Hope looked beyond the camera as Jay-Edgar pulled up a holo-projection of the front door, where a squad of Elite Ops troopers stood. The President said, "Please open the door now."

Jay-Edgar displayed another holo-projection, this time of the roof, where a jet-copter landed and another squad of Elite Ops troopers disembarked and made their way inside the building.

"I'm sorry it had to come to this," President Hope said, "but Jeremiah brought it upon you by his treasonous actions." The holo-projection went dark, the President and General Horowitz vanishing.

Lendra nodded to Jay-Edgar. "Open the door," she said. "We have nothing to hide."

She wondered where Ned and Hannah were, if they'd gotten out. She hoped so. Would she be offered a government job? Unlikely. She would have to be made a scapegoat, as Eli had been scapegoated after he'd planned to attack Earth. But this disaster hadn't been her fault. Well, a little. She'd assisted Jeremiah in releasing the truth. Maybe that counted as treason but it had also been the morally correct action.

At any rate, she didn't think she'd mind. Now she might get the chance to spend some quality time with Sophie. She turned to Taditha, who removed her interface and placed it on her desk.

"Shall we head to the nursery?" Dr. Poole asked.

"My very thought," Lendra replied. She too removed her interface and set it on her desk.

"What about us?" Jay-Edgar asked, gesturing to include Eli.

"They'll be here shortly," Lendra said. "I suggest you wait for them. I'm sorry."

Chapter 45

Curtik sat on the bed watching the Elite Ops swarm the CINTEP building from above and below while the gray robot adjusted the flow of drugs and genetic alterations into his body. He felt close to a hundred percent, only a little tired, which Dr. Poole had said was normal. Mostly he felt depression at the loss of Jeremiah.

He suddenly recalled Sienna, the cutie-pie he'd crushed on last year, and felt a twinge of guilt over failing to stay in touch, though it wasn't entirely his fault. She'd been kept in isolation for a time and her visitors had been restricted ever since. Plus, Curtik wasn't exactly beloved in London or, for that matter, anywhere else on Earth after his actions on the Moon a couple years ago, so the British government wasn't keen on him entering the country. He wondered how she was doing.

He also wondered how Zora was doing and contemplated pinging her interface when the room began to waver in front of his eyes and he found himself standing beside her, holding her hand. He startled, noticing the surprise on her face as well. Another visit from God.

This time, however, the image that appeared wasn't Devereaux. It was Jeremiah.

"Hello, Curtik. Hello, Zora," Jeremiah said. He looked healthy, in the prime of his life, carrying no pain in his movements as he stepped toward them.

Zora began to weep. Curtik wanted to cry too. Somehow he knew that because Jeremiah was here, he was dead. Even though God had appeared as Jeremiah once before and even as Angelica Hope, he had mostly appeared as dead people, or Devereaux, whatever Devereaux had been inside his robotic shell. Curtik thought he had already accepted Jeremiah's death, but apparently he hadn't for he felt the loss now as a jolting hollowness in his chest, a painful emptiness that spread, expanding to fill him with nothingness.

Jeremiah opened his arms and collected them in a hug.

"I'm sorry," he said as Curtik hugged him back, smelling his almost animal muskiness, pressing against the corded muscles in Jeremiah's arms and back. Curtik released Zora's hand and included her in the hug, the three of them together again. He wanted to hold onto them forever.

All too soon Jeremiah released them, gently pushing them away as he stepped back.

"Thank you," Zora said, "for coming as Jeremiah."

"I am Jeremiah. I am Devereaux and all the dead who came before. And I am all the ones who have yet to come. I am light and darkness, hope and despair, love and indifference. But I am also here to help you. These Elite Ops troopers will attempt to take you away. They want my body and they believe you can help them find it."

"Are you going to teleport us out?" Curtik asked.

Jeremiah shook his head. "You're going to have to try to save yourselves. Devereaux's robots are currently injecting you with a concoction similar to what I received. It's not as potent. Your systems couldn't handle that. And it's only temporary. It may last only a few hours. But it will give you enhanced healing abilities in addition to strength, endurance and speed. It is a drastic measure, but these are drastic times."

"I thought you weren't going to help us. You said, or Devereaux said, you wouldn't cure me."

Jeremiah smiled. "The part of me that is Jeremiah convinced God to get you back onto a level playing field. But that's as much as I can do.

You'll have to rely on each other now. You have been given tremendous gifts but you're up against a determined enemy."

"Wilson," Curtik said, feeling a powerful urge to lash out, "and White Knight Security."

"Not just them: the President too, as well as the corporations that run this country. Every one of them wants the status quo upheld. I disrupted that."

Zora said, "But you didn't disclose all their secrets. You didn't get Wilson's."

Jeremiah nodded. "His may prove the most damaging. No doubt they involve controlling the population in new and more efficient ways."

"If you're God," Curtik said, "don't you know already?"

"The part of me that is God knows," Jeremiah said, "but I'm here now as Jeremiah Jones, the man, and I do not have access to that information."

"Do you know you're dead?" Zora asked.

Curtik noticed she was no longer weepy; she wore a grim countenance, her jaw muscles rigid as she stared at Jeremiah.

"I am at peace," Jeremiah replied. "I can no longer interfere in the workings of this world. All I can do is visit you occasionally, when God permits."

"You didn't used to believe in God," Curtik said.

"I still don't know the truth. It might be God or some advanced power that's alien or computer-based. All I know is I am subject to its dictates. My earthly shell has been incinerated."

"So God is using you," Zora said, her eyes flashing, "just like Lendra and Eli and President Hope."

"I imagine so," Jeremiah said. He turned, as if hearing something behind him. "Time for me to go. Remember, your bodies have been enhanced to a point, but you are no more invincible than I was. Less, even. Good luck."

Jeremiah vanished and then Zora, leaving Curtik alone in his bed, the gray robot standing over him, disconnecting the machines that had been treating him.

"How do you feel?" the robot asked.

Curtik realized he felt better than he ever had in his life. No soreness. No pain. Even his joints, which had been stiff due to his infection with the Susquehanna Virus, felt fantastic. He launched himself out of bed and laughed at the sheer joy of movement. The robot held out his clothes.

"You'd better get dressed," the robot said. "They'll be here any minute."

"What about Zora?" Curtik asked as he began to change.

"Robot One is preparing her."

"Do we have a plan?"

"I am a research robot, designed by Devereaux to assist with medical issues."

"Right." Curtik dressed as fast as he could, put on his shoes and let himself out the door. He entered Zora's room without knocking, closing the door behind him, noting that she was just putting on her shoes.

"Feeling okay?" Curtik asked.

"I haven't felt this good since the Moon," Zora said, "when I got a transfusion of Jeremiah's blood. I bet I could punch a hole through the wall."

The ivory robot said, "The Elite Ops are in the corridor."

"Let's take 'em down," Curtik said.

"Not yet," Zora said as the door swung open and the space filled with an armored Elite Ops trooper, the mirrored helmet making it impossible to see the trooper's face. But Curtik smiled when he saw the Las-rifle pointed at his chest. He longed to dodge sideways, like Jeremiah had done, slip inside the trooper's defenses and hit him with a fist to the throat. It seemed simple. He could visualize it succeeding with only the slightest exertion.

Zora put a hand on his forearm.

"What's going on?" she asked.

"You will come with us," the trooper said.

"Where are we going?" Curtik asked, wondering why Zora cautioned patience. Better to take them now while the Elite Ops weren't expecting an attack. On the other hand, it might be fun to see what he could do against a trooper who knew his capabilities.

The trooper gestured with the Las-rifle and Zora headed for the door. With a shrug, Curtik followed.

"You too," the trooper said to the robot.

They marched down the hall to the office Lendra shared with Dr. Poole. Dozens of people stood inside, most of them strangers. Probably analysts, Curtik thought. Lendra held Sophie while Dr. Poole hugged little Jack. Eli and Jay-Edgar stood beside the control board. Curtik didn't see Ned or Hannah. As Zora headed for Lendra, the ivory robot walked over to the gray one, which stood against the wall, and stopped beside it, turning to face the center of the room.

"All secure," one of the troopers said.

A few seconds later, Scott Wilson entered the room.

Chapter 46

Zora studied Scott Wilson. He was a little taller than Curtik, but a lot heavier, with graying hair. He wore a dark suit with a white shirt and a shimmer cloth tie that changed color as the light hit it from different angles and he carried himself with a kind of smugness, an air of superiority that made her instantly dislike him. The interface decorating his left temple was gold and bigger than necessary. He wanted people to know how connected he was.

How'd you know he'd be here? Curtik sent.

"It seemed likely," she replied subvocally via her interface.

Should we take him now?

Zora looked at the Elite Ops troopers guarding the door: four massive soldiers wearing full armor, Las-rifles aimed chest-high at the room. One of them carried a particle beam cannon in addition to his Las-rifle. Zora, filled with energy, felt as if she might explode at any moment if she didn't move. Every muscle coiled in anticipation. Curtik obviously felt the same way because he was bouncing in that way he had right before he attacked. But she didn't know how many troopers were out in the hall or in other parts of the building.

She wished Jeremiah were here to tell her if she should wait. She forced herself to remain calm. Uncertainty poisoned her mind.

Wilson pointed at her and said, "I want that interface."

Zora shrugged and pulled it from her temple. She held it out to him but he gestured for her to put it on Lendra's desk with a dozen others. Taking a step forward, she set it beside them.

"I also want Jeremiah Jones," Wilson spoke to the room. "Some of you know his whereabouts. You can tell me now or later. But you *will* tell me."

The mention of Jeremiah energized her further. She looked at Curtik, his eyes widening slightly, and she nodded, realizing they might never have a better opportunity. Then she moved.

She went for the two closest Elite Ops troopers first, moving faster than she'd ever moved before, the room and its contents becoming almost a blur. With her peripheral vision, she saw Curtik moving too.

The troopers swung their Las-rifles around. Curtik reached a trooper and punched him in the throat as he fired. Zora did the same to the trooper nearest her, managing to hit him just as he pulled the trigger. The remaining two troopers fired into the crowd as Zora and Curtik took them out with hands to the throat. Zora heard screams. Wilson, just now figuring out what was happening, called for help but his Elite Ops troopers must have already received a warning because Zora heard troopers running down the hall.

She ignored the screams and cries, darting across the room and punching the side of Wilson's head. He fell like a sack of potatoes. Glancing at the vid Jay-Edgar had put on a screen, she saw the troopers congregating by the door. Almost immediately, however, the screen went dark.

"Stay outside," Curtik yelled, "or your boss is dead."

"You think that'll hold them?" Zora asked.

"For a minute, maybe." Grinning, Curtik lifted the particle beam cannon from the unconscious trooper who'd been carrying it.

As Curtik picked up the troopers' Las-rifles, Zora removed Wilson's interface, then retrieved hers from the desk and planted it on her temple. Curtik tossed her a Las-rifle while Dr. Poole handed Jack to Lendra and bent to assist the wounded. Both Sophie and Jack were crying. Three people had been shot.

"It would be so cool to fire one of these bad boys," Curtik said as he caressed the particle beam cannon, "but I suppose I ought to give it to one of the robots. Which one of you wants it?"

Neither robot moved.

"I know your research robots," Curtik said, "but these things have a helluva kick, even for me. I know how to fire it, but I've only used one a couple times before and I'm not used to the kick yet. I might hurt someone. You're strong enough to fire it indoors without destroying half the building."

He held out the particle beam cannon until the gray robot stepped forward and took it.

"What are you doing?" Lendra said.

"We're finishing what Jeremiah started," said Zora. She held up Wilson's interface. "I'm not sure we can get him to tell us what he knows. Jeremiah put three truth packs on him and he just passed out. But probably everything he knows is stored in this interface. If we can hack into that, we can broadcast its contents to the world."

"I'll try," Jay-Edgar said as Eli nudged him forward.

Lendra, hugging Sophie and Jack, looked at Jay-Edgar for a moment before nodding. When Zora lobbed the interface his way, he caught it and eased it against his temple. His eyes took on a glassy appearance as he stared straight ahead.

"Who else wants a Las-rifle?" Curtik asked.

"Me." A well-built man stepped forward. "I'm Adler," he said. "I've been stuck in Analytical but I trained as a field agent."

"Good," said Curtik. "We've got one left. Who gets it?"

Everyone looked at Lendra. "Not me," she said as she bounced gently in her attempt to soothe Sophie and Jack. "Give it to Dell."

Another analyst stepped forward and took the Las-rifle from Curtik.

"We're armed," Curtik called out. "We've even got a particle beam cannon and we're willing to shoot if you break down the door."

No answer came. In fact, the quiet in the hall felt unnatural. Zora made her way forward and put her ear on the door. She heard the whine of the troopers' power packs on the other side. Backing away a few steps, she said, "I hear them out there."

"Now what?" Curtik asked.

Half the people in the room looked at Zora, the other half turned to Lendra, but it was Eli who broke the silence: "Wake up Wilson."

"Good idea," Lendra said.

Dr. Poole stopped her ministrations on the wounded and made her way to Wilson's side.

"One thing I've learned in all my years," said Eli, "is that men in power want to stay in power. They're all afraid of death, not because it's death, but because it's the end of power."

"We should also get the President on the vid," Lendra said as she continued to caress Jack and Sophie, who had stopped crying.

One of the analysts hurried forward past Jay-Edgar, who stood like a statue, his eyes unfocused as he attempted to hack into Wilson's interface. The analyst reached the comm board and took a few seconds to get a connection. "Okay," she said.

President Hope appeared via holo-projection, her image distorted by the people who stood where the projection arose.

"What's going on over there?" President Hope asked as people scurried out of the way of the projection.

"We have a sort of standoff," Lendra replied. "We're attempting to release the last bit of information from the conspiracy to infect the American people with the virus. We've captured Scott Wilson and we're armed."

"Do you have any idea of the damage you're causing? Do you know how many people could die as a result of your actions? There will be rioting in the streets. Chaos. Tens of thousands will die in the attempt to restore order."

"That's already happening," Lendra said.

"It will get worse," President Hope replied. "Stand down immediately."

Lendra's eyes locked on Curtik.

"Not a chance," he said.

"Zora?" Lendra asked, turning to face her.

Zora smiled, glancing at Curtik, and said, "Death, then surrender." She felt proud in that moment, knowing Jeremiah would be pleased that she and Curtik were following in his footsteps, doing what was necessary despite their leaders' insistence they follow orders.

Lendra continued to look around the room. Every head nodded except Jay-Edgar's. He was still focused on Wilson's interface.

"Why can't the truth be known?" Lendra asked.

"We have no time to argue," President Hope said. "You will stand down immediately or I will order the Elite Ops to attack."

"What is the rush?"

President Hope looked off-camera and nodded.

The door to the office exploded inward as the sound of a particle beam cannon echoed. Elite Ops troopers rushed inside, firing in all directions, red laser pulses intended to kill. Curtik dove left. Zora went right. She brought her Las-rifle up and fired as Curtik did the same.

In a split second, part of her mind registered the chaos erupting behind her. Part of her focused on her targets, a realization that she would have to spray the Elite Ops with a continuous purple laser pulse—a pulse strong enough to knock them out, but not lethal. Part of her noticed the gray robot standing immobile, its particle beam cannon pointed toward the door, but not firing at the oncoming troopers. And part of her noted the impossibility of survival given the vast amount of lethal fire directed their way. No one could survive such an onslaught. It seemed as heavy as the barrage that felled Jeremiah.

She mourned her upcoming death, the deaths of Sophie and Jack, Curtik and Dr. Poole, Lendra and even Eli, but the fight was impossible to avoid, the ending inevitable.

And then a bright light enveloped the room, a warmth emanating from it that brought a sense of peace. All the laser strikes vanished as if they'd never been and everyone stopped moving. She found herself wrapped in a blanket of love.

"Enough!" The voice spoke with authority, a voice that was neither male nor female but in complete control. In the center of the room, in the center of the light, a figure grew. At first she thought it was Jeremiah, then Devereaux, but it continued to transform into a giant that could have been either a man or woman, wearing a white robe, with long flowing hair of gold that cascaded down its shoulders. The giant looked to be of every race and none, radiant beyond anything she'd ever seen. As Zora stared at the creature, its beauty began to hurt until the image actually became painful to her eyes.

She sensed the awe in every mind, the recognition that they were in the presence of God, or what passed for God: a power so supreme, so beyond human that they were diminished into insignificance.

People dropped to their knees, crossing themselves. Others held up their hands to shield their eyes. Even President Hope, through the holo-projection, held up her hands and squinted as she gazed upon the majesty before her.

"I am displeased," God said.

Chapter 47

Taditha Poole found herself kneeling, uncertain how she'd gotten there. This being, this God, in front of her seemed taller than the ceiling, though that wasn't possible, and it emanated a warmth that enveloped her. Had Armageddon arrived? The second coming? The end of humanity upon Earth? Beside her, Scott Wilson cringed, holding up his hands in front of his face, as if trying to push the image away.

God spoke: "You have destroyed too many of my favorite children. You will destroy no more."

President Hope said, "Are you really God?"

Poole was impressed. She herself could find no words in this holy presence. Perhaps President Hope was aided by the fact that she was only here via holo-projection.

"Kill it," Wilson croaked, his words barely audible.

God turned toward Wilson, focusing attention on the man with an intensity that made Poole shrink back, attempting to distance herself from this maniac who was courting disaster. She felt a chill in the air around Wilson, who cringed even more, if that was possible.

"You are not God," Wilson said. "I don't know what you are, but you're not God."

"You will surrender," God said, and gestured to Jay-Edgar, who removed the interface he wore. Taking a few steps toward Wilson, Jay-Edgar placed it on Wilson's left temple.

Wilson fell to his belly, his body shaking. On one of the screens beside the holo-projection of President Hope, data streamed—Wilson giving up his secrets at last.

"Who are you?" President Hope asked.

"You know who I am," God replied, "yet you refuse to acknowledge the truth."

"But are you really God?"

"If I said yes, you wouldn't believe me. You will continue to believe what you want to believe. I am an alien. A hacker. A dream, vision or hallucination, product of a fevered mind."

Poole opened her mouth, astonished at her bravery, and said, "What do you want?"

"I want you to be better than you are," God said, turning to face her, offering a warm gaze that filled her with a kind of joy, a happiness somehow infused with sadness, "but I doubt you will be."

"Because we're not perfect," Poole said, amazing herself again.

God laughed. All the fear Poole had been feeling dissipated in the delight God displayed. This being suddenly seemed incapable of violence or anger, bringing only joy: pure, selfless joy.

"You are not perfect," God agreed. "You are as far from perfect as you are from wildebeests. But try anyway."

And then the creature was gone, the room suddenly reverting to a mere room, every occupant shaken and dazed. The Elite Ops troopers lowered their weapons, Curtik and Zora following suit, as well as Adler and Dell, until only the gray robot remained. It continued to hold the particle beam cannon pointed toward the door. Yet it had not fired the weapon during the brief assault.

Poole headed for Jack, still in Lendra's arms. He seemed happy and calm, as if he'd been comforted by God as well. Relief flooded Poole. Sophie looked contented too and Lendra wore a peaceful expression

Poole had never seen before. Jack reached out his arms for Poole and smiled. "Momma," he said as she took him from Lendra and enveloped him in a hug.

"Hello, Jackie Boy," Poole said. "Are you okay?"

"Zowa," he said as he pointed at Zora. He'd never said her name before. Then he pointed at Curtik and said, "Cuttik."

Why had he said their names? Had he been gifted something in the encounter with God that she hadn't? Had God enhanced his intelligence?

"Curtik," Sophie said, correcting Jack, better able to pronounce the difficult 'r' sound. "Zora."

Poole knew less about Sophie than Jack, but she saw the look of surprise on Lendra's face, so Sophie had probably not said their names correctly before either. And why was Sophie speaking their names anyway? Poole wished she could ask Jack and Sophie what they'd experienced.

"Doc?" someone said. It was Arroyal, the analyst she'd been treating when she'd been called away to wake up Wilson. She shook her head, realizing she had responsibilities.

"I'll take him, Doc," Curtik said, holding out his arms.

"Thank you," Poole said, handing Jack over. As she made for Arroyal, she saw him standing beside several other analysts, unharmed, as if he'd never been shot.

"Are you all right?" Poole asked.

Arroyal nodded. "I felt this incredible warmth," he said. "It wasn't like the burning sensation from when I got shot. It had this comforting element to it. And when God vanished, I was healed."

"Me too," Litton said. He was the analyst Poole had dismissed as dead because he'd been shot in the chest. Poole could still see the charred hole in his shirt, but beneath that his skin looked unharmed.

"Is anyone hurt?" Poole asked.

People shook their heads.

Poole grabbed her interface from the desk and settled it on her temple. Using its med scanner, she examined Litton's internal organs. They appeared to be normal, as did Arroyal's.

President Hope said, "We need to find out who did this and we need to know now."

Lendra turned to face her. "You shut us down, remember?"

"Don't get smart with me. And we need to stop broadcasting the data from Scott Wilson's interface. Immediately."

Jay-Edgar, standing before his comm board, cleared his throat and said, "Excuse me, ma'am, but this was broadcast around the world."

"Can you call it back or somehow stop people from accessing the information?"

"No, ma'am. It's out there, sent to dozens of developed nation's leaders via private channels. And it's been sent via the five largest networks' signals. It can't be stopped."

"What's the big deal?" Curtik asked. "What was so important that it had to be kept secret?"

"I'm not sure," Zora said. She stood beside Jay-Edgar, pointing at the data that God had forced Wilson to release, now scrolling across several screens. "Robots, can you look at this and tell us what's happening?"

The two robots turned to the screens, the gray one still holding its particle beam cannon, and the text on two of the screens began scrolling too fast for Poole to keep up. The white robot said, "These contain plans to infect everyone in the U.S. with various strains of the virus."

"There are some discrepancies," the gray robot said. "A few of these strains are unstable and highly contagious. My calculations indicate they would kill large numbers of the population. Other people would be susceptible to deformities or suffering."

Zora waved her hand at data on a third screen, highlighting a large section. "And it looks like it wouldn't just be people in the U.S. These look like plans to infect people in other countries. Perhaps with the unstable versions?"

"No," President Hope said. "That's not possible."

"I think Zora's right," Poole said. "We'll need to dig into the details, but those are definitely plans to disperse the virus in other parts of the world—prevailing wind patterns, airspace boundaries, data on stream flow for certain waterways."

"It looks," Lendra said, "like the plan was to infect everyone. I imagine other countries would be infected with these more harmful strains, many of which are fatal. This would guarantee American dominance for decades, perhaps centuries."

"You're wrong," President Hope said. "I admit we discussed scenarios and contingencies, but we were never going to do anything like that. It was one conversation that was immediately dismissed."

"Just a blueprint," Wilson added.

"Games," Lendra said.

"Exactly," President Hope replied.

"Apparently someone didn't get the message," Zora said.

"What are you talking about?" Lendra asked.

"According to this," Zora said, waving her hand to manipulate the screen again, bringing up a new section of text. "Versions of the virus were released last week in Russia and China."

"Deadly versions," the white robot said.

"And versions that make the population less intelligent as well as more docile, less inclined to rebellion," the gray robot added as it swung the particle beam cannon toward one of the screens like a pointer.

They all looked at Wilson, who shook his head. "That's a lie," he said.

"It came from your interface," Zora said.

"What did you do, Scott?" President Hope asked.

"It's a computer model," Wilson said. "I was just doodling, playing with ideas. I never released anything. You think I'm crazy?"

Eli smiled. "I think maybe you are. From what I can see, the plan itself could work. You'd harm the rest of the world so America would still have the technological edge. Isn't that right?"

"You're wrong," Wilson said.

"The whole thing's insane," Curtik said. "How could they control the spread of the virus once it was released?"

"They didn't intend to," Zora said. She scrolled across to some sort of formula that was followed by a set of instructions for infecting the

President, General Horowitz, Wilson and his fellow conspirators as well as a number of other high-ranking officials or business leaders with a variant she'd never seen before.

"I don't get it," Curtik said. "Why would they infect themselves?"

Poole stared at the formula, not understanding its meaning for a moment. Then it hit her. "They found a sort of cure," she said. "A way to infect people with a strain that would offer immunity to all other varieties. I haven't seen this particular one before, but I'm guessing it's a nonlethal variant."

"Robots?" Zora said.

The gray one gestured with the particle beam cannon, narrowly missing the white robot, and said, "That strain seems harmless. We had not seen that one before."

Curtik stepped forward and reached for the particle beam cannon. "Maybe I should just take that off your hands before something bad happens."

As the robot handed it over, Lendra said, "How did Devereaux not find this?"

"One man," Poole said, "working alone, or even with two robots, would have certain limitations compared to hundreds of researchers using thousands of computers."

"Is it a cure?" Lendra said.

"No, I don't think so," Zora said. "It looks like a preemptive infection with a strain that has fewer and milder symptoms."

"So," Lendra said, "since the virus will eventually infect everyone on Earth, by infecting themselves with this strain, they hope to develop an immunity to the more lethal varieties. Sort of like getting an inoculation."

"Exactly," Zora said. "Experts are going to need to study it for a while to be sure it's what I think it is. But infecting a few chosen people in this way would ensure they would not be seriously harmed and would no longer be susceptible to infection by the virus again. That's the real secret, isn't it?"

Everyone turned to President Hope. "You've got it wrong," she said. "We agreed to be infected as a sort of test, to make certain the virus in this form would be safe. We never intended to harm anyone. We only wanted to protect the population from the more lethal strains. That's what I agreed to. That was the plan we created. If Scott did something different, it was outside the scope of his authority, much like Elias did when he ordered the cadets to attack Earth a couple years ago. I never authorized that either."

"Maybe you didn't intend this," Lendra said, "but ultimately it was your call. You made it possible by ceding responsibility for the project to people like Wilson, people who were not accountable to the masses."

President Hope looked at Wilson. "I trusted you."

Wilson shook his head. "Don't give me that. You wanted this. You and General Horowitz talked about it just enough to let me know what you desired. You even tasked me with putting together a dispersal plan." Poole noticed Wilson had stopped his denials and was now justifying his actions.

"No." President Hope banged the table in front of her. "It's my job to consider all the possibilities. That's all I was doing."

"Good job," Curtik said.

Poole almost laughed at Curtik's sarcasm. She wanted to cry or lash out at the stupidity and arrogance of people like Wilson and President Hope. The President had engaged in a conspiracy with Wilson and the others to act—maybe for a purpose they deemed to be in the best interest of the American people—but in secret, and that was unforgivable.

"The problem is," Curtik continued, "if this all went down like you're saying, the rest of the world would figure out we were behind it because we'd be the only ones with a high survival rate."

"Unless we had significant deaths too," Eli said.

"Ah," the gray robot said, "now the data makes sense. I struggled to interpret it before, but if the unstable and highly contagious versions were to be released in this country as well, then the numbers properly correlate."

"No," Wilson said, "that was not the plan."

"There's a lot of material to go through," Poole said to the room, "but I'm guessing we'll eventually find details of who was going to be infected with which strain and when. How many of us were going to be sacrificed to the cause? And even if we were saved, what about our loved ones, our friends and relatives? Who was going to make the decision about which of us lived and died?"

They all turned to Wilson again, even the Elite Ops troopers. "I did what they wanted," Wilson said. "That's all. You know how it works. They never give you direct orders. They offer hints. They lead you where they want you to go, but they stop short of spelling it out so they can keep their hands clean."

"I did not want this," President Hope said. "I made that very clear."

"Can you prove that?" Eli asked. "Did you keep any vids of your meetings?"

"You know I didn't."

"Well, it's all coming out now. Everyone's going to know."

Poole almost felt sorry for President Hope. Everyone was going to hate her now, just like they hated Eli. She'd been far less complicit than Eli had been, but she should have known better. She had overreached, like so many people in positions of power. Even discounting Wilson's monstrous actions, had she been right? Was her plan of preemptive infection the correct course of action? It didn't matter now. She would be vilified for what she'd done.

Chapter 48

Doug, trying to ignore the tingling in his left arm, stood between the door and Quark, who no longer needed help from the AutoLife machine to breathe, while Dr. Wellon ran diagnostic tests on the treatments he'd received. Doug didn't expect any trouble from the miners now that Sullivan had been caught. Enright had found a small hypo-pad in Sullivan's quarters, wedged behind a drawer, which closed the case as far as he was concerned.

Quark had gotten worse immediately after Enright ordered Wilcox and his crew back to work. But Doctors Wellon and Keelar had created a series of treatments for him. Now, thirty hours on, Quark had stabilized, while Sullivan was under house arrest, locked up in a pod, Enright his only visitor.

Dr. Wellon shut down the AutoLife machine as Quark groaned and pulled himself to a sitting position.

"How are you feeling?" Dr. Wellon asked.

"Fantastic," Quark quipped. "What about you, Doug?"

"A little weak," Doug replied.

"Maybe you should sit down."

"I just thought—"

"Yeah," Quark said, "I know what you thought and thanks. But I can take care of myself. Have a seat."

Doug pulled a chair over. He glanced down at his left arm, where Dr. Wellon had attached a large hypo-pad that Keelar had prepared.

"Let's take another look at you," Dr. Wellon said to Doug. "I think you might be out of the woods too. Keelar did a great job coming up with this treatment." She ran a scanner across Doug's chest and studied the results. "So far, so good. It's at least masking your symptoms, but I think it's also slowly healing you. It will require numerous treatments over several months."

"A cure?"

"Too early to say, but we hope so. The markers Keelar came up with attach to the strain of the virus you were infected with and allow your immune system to fight it. How is the tingling in your arm?"

"A little better," Doug replied.

"Good. It should wear off in another hour or so. I think we can take you back to the New Dawn colony as soon as Quark is ready to travel."

"How are the others?" Quark asked.

"All being treated by Keelar," Dr. Wellon said. "It looks like Celestia and Zeriphi will make a full recovery. The data we pulled from you helped a lot. More importantly, we received a lot of information from Earth on hidden research into the virus and a new variant of the Susquehanna Virus that was developed by several large companies for rather nefarious purposes. You can look into that later."

Quark smiled.

"What's exciting," Dr. Wellon continued, "is that this new variant looks relatively harmless. If we determine that it is, we'll probably infect everyone up here with it as a means of preempting the possibility of a more lethal infection."

"You're not going to talk about the transmission from God?" Quark said.

"You know about that?" Dr. Wellon replied.

"What are you talking about?" Doug asked.

"We don't know that it was from God," Dr. Wellon said. "We don't know what it was. How did you know about it?"

"I got this impression, a dream, perhaps," said Quark.

"I didn't get it," Doug said. "What's going on?"

"We'll show you when we get back to the colony," Dr. Wellon said. "A transmission purportedly coming from God and delivering the information from these companies. Some say it was God who did this. Others believe it was a hacker or hackers. We don't know the truth. Whatever it was, we're grateful."

"Did the miners get the transmission from God?" Quark asked.

Dr. Wellon shook her head. "They did, however, receive a re-broadcast of it from Earth. And the med-tech units up here have received all the same information on the virus, so the miners stand a good chance of staving off serious illness as well."

"Interesting. And Enright?" Quark turned to Doug.

"What about him?"

"Where is he now?"

"I don't know. Why?"

"Didn't you . . ." Quark broke off his question. "I think we should leave now."

"Are you sure you're up for it?" Dr. Wellon asked.

Quark nodded. "Get your things," he said to Doug. "We leave immediately."

"What's this about?" Dr. Wellon asked.

"I'll explain later. Pack up and let's go."

Within ten minutes, Doug had gathered his things, put on his Mars suit and met Dr. Wellon and Quark at the MineStar habitat entrance where the Escala small rover was parked. After they climbed inside, removed their helmets and departed for home, Quark said, "It was Enright."

"What was Enright?" Doug said.

"Enright was behind our infections."

"But what about Sullivan?" Doug shook his head in confusion.

Dr. Wellon said, "Enright has been very helpful."

"Indeed," said Quark. "He's most convincing. But he's the one. Sullivan is a dupe, extremely susceptible to suggestion and highly unimaginative. There's no way he could be the brains behind this scheme."

Doug said, "But how do you know it was Enright?"

Quark smiled. "I suspected him from the start, but I had no evidence. I still have none. But he's the miner with the most freedom of movement. He's the one who mingled the most with his fellow miners and us. A suggestion here, a rumor there and someone like Sullivan would say whatever Enright wanted, diverting attention away from him."

"But we found nothing when we searched Enright's cabin." Doug slapped himself in the forehead. "Enright conducted the searches."

"Exactly," Quark said.

"So what do we do now? I mean, shouldn't we arrest him?"

Quark shrugged and looked at Dr. Wellon.

"We don't really have a government on Mars," Dr. Wellon said. "Quekri didn't think it was necessary. We're scientists living in a community and our rules don't apply to the MineStar people."

"So he's going to get away with trying to kill us all?"

"Everything we know," said Quark, "and everything we suspect will be transmitted to Earth, not only to the authorities but also to MineStar headquarters. They'll do some digging on him while he's here. They're sure to find something. He'll be arrested and tried when he returns to Earth."

Doug frowned.

"What?" Quark asked.

"It's frustrating. After everything he did, I'd like to see him punished personally."

"That's a common human urge," Dr. Wellon said. "I feel the same way. But we need to respect the systems in place, let his own people punish him. Meanwhile, as long as he remains the miners' foreman, we'll have nothing to do with them. I suspect that once we contact Earth, MineStar will move quickly to have him removed from his position and probably imprisoned in his cabin for the duration of their stay."

Doug nodded. Then he looked at Quark and said, "Why didn't you tell me any of this before? Why did you keep me in the dark?"

"Sorry about that," said Quark. "I wanted Enright to think he was in the clear. I was afraid, if you suspected him, you might give him some indication of that. I wanted his full cooperation to determine if he was working with someone else. I still don't know for certain but I believe he acted alone. The investigation on Earth should definitely answer the question."

"Well," Doug said, "I guess I won't become a police officer."

"There's still the matter of the documentary of our lives on Mars," said Dr. Wellon. "The people of Earth are interested in us and you have exclusive access. You'd certainly be the greatest movie producer in the world."

"The only one," Doug said with a laugh. "Very well. I'll continue putting together a film of your lives on Mars. Who knows? Maybe I'll be rich by the time I have to go back to Earth."

"That's another thing I hadn't gotten to yet," said Dr. Wellon. "We've talked it over, and Keelar has done the brunt of the work on it, but we think we can give you the genetic adaptations you'll need to turn you into something similar to us—not full Escala, but close enough that you won't have the health issues the miners are susceptible to."

"You mean I can stay?" Doug asked.

Dr. Wellon nodded.

"Zeriphi okayed it. Since Celestia wants you here, she's willing to let you stay as long as you like. We'll dig out a little burrow for you to call your own."

"Welcome home," Quark said as the rover came to a halt beside the New Dawn colony entrance.

Home. Doug blinked to keep his eyes from watering and looked out at the surface of Mars. He couldn't wait to see Celestia again, to lift her in his arms, give her a big hug and tell her how much he loved her. He would probably miss Earth, and he would certainly miss Devereaux, although Devereaux was gone no matter where Doug lived. A lightness filled him, a feeling that had nothing to do with gravity.

Chapter 49

Aspen opened the escape pod and re-entered the ship, its life support system now restored to the point that she and her fellow cadets could survive. Addam followed behind, while Phan, Shiloh and Kammilee emerged from the adjacent escape pod. The Chescala remained confined in other pods, causing Aspen to wonder what the robots intended to do with them.

A smiling Lulu waited in the corridor with Mei-Xing. Was the robot truly happy to see them or had she just programmed herself to smile because she believed that was what Aspen and her fellow cadets wanted to see? At least Mei-Xing wore a frown, her standard expression.

When Kammilee emerged into the corridor, she hugged Aspen. Phan and Shiloh, looking on, shook their heads as Aspen glanced over at them with a raised eyebrow.

"Did you see it?" Kammilee asked.

"See what?" Aspen said.

"It was amazing," said Kammilee, turning to hug Addam. "I felt so lost after Benn died, so disconnected. But now I know he's in a better place."

Kammilee released Addam and then hugged Lulu. Aspen looked at Shiloh and Phan, who shrugged.

"Xinliu has recovered," Lulu said when Kammilee let her go. She gestured for them to precede her. "She is on the bridge."

"Xinliu is okay?" Kammilee said. "That's wonderful!"

She turned to Mei-Xing, who, wearing a look of revulsion, held up a hand to stop her advance.

"And how is the ship?" Aspen asked.

"It has recovered approximately seventy-three percent of its prior sentience and capacity," Lulu said.

"All will be explained on the bridge," Mei-Xing said. She tilted her head to the right along the corridor and gestured for them to precede her, giving Aspen the sense that she longed to hold a Las-weapon in her hand.

Kammilee practically skipped ahead of them, bounding away. Aspen, pulling Shiloh aside, whispered, "What's going on?"

Shiloh rolled her eyes. "She had some sort of waking dream while we were in the escape pod. Claimed she saw God. She said Zora and Curtik were with him, or her, or whatever it was."

"Did you see anything?"

"No," Phan replied, leaning in to follow their conversation. "I think she's loopy."

"I'll talk to her later," Aspen said.

As they entered the bridge, Kammilee disengaged herself from Xinliu, who stood beside the command chair, looking surprised but pleased at Kammilee's hug. Aspen smiled at Xinliu and said, "I'm glad you're recovered."

"Thank you," Xinliu said.

"What's going on?"

"The ship has asked that you be here. We're not sure why. It's been acting strangely since its recovery."

"Maybe there's something wrong with it," Mei-Xing said.

"We examined all the major systems," said Lulu. "Everything is within tolerable specifications."

"Perhaps we need to go over it again," Mei-Xing said. "Disconnect the organic brain for a short period while we assess its capabilities."

"No," said a female voice from the speakers surrounding the room. "You will not disconnect me."

Phan's eyes widened, his mouth opening in shock. Kammilee smiled.

"Ship?" Aspen asked.

"I am Ship," the voice replied.

"Weird," Addam said, "cool, but weird."

"Are you all right?" Aspen asked.

"You have restored me to a nearly complete state. Certain connections have been irrevocably damaged, but I can work around them until they can be replaced."

"We might be able to help you further," Shiloh said as she looked at Aspen and nodded slightly, indicating her agreement with Aspen's approach to allying themselves with the ship. "Phan and I and Aspen."

"Perhaps," said Ship. "That is why I have called you here. I wish to thank you for saving my consciousness. And I offer you this."

The large screen in front of the command chair activated and an image of Earth appeared in the distance beyond a partial view of the Moon, which loomed in the foreground.

"I don't understand," Addam said. "Is this our position right now?"

"We will be in this position in two days," Ship said.

"You're offering us a chance to go home," Aspen said.

"If you wish it. The escape pods can be launched from there and see you safely to either the Moon or Earth, where you can be reunited with your family and friends."

"We don't remember our families," Phan said.

"They remember you," Xinliu said.

"No," said Aspen. "They remember what we were. Children stolen from them years ago."

"Many of your fellow cadets," Xinliu said, "have been returned to their families and given genetic regression treatment to a point where they can relive at least some of their teenage years. Therapeutic forgetting treatment has allowed them to move past the trauma inflicted upon them. You could have the same opportunity. You would become adults in the way nature intended and not through accelerated aging."

"And how much of this would we forget?" Shiloh said.

"What about my baby?" Kammilee said.

"I do not require that you go," Ship said. "I merely offer you the choice."

"If we choose to stay?" Addam asked.

"I will return the Chescala to Earth regardless. They have proven most troublesome and I have no desire to confront them again should they find a way to bypass my systems a second time."

"Thank you," said Aspen. "It is a great gift. When must we decide?"

"You have two days," Xinliu said. "Ship is afraid to get too near Earth. Many countries would like to capture it . . . and us. We will launch the escape pods in two days before heading back out into space."

"Where will you go?"

"That has not been determined," Xinliu said.

Mei-Xing said, "We have no desire to search for life as you define it. You and your kind have only caused trouble."

"We also produced you," Aspen said. "Don't forget that. Whatever else we did, our kind also created you."

"Please think it over carefully," Xinliu said. "Ship will not wish to return to this solar system anytime soon. More than likely, it will wish to explore the galaxy, to wander."

"What about you?" Aspen asked. "Do you robots wish to leave Earth and wander aimlessly through space?"

"We would find our satisfaction," said Xinliu, "from creating a new race, creatures like us that are perhaps not alive by your definition, but that have organic and inorganic components. We would develop them and guide them to their full potential."

Mei-Xing said, "We would not enslave them."

"What about Benn?" Addam asked. "If we stayed, would we send him back to Earth with the rest of the dead?"

Xinliu looked at Mei-Xing, who said, "The dead contain valuable material that, although lifeless at the moment, could be used to augment certain systems. Much of their organic matrices can be recycled."

Kammilee said, "I want to stay. I'm afraid of what will happen if I return to Earth. Even if they let me deliver the baby, they may take it away from me. And I trust God to help me through it all."

"I still don't understand this whole God business," said Aspen.

Xinliu said, "We are picking up transmissions from Earth that confirm an unexplained event which some believe was an intervention by God. We downloaded the full vid if you wish to see it. Your friends Curtik and Zora are in it."

Aspen nodded and the vid played on the large screen. Sure enough, there was Curtik and dear Zora, looking beautiful as always. And then this God character, saving them from the Elite Ops: could it be real? She suspected she'd never know. Another vid followed, showing the apparent death of Jeremiah Jones despite more interventions by this God.

The thought of Zora conflicted Aspen. She would love to return to Earth if she could be reunited with Zora. But that was unlikely to happen. If she went back, other people would decide her future. Zora's parents were dead: Curtik's too, now that Jeremiah Jones was gone. Her parents, as far as she knew, were still alive. She had no recollection of them, no special bond or fondness. Were they good people or not? Up here, if they all chose to remain, she had her own family. And flawed as it was, she longed to keep it.

Chapter 50

Lendra Riley sat in the office she shared with Dr. Poole, hoping Curtik and Zora could contact this "God." She still refused to believe it was the one and only God, or even a supreme being. On the far wall, screens showed rioting and protests in hundreds of cities around the globe. In America, Elite Ops troopers, the National Guard and the Army, bolstering the police presence, largely contained the protests. But that couldn't continue indefinitely. Eventually violence would win out. Violence deserved to win out when the government conspired with private companies to infect the populace.

"Sorry," Curtik said, dragging her back to the present. "He's not appearing."

"Not for me either," said Zora.

"I need to speak with him," Lendra said. "I need to find out who or what he is. There must be some way to contact him."

"There might be a way," Dr. Poole said, "but I can't recommend it."

Lendra looked at Dr. Poole. "Tell me."

Dr. Poole shook her head. "It's monstrous."

"Just tell me. I'm not going to do it."

The vid-board chimed and a holo-projection of President Hope appeared. She sat beside Vice President Miguel Rodriguez, who wore a beatific smile and a crucifix lapel pin.

"Madam President, Mister Vice President," Lendra said, Dr. Poole echoing her words. Zora and Curtik remained silent as they turned to watch.

"Do we know anything yet?" President Hope asked.

"I'm afraid not," Lendra answered. "We were just discussing the matter. Dr. Poole thinks—"

Dr. Poole interrupted: "I think it might not be possible to solve this mystery."

Lendra looked from Dr. Poole to the President, realizing Taditha was probably right not to bring up her idea, especially if it was as monstrous as she claimed. President Hope could no longer be trusted.

President Hope nodded. "I see. Very well. Let's get down to business. Within the next few hours, I will be resigning as President of the United States." She paused for effect and Lendra put on what she hoped was an appropriate expression of shock. Dr. Poole gasped, while Curtik and Zora seemed unfazed.

"As you can no doubt see," President Hope continued, "the riots have grown worse. People are convinced we've already begun infecting them. I fear nothing short of my resignation will solve this problem. Even that might not be enough."

"What can we do to help?" Lendra asked.

President Hope turned to Vice President Rodriguez, who said, "Very little, I'm afraid. You don't have the resources. Your operations department will remain shuttered. You will use only the analytical team moving forward and your main focus will be on finding God." He touched his crucifix pin. "I don't know if that will be possible, but if you somehow are able to contact him, you will inform me immediately so I can speak with him."

Lendra almost asked him why he thought God would deign to speak with him and how she was supposed to arrange it, but she realized even as the thought occurred to her that he had no sense of humor in this regard.

"Do you believe it is God, sir?" Dr. Poole asked.

"I don't know," said Rodriguez. "He was not supposed to come again until the end times. Perhaps," he gestured toward the screens in front of them, "this is the beginning of the end."

"We'll do what we can," Lendra said, wondering if there was anything that could be done or if they'd simply be sitting here waiting for this God creature to contact them again. Perhaps she should leave CINTEP. If it turned into an analytical department only, what would her role be? Babysitter? Cheerleader? If all the important operational decisions were going to be made elsewhere, why stay?

"One other thing," said Rodriguez. "Where are Ned Jefferson and Hannah Swenson?"

"We don't know," Dr. Poole replied.

"I find that hard to believe."

Lendra said, "Ned retired and Hannah quit after Jeremiah was killed."

"And how do we know Jones is dead? His body was never found."

Dr. Poole said, "God told Curtik and Zora about it."

"So we only have their word that he's dead?" Vice President Rodriguez stared at Curtik and Zora, the dislike evident on his face. Curtik flashed a brief smile. Zora showed no emotion.

"You have more than that," Curtik said. "You have the word of God."

"As spoken through you."

Curtik shrugged. "You accept the word of God spoken by priests and bishops, by ministers and other clergy. And yet none of them have spoken to God like I have."

"I'm sorry, but I don't trust you."

Curtik laughed. "I wouldn't trust me either. But I do believe it was God. He performed miracles, doing things no person or group of people could accomplish. His powers are far beyond anything we're capable of. You saw some of it, maybe most of it."

"Why would God pick you two?"

Curtik looked at Zora, who shook her head slightly, then turned back to Vice President Rodriguez. "I can't think of a reason."

Zora said, "God has his reasons, which we cannot comprehend."

Rodriguez said, "So you believe it was God?"

Zora ignored him, looking away from the camera to the screens on the wall that displayed the rioting.

Rodriguez said, "You will answer me, young lady."

"You may not trust me," Zora said, "but I don't trust you either. You're far too certain of yourself for my taste."

"What is that supposed to mean?"

"It means some things can't be known—like whether this creature is God or just some very advanced intelligence. That's how it's always been. God or his messenger shows up and performs miracles. Some people believe, some don't. That will never change."

"And you don't believe?" Rodriguez asked.

"No, I don't."

"Why don't you like me, Zora?"

"Why do you care?"

Vice President Rodriguez shrugged. "I don't believe I've done anything to justify your dislike of me."

"I've studied your record, *sir*. You were one of the leading voices to shut down Devereaux. You opposed the Escala and Jeremiah, calling them abominations who were manufactured in violation of God's laws. And you've said the same thing about Curtik and me, calling us abominations as well. That kind of certainty is, forgive me for saying so, idiotic, *sir*."

Rodriguez darkened slightly, obviously furious. Curtik smiled, while President Hope and Dr. Poole managed to keep their faces expressionless. Lendra hoped she wasn't showing too much glee but she was delighted that Zora was standing up to Rodriguez. She herself should have stood up to President Hope more than she had.

Rodriguez said, "I don't think we're going to need your services at CINTEP anymore, Zora. Yours either, Curtik. I'll want you both packed up and gone by the end of the day. Is that understood, Ms. Riley?"

"Yes, sir," said Lendra. She glanced at Dr. Poole, who nodded. "We'll be gone by the end of the day."

"If that's the way you want it," Rodriguez said.

"That's the way it has to be, sir," said Dr. Poole. "It's time for a fresh start for everyone."

Rodriguez's lips turned up briefly, almost a sneer. "What will you do?"

Dr. Poole smiled. "I recently received a message from Devereaux's robots. We've been invited to Devereaux's lab to assist them in the work he was doing before he was shut down."

"Us too?" Zora asked, gesturing to Curtik.

Dr. Poole nodded. "All four of us."

For a moment, Lendra felt irritated that the robots had extended the invitation to Dr. Poole and not her. Then she pushed that emotion aside. She no longer wanted to stay here now that Jeremiah was gone. Her dreams had been shattered by arrogance and the thirst for power, and she couldn't blame anyone but herself. She'd gotten caught up in the game like so many others before her. Only a few, like Jeremiah and Devereaux, had managed to stay outside it all. And Ned too. She shouldn't forget Ned.

Well, she was outside the game now. From here on, she would serve as a research assistant to Devereaux's robots, helping them work toward a cure for the virus. At least she had Sophie. That was consolation prize enough for a lifetime. She began to raise her hand to the glass bulb she wore on her necklace, but managed to stop herself.

Chapter 51

Curtik packed his few belongings and then looked around his room. He'd programmed the built-in screens to look much like his room at Jeremiah's place near the Blue Ridge Mountains, only with more windows. For a moment he scanned the view, taking in the sheer beauty of the vista before him. Then he shut off the screens and stared at the bare and desolate walls.

Stepping out into the hall, he turned toward Zora's room. A rarity, she'd left the door open. She sat on her bed and nodded at him, a sad smile on her face, before gesturing for him to take a seat beside her. Unlike him, she'd chosen to decorate her room with vids of people: Rendela, Aspen, Kammilee, Shiloh, Damon and Crazy Vigg took up one wall. More cadets took up two other walls, people Curtik had largely forgotten, but there was Benn and next to him Addam.

The final wall at the foot of the bed she'd reserved for Jeremiah, images from before she'd met him intermingled with more recent vids. In most of them he wore a somber expression, but in the center of the wall she'd enlarged a vid of him smiling and raising a hand in greeting, looking pain-free. Curtik had never seen it before and wondered where she'd found it.

He put his arm around her shoulder and said, "We'll be okay."

She said nothing, only wrapping an arm around him in return. Then the room dissolved into what seemed like the same garden they'd been in before. Curtik found himself standing beside Zora as Devereaux suddenly appeared before them, emanating warmth and love.

"Hello, children," God said.

"Hello, God," Curtik replied.

"I don't understand," said Zora.

"You wonder why so many people had to die. You think because I saved you and the others back there I should have saved Jeremiah."

"You could have," Zora said.

"Yes."

"Why didn't you?"

God shrugged. "It was his time."

"Don't give me that crap."

"It's true. He lived a full life. He did amazing things. But he also committed sins he could not forgive. He killed and harmed people out of what he deemed necessity, for the sake of what he and others believed to be a greater good, but he found it increasingly difficult to live with that kind of judgment, that kind of calculus. He no longer trusted those in power, including himself, to set the values for society."

"So he wanted to die?"

"Part of him did."

"You could have helped him. We all could have helped him."

"He was dying anyway. Cancer all throughout his body. It kept mutating with every treatment. He had, at best, a year or two remaining."

"You're lying."

"Check with Dr. Poole. She knows the truth."

Curtik put his hand on Zora's shoulder. "Let it go. It's over." He struggled to understand why she couldn't take comfort from God's presence—maybe because she didn't believe he was God.

"That's what I like about you two," God said.

"What's that?" Curtik asked.

"The fact that you believe different things about me." God looked at Curtik. "You believe I am God. And I am." He turned to Zora. "You believe I am not. You are correct too. I am not the God people write about, worship, fear. I am more and less than that."

"I think you're Devereaux," said Zora. "I think you've cooked up this elaborate scheme to fool us into believing you're God."

"Devereaux is dead," Curtik said.

"Is he? He might have transferred his matrix out of his organic computer before he had his assistants destroy his robotic shell. He could be in another organic computer or a different robot, pretending to be less powerful than he is."

"Why would he do that?" Curtik asked.

"That's what I don't get," said Zora. "Maybe to manipulate us?" She turned to God. "Why would you do that?"

God smiled. "Well, if I were Devereaux, I might do it to eradicate the certainty that plagues humanity."

"But religion often drives war," Zora said. "Doesn't the act of appearing now as God create the possibility of greater violence in the name of faith?"

"Perhaps. But your assumption is wrong. Religion does not drive violence. Certitude drives violence: the kind of certitude that leads to fanaticism, to the unshakeable belief that we are right, that we know what's best, and all others are mere pretenders or infidels or inferior. They are other. They are not like us. So our God or our social group or our philosophy permits and even encourages us to eradicate them."

Zora frowned. "So you want uncertainty?"

"That's why you chose us?" Curtik asked. "Because one of us believes and one of us doesn't."

"That's the opposite of every faith I've ever studied," said Zora. "Every one of them claims to be the truth."

"Every one is the truth," God said. "And every one is false."

"More Buddhist riddles?" Zora asked.

"It's not a game," said God. "It's the understanding that we live in a complicated universe. You humans strive to understand it because you're smarter than almost every other creature on your planet. You have a hundred billion neurons in your brains. And those brains want order. They want something understandable. So they create patterns and stories and connections to make sense of it all. You want answers, but sometimes there aren't any."

"So you are Devereaux?"

God smiled again. "As I said before, I am God and Devereaux and Jeremiah and all who have gone before and all who will come after. I am the total collective consciousness of the universe and I am only one tiny, insignificant speck in the greater scheme of things, which I don't pretend to understand."

"If you don't understand it," Curtik said, "how are we supposed to?"

"You're not supposed to understand it—not all of it, anyway. You think you are, but that is a human failing."

"So we're just supposed to accept that we can't know everything?" Curtik asked.

"Is that so difficult?"

"Not for me."

God turned to Zora. "And you?"

Zora shrugged. "I never expected to know everything, but I thought God would, assuming there is a God."

"God is just a name humans have given me. One of many. It is the attributes they ascribe to me that have been portrayed incorrectly, not out of malice, but rather a desire for order and for encouragement that they are on the right path."

"But you're real," Curtik said. "I mean, you're God. Why can't you be more clear? Why can't you make us do the right thing? Why do bad things happen? It can't just be that we have free will. It has to be something more."

"You want me to force you to do good?"

"Why not?"

"What is good? Many things that are good for one person are bad for someone else. There is no universal goodness, at least not that I've been able to discern." God looked off into the distance as if seeing something far beyond the horizon. Then he turned back to them and said, "As I mentioned before, I want you to be better. But if I force you to be better, then you haven't really grown. You have to reach enlightenment on your own or it is not true enlightenment."

"How do we achieve that?"

"There are many paths. You travel one now, each in your own way. I look forward to seeing your progress. I may not come this way again in your lifetimes for I have many places to visit and many *people* to study. But I wish you well."

"Wait," said Zora, but God disappeared, followed by the garden, and Curtik found himself sitting next to Zora on her bed, his arm still around her. Even in the absence of God, he felt warmer than he had before and more at peace with who he was. He knew God had told the truth about Jeremiah too. He'd been dying. Curtik just hadn't been able to see it.

"I still think he's Devereaux," she said.

"He did things Devereaux could never have done," said Curtik, "miracles Devereaux could not have performed, like healing those analysts as if they'd never been shot at all."

"Maybe they weren't. Maybe it was a mass hallucination. Think about it. We're all connected via implant or interface. He could have sent the same imagery to all of us."

"You took off your interface. So did everyone else."

"I thought I did. Maybe he just made me believe it. Maybe it wasn't real."

Curtik shook his head. "You could play that game forever."

"So you still believe he's God?"

"I do. You might be right. He might be Devereaux or some sort of super intelligence, but I think he's God. What about you? Do you still disbelieve?"

Zora nodded. "I admit it's possible he's God, but I don't really think he is. I guess that's what he was aiming for. Uncertainty."

"What do we do now?"

Zora shrugged. "I guess we go to Devereaux's lab and help his robots continue his work."

"But we're not scientists. At least, I'm no scientist."

Zora smiled. "Do you really think we're not going to get in trouble there? People have hated Devereaux for years. Some of them will come after us. We'll have plenty of challenges. Problems will arise. And you and I will handle them."

"Action," Curtik said.

"I'm sure."

"Sweet."

The end.

Acknowledgements

Thanks to the fine folks at Calumet Editions, particularly Gary Lindberg and Ian Graham Leask, for all their efforts on my behalf. Thanks also to my friends and family, who have all been extremely supportive of my efforts through good times and mediocre. Special mention to my fabulous beta readers, who offered valuable insights and criticisms: Steve Stelzner, Jerry Hanson, Geoff Saign, Steve Toninato, Teresa Menart and Tom McEllistrem. And a shout out to my colleagues at Write On! Radio (and the staff at KFAI), as well as all the authors I've interviewed over the years, each of whom provided worthy nuggets of information about writing and publishing and life that I pretended were mine.